JERRY STORY

ROBERT W. SCHRADER

outskirts
press

Outskirts Press, Inc.
http://www.outskirtspress.com

Paperback ISBN: 978-1-9772-0734-0
Hardback ISBN: 978-1-9772-0735-7

Cover Image by Robert W. Schrader

Outskirts Press and the "OP" logo are trademarks belonging to Outskirts Press, Inc.

PRINTED IN THE UNITED STATES OF AMERICA

DISCLAIMER

This is my book. I started writing Jerry's Story as part of my personal therapy for Vietnam Service and recent job termination. Then it turned into a challenge, and kind of fun! Of course, there are things in my memory that probably transferred sub-consciously to my writing. Some of my almost three quarter century memory may have been accurate, or not; so I have included, with permission of those great people (see Acknowledgement Page) some real events, although I also changed names and events. I took great joy in creating an alternative history in this book.

I have not intentionally tried to portray any of my characters as having done what I write they did (Unless, of course, they did).

ACKNOWLEDGEMENTS AND THANKS

Many people encouraged and helped me in my quest to write a book, a project that took a long time between times I worked on it. I probably started writing sometime in 1986. I was between jobs and needed something to occupy my time. Many thought it was a decent book, including a book agent, but thought it was too short and didn't like the ending (I didn't either!)

About 30 years later, during my retirement years, I started over. I added to the beginning and end, fixed up some of the middle and had fun. I asked several people if I could use their names in my book (and of course they always said "sure"). Others were willing to read at least what I had written (to that time) and gave me encouragement and helpful suggestions.

THOSE WHO ALLOWED ME TO USE
THEIR NAME AND PERSONALITY:

COL John R. Burks: Colonel Burks was always the Colonel to everyone who knew him. My wife and I had the pleasure of knowing, working for, and being friends of both the Colonel and his wife, Rose. COL Burks was my first commanding officer. At that time He was the Commanding Officer of 6th Battalion 8th Artillery at Fort Carson, Colorado. He was impressed by my Regular Army Commission (career, rather than Reserve) and overlooked my many flaws. A few years later, I was proud to serve under Colonel Burks at Fort Riley, Kansas. Many years later, we became friends, and although we didn't see each other often, we talked on the phone frequently. During one of those visits, I asked the Colonel if I could use him in my future book. The Colonel said, "Of Course!" (After that, I had the opportunity to invite others.) The Colonel was never, except for his core values, the person in the book. He was never President but would have been a good one. He was, however, the quality person I've tried to portray. Honest, stable, leader of troops and a good man to know.

Rose Burks: I didn't have her permission to use Colonel Burk's wife, Rose, as a character (she had died several years earlier), but since she was the Colonel's wife, a friend, and a Grand Lady, and the Colonel approved, I stuck her into the book. (Hope she likes it!) COL Burks, in my mind, and his Lady, are a package. I always think of Mrs. Burks, when I think of the Colonel. She was the model for a career officer's wife, gracious, charming, and fun. Unlike many commander's wives, Mrs. Burks never assumed her husband's rank or tried to be 'Mrs. COL'. She was always Mrs. Burks; we never called her by her first name! [Unfortunately neither Colonel Burks, nor Mrs. Burks, lived to see the Colonel become President in this book.] I kidded him that he would get that promotion in one or two of our phone calls, but I didn't get the book done in time to have it read to him. My fault, not his! Betty and I miss our phone calls with the Colonel.

Dr. Robert (Bob) Weisberg: In an e-mail, I asked if I could use him in the book and he graciously permitted me to use his name. Bob was/is a highly competent Surgeon, as portrayed in the book. He may not have been on the combat operations described, but it wouldn't surprise me if he had been on similar missions. I served with Bob as his Battalion Surgeon Assistant on board several Navy ships. Good Man, Great Doctor, and an excellent friend.

William H. Jones: Bill is my neighbor in Casa Grande, Arizona, where Betty and I have a vacation home. He is a great friend, and my go-to guy whenever I need help with a project or things around the house, which is often. He responded to my request to use his name, and he just said "sure," which is what he says when I ask him for other help.

Kathleen Jones: She got her "cameo" appearance in the book for two reasons: she encouraged me, read part of the book, did proof-reading, and helped get the darn thing finished. The other reason was to give a name to 'Bill Jones's wife' when she went to the White House!

Charles D. Williams: Chuck is my other go-to guy. He is my foreman at our ranch in Cheyenne, Wyoming. Chuck is an avid Ham Radio Operator, and his part in the book is realistic, but not something he had done. Chuck was never in the Army but is a career retired Air Force Staff Sergeant (he thanked me for the promotion I gave him in the Army). He readily agreed to be a 'character' when he was tired from working around the ranch, and I caught him in a weak moment.

Joseph Pawlik: Joe is a long-time friend and hunting partner. He lives in "upstate New York" part of the time and in Wyoming during hunting seasons. An Army Vet, but never a Deputy Sheriff. He would have done well there too. Another friend who was willing to be one of my 'characters'."

Christina Lynn Schrader: Chris is my daughter. She asked me to put her in the book. She has done many of the things attributed to her in the book but wasn't a Deputy. I told her I couldn't use her name, because it would be confused with another character, Bob Schrader, (who didn't do many of the things he accomplished in the book either, but a few). She readily accepted her new name 'Carlita Christina Camino' after hearing the name description used by Sheriff Tom. Camino is Spanish for road, so the alias name worked out. Thanks, Chris.

Tashana Lynn Schrader Gonzalo is my other daughter. Both my girls are great, and both were happy to be included. Tashana, who is frequenty called T.D., and uses her departed husband's last name; Tashana became Tashana (T.G.) Gonzalo, Court Reporter.

Mr. Dumb John: There were several, always good guys, and you know who you are!

Everyone is entirely fictional and "figments" of my imagination

THOSE WHO HELPED:

Betty A. Schrader: My wife of more than 50 and less than 100 years (yet). She has always encouraged me. She helped put me through school, became a great Army wife, typed and corrected my first drafts, proofread the book, typed the final version, and did anything she could to help me in whatever I attempted to accomplish. It will take another book to give her proper credit. Betty, I love you!

Figgy: Sometimes known as Kathleen Jones (I know that sounds like an alias too). Figgy got her name because Betty and I thought she was a figment of her husband's imagination since she was always gone to help her kids. She is a loyal proofreader and critic.

William H. Jones: Bill did any project I asked him to do.

Charles D. Williams: Chuck proofed my error-filled spelling and helped put the book in final form.

Donald G. Pruter, my favorite brother-in-law, actually my only brother-in-law. I was looking for a name for a Pentagon Colonel, and my wife suggested I use Don since I already had family in Jerry's Story. He readily agreed. He was quite pleased to be a Colonel. "I was only a Sergeant in the Army, and now I'm a Colonel."

Carol S. Ray, my favorite sister (also my only sister). I was trying to determine whether to use her or her late husband Mike. When I talked to her on the phone, she said, "Mike is too quiet, and good mannered be a Prosecutor. I'm the one who likes to argue." So Carol is the Trial Prosecutor near the end of Jerry's Story.

NAMES AND MISTAKES:

Many of the names I have used are composites of familiar names. No name (or person of that name) did anything set out in the book, even the names used with permission. My characters are all figments of my imagination and are not real (except for those that did that!) All mistakes are mine alone.

THANKS:

Thanks for the help, encouragement and kind words about my amateur efforts to write a book. Writing this book helped me through some rough times, PTSD from Vietnam, the effects of Parkinson's disease, and in the process became a fun thing to do. Thank you all!!

DEDICATION

Bob and Edie Burkley: They were a second set of parents to me during high school and after. Bob taught me about horses, how to do many of the different chores around a ranch, and how to back a semi-truck up to a loading dock. Bob was and is my role model. Edie wrote to me every week when I was in Vietnam. Great Friends - I miss them!

Friends who have gone before, and others:

Jim McCue, my best friend in high school and the Best Man at my wedding.

Joe Creel, a chariot driver (two fast horses pulling an oil drum on wheels) who brought the contest to Cheyenne Frontier Days and became a good friend.

My ROTC instructors, high school and college, who significantly guided my future.

Good military leaders, and those I served within the military.

LIST OF CHARACTERS

NAME	CHARACTER	MISCELLANEOUS
Jerry Robert Burkley	*WOC (Warrant Officer Candidate)*	*Rotary and Fixed Wing Aviator*
	Warrant Officer Pilot	*191st Assault Helicopter CO, 9th ID RVN Fixed and Rotary Wing*
		Bounty Hunter 20
		Dustoff 20 (special mission)
	1022nd Medical Helicopter *Helicopter Co. WARNG*	*WO3 (Cowboy 26)*
	2nd Artillery Division	*RW Aviator, Promoted to WO4*
	1022nd Medical Helicopter *Company, WYARNG*	*Cowboy 5*
	Deputy Sheriff	*Charlie 5*
	Banner County Sheriff	*Charlie 1*
Cheryl Hefner Burkley	*Banner County Hospital*	*Phlebotomist*
	Jerry's Wife	
Colonel Donald G. Pruter	*Master of Ceremonies-*	*White House*
	Chief of Staff's Office, Secretary of the Army	

NAME		CHARACTER	MISCELLANEOUS
WO1 William H. Jones		*Rotary Wing Aviator*	*WOC Flight Training*
			191st Assault Helicopter Co. Dong Tam, RVN
		WO3 Volunteer Pilot	*247th Helicopter Ambulance Co.*
		Dustoff Missions (volunteer)	*KIA*
SSG Frances Tucker		*Fort Benning, Georgia*	*Basic Training Drill Instructor*
Gate guard (Corporal)		*Fort Rucker, Alabama*	
CWO5 Sam Schneidmiller		*Fort Rucker, Alabama*	*Officer in Charge-Post Supply*
Captain John R. Burks		*CO, B Company, 187th Training Battalion*	*IP Pilot, Artillery Officer*
	Major	*9th Infantry Division G-3*	*Fort Riley, KS, and RVN*
	Lieutenant Colonel	*9th Infantry Division G-2/3*	*Special Missions Officer*
	Colonel	*The Pentagon*	*Artillery Plans & Operations*
	Brigadier General	*Commander*	*2nd Artillery Div*
	Major General	*Pentagon*	*Deputy Chief of Staff, Joint Chiefs*
	Lieutenant General	*Pentagon*	*Chief of Staff, Joint Chiefs*
	General	*Retired*	*Ready Reserve*
	United States Senator for the State of Oklahoma		
	President of the United States (two terms)		
WO2 Roy Henderson		*RW Pilot-RVN*	*191st Assault Helicopter Co.*
WO2 Dave Flagg		*RW Pilot-RVN*	*9th Aviation Battalion, 9th ID*

NAME	CHARACTER	MISCELLANEOUS
Major Winston Quincy	IP-WOC	
	CO-191st Assault Helicopter CO	Dong Tam, RVN
1LT Lester (Les) Moore	RW Pilot	Dong Tam, RVN
	191st Assault Helicopter Co.	247th Med Det
	Promoted to MAJ (Cowboy 6)	KIA
1LT Robert W. Schrader	MSC (BN Surgeon's Assistant)	D Co. 9th Med BN, 9th ID
	Combat Medic	Dusty Papa 5
	Executive Officer	On Board USS Colleton
	Promoted to CPT	
	Promoted to MAJ	Rotary Wing Flight Trn
	Promoted to LTC Division G-1	2nd Artillery Division
	Commander	6/8th Aviation Battalion
	Promoted to COL	Letterman Army Hospital
CPT (DR.) Robert A. Weisberg	Army MC physician/ surgeon	D Co. 9th Med BN, 9th ID
	LTC-Surgeon	Letterman Army Hospital
	COL-Chief of Staff	Letterman Army Hospital
Betty A. Schrader	Bob's wife	
Rose Burks	Major Burks's wife	
SSG Toby Marks	Motor Sergeant	9th Med BN, 9th ID
SPC4 Tim Cotton	Motor Pool Driver	9th Med BN, 9th ID
SPC5 Conrad Thompson	Chief Delta Co Radio Operator	D Co, 9th Med BN, 9th ID

NAME	CHARACTER	MISCELLANEOUS
SPC5 Scott Anderson	Duty Radio Operator	`D. Co, 9th Med BN, 9th ID On Board Colleton
SGT Avery Silverman	Army Combat Medic	D Co. 9th Med BN, 9th ID
SGT Albert Satterfield	Door Gunner	191st Assault Helicopter Co.
SSG Cory Henderson	Army Combat Medic	D. Co, 9th Med BN, 9th ID
2LT Dan McKane	Army MSC Helicopter Pilot	191st Assault Helicopter Co.
LT Jack Long [Navy Rank equivalent to Army Captain, Later promoted to LTCMDR (equivalent to Major)]	Navy Doctor	Colleton Medical Officer
MSG Charles D. (Chuck) Williams	Army MARS Radio Operator [Military Amateur Radio Station]	Dong Tam (AB8AZ)
2LT Joe Creel	MSC	D Co., 9th Med BN, 9th ID Colleton, then Dong Tam
1LT Rios Rivera (Nicknames: "Law West of the Rio River" and "Judge Rio"	MSC	D Co. 9th Med BN, 9th ID Colleton
	CPT	D Co. Executive Officer
	Undersheriff	Banner County SO
SPC4 Lawrence (Larry) Sanders	Radio Operator	D Co, 9th Med BN, 9th ID
WO1 Bill Williams	Rotary Wing Pilot	9th Aviation BN, 9th ID
Jimmy Connors	Local Drunk	Caribou, WY

NAME	CHARACTER	MISCELLANEOUS
Joe Pawlik	Deputy Sheriff	Banner County SO
	Lieutenant, Shift Supervisor	C-4
Mick Nicholson	Deputy Sheriff	Banner County SO
		C-17
Big Tom Flannigan	Sheriff	Banner County SO
		C-1
Edna Flannigan	Sheriff's Wife	Caribou, WY
Julie Burkley	Jerry's ex-wife	California
Fred Hanks	Former Police Officer/Jerry's Business partner	
Joe Chambers	Deputy Sheriff	Banner County SO
		C-27
Jenny Abbote	Dispatcher	Banner County SO
Sally Marton	Dispatcher	Banner County SO
Silas (Old Man) Ferguson	Banker	Ferguson Federal Savings
Davis Ferguson	Banker and Bad Guy	Ferguson Federal Savings
Jeremy Witters	Major bad guy	Bank Robber
Patrick Torkelson	Witters' Partner	Bank Robber
SGT Jack Falls	Deputy Sheriff C-15	Banner County SO
Ed Plant	Owner – Rusty Nail	
Ester Hefner	Cheryl's Mother	
Larry Hefner	Cheryl's Father	
LT Lynn Tibbets	Deputy Sheriff	Banner County SO Day Shift
Cecil Atwell	Civilian Pilot	Caribou, Wyoming
Grant Baldwin	Patrolman	Wyoming Highway Patrol
Len Cody	Police Officer (City 6)	Caribou Police Department
Carl Tafoya	Hunting Guide	Caribou, Wyoming

NAME	CHARACTER	MISCELLANEOUS
Les Bowdon	Sheriff	Canyon County, Wyoming (County 26)
SPC4 Randy Billings	Combat Medic	247th Helicopter Co (Det)
SPC4 Dale Steiner	Combat Medic	247th Helicopter Co. (Det)
SSG Luther King	Helicopter Crew Chief	247th Helicopter Co. (Det)
SSG Marvin Kline	USAF Forward Air Controller	
Carlita Christina Camino AKA Chris Roads	Civilian Pilot/Deputy Sheriff (C-40)	Banner County SO
Judge James F. Brodrick	District Judge	Banner County District Court
Tashana (TG) Gonzolo	Official Court Reporter	Banner County District Court
Carol Ray	County and Prosecuting Attorney	Banner County
Harley Chatham	Defense Attorney	Caribou, Wyoming
Terrance (Terry) Fordham	Bank Teller	Ferguson Federal Savings
Franklin Roosevelt	Jury Forman	Witters Trial
SGT Fred Carson	Deputy, C-10	Banner County SO
SGT Casey Brown	Deputy, C-12	Banner County SO
SGT Don Fredericks	Deputy, C-11	Banner County SO
LT Sid Koslowski	Deputy, C-3	Banner County SO
Sara Alzate	Secretary to Sheriff Burkley	Banner County SO

NOTES ON BANNER COUNTY AIRCRAFT:

- Cessna 206 - N33SD
- Bell Jet Ranger - N3320SD

PREFACE

The Master of Ceremonies, Colonel Donald Pruter, stepped to the mike on the stage, "Welcome to the White House. Today we honor a Sheriff, a Chief Warrant Officer, and one of our nation's heroes. That is not three people, but a single man, Jerry R. Burkley. He has been the Sheriff of Banner County, Wyoming, for over twenty years. Jerry served on active duty with the Army as an aviator on active duty and in the National Guard for more than twenty-six years, retiring as a Chief Warrant Five, with awards of the Silver Star, two Bronze Stars, one with a V for Valor, ten Air Medals and the Army Commendation Medal while in Vietnam. Since Vietnam, he has been awarded the Army Distinguished Service Medal, The Legion of Merit, a Distinguished Flying Cross, and three Meritorious Service Medals. These were for service in the Army National Guard and a tour during Desert Storm."

Jerry looked at his wife, Cheryl, and just shook his head. She jabbed him in the arm and whispered: "behave yourself." Jerry smiled and set back to listen as the Master of Ceremonies continued, "Ladies and Gentlemen, the President of the United States!" Everyone stood. The Marine Band began to play Hail to the Chief, as the President made his way to the microphone. The applause went on for an extended period. This was a well-respected President if not well liked by all of the voting public. He had won office on the concept of putting government back into the hands of the people, and in the last term and a half had done so, to the dismay of many who expected something for nothing from the government. Jerry had worked on several mission projects for the President; in fact, he had been in charge. The two were good friends. This ceremony was kind of a payback to Jerry for having gone out of his way to ensure those projects had been successful. Jerry would have gladly passed on the recognition. He and the President had met while Jerry was a Warrant Officer Candidate (WOC) and the President was just beginning his highly successful military career.

"Thank you, thank you! I appreciate the courtesy you are extending me. Today is the Fourth of July, and we celebrate our country's independence. But, tonight is about Sheriff Jerry Burkley. "Jerry, please join me at the podium." Jerry moved smoothly from his chair on the stage to stand beside the President of the United States. "Sheriff Burkley has performed honorably for the State of Wyoming, the United States Army, and the United States of America. I am pleased to award Sheriff Burkley with the Presidential Medal of Freedom. This medal is the civilian equivalent of the Medal of Honor that Jerry probably also richly deserves. The Medal of Honor is the highest personal military decoration and is given by the President in the name of Congress for military members who have distinguished themselves by acts of valor. The Presidential Medal of Freedom is an award bestowed by the President of the United States. It is the highest civilian award of the United States for especially meritorious contribution to the security of national interests of the United States and other significant public or private endeavors. Although it is called a civilian award, it can be presented to the military and worn on the uniform. Sheriff Burkley earned this medal by his service to the United States as the Sheriff of Banner County, Wyoming. His exploits would fill the pages for many writers of thriller books. He served admirably in both Vietnam and during Desert Storm. Few people are nominated for this award, and even fewer are as deserving as Jerry Burkley."

The President explained the award as he was placing it

around Jerry's neck. Standing behind Jerry, President Burks commented, "The Presidential Medal of Freedom is worn around the neck on a blue ribbon with white stripes. The medal has a gold star with white enamel within a gold ring. A Golden Bald Eagle is in the center. Pretty good looking necklace! Few are awarded this Medal. It gives me great pleasure to award it to Jerry R. Burkley."

Jerry just merely grinned, and modestly said, "thank you." The ceremony went on for quite a while after that, but Jerry and Cheryl just took it all in, enjoyed what was being said, and waited for the end. Finally, the President United States left the stage, and the gathering slowly broke up with many people shaking Jerry's hand and congratulated him on the honor. Jerry just smiled, shook hands and said thanks!

CHAPTER 1

Hi, my name is Jerry, and I guess this is my story. Actually, it is a story of a lot of people that I knew, worked with, loved, and ultimately shared my life. I think it started when I was trying to decide what to do after high school. My best friend was not happy with my choice to go into the Army. He had a great argument. Vietnam was not only just getting started, but was getting dangerous. He had a good point!" At any rate, his argument didn't change my mind. I joined the Army at the Army Recruiting Office in my hometown, Cheyenne, Wyoming.

It was a fast-moving process, I was sent to the Army Recruiting Center in Denver, Colorado, where I was subjected to many tests, probes, pokes, and other indignities, before the medics thought I might make a good 11 Bravo (Combat Rifleman). I wasn't totally unhappy with their decision. I figured that 11 Bravo might be an acceptable MOS (Military Occupational Specialty) if I was going to try to get into flight school. After all, both of those get you into active combat. I really wanted to fly.

As soon as I got to basic training at Fort Benning, GA, I put in for flight school, either fixed wing or rotary, hoping that I would get accepted to one of them. I didn't care which one; I just wanted to be taken into one of them so that I could fly. I was asked why I didn't apply to the Air Force or one of the other flight programs. I wanted to fly close to the ground with small aircraft, not way above everything that was going on. Those other guys flew way above combat and didn't even really know what was going on in the war. I did!

I got my wish! Soon after basic training, I got my orders for primary flight training. But, first I had to survive basic training, Warrant Officer Candidate School, and be eligible for flight school, physically, and within the parameters of what the military wanted to draft at that time. What the military required at any given point depended upon how many helicopter pilots or fixed-wing pilots had been killed in Vietnam. It was a numbers game!

Army Basic Training hasn't changed much over the years. Basic training was as bad as I expected. I reported into my training unit early and was treated with a great deal of respect; I was given a bed, actually the bottom half of a bunk bed, instructions to the mess hall, and told to get a good night's sleep.

Respect ended the next morning. Training cadre entered the room loudly banging on the trash cans and shouting at the recruits. We were ordered, not very politely, to put on our fatigue uniforms, make up the beds, and fallout for formation. The timeframe was very short, and we all had to hustle to make it to formation on time. Once we were in formation, we were yelled at some more and then marched to the mess hall for breakfast. We formed a long line, picked up trays, silverware, and started down a long line to where the KP's were spooning scrambled eggs, biscuits and gravy onto our trays, whether we wanted it or not. Before we could really begin eating, the drill sergeants were yelling, "hurry up, your buddy needs a seat!" I thought this was pretty bad until we survived to lunchtime, where we had to do pull-ups before we could enter the chow line. Pull-ups continued for the entire time we were in basic training. You either got good at them, or you got hungry. If you couldn't do the required number of pull-ups, you were sent to the end of the line and given the opportunity to try again when you got close to the front of the line. This, of course, cut down on the time you had for that meal.

When you finish eating, you are required to take your tray to the cleanup area and forced to eat any food you had remaining on it. Remember, you didn't get to choose what food was on your tray or how much. We reformed into ranks and were marched to the athletic field where we underwent physical training. We were lucky on the first day because we got to eat first. The rest of the time we performed PT right after formation and then, when we were tired out, marched to the mess hall, required to do pull-ups, and then got to eat breakfast.

PT (physical training) was lots of fun! We did jumping jacks, sit-ups, running in place, leg thrusts, and some innovative things the training cadre thought up on the spot. Then we went for a little run. It started at 1 mile, and by the end of basic training, we were running at least 10 miles every morning. That did get us in pretty good shape.

Our days moved quickly. There were fun things like the rifle range and boring things like marching. There were classroom sessions that taught everything from infantry tactics to the complete understanding of military law. In our free time, haha, we cleaned the barracks, picked up trash (called policing the grounds), cleaned our rifles and our personal gear including polishing of the brass that went on the class A uniform we never got to wear.

But, the big day finally arrived. The morning started as usual with PT, breakfast pull-ups, and being yelled at by our drill instructors. "Get into your class As and make sure your shoes are polished," SSG Frances Tucker ordered. We did, and based on our past experiences did it very quickly.

This formation was different. The start was the same, marching to John Phillip Susa music, and saluting the reviewing stand. Instead of marching off at the end, we marched back into our original positions. The Adjutant, (S-1 personnel officer) advanced to the right front of the formation, and in a loud, clear voice, ordered: "ATTENTION TO ORDERS: and we were assigned our first post. I was attached to WOC (Warrant Officer Candidate) Pilot Training Class #130526, Fort Rucker, Alabama, with a reporting date and authorized POV (Privately Owned Vehicle) travel, which was a real bonus, except the travel time was very short. Military travel is based on the idea the first day doesn't count, and the check in time is any time before midnight on the last day, so if I hustled, I could make it in time.

"Jerry, what are your orders?" shouted my roommate, Bill Jones. "I'm going to WOC Rotary Wing Air." We embraced and patted backs.

"Same place, and I have a car. Are you going with me?" He threw his suitcase toward me and said, "Who's driving?"

"We both are if we are going to sign in on time."

"You get to drive first; I've been celebrating," Bill advised, "and I have a little bit to finish up."

I figured he was about half in the bag and it was my car. "OK, get loaded, the car not you."

Soon we were past the gate and on the road to Fort Rucker, an old, but new post dedicated to Army Aviation helicopter activities and also used to train WOCs, most of whom would be pilots. In the early 50s, Camp Rucker was a deserted army training post left over from the big war, WW2. Soon after its designation as Fort Rucker, the old two-story wooden barracks were knocked down, and more modern Army structures were built. Housing for the cadre and Post Headquarters personnel followed, but not on the grand style older Army Posts had for its command officers. It was functional, but not grand.

Chapter 2

The next day we drove up to the Guard Shack at the Main Entrance to Fort Rucker. A large sign identified the Post, the Commanding General's name, as well as that of the Deputy Commanding General and the Command Sergeant Major, a list of the Aircraft on the Post, and a large Aviation Branch insignia (a set of wings with a propeller in the center). Looked kind of Disney to me, but Bill was duly impressed.

"Think we will get to fly all those?" Bill inquired with wonder.

"Hardly. We will be lucky to fly the UH-72 trainer, and probably the Huey, but not any of the fixed wing stuff. If we make it through training that is!"

The gate guard gestured me to roll down the window so he could talk to us, and boy did he. We were in the wrong uniform, not properly shaved, and didn't have a vehicle sticker to allow us onto the post and some pointed remarks about our ancestry. It may have been his general good nature or the fact we were both not wearing OX's on our collar (warrant officer candidate insignia) and wearing stripes on our uniforms. Whoops, lousy error on our part.

After giving the Corporal our orders, and his discovery we were Warrant Officer Candidates, his demeanor changed dramatically. He became quite helpful.

"Gentlemen, welcome to Fort Rucker, Alabama, home of Army Aviation. As you can see on our sign, a wide variety of aircraft are used here, both fixed and rotary wing. Our Moto is 'Above the Rest', probably because you will be flying over everyone." The Corporal then went on to give us detailed instructions to Post Headquarters so we could sign in, and how to get to the WOQ (Warrant Officer Candidate Quarters). Gave us a snappy salute (which we didn't deserve yet) and waved us through the gate. We both returned his salute and quickly drove onto our new home. After each presented his orders to the clerk at the sign-in desk, signing the official rooster book, and receiving a packet of information, which gave them their room assignment and the welcome news they didn't have to report for training until the next day, Jerry and Bill began to make plans.

Both their WOQ and Warrant Officer Flight training were on the far side of the post.

"I'll drive," stated Bill.

"Of course, you have a car, and I don't," said Jerry to remind Bill it was his car. "But first we need to go to the PX (Post Exchange) and the Class 6 Store," Jerry retorted."

Bill chuckled, and inquired, "what's Class 6?"

"Didn't you pay attention in class? There are five military classes of supply for food, fuel, ammo, clothing and something else. Class 6 is used informally for the place you can buy booze."

"Why not just call it a liquor store?"

That caused Jerry to laugh too. "Probably because the Brass doesn't want civilians to know soldiers drink. For some reason that upsets the civilians."

"So what," Bill commented, "we can't drink during training anyway, it says so right in the handouts."

"True story, but we still need to go to Class 6 and the PX," Jerry persisted.

"Not my car, but I still want to know why."

"Again, you didn't pay attention during class," Jerry lectured. "As you may recall, all good officers, and I think we qualify, at least right now, is to perform a recon (reconnaissance) before conducting any mission. You may recall I was at Fort Rucker on a supply run. As were you, as I recall. When I was here, I had the time and the intelligence to do a recon."

"What mission and why Class 6 and the PX?"

"Mr. Jones, listen to me, I will explain in terms a newly minted Warrant Officer, Junior Grade, such as yourself, should be able to understand," Jerry intoned much as one of their instructors began their many classes in basic. "First, our new quarters, the WOQ, while much, much nicer than the barracks during basic, only has one refrigerator and one ice machine. The WOQ, on the other hand, has 42 residents in the building."

"Great!" Bill exclaimed. "We will have ice and a place to keep snacks!"

"Not true, and don't interrupt," Jerry ordered. Bill shut his mouth and gestured with his hands for Jerry to continue. "In cases of short supply and large demand, it means there won't be any ice available when we want and probably need it, and someone will pilfer our goodies out of a communal refrigerator, even with our names on them. That means we need our own refrigerator."

A light went on over Bill's head, "so that's why we are going to the PX!

"No, Mr. Dumb-John. We are going to the PX for cleaning supplies. My Recon shows there is no maid service or snacks. We are going to the Class 6 for a fifth of Scotch and a fifth of Whiskey, good stuff," Jerry explained.

"But we can't drink!"

"I know that, and we aren't going to drink." Once again using a training voice, Jerry explained, "my Recon also discovered that a CWO (Chief Warrant Officer) is in charge of supply. What you also may not know is that most Warrant Officers are not young and new to the military like us. Most Warrant Officers get a Warrant after long and successful service as an enlisted soldier, a sergeant or more likely a senior specialist, who gets a Warrant as a reward for long and faithful service. If that Warrant Officer then really is good at his specialty, like S-1 (administration), S-2, (Intelligence), S-3, (Operations), or S-4 (Supply), than he or she, moves up in rank to Warrant Officer 4, Chief Warrant Officer, just like regular officers move from Lieutenant to General. A Chief Warrant Officer 4 is about the same pay grade as a Major, O-4."

"So how does that affect us?"

Jerry explained, "this Chief Warrant Officer is in charge of Post Supply, and he has lots of brand new little refrigerators. We are going to each take CWO Schneidmiller a gift and engage in friendly talk and eventually ask his help in getting one of his extra refrigerators."

"You mean we are going to try to bribe a senior Warrant Officer?"

"No, Dummy, we are going to become a friend he wants to assist in alieving your allergy to heat and to allow us to make friends with others in the WOQ, who also have similar problems."

They did and got a new compact refrigerator just perfect for a WOQ room.

Chapter 3

Jerry and Bill drove to Building 102, the WOQ, with the refrigerator loaded in the trunk, with the top up, and the back seat full of late night snacks. They checked in and found a spot to park in the crowded parking lot. As they started to unload, a Captain in an impeccable flight suit with embroidered Senior Army Pilot Wings, the crossed cannons designating Field Artillery and the twin tracks of a Captain sewed in the appropriate locations.

"Gentlemen, is that wreck, which may be a car, parked by the red sign yours?"

Jerry and Bill both jumped to the position of attention, saluted, and replied, "Yes Sir".

"Perhaps you can tell me your names, the reason for being here and since you parked in front of it, what is written on the red sign."

Jerry and Bill gave their names, rank and that they were reporting to Flight Training and assigned to this WOQ. Both admitted they didn't notice the sign since they had been distracted watching the two young women driving by in an open convertible. "You may see those ladies again. They live in the adjacent WOQ. Of course, you are not permitted to enter the women's WOQ."

Jerry volunteered to read the sign - - - He did:

RESERVED FOR COMMANDING OFFICER
B COMPANY, 187TH TRAINING BATTALION
CPT JOHN R. BURKS

"Gentlemen, let me introduce myself. I am Burks, John R., Captain. I am your new CO, Training Officer, and senior officer in charge of this WOQ." Captain Burks then went on to explain in great detail what would be required of the two Warrant Officer candidates during training, in the WOQ, and their conduct when not on duty. He then ordered them to move into the room across from his in the WOQ so he would be available to advise and assist them (and to keep an eye on them). "You are already troublemakers who don't know where to park," he advised them. Captain Burks then helped them park in appropriate space and assisted them in moving into their quarters while admiring their new refrigerator still in the box.

Days were consumed learning to fly; nights, weary and worn out, learning the theory of flight, rules of flying and the regulations that govern combat operations. All, that is, except for one Warrant Officer Candidate Burkley, who turned out to be a natural pilot. From the first time he sat in the left-hand co-pilot's seat in the cockpit of a TH-67 training helicopter, he could feel how the controls and the chopper connected. Not that he was an expert or even a skilled pilot, but he could fly the darned thing. During his first instruction period with CPT Burks Jerry was asked, "OK Mr. Burkley, how many hours do you have in helicopters?"

Jerry replied, "first time I've been in one, Sir." Disbelief was evident on CPT Burk's face. He took Jerry out to the practice area and worked him out. Jerry learned a lot about flying helicopters and impressed the hell out of CPT Burks. After just a few more training sessions, Jerry was passed to the next level of training in the UH-72 Lakota light utility helicopter and then introduced to the Huey, the famous HU1D helicopter being used in Vietnam. From that, he progressed to flying solely by reference to instruments on the panel before him, while his vision was restricted to that area by a visor hood on his head. This training was harder, but with extra book work in the WOQ at night and a determination to get it right, Jerry learned to orient himself to the outside world by instrument reference only. He was above the average student in this area of training as well.

Unfortunately, theory wasn't easy for Jerry at all. Jerry had a difficult time with classroom work and tests. He spent a lot of time during class, study periods, and even late at night pouring over the books. Even the Army method of:

1. Tell the class what they would be taught.
2. Teach.
3. Review.
4. Tell the class what had been taught,
5. Review again.
6. Test.

It is a tedious way to learn but is usually effective. Not so for Jerry. After numerous counseling sessions by instructors and CPT Burks, a solution was found.

Bill was almost a mirror image of Jerry. He was a natural at the books but had difficulties in applying that knowledge to flying a helicopter. It turned out that both Jerry and Bill were good teachers. CPT Burks paired the two, almost as a separate unit, to teach each other. It worked! Bill stood ranked 3rd in academics and 7th in flight; Jerry was first in flight and 10th in academics at graduation.

Jerry had one major error during flight training, blame it on theory or his quick adaption to flying. He mixed up some airports. On a dual cross-country flight, he was supposed to land at his filed destination airport but started to put down at an airport on the same flight path, but 20 nautical miles closer, not the place he was cleared to land. His Instructor

Pilot pointed out his error, and Jerry quickly noticed it on his JEPP chart (the official charts, or maps, used by pilots everywhere). They flew on to the proper airport several miles to the west. Jerry rather enjoyed reading many years later about a commercial airline captain who landed at Buffalo, Wyoming, instead of Sheridan, Wyoming, about 30 miles difference, just as he had done as a young Warrant Officer student. A good ending for both pilots, but not a good way to fly. It made Jerry pay more attention to his JEPP Charts and the cross-reference to the instrument flying information.

Since both Bill and Jerry were doing extremely well at the three-quarter point of the training period, both broadened their training. Bill was assigned to provide extra-duty tutoring for other struggling, but promising pilots. Jerry was given advanced instrument instruction and then sent TDY (temporary duty) to Fort Wolters, TX, to transition into fixed wing C-172, the push-pull Cessna, and finally familiarization with the Caribou.

Jerry returned to Fort Rucker to discover he had a new company commander. CPT Burks had been promoted to Major and assigned 9th Infantry Division G-3 (operations) Artillery, and transferred first to Fort Riley Kansas, and then to Vietnam when the Division was reassigned there. It was rumored by the Class that the Old Man, CPT, now MAJ Burks was in charge of some mysterious projects for the 9th Infantry Division G-2 (intelligence Office).

At Fort Riley, Kansas, the 9th Infantry Division prepared for a new kind of war, where helicopters and armored assault boats chased Charlie into the back waterways of the Mekong Delta. The 9th was headed to Vietnam; first to Bearcat near Saigon, and later to a man-made location called Dong Tam west of My Tho. The 9th became the first American infantry unit to establish a permanent post in the enemy-infested Mekong Delta.

WOQ graduation came with wings and a single bar designating a Warrant Officer, Junior Grade.

CHAPTER 4

D ue to Jerry's advanced training, he was the first of his Class to be posted to The Republic of Vietnam. His orders read:

RPT 9th ID, Bear Cat, RVN, en-route 191st Aviation Helicopter Co., 9th ID, Bear Cat, RVN.

The orders weren't that clear in English, but printed in military jargon. The orders were clear. Mr. Burkley was going to Vietnam to fly in combat. He had mixed feelings. "I am proud to be the best of my Class, but I'm scared to shit." A lot of it was the unknown of being in combat and maybe buying the farm (getting killed). Jerry knew flying was inherently dangerous and he could be killed just flying. In Vietnam the enemy would be shooting at him and trying to kill him. Most of the 9th Infantry Division units had originally trained together, but Jerry was going by himself as a replacement. At least I know what I am going to do and what Unit I will be assigned. Maybe I will see the Old Man. He would eventually see Burks, and he wouldn't like the whole experience either.

The Military C-141 troop and equipment transport aircraft landed at Tan Son Nhut Air Force Base in Vietnam and taxied to a parking spot about 100 yards from a group of steel buildings. The passengers on the C-141, all military troops, (including the crew), felt the hot, humid heat encase and engulf their bodies almost as quickly as the aircraft doors were opened. Sweat broke out as each soldier deplaned and found his gear stacked near the rear of the plane.

Jerry decided he had never been that hot and sweaty, not even at Rucker or Benning, during his life as a rotary wing aviator in the United States Army. A Major drove up in a jeep and ordered everyone into a group formation. Jerry thought but was smart enough not to articulate, "Sure happy I'm only a Warrant Officer" (Jerry had all the privileges of an Officer, but none of the responsibilities). Jerry and 12 other Warrant Officers, all rotary wing aviators, grouped themselves. A Second Lieutenant was acting as their Platoon Leader. The Major, a career Quartermaster Officer by his insignia, ordered the assembled troops to "Attention, at Ease" then gave them pertinent information about Quarters, transportation to the 'Old Reliable Academy' in Bear Cat, the things they could or may do, and the many things they could not do or even think about doing. He then called the assembled troops to attention and dismissed them.

The sounds of combat, the roar of jets and the frenzied activity on and off the field at Tan Son Nhut continued. Jerry thought and maybe vocalized his primary concern, "A fellow could get killed here," he murmured. One Senior Airman heard Jerry and commented, "that's all a long way away, don't sweat the small stuff. Where you can get killed is out in the field or up in the air."

"NO SHIT!" another Warrant Officer exclaimed.

"Maybe," Jerry responded, "but I don't like being bunched up, out in the open. That goes against everything I was taught in basic."

A voice from the rear shouted, "Sounds like an infantryman."

Jerry shouted back, "No Way! Just listened in basic."

"Gentlemen," ordered the Second Lieutenant, "Good Advice! Now SHUT UP!"

They did, but Jerry didn't stop thinking about it.

Soon the formations were broken, and the troops loaded onto buses with bars and screens on the windows. They already knew the screens were supposed to keep out hand grenades thrown by enemies of the United States Army. No one explained what would stop bullets or RPG's (rocket-propelled grenades). The buses moved in a stop and go manner since the road called Highway 1 was crowded with local farmers, buses carrying civilians (maybe) and both ARVN and US military vehicles. Eventually, the buses arrived at the home of the Old Reliable Academy, the Academy having been assigned the ominous duty of preparing new soldiers for what they might expect during their assignment to the 9th Infantry Division Units. It was training that was developed by experienced combat troops who had served with the 9th, but a significant failure in the sense that combat is a continually changing environment the NVA were quick to adapt and adjust to take advantage. It was invaluable in a sense it gave the 9th Soldiers a real heads up on what to expect. Several days were spent attending lectures, firing and familiarizing with various common infantry weapons, and being correctly scared and afraid of the enemy, who was called many names, but most commonly, "Charlie".

Jerry's first night, or rather the next morning, was humorous to all, except Jerry. Some felt sorry for him, but everyone thought it was funny. Jerry had a beer at the Officer's Club, but was soon bored, and went to bed. His was the top bunk, and he pulled the mosquito netting around his bed, punched the pillow into an acceptable shape, and shut his eyes. The long travel, boring reception, and the change of time zones put Jerry immediately to sleep. He woke late the next morning. The other officers had gone to breakfast, meetings, or were wandering around. Not Jerry, he slept in. He heard movement, opened his eyes and discovered he was alone in the large barracks with an Asian woman with a stick. Fear, self-preservation, and a great deal of confusion led Jerry to respond in accordance with his Infantry Basic Training. Jerry jumped from his second level bed, his Gerber combat knife firmly gripped in his right hand. The Mama-san was as startled as Jerry had been scared. When Jerry recognized the situation, he put his Gerber back in its holster, bowed to the Mama-san, grabbed his dopp-kit (razor, toothbrush, etc.), and made tracks to the latrine.

Two of Jerry's fellow Warrant Officer Pilots, Ray Henderson and Dave Flagg returned to the barracks from breakfast just in time to catch the end of Jerry's wake-up call. They followed Jerry into the latrine, laughing out loud and giving Jerry a hard time; "Were you worried Mama-san was going to jump on you and give you a good time?" chuckled Dave. (Mama-san was old, at least for a Vietnamese, had bad teeth from chewing beetle nuts, and she even had some running down from her mouth) "Yeh, sure," Jerry replied.

Dave continued but in a different direction. "I just took the mandatory in-country flight check."

"How was it?" Jerry responded, hoping to turn the conversation away from the Mama-san fiasco.

"Not great! I had one of those overbearing flight instructors who liked to bang on the controls to emphasis his instruction."

"I had one of those in basic flight. I spent more time thinking about how to shove the IP (Instructor Pilot) out the door than I did about learning to fly that piece of junk." Ray was about to go on, but Jerry interrupted with his announcement that Major Quincy, the 191st Assault Helicopter Company Commander, located across Bear Cat from Old Reliable, had an officer on a familiarization flight who tried to land at the wrong airfield. He had his VOR tuned to the wrong frequency, didn't have the volume up, and so couldn't verify the Morse code identifier. Major Q stopped him before he touched down on the taxiway at Tan Son Nhut," Jerry grinned.

"Who was the lucky Warrant Officer?" Dave demanded.

"It wasn't a warrant officer, it was that smart ass, 1LT

Moore," Jerry said triumphantly. "And he got sent back to refresher training, so we won't have to put up with him for a while."

Jerry wasn't as smug as he acted. He knew he had done the same thing in training, but being in a combat unit, and being lost were a horse of a different hue. There was also a big difference in rank and experience. Jerry had been a new Warrant Officer in flight training. Moore was a First Lieutenant, with more flight hours and supposedly more experience flying. Here people were placing their very lives in the hands of the pilots. The pilots were expected to be competent.

"I almost did that in training. Fortunately, my IP gently informed me of my grievous error before I turned onto final," admitted Ray. They all laughed and prepared for class.

Soon orders were posted on the bulletin board; Jerry and Ray were assigned to the 191st Assault Helicopter Company. Dave was assigned to the 9th Aviation Battalion. All three would be in Dong Tam, but doing different jobs; two of them in attack helicopters and Dave probably doing trash haul duty in a slick (an unarmed Huey). All three were apprehensive about their assignments and what the future would bring. They didn't have to wait long.

Bear Cat was a combination training and operational base near Bien Hoa, with a 5,000-foot runway and an elevation of 140 feet. Dong Tam was all new, built on dirt dredged from the Mekong River, and all operational. It had a 2,300-foot runway and an elevation of 5 feet when all the dirt stayed in place, located just west of My Tho. There was a vast harbor used by the Navy and the Army for a Joint Operation called The Mobile Riverine Force, a large and serious military operation comprising the 2nd Brigade of the 9th Infantry Division, and the Navy's River Assault Squadron 9 and 11, (part of the Navy's River Assault Flotilla One Task-Force 117), along with various support units (D Company, 9th Medical Battalion and others).

Jerry received an intense indoctrination to the Mobile Riverine Force and Delta Company, 9ᵗʰ Med.

Standing at the bar, Jerry told his current war story. "I was flying #2 (co-pilot) into Dong Tam when the excrement hit the rotating blade. "The crap hit the fan, not my Huey rotor blades," Jerry told his enraptured audience at the Ton Son Nhut Officer's Club Bar. Jerry continued his story as if it was just happening.

"Bounty Hunter 20 (the radio call-sign for the armed Assault Huey helicopter Jerry and the Aircraft Commander, Major Quincy, were flying), Bounty Hunter 33 (the call-sign for the 191st Assault Helicopter Company operations center), break off approach to Jayhawk (9th Aviation) and proceed to Killer Alpha (U.S.S. Colleton, a Navy ship of the Mobile Riverine Force). I say again, break off approach to Jayhawk and proceed to Killer Alpha. Contact Papa Delta 33 (D Company 9ᵗʰ Med BN, 9ᵗʰ ID) for further."

Major Quincy keyed the intercom, "What is that all about?"

"Not sure," Jerry reported, "but it looks like we might have a mission."

"Acknowledge Bounty Hunter 33," said Major Quincy. He turned our Huey towards the Colleton, wondering why they were being sent to Delta Company's Army Surgical facility on board the Colleton. Not as effective as the 3ʳᵈ Surgical Hospital, which was a larger surgical hospital in Dong Tam, but pretty close.

The sick bay on the Colleton consisted of three separate areas on three levels of the ship, with ramps from one level to the other. Level one was a flight deck for helicopters, Level two was a triage area below the flight deck, with six treatment positions. Level three contained a two table surgery, recovery area, 18 bed ward, pharmacy and a one-chair dental clinic.

Approaches by air were controlled by Navy radio operators. Dispatch of medical Dustoff (helicopter medical evacuation from field locations) were coordinated and controlled by D Company 9th Med Operations Center on the Colleton.

"Roger, Sir," Jerry complied.

"Bounty Hunter 33, Bounty Hunter 20, affirm. In-route Killer Alpha." Jerry changed his radio frequency and called, "Killer Alpha, Bounty Hunter 20."

"Bounty Hunter 20, Killer Alpha," came a strong radio signal.

"Bounty Hunter 20 inbound to your location." The ship moved around on the Mekong, so we had to track it by our navigation equipment.

"Bounty Hunter 20, Killer Alpha, your call sign is now Dustoff 20, cleared to land medivac pad. Expect VO (verbal orders) from Dusty Papa 5 on landing".

Specialist 5 Thompson, the chief Delta Company Radio Operator, who was monitoring the ship radio frequency, picked up the handset of a field telephone and cranked it several times. The phone was quickly answered by 1LT Schrader in his stateroom/office several decks below on the Colleton.

"Have you got our lost bird,?" 1LT Schrader asked.

"Yes Sir, he is on the way."

"Thanks, I'll meet them on the pad."

Meanwhile, Major Quincy grunted, "What the Hell!"

"Yes Sir, sounds weird," Jerry replied.

CHAPTER 5

Lieutenant Schrader was an R.O.T.C. (Reserve Officers Training Corps) graduate from the University of Wyoming. He graduated near the top of his class as a Distinguished Military Graduate, which made him eligible to receive a Regular Army Commission. In simple terms, Bob got the same Commission West Point Graduates received and given his choice of Army Branch. He elected to be commissioned in the Medical Service Corps due to his prior training in medicine. He was ordered to Fort Sam Huston, Texas, for the Medical Service Corps Officer basic course, with added training as a Battalion Surgeon Assistant (the original Physicians Assistants you see now routinely practicing in hospitals, clinics, and doctor's offices). That instruction was routinely referred to as 'How to be a doctor in thirty days course'by those attending.

When the intensive medical training was completed, 2LT. Schrader was sent to Fort Riley, Kansas, for his initial tour of duty with the 9th Infantry Division. He was assigned as a medical platoon officer, which really meant he was in charge of a bunch of jeep and ambulance drivers and their vehicles. With typical Army efficiency, he was an almost a medical doctor and assigned to be in charge of a motor pool.

The job had some perks; he had his own office, a jeep, and driver, and was actually in command of about 90 soldiers. Although it was probably against regulations, the good Lieutenant and his motor Sergeant, Staff Sergeant Toby Marks, conspired to paint "BETTY ANN" on the panel beneath the front window. Betty was the Lieutenant's wife. He reasoned that many of the artillery pieces and other motor vehicles had names, so his jeep should also have an appropriate one. The title served a valuable and time-saving expedient. Schrader could find his jeep, which looked exactly like the several hundred on the post, with little or no effort. Since he had a driver, that expediency wasn't necessary, but provided a reasonable explanation when questioned by senior officers, especially those conducting inspections!

Unfortunately, one of those Senior Officers, was Major John R. Burks, now the assistant to the 9th Infantry Division G-2 (Intelligence). Major Burks was intelligent, knew the regulations by heart, and was in a position of leadership not attained by many Majors.

"Sergeant, why is there writing on this jeep?" he inquired of Staff Sergeant Marks after parking his jeep next to it at Post Headquarters.

"Sir, that is the Lieutenant's wife's name. He uses it to be able to find this jeep in areas where there may be many other similar vehicles".

"You mean he doesn't recognize the antenna farm (all the radio antenna's mounted on the jeep to provide command communication radio capability), and how you and the driver look? Doesn't sound like a very intelligent Lieutenant."

"Sir, Lieutenant Schrader is one of the most intelligent and best officers I have ever served. He and I just thought it would match in with the other named vehicles on the post, like the names painted on the barrels of the self-propelled artillery cannons."

"Oh, both of you did, did you? When this Lieutenant returns and perhaps finds this jeep, his driver and you, tell him I said to report, with you, to my office at G-2 in Post Headquarters. My name is Burks."

"Yes sir," replied Staff Sergeant Marks, giving Major Burks a snappy salute.

When the Major departed, Sergeant Marks commented to the driver, Specialist 4 Tim Cotton, "I think maybe we better get the name off before we report." The two of them took out pocket knives and began scrapping the white letters off the OD Green paint. They were still diligently performing this self-imposed task when the Lieutenant walked up to the jeep.

"What do you think you are doing?" he said in a calm, steady, and stern voice.

"Just trying to reduce the amount of trouble we may have, Sir." Replied SSG Marks. The Sergeant went on to explain what the Major had said, how he said it, and why taking off the markings would at least ease the problem when they had to report to Major Burks.

"Good call Sergeant. Let's finish this up, and then go meet the G-2 Major." One Lieutenant, a Sergeant, and a Spc4 quickly finished the obliteration of the name on the jeep, went by their orderly room, obtained some OD Green paint and finished the job in style.

After a long search of the headquarters building Lieutenant Schrader and Staff Sergeant Marks discovered Major Burks' office on the third floor, somewhat closer to the Commanding General's Office then they had initially believed it would be, and a long way from the main G-2 Office. LT Schrader knocked on the door, was told to enter, and he and his Motor Sergeant marched into the sparse office, saluted, and LT Schrader announced, "Reporting as ordered, Sir!"

"You must be the Lieutenant with his wife's name emblazed on his jeep," the Major said as he returned their salutes. "I regret I haven't met the lady, but I am sure she does our Post proud if she has her name on one of our jeeps."

"Sir," SSGT Marks injected, "the name has been removed."

"Why? It was properly done and readily identified Lieutenant Schrader's Jeep as you told me earlier".

SSG Marks was awed by the Major's comment. "I thought you wanted it removed, Sir."

"I neither did nor not, wanted it kept. That is a command decision, which should be made by your Platoon Commander, who I presume is Lieutenant Schrader," said Major Burks.

"Major Burks, I assisted SGT Marks and my driver in removing the name. I felt it was best since there wasn't a reg (regulation) that authorized it," volunteered LT Schrader.

"Good call, Lieutenant. Maybe you aren't as dumb as I first thought. Sergeant Marks, you may be dismissed. Lieutenant, have a seat," said Major Burks.

Bob sat, dumbfounded by this turn of events and wondering what was going to happen next. What was happening next came quickly.

"Lieutenant Schrader, I understand you are a Battalion Surgeon's Assistant, a medic trained to be a doctor substitute, is that right?"

"Yes Sir, that is what I was trained to do while I was at Fort Sam."

"Is that what you are doing at 9th Med.? Or are you a glorified Motor Office with additional duties such as VD Officer, NCO Career Officer, Minority Affairs Officer and the like, but no duties in the medical treatment field."

"That about sums it up Sir. I am also the Savings Bond Officer and the paymaster once a month," admitted the Lieutenant.

"That's what I thought. Well, maybe I can make life a little bit more medical, if not enjoyable for you. Would you be interested in working for me on special assignments? "asked Major Burks.

Bob thought, "in for a Penny, in for a Pound, whatever that meant." What he thought it might mean was that he would get out of the motor pool and get into being a medic like he was trained. "Yes Sir, I would be most happy to work for you." Lieutenants, even West Point Graduates or their R.O.T.C. equals, are never very smart when it comes to decisions like this. Schrader was no exception. What Major Burks had in mind was nothing like what Bob expected, but after all, he was just a lowly Second Lieutenant, or as that group was generally referred to in reference to the single gold bar as 'butter bar' Lieutenants. He made the decision, but now he might have to live with it.

"You and your wife report to my quarters at 1915 (7:15 p.m.) for your Commanding Officer call. I will have your orders ready by then. You do know how to attend do you not?"

"Yes Sir, we practiced that during my senior year at Wyoming, and my wife and I made an officer's visit to my commanding officer at 9th Med.," said Bob, his head moving up and down in agreement with his comments.

"Good, we will anticipate your attendance tonight," Major Burks said, as he gestured for Bob to leave. The Lieutenant saluted, make a crisp about-face and marched himself out of the office.

Lieutenant Schrader and his wife, Betty, arrived at the Major's quarters at 1900 hours, Bob having been long trained in R.O.T.C. and Medical Service Corps basic training, that if you weren't at least 10-15 minutes early, you were late. Both Betty and the Lieutenant, were dressed in formal attire, Betty in a dress, and the Lieutenant in a Class A Green uniform, his shoes highly polished and his branch insignia, rank and his lone decoration, the National Defense Service Ribbon (which every soldier had issued after a short time in service), in the proper location on his uniform jacket. In his hand the Lieutenant had his calling card, a business card with his name and rank embossed, and with the corner turned up (so the Major would be able to separate it from any others that may be in the silver tray Lieutenant Schrader expected to be readily available for him to deposit his card upon arrival at his new commander's residence. The expected tray was on a table next to the door, and after Major Burk's wife, Rose, answered the door and invited them into their quarters, Lieutenant Schrader placed his card in the tray according to ancient Army Protocol.

Mrs. Burks was charming and invited them to come in and have a seat. She called to Major Burks, "our guests are here John."

Major Burks also welcomed them, introduced himself and Mrs. Burks to Betty and Mrs. Burks to Lieutenant Schrader, and then asked if they would like something to drink. Betty made her first error (or at least she thought so) by replying "I would like whatever you're having, Sir" (Betty had learned a lot about Sir and senior officers, especially Commanders, from the Lieutenant). She later learned what Major Burks was having was a Gin Martini, about ten parts gin, one part dry Vermouth and a small splash of Scotch, which Major Burks generally kept in a pitcher in his refrigerator. The Lieutenant compounded Betty's error, by saying, "I would have the same, Sir."

What should have been a five to ten-minute conversation over coffee or tea, lasted for 2 hours over Martinis. The good news was that it gave the Commander, his wife, his new subordinate and his wife, an opportunity to get to know each other as individuals. The bad news was an inspection early the next morning, with Major Burks in the field and Lieutenant Schrader the rear echelon commander (meaning he got to answer the phone, work the command radio, and take care of anyone who appeared at headquarters). Pretty easy for the Major, who had done this many times before. Not so easy for a slightly hung-over Lieutenant, who did have the faintest idea what to expect. Both were successful, however.

Two days later, Lieutenant Schrader was summoned to Major Burk's office. "Lieutenant, I am going to grant part of your wishes. You wanted to work as a Battalion Surgeon's Assistant. To that end, I have had you assigned to Delta

Company, 9ᵗʰ Medical Battalion, which is one of the units in this Division. You will be assigned as the Company Executive Officer, with duties as assigned. You will be the second in command of an army surgical clinic onboard a U.S. Navy ship in Vietnam. You will deploy with the rest of the 9ᵗʰ Infantry on Wednesday. You may tell your wife your assignment, but no one else who does not need to know. Those who need to know will have been provided with a copy of your orders, so you will only tell your wife and advise her that she is not to disclose to anyone what you tell her. Do you understand?"

"Yes, Sir."

"While so assigned, you will, from time to time, act as my intermediary or voice, for classified assignments to others. What they are going to do does not concern you. You will keep this information Top Secret from all others. Do you also understand this?"

"I understand Sir, but I only have a Secret Clearance, I am not cleared for Top Secret," answered Lieutenant Schrader.

"As of 0800 this date, you were granted a Top Secret Clearance. That is not a problem. You are going to be acting for me in several classified military operations, which are not the usual combat military operations. I am sending people on special missions to assist our Combat Commanders. You will be the one to brief and de-brief those leaders."

Bob thought, "oh, shit, what have I gotten myself into." Bob brought his attention back to Major Burks, with his full concentration being centered on what he was being told.

Whether Major Burks was being a good Commander, or because he sensed the Lieutenant's discomfort, he went on, "You will be provided with a Sat-Phone, current SOI.s (Signal Operating Instructions, a daily to authenticate radio communications authority), and my instructions to you about messages to others. It will become clear to you, as we progress, what you need to be doing."

Like hell, throught Bob. I don't know what I'm doing now, what makes him think I will figure it out by myself. Never happen. "Sir, I am a medic, not an operations officer."

"In this situation Lieutenant, you may be both."

Major Burks went on to explain that Lieutenant Schrader was assigned to Delta Company because the 9th Med Company was the unit that comprised the surgical clinic for the Mobile Riverine Force, attached to whatever Navy ship had the best medical facility on board (much to the dismay of both officers and enlisted members of Delta Company who had to move the clinic to each ship in turn, as they returned from Subic Bay Naval Facilities in the Philippines after upgrades.) In addition to your duties as XO (executive officer), you will brief the operations officers I assign to special missions from time to time. You will probably not be given any operational duties unless you request them" Major Burks advised. "I will send you the information you need through the Navy classified document officer on the ship. He will advise you when there is a message from me. You will convey that information to the special mission action officer for that mission when that officer identifies himself, or I identify him for you "Yes Sir," was all Lieutenant Schrader was able to reply. The Lieutenant knew he was way in over his head.

CHAPTER 6

"Ok, Mr. Burkley, you have the controls. We are cleared to land on the Killer Alpha," advised Major Quincy.

"On the what?" Jerry asked, hoping it wasn't the ship with a little pad between the two big parts, with a big red cross painted across the pad, and the radio frequency painted on both ends.

"That big grey thing with the big red cross in the middle of the landing pad. Think you can put this bird down there?" Major Quincy inquired.

"Sir, I've never landed on a ship before," Jerry protested.

"You have the controls, Mister. You have to learn to do this before you can be PIC (Pilot in Command) of helicopters in the 9th Infantry Division. This is pretty easy, wait until you have to land on one of those little boats like the ones docked next to the Colleton, which is the name of that big boat you are going to land upon." Major Quincy hid his grin by looking away from Jerry towards the ship.

"This ship isn't moving, so you don't have to worry about the superstructure catching up with you. This is just like landing at 3rd Surgical (the inflatable surgical hospital at Dong Tam, which was kind of like a large, air-conditioned, kid's bounce house). It isn't even dark yet, so piece of cake," remarked Major Quincy.

It was a piece of cake after Jerry sized up the situation and deftly maneuvered his Huey onto the landing pad deck, shut down, and awaited further instructions, which soon followed. A Second Lieutenant approached the chopper and waited for the pilots to recognize his presence. When Major Quincy did so, the Lieutenant saluted and requested the pilots to accompany him. Neither Major Quincy nor Warrant Officer, Junior Grade, Burkley, were comfortable leaving their Huey unattended.

The MSC Lieutenant seemed to anticipate their reluctance (in fact Major Burks had advised him this problem would probably arise). He told Major Quincy, "your Huey will be watched by my staff, right here on the pad. We won't be gone long." Eventually the Major accepted the situation and agreed to accompany the Lieutenant.

Lieutenant Schrader led Major Quincy and WO Burkley off the pad, down a curved ramp into an air-conditioned medical facility one deck lower, pointing out the features of the Surgical Clinic, and introduced them to his duty radio operator, Specialist 5, Scott Anderson, who gave them a brief orientation of the communications center, which was mainly a couple of military radios. The Lieutenant then led them down two more decks to Officer's Country, where his cabin was located.

The Lieutenant shared a four-person cabin with one of the Army Doctors, Captain Robert Weisberg, a talented Surgeon, who had just completed an assignment as the Battalion Surgeon for the 5th Battalion, 60th Infantry Regiment (commonly called 5/60th). After his field duty was finished, Bob was assigned to the ship, both as a reward for work well performed, and to take advantage of his field experience. The cabin had two pair of bunk beds, a desk for each of the two officers, and a sink. Both officers stored their field gear (pack, helmet, ammo, rifle, and the like), on the top bunk and slept on the lower. The Lieutenant also had a fully packed field medic pack stacked there. They stored their handguns and knives in a locked cabinet over their desk. Lieutenant Schrader had a crank operated field telephone next to his bed, which was connected by wire to the Company communications center. The Lieutenant also had a short-timers calendar (a drawing of Snoopy with numbers running from 365 to DEROS; DEROS being the estimated date of return to the Real World-the United States). As each day was served, one of the numbers was colored. There were a lot of uncolored boxes on the calendar.

"Lieutenant, why are we here and who are you? I am a Major and I don't routinely report to Butter Bar Lieutenants," demanded Major Quincy, holding his temper in check for the moment.

"Sir, I am Lieutenant Schrader. I am acting for Major Burks, 9th Infantry Division G-2 Special Operations Officer. He has selected me to be the briefing officer for a special mission which you and Mr. Burkley have been selected. "

"Why us, and why do we have a medical evacuation call sign? We are Assault Helicopter pilots," demanded Major Quincy. Mr. Burkley nodded in agreement.

"Sir, the easy answer is Major Burks ordered it. I believe Mr. Burkley worked for him earlier, and that you were part of the Warrant Officer Training Company he commanded."

"That's true," Mr. Burkley volunteered. This time Major Quincy shook his head in agreement.

"Major Burks feels that this method of assignment will give the mission better cover, and more chance of being successful than if everyone was ordered to 9th Infantry HQ for a briefing, where all the prying eyes and nosey Vietnamese could speculate about why you were there. Let me explain what is planned; I think that may answer your questions."

The Lieutenant gave the two pilots the mission information:

1. "The mission is to medically evacuate a Viet Cong General from the Cam Son Secret Area. That is the map designation of the area, not a play on words," added Lieutenant Schrader.

2. "Two of my medics and I will accompany you. I think I volunteered, but regardless I will be on this mission. The addition of three crew will mean you have to adjust for weight and balance."

"No way, that would mean removing ammo we might need," objected Major Quincy. "I am the aircraft Commander, and you don't have the authority to tell me to download ammo."

"No Sir, I don't, but I think Major Burks does have that authority."

3. There are two Cobra Gun Ships from 9th Aviation Battalion assigned to provide additional support. You will be provided with call signs just before departure from the Colleton.

4. Objections will be entertained by Major Burks at the conclusion of the mission.

5. This mission will commence at 1600 hours this date. "It is now 1500 (3 p.m.) hours. I would suggest mission prep begin immediately," suggested the MSC officer.

Major Quincy left in a rage, headed for his Huey to get on the radio to his command. He was frustrated to hear, "Assault 20, you will follow the mission orders you have been given."

The Crew of Assault 20, now Medivac 20, began offloading ammunition and other items that would reduce the overall weight of the Huey, to accommodate the weight and equipment of Lieutenant Schrader and his two medics, including a litter and medical supplies. Major Quincy was still fuming, but Mr. Berkley was feeling pretty good about being selected by the Old Man for a special mission.

At 1545 hours, the Colleton's PA system announced, "All special mission personnel report to Officer's Mess." In Navy terms, the Officer's Mess was the place where officers were served meals, and at other times used for meeting or just conversations. This was a small meeting; one Army MSC (Medical Service Corps) Lieutenant, two Army Combat Medics, two recently designated Army Dustoff Pilots, a representative from the 9th Aviation Battalion, the Navy Mobile Riverine Commander, and Major Burks.

"Gentlemen, my name is Burks. I am the 9th Infantry

Division G-2 special operations officer. You are about to constitute Operation 'Freedom Win.'. Your mission is to locate a wounded Viet Cong General. General Giap has been shot in the chest. For this mission, he is designated 'Win one'. He will require further medical treatment. Lieutenant Schrader, Sergeant Billings, and Specialist 4 Steiner have been assigned to see that part of the mission is successful. As a team, Freedom Win will locate the General, who is being held by elements of the 5th Battalion, 60th Infantry, in the Cam Son Secret Area, approximately 20 miles or 32 kilometers east of this location. The coordinates are 15.783 Latitude 108.250 Longitude. 5th of the 60th is in contact with enemy forces, who presumably are trying to rescue Win One. You will probably encounter a hot LZ (a helicopter landing zone receiving enemy fire).

Two Cobra gunships (the first actual attack helicopter, the Bell AH-1G Cobra) from the 9th Aviation Battalion, call signs 'Freedom 1 and 2', will fly both operational lead and general support.

Dustoff 20 will load, treat Win One if necessary, and transport to Killer Alpha (the Colleton). Boats of the Riverine River Assault Squadron 13 will be in reserve standby if deemed necessary for additional assistance to Freedom Win.

Lieutenant Schrader, call sign 'Dusty Papa 5' will be in overall command of this mission (medical service corps officers don't command missions). He and his medics will also load and treat Win One.

"Good luck," Major Burks ending the briefing.

On Deck, Warrant Officer Burkley made sure the MSC Lieutenant and the two medics were strapped into their seats and tested their headphones and push-to-talk mikes were on "intercom" (so the AC, aircraft commander, Mr. Burkley and

SGT Potter, the crew chief/door gunner, could communicate with them).

The medics, SPC 5 Dale Steiner and SPC 4 Avery Silverman, were seasoned combat medics. Both proudly wore the Combat Medical Badge (equivalent to the Bronze Star with V for Valor) which was awarded for performing medical duties while in combat. (For putting on band-aids while the enemy is shooting at you). This was not their first combat extraction. LT Schrader was still worried about how he would perform executing his first combat.

CHAPTER 7

S GT Satterfield, the door gunner, thinking about the upcoming mission, thought to himself (he wouldn't dare voice this opinion for a lot of reasons, probably because he would get a lot of kidding about becoming a 'lifer', a career 20-30 year retiree). Some Lieutenant Colonels are a lot like full Colonels; squared away, sure of themselves, and confident, like Major Burks, who wasn't even an LTC yet, would become if he didn't get killed first. He wouldn't quit. Those officers had a Duty to Country, Family, and most importantly, to their Brothers-in-Arms of whatever rank. Loyalty went both up and down the ranks. They were men who could be counted upon! It was apparent in the way they walked, spoke, and acted. You felt safe following them where ever they led. The 9th Medical Battalion has a saying that voices this value: "Where you lead, we follow." Other soldiers, and especially some Commanders were much the opposite. You couldn't trust them with your life!

Many were like Major Burks and good Colonels too. They were loyal, brave, and trustworthy. SGT Satterfield mumbled to himself; "These are the pilots I want flying me!" They were generally also great pilots which added to the equation. SGT Satterfield thought both Major Burks and Warrant Officer Burkley fit the mold. Missions succeeded because they were the rule, not the exception. He was proud to be working with them.

He didn't work for Major Burks or Mr. Burkley, but it was the Major's mission, and Mr. Burkley was his aircraft pilot, so he felt he worked for both.

Major Quincy and Mr. Burkley were surprised when a medic, SSG Henderson, was assigned to the mission. They were more surprised by the equipment he insisted on putting in their Huey. There were no red crosses (to identify medical aircraft, on the doors and nose of their assigned Huey). Jerry was assigned to fly the medical Huey, and Major Quincy was re-assigned to a spare gunship. Jerry's co-pilot was a Medical Service Corps Second Lieutenant, with McKane printed on a name tag with a Combat Medical Badge and pilot wings sewn over his name tag on a baggy green flight suit. SSG Henderson and 2LT McKane gave SSG Satterfield an extensive medical briefing and training on the equipment and made him practice until he was proficient. Later he discovered 2LT McKane had been a Dustoff (medical helicopter evacuation) pilot before Major Burks conscripted him for special missions.

Major Burks summoned the crew and pilots to a briefing room and after everyone was introduced by name and mission duties, advised them: "this is a very critical mission, which must be carried out with precision. You are tasked with the responsibility of removing a high ranking North Vietnamese General from the Cam Son Secret Zone about 20 to 40 klicks (kilometers) east of Dong Tam, and bring him, under your medical care and treatment, to the Delta Company, 9th Infantry Division, surgical facility on board the U.S.S. Colleton, radio call 'Killer Alpha', located in the Mekong River about the same distance west of Dong Tam. Maps and coordinates are included in mission packets the G-2 will give you. Your Rules of Engagement on this mission allow the gunships to fire at any enemy targets, and individuals to initiate fire if felt necessary. It is imperative this General be subjected to interrogation. He has current information on enemy forces and plans. Our troops will benefit from any information we can obtain. Move him from the Battalion position where he is being held, provide any necessary medical care and treatment, and get him 'Killer Alpha'." Major Burks closed the meeting, saying, "be careful, come back safely," and left the briefing room, as all stood to attention.

The Mission, Code Name for radio reference, GENINFO, lifted off on schedule. All went smoothly until the advance Loach teams (Hughes OH-6 Cayuse) approached the LZ (Landing Zone) at 5/60th. Then all hell seemed to break loose. The radios filled with warnings to the other helicopters, "abort, dodge right; you have RPG (rocket-propelled grenade) fire from 260 degrees; so much radio traffic that none was intelligible." The Cobra gunships (Bell AH-10 Cobras), quickly shut down the defensive positions and radioed, "all clear for now, hurry!"

On the ground, several U.S. and VC units were engaged, and the gunfire was heavy. The sounds of hits on the medivac helicopters could be heard through the Dave Clark style headphones worn by the crew members, and even louder to the passengers not so equipped. Jerry and Major Quincy both zig-zagged towards the LZ.

"I'm hit," cried Silverman, holding both hands over his lower leg. Lieutenant Schrader unstrapped and crawled across the Huey floor to Silverman. "Easy does it, Avery, I'm here to help."

"It hurts, Sir," Silverman responded, then reached into his own medical kit for a field dressing to cover the wound and allow Schrader to apply pressure and then a bandage to hold the dressing tight against the wound on both sides.

"You'll be fine. Get ready to receive WINONE; I will get out and assist, you take my place here."

Enemy troops could be seen from Dustoff 20, as Jerry dropped in a steep vertical descent into the LZ. The red smoke from the smoke grenades used to mark the area of the LZ to land, limited visibility. Since most of the ammo had been removed from the Huey, LT Schrader, the medics, crew chief and the co-pilot, were firing their personal weapons (M-16, .45 automatic pistols, and a shotgun) out the door openings as the Huey touched down. LT Schrader, the crew chief, and SSG Henderson jumped out and ran to the troops bringing a litter to them. All assisted in shoving the litter into the passenger compartment in the Huey. LT Schrader was strapping the litter to the floor as Jerry put on full power, lifted and tilted pitch forward to gain flying speed and gain altitude. Soon Dustoff 20 was airborne and headed towards the 'Killer Alpha.'

"All crew report," ordered WO1 Berkley.

"WINONE secured on-board, all crew onboard. One friendly, Silverman, wounded, treated and able to continue," LT Schrader reported. "In order, all the rest of the crew reported good to go!"

LT Schrader and the two combat medics gave the General a thorough examination, changed dressings, and started a new IV drip of saline and water. "AC, the patient is in good shape and can be taken to destination."

"Thanks, Bob. We will be there in 10 (minutes). Good job to you and your team".

"Everyone did well. Thanks to all," Schrader praised.

After the General was offloaded at 'Killer Alpha', and turned over to the MPs for security and the Colleton medical staff for medical care, Major Burks assembled all the crews (most of whom landed at Dong Tam and were moved to Colleton by Navy boats, (no parking space on the small Colleton landing pad), and also congratulated the crew on a highly successful mission. "You did extremely well today. The 5/60th did amazing work both in capturing an important enemy general and proving support to allow his transport to this ship. We had only three wounded, none seriously, lost no-one and no aircraft. Great Job! Please attend your debriefing sessions and get your reports finalized. No job is done in the Army until the paperwork is done. Be assured your service records will reflect the excellent performance of every one of you. As the Navy would say, Bravo Zulu (2 flags flown on the ship meaning B and Z, pronounced Bravo Zulu, meaning well done)."

The entire team left, wondering who Major Burks was and why was he in charge. Jerry learned more later.

WO1 Burkley and 1LT Schrader went back to slightly different quarters (place to live). Burkley went to Dong Tam, where he was quartered in a two-story barracks with separate rooms for each officer. As he had previously accomplished, Jerry had a refrigerator in his room (which made him popular with other officers, and some senior NCOs). Schrader, on the other hand, had a stateroom on the Colleton, which he shared with Dr. Weisberg. The Lieutenant was not bashful about carrying Class 6 items onboard (no Navy officer would dare do so). That made his stateroom popular for the doctors, some visiting Army officers, and even the Navy Chaplain. Their duties were routine, and almost boring most of the time. Schrader got to perform surgery on American and RVN troops wounded in the field and brought by Dustoff to 'Killer Alpha'. Jerry flew many air assault missions within the Delta AOO (Area of Operations), but none as dangerous as the mission into the Cam Son Secret Area. The area isn't secret, everyone on both sides knows where it is and that it is a haven for Viet Cong units.

One day, 1LT Schrader and the Colleton medical doctor, LT (CPT in Army Rank) Jack Long, inspected the ship's galley (the kitchen). Both Bob and Jack had noticed the menu for the Officers Mess that night was cold cuts. They also saw the galley Chief had lobster tails in the refrigerator. After a short negotiation with the Chief, the galley passed inspection. Bob and Jack carried some lobster tails and butter to the surgical area. Lobster tail was wrapped in a surgical towel and put in the autoclave at its lowest setting, butter melted in a bowel over a Bunsen burner, and both officers had a delicious meal. The towel, which could never be salvaged, and the lobster shells were placed in a paper bag. During "trash call," which is when garbage was tossed overboard into the Mekong River, the bag was thrown out as well. A sampan (Vietnamese flat boat) was paddled quickly to the bag. Once the Vietnamese looked inside, the bag was thrown back into the Mekong River. A delightful evening for both officers!

Jerry wasn't nearly as comfortable in Dong Tam. When he was not flying missions, he had his choice of volleyball, an outdoor movie, dinner on a tray in the mess hall, or a warm beer, if he wasn't on call.

Both were bored to tears. The adage about war being long periods of stark boredom, interspersed with moments of stark terror, became real.

Dong Tam was dust in the dry season, and you could see fat drops of rain in the monsoon season when the dust turned into sticky mud. Both were miserable. In the "Real World" (The United States) there were draft-dodgers going to Canada, and many draft-eligible young men and others staging objections to the war!

"Why is it that people object, in the names of soldiers fighting the war, then object and despise the same soldiers when they return from that war?"

Perhaps the answer lies in the songs of the time, like 'Blowing in the Wind':

"Where have all the soldiers gone, blowing in the wind?"
And other protest songs of the 60s.

Conversations around the bar could get heated or interesting! Usually, it got started with a demand, not a request, for pilot qualifications.

"Jerry, did you go to flight training at Walters, Hunter, or Rucker (the three primary training locations for both Warrant Officers and Commissioned Officers)?"

"Yup!'" was Jerry's casual reply.

"No one does all three," several of the assembled pilots exclaimed!

"He did," stated a Major with wings of a Senior Aviator on his utility uniform. "I was his IP at Rucker and the Advanced Course at Walters. He learned fixed wing and instruments at Hunter. Mr. Burkley, may I see you for a moment? You may tell these Gentlemen before you come with me, they all signed up for their first job to fly helicopters and to get shot at, since you already have done that."

"Yes, Sir."

Major Burks went on, "Mr. Burkley also went through the equivalent of three basic training courses at each of those schools. Feel lucky you didn't lead such a charmed life. Mr. Burkley."

"On the way Sir! It's true that about sums it up," commented Jerry as he left. "Fly, get shot at, and hope they miss."

Laughter followed them out of the Club.

"How much have you had to drink Mister?" the Major inquired.

"Coke and water only Sir, I have a check ride at 0600,"

"That will be canceled. Go to Ops (operations), check out our bird, wind the rubber band, and be ready to fly with me at 2300 (11:00 p.m.).

"What about the crew members, Sir?"

"Already laid on and working. I suggest you do likewise. I will file our flight plan."

Jerry was left standing, then ran to Ops. He was both puzzled since the old man wasn't really in his chain of command, and proud to and pleased to be flying with Major Burks, if he was. The Major worked in mysterious ways!

The urgent mission was pretty routine. In fact, it was downright dull. Major Burks and Jerry, plus a door gunner and a crew chief, flew 'Chick One' and 1Lt McKane and WO1 Bill Williams flew 'Chick Two' from Dong Tam to Bear Cat, where part of the 9th Infantry Division was still stationed.

Jerry had questions to ask Major Burks during the short flight.

"Sir, what is going on in Bear Cat?"

"Just a paper shuffle."

"Then why, at this time of night, with two Hueys?"

"That's when I was free to go," Major Burks replied, his tone of voice ending this area of questioning.

Shortly after that Jerry asked, "Chick is a strange call sign. What does it mean?"

"Son, all calls are strange, most have no meaning. In this case, it refers to Chickasaw, Oklahoma. You need to get Approach on the horn so we can land."

"Yes, Sir. Python 33, Approach, Chick One, five south with one for landing."

"Cleared number 1 to helipad. Watch for other traffic," answered Bear Cat Approach Control. Contact tower on SOI (signal operating instruction) frequency." (Frequencies were usually not given in the clear to prevent unauthorized use or jamming of the radio frequency.)

Both Hueys landed and moved to parking revetments.

Major Burks left with a briefcase in his hand and boarded a waiting jeep. After refueling, and checking the aircraft, both crews did what was common in the Army, hurry up and wait.

When Major Burks returned, he was wearing the silver oak leaf of a Lieutenant Colonel. The oak leaf stood out on his uniform as they were the regular pin on insignia rather than the subdued sew on kind. This leaf was pinned through his old Major sew on rank.

LT McKane was the first to notice, "congratulations Colonel."

The rest soon got the message and congratulations were voiced. LTC Burks waived it off, said thanks, and asked, "are we ready to go?" Four "Yes Sirs" replied.

Shortly after takeoff for the return trip to Dong Tam, a radio call for a Dustoff Mission was heard: "Dusty Papa 33 (9th Medical Medivac Control), Panther Charlie 3-5 (3rd platoon Sgt, C Company, 2/47th), request Dustoff; 4 litter, 2 ambulatory, 10.35 N, 104 E (map coordinates of LZ)), Red (LZ receiving enemy fire), Over."

"Panther Charlie 3-5, Dusty Papa 33, copy, standby, break (the radio operator indication he was going to talk to someone else), any available aircraft, no Dustoff available, over."

All helicopters would divert for this mission if their mission didn't have a higher priority. Jerry didn't even think about it. He was doing a trash haul mission. In his mind, a paper shuffle wasn't a mission. He pressed the mike key on his stick, "Dusty Papa 33, Chick One and Two will respond."

McKane keyed up, "Rodger Chick Two."

"Chick One and Two, Delta Papa 33, contact Panther Charlie 3-5, on their push (radio frequency). Advise further."

"Roger 33."

Only then did Jerry look over at Major, no, he remembered Lieutenant Colonel Burks. The Colonel raised a 'thumbs up' and pointed forward.

Jerry was relieved, proud and scared all at the same time. He and McKane pushed on to a presumably hot LZ. He hoped there was also some gunship or fast mover (Air Force jet fighter) support, but he doubted it. Panther Charlie 3-5 had suppressed most of the VC fire by the time the two Hueys arrived. Panther Charlie 3-5 lit up a strobe light to mark the LZ; Chick One and Two homed in on it, safely landed, and the six wounded and one KIA (killed in action) were loaded on the two helicopters, the Huey crew members quickly directing the infantry troops in loading. Both Hueys lifted, rotated forward and gained flying speed. Both choppers received hits, but with no real damage.

"Killer Alpha, Chick One with one, inbound your location 4/2/1 (4 litter, 2 ambulatory, 1 KIA)," Jerry radioed.

"Roger Chicks, cleared for landing."

"Chick Two land first," advised Jerry on the Chick operations frequency, switched his radio to the preset frequency for Dusty Papa, and transmitted, "Dusty Papa 33, Chick One with one, for landing with Evac 4/2/1."

"Cleared to Pad," advised Killer Alpha. Chick Two quickly landed. Litter bearers from the ship removed the wounded from Chick Two and carried them down the ramp to surgery. 1LT McKane lifted off and circled the ship while Jerry sat down with his load. He was also quickly unloaded. As the patients and the KIA were removed, Lieutenant Colonel Burks instructed Jerry to shut down and follow him.

1LT Schrader met them halfway down the ramp. "If you aren't needed in treatment, let's go to your stateroom," LTC Burks told the Lieutenant.

"Yes Sir, surgery is covered right now, I've been monitoring the radio."

LTC Burks led the way out of the surgical area below to LT Schrader's quarters, which indicated to Jerry that the Old Man had been on board the ship before, and probably more than once or twice. Jerry had only been on board once before, and he was totally lost after the first or second change in direction (below, left, right).

"Colonel, congratulations!" said LT Schrader when they reached his office.

"Thanks, the General just pinned it on tonight. He was even able to get Rose on a comm radio for a short time. Great ceremony! Jerry, I'm sorry you couldn't be there too, but Chick One had to be manned with a pilot."

"No sweat Sir, I too am pleased to see your silver oak leaf."

"OK," LTC Burks moved on, "I wanted both of you to meet. The Dustoff was a good opportunity, and we don't have long. We may have to clear the deck soon."

"Mr. Burkley and I were on the WINONE mission together. I think we made a good team," LT Schrader told the Colonel.

The Colonel went on to brief the two young officers about what LT Schrader's involvement with the Colonel's missions involved, and that Mr. Burkley was going to be his backup. Just as the three were returning to the deck, the PA system announced, "Clear the deck for incoming medivac."

As Chick One hoovered, lifted off the deck, and departed for Dong Tam, LTC Burks mentioned to Mr. Burkley and gave him one more jolt for the night. "I have another mission for you, LT McKane, and your crew. I will need you available Saturday afternoon and evening. Please clear that time for all personnel and aircraft."

"Yes Sir, but that won't make anyone happy."

"Why?"

"Sir, that is when Bob Hope will be here with the U.S.O. to perform!"

"That should work out well," advised LTC Burks. Talk to me when we land."

Jerry shut up, fuming over the injustice of a special mission when Bob Hope was going to be there in person. Oh, well, he determined, the task must be critical, and it was what the

Old Man wanted him to perform. Jerry made a significant attitude adjustment before they landed and secured their aircraft. LTC Burks informed him his team would be in charge of transporting Bob Hope, and three of his star performers. The rest would be carried by Air Force aircraft. Jerry's attitude took a big swing up, and he was extremely pleased to be the one to announce the mission to his crew.

Bob Hope made the mission even better when he called the entire crew onto the performance stage to be introduced, and then seated them in the second row, stage front for the show. They had to leave early to crank up the helicopters (or as Mr. Hope called it, winding the rubber bands-not the first time that reference had been made) but all were 'Happy Campers'.

The next few months were exciting, boring and rewarding. First Lieutenants Schrader and McKane were promoted to Captain; Warrant Officer Burkley was promoted to Warrant Officer Two. The promotions were not all at the same time, so there was time to celebrate all of them in a timely and Army fashion (the promotee got to buy the drinks to 'wet down the bars.'). LTC Burks joined in the celebrations to also wet down his leaf.

All of them performed missions for the Colonel, fortunately with only two casualties, one killed and one not critically wounded. Many medals and decorations were awarded, and presented, with Jerry, Dan, and the other crew members receiving more than their fair share.

As is normally true in the Army, everyone was transferred to other assignments at the end of their Vietnam tour. They went different directions and all said farewell (not goodbye because they expected to see each other in future postings).

CHAPTER 8

O f course, not everyone transferred at the same time. Lieutenant Colonel Burks was the first. He was sent to the Pentagon in Washington, D.C. with a TDY (Temporary Duty) delay en-route to allow the Colonel to attend the Army War College at Fort Leavenworth, Kansas. This assignment was excellent news for the Colonel. The War College was a significant step in getting his next promotion, but he had mixed feelings about going to the Pentagon (the five-sided headquarters building which is Headquarters for the military services). As he told Rose much later, "I could carry coffee to Generals where I was!" Upon getting these orders, however, LTC Burks walked to the M.A.R.S. (Military Amateur Radio System) radio building, not far from the flight line at Dong Tam. The line was short, and he was soon sitting in a small room equipped with a speaker, microphone on a stand, and a two-way switch fastened to the table. Master Sergeant Chuck Williams greeted LTC Burks with enthusiasm, "good morning Colonel, and welcome to MARS! We are part of the Amateur Radio net and provide communications services between Vietnam and various locations in the United States, hopefully, a location close to where the person you are calling lives or works. Since we are not a military radio facility, you can be almost as personal as you wish during your call. I am a Licensed Amateur Radio Operator. My call sign was, and is, N7MZW. You will hearA-B8AZ, the call-sign of the Dong Tam MARS station, and that of any station I can contact in the States. When we are connected you can talk like you do on an aircraft radio; only you don't have to push a transmit button, I will be doing that for you since you technically can't operate a HAM (amateur radio station) radio. The operator on the other end will do that for the person you are calling. I understand you wish to call your wife, Rose, in Junction City, Kansas, is that correct?"

"Affirmative Sarge. I appreciate your help," he replied, as he got settled into the tableside chair.

"No sweat, Sir. I exist to do this job. I'm lucky. This is my hobby, I love HAM radio, and the Army assigned me to this job when I got out of the field. The band conditions are great today, and we have good propagation to the states," MSGT Williams grinned. "Say 'over' when you want to let your wife talk. When you hear her say over, you can talk." LTC Burks only understood the first part. Didn't matter, he just wanted to talk to Rose.

Sergeant Williams went out of the room, closed the door and began the process. "CQ, CQ, AB8AZ Army MARS looking for any MARS near Junction City, KS. Over." He received an almost immediate response.

"AB8AZ, W7UAG in Paradise Valley, AZ, is available for and ready to relay. Over."

Sergeant Williams gave the contact information, and within just a few minutes LTC Burks heard, "AB8AZ, W7AUG, your contact is on the line."

"Thank you, Sir. AB8AZ," LTC Burks heard over the radio, then over an intercom heard, "Colonel your wife is on. Go ahead and talk, say over when you wish to listen.

"Rose, can you hear me, over?"

"Yes Dear, are you ok John?" There was a long silence, and after apparently being told to say over, Rose did.

"I'm great. Going to AWC (Air War College) and then DC. I'll be home soon. Get ready to move. Just wanted to tell you myself. Love you. Got to go, over."

"I love you too," Rose replied. The band conditions starting to deteriorate and LTC Burks said, "what did you say, over?"

A deep male voice came over the radio; she said, "I love you too."

The two amateur radio operators closed down the connection, and MSG Williams escorted the Colonel out. "You got two home runs on that call, Sir."

"I did what?"

"You got to talk to your wife, and Senator Goldwater as well. The Senator was the other radio operator. He has a great station in Arizona and likes to make contacts when he can. You or your wife will have to pay the long-distance collect call from Arizona to Kansas

"Sarge, thanks for the information and your help. If I can ever return the favor, let me know."

"I will Sir," MSG Williams replied, saluted the Colonel and went to try and help the next soldier waiting to make a radio call on MARS.

The Warrant Officers flew missions, but sort of missed the adrenaline rush from the Old Man's missions. Other diversions were devised. Warrant Officer Flagg found the opportunity to even the score with the control pounding Instructor Pilot, 1LT Les Moore (now CPT Moore). Several Hueys, 2 Cobras and a lone Loach, were in a remote location awaiting missions. Feeling the urge of nature, CPT Moore removed the tiny role of toilet paper from a box of C-4 rations and walked down the hill into the high grass.

Warrent Officer 2 Flagg received a radio transmission to transport a Battalion Commander to oversee an operation (a means of observing what was happening on the ground while remaining safely above combat. Dave (WO2 Flagg) took off directly over the route CPT Moore had traveled, hovered over him, and was pleased to see the grass blow flat exposing the Captain with his flight suit around his ankles and squatting. The toilet paper (which many call Air Force Form One), flew up through the blades of Dave's Loach, leaving the arrogant Captain without the paper to finish his private mission. The laughter of the other pilots was joyful. (Moore finally had less!)

Keeping one's nerve, In spite of fear is Courage!
Dying in the attempt is incompetence!!

Jerry received his first experience at landing on a Mobile Riverine Force 'Tango' (LCM-6 Armored Troop Carrier, which had been converted to a floating landing pad for helicopters by covering the top of the troop transport area with a heavy metal top). The Army medics arranged the lower area to accommodate and treat wounded patients while awaiting dust off evacuation. Landing on this small target took skill in hovering, and patiently waiting for patients to be loaded or unloaded, as required by the mission.

The Alpha Boat configured with a hard top was used by the medical platoons in each Battalion, and by Delta Company, 9th Medical Battalion, 9th Infantry Division, as floating medical facilities in support of the Mobile Riverine Force. Bunks on the walls were used for up to five litter patients. There was limited room for ambulatory patients. The ten feet between the landing pad and the cargo deck made it necessary for ambulatory patients to climb up and down, litter patients had to be lowered by hand. Treatment was limited, and the small area made it necessary to move patients in and out quickly. That involved a number of helicopter trips, which exposed the medical crew, usually a Medical Officer or a Battalion Surgeon Assistant (a Medical Service Corps Officer with medical training, now called a Physician's Assistant), seven enlisted medics and a radio operator, to enemy attention and other attempts to neutralize the Tango-Med. The small landing pad made it difficult to land a helicopter, keep it in place, and the air disturbance of the rotor blades made it hard for the medical personnel to move patients and themselves.

It was also Jerry's first experience at sitting in the right seat. Jerry was the co-pilot but training for AC (aircraft commander). Their helicopter was a UH-1C (improved engine and some other modifications) with a nose-mounted grenade launcher, and side mounted machine guns and rockets. The mission was to provide close air support, together with another similar helicopter, for six slicks (unarmed Huey HU-1B is used to transport troops into and out of combat areas), inserting a part of Alpha Company, 5th/60th Infantry Battalion, 9th Infantry Division, on a sweep and destroy mission designed to find and naturalize a VC in the Parrot's Beak area of the Mekong River. The LZ was quiet when the first two Hueys touched down and discharged troops but soon exploded with heavy mortar and machine-gun fire.

The first two Hueys lifted safely off, the troops safely on the ground. The next two troop ships moved west to a clearing and so safely discharged all troops. Sticks (the following groups of helicopter troops) five and six took heavy fire in the original LZ, despite the massive fire assault of Bounty Hunter 20 (MAJ Quincy and WO2 Berkeley) and Bounty Hunter 34 (the other gunship). Stick five and six got everyone safely off, but Stick 6 pulled up hard, partially stalled, and turned into Assault 34's path. Both exploded upon impact with each other. Jerry learned later, all on board both aircraft were killed. Jerry and Major Quincy both felt responsible, although neither could have prevented it from occurring. Both drank a lot at the Officer's Club in Dong Tam that night. The new

Battalion Commander of 214th Aviation Battalion, LTC Ben (Smitty) Smith, gave up flying.

COURAGE IS NOT THE ABSENCE OF FEAR BUT THE ABILITY TO CARRY ON WITH DIGNITY IN SPITE OF IT. DOING WHAT YOU HAVE TO DO!!

That day, the Delta Company, 9th Medical Battalion, Mobile Riverine Force Medical Boat (Dusty Papa Mike) only added to Jerry's misery. "Bounty Hunter 20, Dusty Papa 33, can you take 2 Lima (litters) from Dusty Papa 5 Mike (the Medical Tango Boat)? Over."

"Roger Dusty Papa 33. Coordinates?" Major Quincy responded.

The necessary information was exchanged. Jerry got his first mission requiring him to land sideways on Dusty Papa 5 Mike, Lieutenant Schrader in charge."

This task helped lessen the image of his six friends exploding in a ball of fire and crashing to earth. The flight line was two helicopters short when Bounty Hunter 20 returned from Killer Alpha.

After all the combat at the LZ, Alpha Company didn't find a single target. All felt the loss of two aircraft and six crew members, none more than Jerry.

The hard-topped Tango Boat medical crews had mixed feelings about Huey Helicopters, especially Huey pilots. Some pilots were ok; many were not. When a Huey was grounded (watered, whatever) on the hard-top of the Tango Boat (most were used as medical aid stations so patients could be moved for immediate medical care, treated on board, or transported by any Huey to a better treatment facility). The pilot could move the Tango Boat by changing pitch on the blades while landed side-ways on the mini-deck the hard top provided. (The Huey hung over on both sides, with the cockpit on one side, and the tail and rotor on the other.)

The Navy boat "Captains" (an enlisted man, E-4 to E-6 most generally, in charge of the boat), really disliked pilots who performed this maneuver, on purpose or by accident! Boat Captains could make it hard for a pilot to find a stable landing platform, by moving the boat. The problem was usually solved by sharing a beer or when the Army crew needed a ride to shore from the boat.

By the way, this game was never played in combat.

1LT Schrader leaned over his bunk and pinned new Captain Bars to his Khaki uniform shirt. Bob was pleased to get the promotion but didn't want to have new insignia sewed to his uniform. Officer rank came quickly in the Army. One year from 2LT to 1LT, another year to CPT. The service uniforms, Dress Uniform, and Ceremonial Uniforms had pinned on gold and silver insignia. The field uniforms all had sewn on insignia; a subdued bronze for gold insignia and black for silver insignia. The sew-on was a significant problem. It was hard to get aligned, and you usually had to pay a professional to sew it on. You also had to pay for separate insignia for each uniform. The pin on could be transferred easily from one uniform to another. When he promoted to 1LT, Bob simply took a black sharpie and colored his bronze bars black. He couldn't do that from a single bar to the twin-track bars of a Captain. "Oh, well, the pay increase should pay for all that!"

Bob was leaving on a long-delayed R&R to Hawaii. He and Betty had been planning this occasion for a long time and saving money to pay for Betty's travel to Honolulu, Hawaii, and their entertainment while they were there. He was humming as he got packed.

Dr. Wiesberg was going on R&R too, but he got snagged for one more mission before he left the Colleton. "Doctor W," the ship's PA announced, "report to the flight deck for medical Evac mission." What the hell, he thought as he heard the announcement, I've already got R&R orders. Is this going to mess them up?

On the Heli-pad, he found 2LT Joe Creel, WO2 Bill Williams, and CPT Dan McKane, discussing (arguing) loudly. "Dr. W. are these two working on me," an agitated Creel demanded, "or am I being sent to Graves Registration?"

"When did that happen?" inquired Doctor W?

"This helicopter jockey just told me," he answered, pointing his fingers like a gun at Dan.

Dr. Wiesberg laughed, "he is a classmate of your absent trainer. He is just having some fun at your expense!"

Bill and Dan were also laughing very loudly. "It's ok, Joe,' explained Bill. Dan is just here to ferry our Doc to Ton Son Nhut."

Now Dr. W. was concerned, "when did that happen?" he asked.

"When you were with me at Parrot's Beak, I think."

"No way, I would have remembered that. I don't think, after Parrot's Beak, I want to fly any more missions with you!" Dr. W. exclaimed.

"Sure you will, I'm lucky," grinned Dan. "Anyway, we've got to get you to your R&R transport."

A short flight later, Dan dropped him off. CPT Schrader was waiting on the landing pad area as Doc got off the Medivac Huey. "Come on Major, I have wheels, and your flight assembly is forming right now. Doc had a short wait for his commercial flight to Australia. Bob had to wait overnight. Shortly after that, Bob ran into LTCMDR Jack Long, USN, the Colleton Medical Officer. Since Bob had wheels, a Jeep, they decided to tour the area while it was still daylight.

The Saigon traffic was something to behold. There were

large military vehicles, including half-tracks, jeeps, armored personnel carriers, and large cargo trucks, from all the various military units in the area. United States Army trucks, Vietnamese jeeps, vehicles from Australia, Korea, England, and other participating nations. Mixed in were Moped scooters, often with a driver and a Vietnamese woman in an Au-Dai on the back, bicycles, 3 wheeled cyclocabs pulled by a bike or in a rickshaw pulled by a papa-san in sandals trotting along with the other vehicular traffic, and miniature buses with chickens, people and cargo hanging on as they all tried to navigate the Saigon traffic. There were large traffic circles around statues, and Vietnamese National Police (called White Mice by the troops because of their white helmets and leather gear) trying to direct the wild traffic. Pedestrians crossed as they wished, whenever they wanted, dodging the mixed traffic.

Jack and Bob came up behind a wreck between a farm truck carrying grain, which had attempted to occupy the same space as an armored Vietnamese troop carrier. The small truck was no match for the multiple-wheeled and heavy vehicle. Grain covered the road. Many Vietnamese with woven baskets scurried to scoop up what grain they could to augment their meal that night. "What a mess. How can they live like this?" Jack commented.

"That's what life is like here. And will be until all this crazy war is over, and maybe not even then," said Bob as he maneuvered the jeep around the mess. "At least no-one appears to be hurt."

As Bob wove through MACV headquarters, Jack and Bob observed how the generals lived; air-conditioned trailers parked near the headquarters area. Bob commented, "Nice digs. Better than the shacks, I mean barracks we have in Dong Tam."

"Yeh but not as nice as our quarters on the ships," observed Jack. "But sure nicer than the troops in the field enjoy."

"For sure! You want to see how the REMF (rear echelon

******-*******) and the press live? We can probably sneak into the Five O'clock Follies (the nightly press briefing at the Rex Hotel in downtown Saigon, which gave those present a bird's eye view of some of the closer combat action and gave the reporters something vivid to report on the evening news)."

"Think we can? Sure, I'm game," Jack chuckled. "Maybe we will get on the 5:00 news!"

"We better not. I'm not sure we should be here, and I don't want to have to beg forgiveness or even worse miss my R&R slot while I'm trying to explain why I wasn't patiently waiting at the BOQ for my flight to be announced. We can drive by, but we don't have any way to secure the jeep."

Jack argued, "we have a chain and lock for the steering wheel, it won't go anywhere."

"Maybe," Bob interjected, "but that won't stop some kid from dropping a hand grenade with rubber bands around the spoon, and the pin pulled into the gas tank, which you will note is right under where I am sitting. I don't want to fish around in the tank to see if I can find it before the gas dissolves the rubber bands or take a chance on driving it without looking. Makes a real mess out of the driver, and isn't too healthy for passengers either! I had to treat one of those incidents just after I got over here."

The look on Jack's face made it clear Bob's description was all too graphic! "Let's go check in the jeep, go to the club and have dinner and a drink," he replied.

"Works for me. Maybe a drink before, during, and after dinner," Bob suggested.

Jack and Bob drove through the security gate at their quarter's area, receiving salutes from the two security guards at the gate. "I wish they wouldn't do that. In the field that can get you shot," Bob exclaimed!

Jack understood. Many of the patients they treated on the ship were identified as officers and became a prime target after being saluted in the boonies. Even the officer insignia on their BDUs (battle dress uniform or fatigues) was changed to a subdued bronze or black, rather than the Gold and Silver worn on regular uniforms back in the world. Or "green" as the Army liked to kid the Air Force who had a longer wait for promotions; gold, silver and green with age.

Early the next morning, Bob and Jack, wearing slightly wrinkled khaki-colored uniforms, the Army and Navy somewhat agreeing on the casual uniforms they each wore, boarded a commercial airplane contracted to take soldiers, sailors and marines from Vietnam to Hawaii for Rest and Recuperation (R&R). Both slept most of the way, anticipating their "vacation."

Chapter 9

S SG Cory Henderson and SPC5 Avery Silverman were engaged in their favorite topic, bitching about the Army, Officers, NCO's, and specifically their present duty assignment. They were boxing medical supplies and equipment for the move of Delta Company from the Colleton to the Benewah. This move was mandated by the fact the Colleton was going to Subic Bay in the Philippians for an overhaul, which would include substantial improvement to the medical/surgical facilities used by Delta Company. The Benewah had just returned from Subic with a shiny new surgical facility under the flight deck and at the aft end of the ship. While the medical staff appreciated their new quarters, they all, doctors, MSC's, medics, and even the radio operators due to the fact they had to move everything from one ship to the other, weren't overjoyed. It wasn't easy. Put everything in the appropriate travel cases, with all cables, connectors and instruction manuals; box all the supplies and then take it to the deck, lower it over the side into whatever boat the Navy could spare at the time; and then reverse the process at the new home.

Missions continued but were made difficult by not having the necessary supplies available on whichever of the two ships were receiving patients and only half the medical staff on each ship.

"Why can't the Navy get their act together, we could move all this quicker if they would help get it packed? After all, they are throwing us off this floating madhouse," Silverman groused.

"That would be great! The Army could make it easier too, give us a Hook (a cargo helicopter with two sets of rotor blades). Then we could move it to the deck, and they could move everything to the Benewah in one trip. Save us a lot of time we could use for patients," replied Henderson.

"Gentlemen," the quiet voice of 2LT Joe Creel, a newly assigned MSC officer who would be CPT Schrader's replacement when he finished training and orientation with CPT Schrader, (which wouldn't even begin until Schrader returned from R&R) reasonably pointed out. "The Navy only has 5 medical people, and they are helping us with patient treatment. A HOOK can't hover over the ship without endangering everyone on board when the blades hit the ship parts that are higher than the deck."

"But Sir, something could speed this move along," argued Henderson.

"Yup, if you worked faster and talked less, maybe it would be a faster process," replied the FNG Lieutenant (a new guy). "But then it wouldn't be as much fun if there wasn't something to complain about, would it?"

Silverman got the drift. "Let's get back to work, or we are going to miss the delicious delights from the Navy Mess. At least they named that right."

Bob had to endure a bus ride from the airport in Honolulu to a reception center where the assembled troops were given explicit orders about their behavior in Honolulu, then another ride to the family reception area. "What a goat-rope," he complained to his fellow prisoners on the bus, "that lecture could have been given on the plane or with a handout instead of wasting our short time in Hawaii."

About that time the bus engine gave a loud backfire. Bob and several of those who had been in the field hit the floor of the bus seeking cover. When they realized their reaction for what it was, general laughter rang around the bus. Those who found cover had their badge of recognition; dirt from the bus floor embedded in their already wrinkled khaki uniforms. All of which was soon forgotten as they were reunited with wives and departed for their respective hotels. Bob and Betty soon checked into the Royal Hawaiian, a large Pink colored hotel on Waikiki Beach.

Bob hadn't seen flush toilets in 9 months. His facilities had been austere, even on the ship. "Wow, look at this," he exclaimed, flushing the toilet every time it filled.

"Don't you have anything better to do?" Betty asked.

"Oh, yes! Want to join me," Bob grinned as he jumped on the bed.

Much later, they went to dinner and then back to their room.

Several fun-filled days later, after driving around the island, seeing all the tourist attractions like Sea World, Fort DeRussy, and Pearl Harbor, including a unique bar with a glass-fronted cage of monkeys behind the bar, and being disappointed Don Ho, the entertainer, was out of town they were facing another three month separation. They also discovered after they had been swimming in the hotel pool, that they had been the focus of many in the basement bar as they played around with each other. The basement bar had a window into the pool where the swimmers could be viewed. Unfortunately, they didn't make this discovery until they were in the bar for an after swim Mai Tai.

Betty and Bob were standing in line to check out when Betty noticed Bob had disappeared. When he returned, she said, "where did you go?

"Took my CP (Chloroquine-Primaquine anti-malarial pill) this morning. It has an interesting side effect you can't ignore, at least more than once. There is an immediate need to find a bathroom. I got caught once in Dong Tam when I was in the motor pool, and the outhouses were on the other side of the compound. I learned my lesson. When symptoms call, I find a facility," he laughed. "No shit, actually just the opposite," he offered in explanation. Betty laughed too.

`   1LT Rios Rivera was from Casa Grande, Arizona. He enlisted in the Army after several years of serving as a Deputy Sheriff in the Pinal County Sheriff's Office, where he was certified as an EMT, emergency medical technician. As a result of his training and experience, he was given a direct commission as a Medical Service Corps Officer. His Army friends called him the "law west of the Rio River" and after he settled a race dispute between some of the enlisted, 'Judge Rio'. Recently assigned to the 9th Medical Battalion, 9th Infantry Division, he went on an orientation flight of the AO (area of operations) on a Huey medivac flight. The helicopter delivered him to the Benewah, then proceeded to deliver other passengers to a nearby Surgical Hospital. After depositing those passengers the helicopter, for reasons not clear, crashed into the Mekong River.

The field phone in CPT Schrader's quarters rang early in the morning. "What do you have?" Bob inquired.

"Sir, this is Specialist Sanders, the Captain requests you come to the pontoon (the dock attached to the ship where the Tango boats were tethered). They have an American KIA (killed in action) in the river caught up in the boats."

"On the way," Bob pointed at 1LT Rivera who was camping in Bob's room until he went back to Dong Tam. "Come with me Rio; you might find this educational if not nice." Both hurried quickly up to the deck and back down the ladder to the pontoon. When they arrived, Rio said in a shaky voice, "that's the pilot I was with yesterday."

"Write up a statement, detailing your flight, where you went, anything you observed and what happens here," Bob ordered. Then directed the removal of the pilot to the surgical area pending transfer to Graves Registration. He consulted with the ship's Medical Officer and the XO (Benewah Executive Officer) about transferring the pilot and sent a medic to the Delta Radio shack to send the transfer request for a medivac.

The crash investigation concluded that the pilots had seen a red flashing light on a radio tower, inferred it was another helicopter, and taking evasive action to avoid a mid-air stalled the helicopter causing it to fall to the Mekong waters. The other crew members were recovered at the scene of the crash.

WO3 Bill Jones had a different day, but the same ending. Bill was flying as the aircraft commander of a 247th Medical Detachment Helicopter Ambulance Company medivac out of Dong Tam. Bill was on his 4th mission of the day and in his 3rd Huey. Despite the damage to his helicopters and shrapnel wounds to right arm and leg. This crew continued to extract patients from heavy combat. The crew encountered heavy enemy fire, both coming and going to the hot LZ. While loading patients in the LZ, Bill held the Huey on the ground to allow three additional ambulatory soldiers to get on-board. Other helicopters and troops on the ground later reported the Huey took a direct hit from an RPG (Rocket Propelled Grenade) and exploded on contact. All on board the Huey were killed.

"Hey Captain," shouted Rios Rivera, as he greeted Bob on the Benewah (Keybrook Echo) helicopter pad, as Captain Schrader walked away from the Huey. Did you hear about Jones?

"No, what did he do now?"

"He was a bonafide medivac hero. Mr. Jones volunteered to take a mission for the 247th Med Det (Helicopter Ambulance) [this unit was quartered next to the 9th Med Tactical Operations Center and provided medivac support to the division]. Ambulance) [this unit was quartered next to the 9th Med Tactical Operations Center and provided medivac support to the division.

"Why would he do that? He was in the 191st Helicopter Assault Helicopter Company with me, not an evac unit."

"One of the 247th pilots broke his ankle playing volleyball; there was a bad combat operation with lots of casualties and the needed an AC (aircraft commander) now!"

"So where is he?" CPT Schrader demanded.

"He's dead sir. His bird was on their fourth mission and took a direct hit from an RPG. I understand he has been recommended for the Medal," Rio sadly reported.

"Shit," was Bob's reply. "He was a super guy!"

CHAPTER 10

The following orders (extract) provided new destinations (and opportunities, good or bad):

9TH INFANTRY DIVISION
ORDERS EXTRACT:

Burkley, Jerry R., WO3, released from 9th Inf Div and transferred in grade to Presidio, CA, wiith delay for hospital medical treatment; upon hospital release travel to Fort Carson, CO, as the closest post to home of record, Cheyenne, Wyoming, for discharge from active duty; assigned to Inactive Reserve.

Burks, John R., COL, released from 9th Inf. Div. and transferred in grade to Pentagon, Washington, D.C. with duty in Artillery Plans and Operations.

Schrader, Robert W., MAJ, released from 9th Inf. Div. and transferred in grade to Fort Rucker AL, with further assignment to Rotary Wing Flight Training Class #OF3312022.

Weisberg, Robert, LTC, released from 9th Inf. Div and transferred in grade to Presidio, CA, assigned to Letterman General Hospital with duty as Surgeon

Rivera, Rios NMI, CPT, transferred in grade to D Company, 9th Medical Battalion, 9th Infantry Division, with duty as Executive Officer.

A few more paragraphs sent troops all over the globe to fill vacancies the Army needed to be filled. Those orders had the effect of changing lives.

Jerry and Doctor W had the same military transportation to Travis Air Force Base in California, via a Caribou from Dong Tam to Ton Son Nhut, a C-141 to Elmendorf AFB, Alaska, and a short refueling stop, then to McCord AFB/Fort Lewis, Washington; and a C-130 to Travis. From Travis, they caught a shuttle to the Presidio in San Francisco.

LTC Weisberg reported to the hospital and was assigned married officer's quarters on Post. WO3 Burkley also reported to the Letterman as a patient and was assigned to a ward, a communal room for eight, which was fully occupied. "Not much better than being in the field," he complained.

Dr. W breezed into Jerry's ward, looking splendid in service dress greens, stethoscope around his neck and carrying an AWOL bag (a small zipper bag with handles, generally used for overnight trips, hence the name, 'absent without leave', used by the troops).

"Come with me Mr. Burkley; it is time for your exam."

"Yes, Sir!" Jerry said as he came to attention. He felt awkward in the almost backless hospital gown he had been given when the hospital took away his uniform at check-in.

"Fear not, young man, you are now in the care and good hands of Dr. W., the world-renown Army Surgeon, and general all-around good guy." Dr. W led Jerry into a small examination room, handed Jerry the AWOL Bag and told him, "Get dressed. You have just finished your post service exam with flying colors, I have signed your hospital discharge papers, and we are going to celebrate by going to dinner at Joe Di Maggio's on the Wharf. Great place, fabulous drinks, and good seafood. I'm going to change into civvies, and I will meet you at the taxi stand in front."

Jerry was amazed at this turn of events but happily pulled

on the clothing in the AWOL bag. Even his personal belongings were there, and he quickly stuffed them into his pockets and hurried to meet Dr. W.

The taxi took them through Golden Gate Park, down Lombardi Street (a narrow single lane street that corkscrewed down a steep hill and stopped at the Cable Car turntable). They boarded the cable car, hung onto the outside pole and rode to the foot of the hill, getting off a few blocks from the wharf area. They walked past Ghirardelli Square. "Smell that chocolate!" Jerry exclaimed.

"Ghirardelli Chocolate, want some?" asked Dr. W.

"Maybe after dinner." And they marched on to DiMaggio's, had a fabulous evening, and caught a cab back to the hospital.

MAJ Schrader was also back in the World, but his dinner was in a mess hall, served on a tray. He was entering into his flight training at Fort Rucker. As an officer, he had much better living conditions than the Warrant Officer Candidates but endured the same rigorous training.

Jerry eventually became a Deputy Sheriff in Banner County, Wyoming. He worked for 'Big Tom' Flannigan, the long-time Sheriff. The primary town in Banner County was Caribou, a town of about 5,000 people. There was a good hospital, an airport with a VOR and an ILS approach system (specialized instrument approach systems for aircraft landing at the airport), and one excellent restaurant, The Rusty Nail, several bars, and a bank, Ferguson Federal Savings and Loan. Jerry was reasonably happy there, at least, as long as he didn't have to get out of his patrol car.

CHAPTER 11

Ever have one of those days when you should have stayed in bed or something. Today must be one of those days. Come to think of it; I have too many of those days when I get out of a patrol car. Every time I get out of the car I have trouble. Not when I get out of it for simple things like going for coffee or dinner, or even when I go home, but every time I do a job that takes me out of a police patrol car.

I noticed that problem right away during Vietnam. It wasn't really my fault. In fact, there really wasn't anything I could do about it anyway. I enlisted, volunteered for WO flight school, and went to Vietnam. It wasn't any fun. Out of the patrol car and off to Southeast Asia. Out of the patrol car and right into trouble. Anyway, as I said, it wasn't my fault.

As soon as the Army set me free, I got right back into the patrol car. Same job, same place. I really was happy to be back. Then I got the wise idea to go into business for myself. That was trouble too, although it took me a while to figure that out. I really thought I could do better in the world of big business. Cops really shouldn't do that. Anyway, I finally got it through my skull that I just wasn't cut out for the eight to five routine or marriage either for that matter. I got out of the business, got a divorce, and just about drove myself crazy. Never mind the details. They weren't very pretty either.

Some good comes out of everything though. I learned how to fly helicopters and airplanes in the Army, and I discovered I like being in law enforcement while I was trying out the ways of the business world. Guess it could have been worse. Not sure how but I think it could have been.

After some wandering around, I ended up back in a patrol car. It took a little doing but I got there. Now if I can just stay on the street, it will all work out. Course the Sheriff may have something to say about the whole thing. He kind of wants me to be his Undersheriff. That sounds like a promotion, and it is, but it's mostly a desk job. I like it out on the street where I can roam around. Besides, it bound to be trouble. After all, I'll be out of the car again, right.

To be sure, you can get into trouble anyway. At least I can. Take last night for instance. I was just working a routine patrol, well usual for our county. About four hours into the shift I got a call on the radio. That's pretty routine. It's really the only way anyone can get one of us. Us being the patrol division of the Banner County Sheriff's Department.

Anyway, I answered the inquiry from the dispatcher, and she told me to check out a disturbance at one of the local county bars. She sent one of the other units along to be my backup in case I needed any help. Routine.

As I said, you can get into trouble getting out of the car at the wrong time. Even in the line of duty. I got out of my patrol car before the backup unit got there. Big mistake. At least this time it was. Heck, I've been to this bar for the same type of call lots of times. The cast of characters was even the same.

Trouble starts with little things. This time it started with a call from the dispatcher. Both the other units were farther out in the county, so I just picked up the mike and took the call. Wasn't much traffic on the road, so I just pointed the Pontiac towards the Moose and drove on down. Didn't even used the red lights or siren.

That's right, the Moose. Probably it's called the Moose because there is a big moose head hanging behind the bar. Or maybe they have the moose head because the bar's called the Moose. I don't know. In small towns, you find all sorts of cute, rustic names for places. Anyway, I knew the other two cars would mosey on over my way as soon as they could even if a backup hadn't been assigned. It had been a boring night, and this was the first real complaint we'd had all night.

I got out and locked up the Pontiac in the spacious parking lot at the front of the Moose. Well, actually I parked in the fire zone at the front door, but it was official business. Jimmy Conners was busy breaking up tables and chairs near the bar. When he's in this kind of mood, everyone pretty much leaves him alone, so the damage gets done to the bar, but not the people. I guess I just got there too soon. Jimmy wasn't breaking up anything when I walked up to him."

Mistake number two! He was leaning over a chair with his foot up on it when I got to him. I thought he was tying his shoes or something else equally innocent. He was wearing cowboy boots. Up came the chair and I ducked under it. At least I meant to. When I gained consciousness, the Sheriff was looking down at me, and I was really hurting. Parts of chairs were everywhere around me. My head hurt, my shoulders hurt, and worst of all, my pride hurt. Most times I just give Jimmy a ride to the jail, letting him pay for the damages and his fines after he sobers up.

"What are you doing down there?" queried Sheriff Flanigan. "Sleeping on the job now. Not at all like you."

"Well Sheriff, I thought I was going to give Jimmy his usual ride, but I don't think he was quite ready. Where is he anyway?"

The Sheriff's ruddy face lit up. I think there was a smile behind all the whiskers. "Joe and Mick gave him a ride back about twenty minutes ago. You were resting so peaceful we just didn't want to disturb you."

That's my Sheriff. Always so considerate of the hired help. I found out later Jimmy was just standing over me saying, "oh shit, I'm sorry," over and over. He didn't do anything else, just stood there until Joe and Mick led him off. Joe and Mick are the other two deputies on this shift. They got there about the time Jimmy hit me and just got to watch. Nothing else to do at that point.

I like working for Sheriff Flanigan. Big Tom Flanigan has been the county sheriff for longer than anyone can remember. I think he may have been the original issue sheriff for this county. Tom probably hasn't been around quite that long since Banner County celebrated its centennial last year, but it sure seems that way. He's one of those people who never show their age after a certain point. He looks like he's in his fifties, but since he isn't talking no one knows for sure. Except maybe his wife and I wouldn't take any bets on that either.

He's an easy guy to spot. I've never seen Sheriff Flanigan without a steel gray cowboy hat set down over his medium length white hair. In fact, there's a rumor that he doesn't even take it off for a haircut. His big bushy mustache bobs up and down as he talks and covers up his mouth, so you don't know if he's smiling or frowning. If you watch closely, you'll discover the crow's feet at the corners of his weather-beaten face turn up and get larger when he smiles. Just watch him laugh sometime, and you'll see what I mean. From there on down he looks like the stereotype of a cowboy from the old days. Whipcord thin, bowlegged and still smokes hand-rolled cigarettes. The tag of his tobacco sack hangs out of his left shirt pocket, even when he's in uniform. Looks kind of funny when the wind whips it around just below the large star that identifies him as the Banner County Sheriff. You know, I don't think I've ever seen him without the badge either.

When he's not in uniform, he looks like some character out of a Louis L'Amour western. Most of the time he wears the same uniform we deputies do. Tan uniform shirt with all the appropriate patches sewn on. Department patch on the left, United States flag on the right shoulder, firearms qualification patch, and nametag on the right front above the pocket and a large seven-point star on the left. He looks sharp in his uniform and demands that we try and look as good. Makes for good public relations is what he keeps telling us.

Brown permanent press pants and cowboy boots round off the uniform. Oh yes, we also carry a .357 Smith & Wesson, model 19, which we are required to qualify with on the firing range each month. We carry the revolver and a lot of other junk like mace, handcuffs, and extra bullets in high-quality black basket weave leather gear. Usually, you end up carrying a nightstick, a two-way portable radio and sometimes a flashlight. It gets heavy and awkward sometimes, but it does give us the equipment we need at the time we need it. Equipment in the car trunk just doesn't seem to be available when you want to use it. Several of us wear a bulletproof vest under our uniform shirt as well, but it is uncomfortable because of the heat build-up under it. That's why you often see our deputies riding around in the winter with the car windows open.

Sheriff Flanigan is probably one of the best law enforcement officers around, even if we are just a small department out in the sticks. I've learned more from him in the two years I've been on his department than I did in the six years I was in the big city department. I thought I was pretty hot stuff when I went to work for Tom. Even though I had been out of law enforcement for a few years, I figured all that big city experience would make me king of the mountain out here in the middle of nowhere. It didn't take long to figure out I didn't know all that much. Big Tom wasn't mean or pushy about it; he just let me make all the mistakes he thought I should and then made a suggestion here and another one there until I wasn't making as many as I did before. Now I know I don't know it all so maybe I can learn to do the job with the same elan the Sheriff has.

I told you I always get into trouble when I get out of the car. What I meant was the job of being a street cop. I had never realized working the streets meant so much to me until I went to work for Tom Flanigan. Oh, I knew I was unhappy and wasn't fitting in, but I didn't know why. That came later.

I first met Big Tom Flanigan on official business. His official business, not mine. I wasn't a cop at the time. I wasn't in business anymore either. I was just one of the dropouts from society who were a little rowdy in one of the lower class bars the Sheriff rides herd. I was probably a little more than rowdy. I had tied one on and was feeling sorry for myself. Not quite as bad as Jimmy Conners, but working hard at it. I hadn't gotten to the place where I was breaking anything or anyone up yet. I was sure trying hard to get into a fight with someone; anyone, but so far no real takers. To make a long story short, if that's possible, the Sheriff put me up at his place for a couple of days. No, not the jail, but the cozy home the county provides for the Sheriff to live in. Big Tom and his wife put me up in the spare bedroom and gave me sympathetic ears to talk to. At least Edna's ears were sympathetic. Big Tom just spent some time pointing out what a jerk I was to waste my life bumming around just because I felt sorry for myself.

Well, I thought I had good reason to feel that way. I had enjoyed being a dropout and wanted to make more money for my wife. I quit and went to work in an office, wore a suit and tie, and generally became another one of the walking money machines. I hated it! I hated it!. I took it out of my wife, the dog and almost anyone around. Julie, that was my wife, decided she could do without my temperament and let me know she could live without me.

I guess she could. Just a few months after our divorce she was married again and moved to California. Soon after that I sold out to my partner and hit the road. I bummed around for a couple of years doing odd jobs here and there. Finally, I ended up in Caribou.

That, no kidding, is the name of this town. The county seat for Banner County. Really, that is the name of this town of 5,000 people. When I first got there, it was a sleepy little town near the mountains with more bars than anything else. I was tired, hacked off, and running out of money. The big problem with dropping out is the limited cash flow. I needed a job, but I had a pretty big chip on my shoulder. Those chips can limit your options for employment. The bigger the chip, the smaller the chance of getting a job. The whole thing becomes mutually exclusive. Without a job your frustration grows and pretty soon you're on the prod, looking for a fight with anyone and everyone. The luckiest thing I ever did was pick Big Tom's town to come to rest. I really don't know how he did it, not to this day. After staying at Tom's for several days, I got ready to move on. Saying goodbye to Edna, I loaded my gear into the Blazer and went to find Tom to say goodbye and thanks. Next thing I knew I was in a uniform, wearing a badge again, and driving a fairly new patrol car around Banner County. It was just the medicine I needed.

It's nice to be a uniformed deputy. Can you believe I get paid just to drive around in a car all day? Well, almost all day, or all night, depending on what shift you are working. Just enough other activity going on to make the job interesting. A few speeding violations, a family fight or two – we call them domestic disturbances, and every once in a while some real crime like armed robbery or burglary.

I didn't know how much I missed law enforcement until I got back into uniform. Now I don't want to get out of the car or do any other kind of work. The only trouble is the Sheriff has other plans for me. You saw how it worked out last time. What the Sheriff wants, he usually gets, and you feel like it's your idea. A desk job is not my idea of what should be my idea.

I don't blame Tom Flanigan for what happened at the hospital. Even he couldn't have worked out the incident at the Moose, my getting hit over the head, and the trip to the hospital. At least, I don't think he could. The Sheriff wasn't responsible for what happened at the hospital. That one was probably my fault, but then you never can tell.

When he got me to the emergency room, I was still hurting all over but not so much I didn't notice the strange lady working there. Strange from the viewpoint of being new or perhaps being so pretty, but definitely not odd. Well, maybe a little odd because I didn't know her. I usually know when someone new moves into Caribou. After all, I spend most of my time driving around and talking to the people who live here. I had never seen this pretty lady before, and believe me, I would have remembered.

She acted as she belonged in the emergency room. She was certainly dressed like she belonged there. She had on the customary white uniform nurses wear, and she had a clipboard in her hand.

The Sheriff, as usual, sees all and knows all. "Cheryl, I'd like for you to meet Lieutenant Jerry Burkley, one of my better deputies when he's paying attention to business. Jerry, this is Cheryl Hefner, the county hospital's newest and prettiest laboratory technician."

My response was probably just above being incoherent. Cheryl just looked at me and then asked Tom for help as I started my slow fall towards the floor. When I regain consciousness, the scenery was much better than it was at the Moose. Instead of looking into the Sheriff's face, I was looking into the most beautiful green eyes I had ever seen.

A light, sparkling voice drew my attention to full lips and then to Cheryl's face. At least I think it was her face, not having had time to fully appreciate it before.

"Feeling any better Lieutenant?" asked the pretty lady in front of me.

Well, it was to my front. I guess I was laying down on a hospital bed at the time and probably didn't know any better. I must have been hit pretty hard at the Moose since I was still having trouble talking. Or maybe it was because she took my breath away. I dozed off dreaming of her green eyes.

CHAPTER 12

Being in the hospital is not my idea of fun! For one thing, I like to sleep in. Not in a hospital. Those people think the day should start before the roosters get up. In fact, it wouldn't surprise me to discover them waking up the roosters as they make their early morning rounds. The worst part is that they wake you up, then make you wait for breakfast. Not even a cup of coffee. Wake you up, take your blood pressure and temperature, then run around the halls keeping you from going back to sleep.

Nights are even worse. Did you know they wake you up in the middle of the night just to give you a sleeping pill? I think they do it so that you know what you're paying for when you stay in a hospital. I'm glad I only spent one night there.

Of course, getting out is tricky too. Even when you're in good shape and could walk out of place, they insist you ride out in a wheelchair. Paperwork to get in and even more to get out. When I put someone in jail, I do all the paperwork, and the prisoner is usually out before I get it done. Something drastically wrong with the system.

The Sheriff was happy to get me back to work. At least I think he was! He waved at me from his office as I came into the station. After giving me a rundown on what had transpired since my little scene at the Moose, he said, "be careful out there." I think he watches too much Hill Street Blues on television. Anyway, I'm back in the car tonight. Typical night. Absolutely nothing going on. Joe and Mick aren't even saying much on the radio for a change. Sally, our dispatcher, has a new book keeping her occupied. These shifts can get downright boring sometimes, but tonight it felt good.

"Charlie 5, this is Charlie 27. Want to get some coffee?"

I'm Charlie 5. Charlie 27 is Joe Chambers, one of the other deputies on the shift. We use code numbers so we can confuse everyone listening to us on their police scanners. Supposedly it keeps everyone from knowing what we are doing. It probably doesn't work for that purpose. Most everyone locally knows that the number of our radio call is simply our badge number. If that's not enough, the number is painted on the outside of the car as well. Most of those who listen to the police frequencies on their scanners also have a copy of the police ten code too, so it's probably more mystic than anything else. The only ones that get confused are new officers and dispatchers.

I told Joe ten-four, which is code for OK and started off towards our usual coffee spot. There aren't all that many places open after 10:00 p.m. and the Coffee Cup serves the best coffee. By best I really mean it's drinkable, rather than good, but the service is excellent, and it's centrally located for all the patrol units when we're spread out at night. Usually Mick will wander on down without the need for an invitation so I figured we could sort out the rest of the door and building checks while we talked. I wanted two of us to check the lake area anyway, and that would give us the chance to draw straws for staying behind. The lake area is the local lover's lane, and that's where the kids do their drinking and romancing. We like to run through every once in a while just to make sure they don't overdo the alcohol and get themselves hurt. I can't remember ever arresting one of them for drinking underage. We just have them pour out all the beer. That usually hurts them enough to take it easy for a while and yet feel like they got away with something.

Coffee. No such luck! I had just pulled up to the curb in front of the Coffee Cup when the radio crackled back to life.

"Charlie 5, SO. Domestic disturbance at the Crane residence. 215 Main. Respond Code 1."

So much for my quiet night too! Putting the Pontiac back into gear I swung a U-turn and headed over to the Cranes. Code 1 means to obey all traffic laws and no sirens or lights, but we usually push the speed limit a little getting there. A domestic disturbance can be anything from yelling and screaming to actual violence. Often a neighbor calls it into the dispatcher, and they don't really know what's going on any more than we do when we first answer the call.

Domestic calls scare me. Traffic stops and domestic disturbances cause more injury to cops than bar fights and bank robberies. You stop a guy for having a tail light out, but he has just pulled a burglary, so he starts shooting when you walk up to the car all unawares. Domestic disturbances are a lot like that. When you get there the abused wife usually wants you to arrest the dumb SOB, but about the time the cuffs go on she figures out that he's going to be one mad fellow when he gets out and the next time will be worse for her. Besides, he'll be off work for a day or two until the courts sort it all out so the paycheck will be smaller and then there is the money for bail and maybe even a lawyer. When all that sinks in, she will suddenly turn on the cop who is going to cause her all those added problems. Sometimes it just verbal - and sometimes she throws things. Once one pulled a knife out of the kitchen drawer and came after my partner. Not a neat spot to be in! Anyway, I'm pretty cautious about these calls even if I know the people. They don't always act very rational.

More bad news from the radio. "Charlie 5, there is a report that a gun is involved. Use Caution."

Just what I needed. At least the radio wasn't pouring out only bad news. "Charlie 5, Charlie 27 will back up. I'm right behind you."

I stopped the Pontiac short of the Cranes front door and hit the electric switch to release the Remington pump shotgun from the magnetic rack next to the radio console. That twelve gauge at least evens up the odds if there are going to be guns around. I jacked a round into the chamber as Joe pulled up behind me. Going between our cars, I motion for him to follow me and moved onto the porch steps. Joe went to the right-hand side of the door, and I stood on the left off to the side.

That way if someone wants to shoot through the door, you aren't right in the line of fire.

I reached over to the door with my left hand, shotgun in my right, and knocked on the door. After a short wait a tall, hefty middle-aged female opened the door.

"It's all right officer. The gun's been put away

We followed her into the house. Standing in the dining room was a large fellow who was bleeding from the head like a stuck pig. There was blood in his hair, running down his face, and forming an icicle on the end of his nose where it was clotting. It took me a few minutes to realize what had happened. Off to the side of the dining room was a tubular metal kitchen chair with one leg bent at a pretty good angle. Later we got all the details, but it was pretty apparent she had clobbered him with the chair. It took most of the fight out of the whole situation. The gun was sacked up in a cloth gun case on the living room couch.

I left Joe with the lady, who turned out to be Mrs. Crane, and I took the man, who of course turned out to be Mr. Crane, to the hospital to have his head examined. Separate the participants, and usually, you don't have any more immediate problems with them. Saves the paperwork an arrest would generate too, although Joe and I will both have to file a report on this case at the end of the shift. Luckily the bleeding had about stopped so he didn't get blood all over the inside of the Pontiac.

I drove into the emergency room driveway and parked in front of the electric slide doors to the emergency room. Crane could walk, so I just escorted him inside and turned him over to the receptionist for all the insurance and admission stuff. She was kind enough to point me down the hallway to the staff lounge where there should be some fresh coffee. Somehow I was going to get my coffee break. Even if I had to handle some more of the hospital breed of coffee.

Just as I got some of what looked like coffee into the traditional styrofoam cup, I heard this angel voice say, "pour me one too, will you?"

Pretty green eyes was standing in the doorway looking even better than the other night. Of course, I was probably looking better too. At least I felt a whole lot better. I almost tripped over my feet getting that cup of coffee to her. Getting a cup for myself gave me time to get my mind working in top form again. At least under the circumstances, it was in pretty good form. We moved to one of the tables and talked for a while about the weather, the time I spent at the hospital after the fight at the Moose and what I was doing there tonight.

The entire time I was just mesmerized by her. That hasn't happened in a long time. I had kind of given up on the female of the species after I got divorced. No real reason. Just didn't see one that sparked my fancy. I was finding myself getting interested in this one. She not only spoke intelligently but her voice was beautiful to hear.

We talked a little about her job too. Did you know that lab techs have to go to quite a bit of school and then pass pretty tough exams before they can work in the hospital labs? I thought they just gave them a little quick OJT, on the job training, on how to stick you with a needle and take all your blood. I was impressed. Course I was impressed anyway but that's different. Cops get mostly OJT. Some of us have appropriate college training, and some even have law degrees, but mostly just OJT. Especially in out of the way places like Banner County.

Just as I was getting into the conversation bit, the admissions receptionist came into the lounge to tell me Crane was all doctored up. Only she did it in that stilted way hospital workers have; "Mr. Crane has been attended by a doctor, and his laceration has been sutured. You may take him now as he won't need to be admitted."

That was just too bad. After all, I have to chauffeur Crane around if the hospital won't keep him, but that's the way the night seems to be going. While I was getting this great piece of information, Cheryl got away to somewhere else. Anyway, she wasn't in the lounge anymore, and I missed the chance to say goodbye and ask if I could see her again. I do not like Mr. Crane any too well at this point.

"Good night Lieutenant. Come back again." The lost was found. She was standing by the door looking at my patrol car. "Why do you park right in front of the door? What happens if the ambulance needs to get in?"

"Well, it is easier than walking. I park there, so I have the least amount of trouble with the person I bring in. Usually, I have someone who either is or should be under arrest, and it's a little hard to keep an eye on them when you are in-between two other parked cars in the parking lot. I usually know about the ambulance before you do because our dispatcher also dispatches them and I would hear it on my portable radio. Pretty neat huh?"

"If you think so. Seems pretty lazy to me!"

"Will you have dinner with me tomorrow night?"

"Will you park in front of the restaurant door if I do?"

"No, I'd rather make you walk. Help you understand the effort involved when you park a long way from where you want to be. Besides the Sheriff frowns on using the patrol car for personal business."

She smiled. "Am I business?"

"No, you are strictly pleasure. Where can I pick you up?"

The smile became a laugh, soft and gentle. "I think you already have. The big apartments on seventh. Number 216 on the second floor."

I wasn't very mad at Crane any more. I was pretty happy with him. If he hadn't acted as a target for a kitchen chair, I might not have a date tomorrow night. I was so happy with him I took him out to his brother's place in the country to spend the night. Nice night!

Going back to town I sang along with the car radio. It was the most delightful evening I've had in quite a while. Attitude affects the way you feel. I felt pretty good. I even got serious about checking for unlocked doors at the school. Usually, they forget to lock one when they leave. We used to call the principal and let him come down to lock up. Finally got him to give me a spare key. Now I can check it out, get it locked, and get on the way in short order.

In case you hadn't noticed, I don't like to do door checks anyway. But - when you feel good, you do your job well. Even dispatch noticed the increased interest. After doing several registration checks, the dispatcher asked me to knock it off. Guess it interrupted her reading. She should have let me do a few more before getting agitated. Bet we would have had a lot fewer problems later if I had run the fancy Continental. But that's getting ahead of myself.

I can get cute on the radio too. We had a new dispatcher on who had not been exposed to some of our shorthand. When I pulled up to the Sheriff's Office, I picked up the mike from the side of the radio console and pressing the transmit button advised dispatch, "SO, Charlie 5. OTL."

That was all. I got out of the car, locked it up with the electric door lock button and strolled into the office. I could hear the dispatcher calling me on the radio. Turning down the volume on the portable, I walked up behind her at the desk and said, "on the lot."

She almost jumped out of her chair. Sometimes discretion is the better part of valor. I left the dispatch office in a hurry.

"What's that all about, Jerry?"

"Just keeping the dispatcher on her toes Sheriff. She didn't know what OTL stood for so I told her. Guess I should have let her know I was in the room before I spoke up. This one seems to get rattled easily."

"You sure know how to make a Sheriff's job easy Jerry. It took me two weeks to find that gal to dispatch and you'll probably run her off on her first solo night."

"Ah Sheriff, she had a regular dispatcher with her most of tonight. Sally only went off duty an hour ago. Besides, she and Sally thought I was making them work too hard on the computer with car checks tonight."

We walked into the Sheriff's office, and I eased into the more comfortable of the office chairs.

"I noticed you were working harder tonight. Maybe we should get that head checked out again. You're not acting normal." Tom lit up his cigar, laughter around the corners of his eyes.

"Got a date with that lab tech you tried to introduce me to the other night. Pleasant expectations make for a happy employee."

"Happy enought to take the Undersheriff's job when Glen retires?"

I chuckled out loud. "Nope, not that happy. I like it in the car. Undersheriffs push paper and stuff like that. Thanks, but no thanks."

"You don't get hit on the head as often," the Sheriff observed.

"True. But it has other headaches that more than make up for it."

You've got to hand it to the Sheriff. He does keep on trying. After sidestepping the Undersheriff queries and getting on to other conversation, I took my leave and headed for home. I think the Sheriff hangs around at the end of my shift so that he can give me more problems to think about.

Not tonight though! I just wanted to get out of the uniform, watch the late night movie, and have a couple of scotches. I backed into the drive next to my humble abode. It's not so humble. A reasonably new 35-foot travel trailer with all the modern conveniences. Better than the back seat of the Blazer. Besides, I've been around a large part of the country in it, and I can leave anytime I want. Just hook the Blazer up and away we go. Should unhook the utilities first. Didn't once. What a mess!

I flipped the TV on and continued back to the bedroom stripping off gun belt and equipment on the way. Sometimes the place gets that lived in look. I hung up the uniform and pulled on a warm terry cloth bathrobe, put the gun belt and equipment where it belonged and made a scotch with lots of ice. Fell asleep in front of the TV. Didn't even get to drink the scotch!

CHAPTER 13

The ringing phone woke Jerry. Still groggy, he answered briskly, "Burkley, what do you want?" Then he softened his tone as he thought maybe Cheryl was calling. "Or what can I do for you?"

The male voice, which certainly wasn't Cheryl inquired, "is this Mr. Burkley, Warrant Officer Burkley?

"Yes Sir," Jerry replied automatically.

"COL Burks calling, stand-by."

Soon, another male voice said, "Jerry, how are you?"

"Good Sir."

"Miss flying helicopters and combat missions?"

"Not really Sir," Jerry replied, starting to feel the adrenalin jolt he had felt during Vietnam.

"Good," COL Burks stated. "I have a flying job for you with the 1022nd Helicopter Ambulance Company with the Wyoming Army National Guard in Cheyenne. You should fit right in."

"Yes Sir, but I'm in Caribou and have a full-time job."

"That's ok; this is just weekends, summer camp, and maybe a couple of missions for me. It will help your retirement later on."

Jerry objected, "I don't know if the Sheriff would give me the time off." But, he didn't automatically say no to the Colonel's suggestion.

COL Burks heard the non-answer, and also had answers to his objections. "I talked to Tom. He is fine with it and thinks it will help the department's image. Even if he didn't, Federal Law requires employers to give you the time off."

"Why are you doing this Sir?"

"Because I need someone I can trust and depend upon who will be in a position to assist me when I need him."

Jerry caved in, as the Colonel expected him to do; so Jerry started flying helicopters again.

Jerry got out of the car once more. He was recalled to active duty. Colonel Burks was involved in several career changes:

DEPARTMENT OF THE ARMY
ORDERS EXTRACT

Burks, John R., COL, is hereby promoted Brigadier General, United States Army. General Burks is ordered to proceed to Fort Carson, Colorado, with duty as Commander of the newly formed 2nd Artillery Division. After training 2nd Arty, will proceed to the Republic of Vietnam in support of 9th Infantry Division.

Burkley, Jerry R., WO3, WYARNG, assigned 2nd ARTY DIV, 6/8th ARTY, RW Aviator.

Schrader, Robert W., MAJ, USA, assigned 2nd ARTY DIV, duty as DIV G-1

"Gentlemen, Welcome to the 2nd Artillery," greeted BG Burks.

"Yes Sir," replied both officers.

"Mr. Burkley and Major Schrader, I am proud and happy to have both of you with the Second. I am also pleased to promote each of you, Major Schrader to Lieutenant Colonel, and Mr. Burkley to Warrant Officer 4." He then proceeded to pin the appropriate leaf and bar on each of them.

"Thank you, Sir, it is a pleasure to be here, and I am even more pleased with the new leaf," grinned LTC Schrader.

"Thank you. I think Sir. This sure gets me out of the car!" Mr. Burkley quipped.

"I do want both of you here. We have a lot to do and missions to complete. You will be happy to know none of them are the special missions of your last tour," BG Burks sincerely told the two smiling officers.

There, indeed, was a lot to be accomplished. A new division, with newly assigned soldiers, had to be trained to work as a team. Even though many of the new soldiers were highly experienced NCOs and Officers, they had never worked together before. Under the General's leadership, the staff, line officers and non-commissioned officers became a combat-ready Artillery unit. The General used Jerry as his Aid-de-Camp, a position usually filled by a commissioned officer, both to run errands and often to fly him wherever he needed. LTC Schrader was challenged by the influx of new troops, the paperwork required by the Army, and giving the General everyday support. Soon the Second was prepared to deploy to Vietnam.

In Vietnam, the challenges grew larger. Not only did the Second need to establish a base camp, but separate firebases in coordination with Infantry units, perform artillery fire missions, and care for all the people assigned while also training them in combat.

Mr. Burkley flew the General, acted as his Aid, and did everything thrown at him to get done. LTC Schrader was given command of the 6/8th Aviation Battalion and flew missions in support of the Second, while training his pilots and insuring his helicopters were well maintained. It was a busy time for them all.

BG Burks got his second star (Major General) before he left Vietnam. LTC Schrader was promoted to Full (or Bird) Colonel, and Jerry pinned on the bar of a WO4. There were also some medals awarded.

Since they all arrived in Vietnam together, they all left together. Jerry went back to being a civilian, but still in the WYANG (Wyoming Army National Guard).and his job as Deputy Sheriff in Banner County. General Burks was returned to the Pentagon. COL Schrader was assigned to Letterman

Hospital, where he joined Dr. W. in tours of the Wharf and other exotic destinations much like the Doctors on the TV series "MASH."

Jerry was looking forward to making another date with Cheryl.

CHAPTER 14

The two men in the office were out of place. Or at least in the wrong positions. The one behind the desk did not look as if he belonged while the one in front had the appearance of one who should be behind the large walnut desk. Not only was their appearance odd but the conversation was also entirely out of place for this office.

Why you may ask should any of that make a difference? After all, an office is an office. Many different subjects are discussed in offices all over the land. In this case, the office is one of a bank cashier; the issue being the robbery of this bank. Even such a discussion would not be out of place for bank officers worried about possible theft or even talk about a robbery of the past. Most bank officers are worried about the possibility of theft. That this was a small bank with little cash on hand most of the time might make such deliberations unnecessary but what was interesting was the fact the two were deciding how to successfully rob this bank, Ferguson Federal Savings, and Loan.

Ferguson Federal Savings and Loan was an institution in the remote mountain community it served. Old Man Ferguson had formed the bank decades ago as a means of putting his own money to work. Silas Ferguson had started life in these mountains as a remittance man from England. He was a hell-raising reprobate whose parents could no longer control. As the son of a high ranking English Lord, he was also the source of great embarrassment to his parents, particularly his father whose position was not always that secure in the English scheme of things. Money was not a problem.

Silas was not stupid, only carefree and wild. The western part of America agreed with his temperament. His native intelligence, coupled with what was for those times an unlimited source of funds, made life easy while he accumulated more and more. After a while, the acquisition of land, businesses and more money was not enough. Silas soon learned that his money could make more money through interest, and with less work than he could with his own efforts. He started lending to neighbors and small business owners. Those who were successful paid him for the use of the money. Those who were not soon learned the price as Silas acquired more land or another business from them. As the years went by the banking operation became more formalized, finally becoming the first of the federally chartered banking institutions in the west.

Rarely was Silas referred to by his name; he merely became Old Man Ferguson. Whether the kids started it or whether it was a derogatory term applied by those who could not pay off their loans no one remembers, but it was used generally during his long and profitable life. He was not a bad man in any sense of the term. Silas just worked harder at collecting the debts owed him than most. On the other hand, he had pride in his small community and was a soft touch for almost any project that didn't involve a loan from his bank. He created parks, built the first city hall, and was active in all the activities that we would term charitable activities in this modern day and age. His bank was a model of contemporary banking. The building that houses the bank is still current and up to date even though it has been standing for many years. The most recent version of several modifications and additions could match the architecture of many of the more recent banks erected in rural areas. It probably exceeded the grandeur of most. The modern facilities combined with the old gave the bank mossy stability. Stability that gave depositors a feeling of confidence in the dependability of the old established bank in much the same manner an old club has a mystic for its members.

Approached across a grassy expanse dotted with statues and memorabilia of the old west, the bank itself was constructed of natural stone, complete with the moss that identifies real moss rock so the bank was impressive. The antique, massive wooden doors have given way to glass and aluminum; the entry into a large, high vaulted, comfortable room covered with dark oiled walnut walls showing years of polishing. The warm wood gives off many varieties of visual response as the light plays upon it. Contrasting sharply are the bright sides of the ultramodern vault and safe deposit boxes which are visible from the lobby. Between the old and the new are newer wooden, or at least wood laminated, counters for the tellers. Off to one side are a series of old-style offices for bank officers. The other side is littered with the desks of lesser functionaries handling the tasks of new accounts, secretaries and the like.

In a central location beside the vault and behind the teller counters is an impressive oil painting of the founder, Silas Ferguson. Dressed in the style of the button-on collar, four-in-hand tie, and modified tails, the picture adds its own measure of elegance. The image also adds to the strangeness of the man behind the desk in the corner office. That office, the cashier's office, also combines the old with the new. The same dark, oiled walnut walls that give such staunchness to the lobby were intricately joined to moss rock walls within the office. A large window looks out upon the mountains to the west. The furnishings and trappings were those of any modern office of a busy bank executive. Expansive solid wood desk, high backed desk chair in the style referred to as a judge's chair, and rocking, swivel guest chairs. The decorations and mementos of both civic participation and professional accomplishments covered the walls and much of the built-in bookshelves on either side of the window.

The man behind the desk just didn't fit the image of the person who should be the primary occupant of this office, the bank's cashier. As you might expect, however, he was the rightful heir to this office. Davis Ferguson, great-grandson of the illustrious founder of Ferguson Federal Savings and Loan, was a throwback to his background. Maybe he had it too easy. Or, maybe, just maybe, Davis was not the person with the character to be where he was. Else why should he be discussing the robbery of his family's ancient and reputable bank?

He certainly did not look like a banker. Davis wore suit and tie,as is the uniform of the banker, but they certainly did not give his portly body any of the unique appearance one would expect from their banker. For one thing the suit looked like it had been slept in for several days. Remains of past meals were rubbed into the fabric of the suit coat, his hair appeared uncombed and wild, although that may have been an appearance generated by the extremely poor haircut. Don't blame Davis's barber though; it had been a long time since the barber had an opportunity to show his talents. Under the coat on those rare occasions when Davis Ferguson took his coat off lay a gargantuan pot belly. That, of course, explains the suspenders. What is not explained is the color. Bright red suspenders held up his dark brown pants against both gravity and the pull of his stomach.

On the other hand, the visitor looked like a banker should look. Dark blue, pin-striped suit, highly polished black shoes and an impeccable white shirt with a dark tie adorned his body. He much more closely resembled the popular concept of what a banker should look like. Jeremy Witters was not a banker. He was not even a customer of the bank in the usual sense. Jeremy Witters specialized in removing money from banks with the help of the rather deadly .45 Colt Government Model automatic concealed in a shoulder holster beneath his neatly pressed coat.

Some have identified him as a cool customer; others only get the impression of a cold machine. Both are correct. Seemingly without nerve, Witters was competent at his chosen profession. He has made his withdrawals at a number of banks without ever being apprehended. His success is probably founded on the degree of prior planning which goes into each of his withdrawal projects. He always seems to know everything worth knowing about any bank he robs long before he puts his plans into operation. It has been rumored his knowledge is more than just observation. As a matter of fact, that is true. In each of his engagements, he has elicited the support of some key insider who is dissatisfied with his employer or has dreams of getting rich quickly. Usually, both aspects are present. This was just such a situation.

Although the bank was busy with customers and bank employees going about their typical day to day business, Witters and young Ferguson were able to discuss their own business freely due to the insistence of Old Man Ferguson that his offices be constructed to be almost soundproof. That there may have been apparent disadvantages had not been foreseen by Silas.

"Look, Mr. Witters, I can give you all the information you want, but I just can't be part of the actual robbery. After all, everyone in the bank knows me, and I would be sure to be recognized. Besides, I don't think my nerves would take being out in front with you. You may be poised enough to do that but not me."

"That's bullshit, and you know it. You're not going to back out now you spineless little wimp. Our agreement was conditioned on your total commitment to this operation. That means you will be with my partner and me during the entire time. We can't afford to leave you in a position to cross us after the hit takes place."

Davis leaned forward in his chair, placing his hands on the desk before him and looking straight into Witters' eyes said, "you know I wouldn't say anything."

Witters laughed, "that's true, you don't have the guts to step forward. At least until you have your share of the money in your hot little hand." Leaning back in the chair Witters continued, "you don't have any choice. The way I see it your father is going to get rid of you any day now because you don't even have what it takes to be the spoiled little rich kid. Even your wife knows that. Why do you think she's divorcing you?"

"It's not because of that," Davis protested.

"Sure it is," continued Witters. "You're nothing but a fat incompetent who's had everything handed to him on a silver platter. You still can't figure out you had it made. Well, now you have a choice." Pointing his finger at Davis, Witters' voice dropped an octave as he made his point. "You can go through with this as we originally agreed and get the money you need to start over somewhere or you can back out now and figure out how to pay back the money you already took from the bank. That's jail time when you get caught and you will. I don't think you can last a whole week before you try to suicide your way out of the attention you'll get at the pen. That's if you even make it through the trial and all the publicity. In a small town that might get rough, but that's your problem. What's it going to be?"

Visibly trembling, Ferguson responded, "you don't give me much choice, do you? Either way, I'm probably going to end up in jail. If I don't do it your way, I get caught for embezzling, and if I do, I still can't stay here because everyone in the bank will recognize me even with a disguise. I'll do it, but not by choice. When will it take place?"

"I'll let you know," Witters grinned, "when I think it's right. But I'm warning you, talk or act before I tell you and I'll kill you myself." Taking a cigar from the box on Davis's desk, Witters swung his legs up plopping his feet on the smooth surface of the expensive desk. "Get yourself a black shirt, work pants, and a black stocking cap that will cover your face like the skiers use. Use some common sense and get them in some other town than this one and not all in the same place. Pat and I will let you know when to use them."

Now that he was again committed to Witters, Ferguson

was in a hurry to get it over with. 'Central Mines will have a payroll to meet this Friday. Those miners like to carry cash, so the bank gets extra cash from the Fed that day just to cash their payroll checks. Why not do it then?"

Witters knocked the ash from his cigar into the thick carpet, carefully ignoring the ashtray next to him on the desk. "Maybe. Maybe not. You get that kind of cash every week, so there's no hurry. Maybe Friday, maybe next Friday, maybe next month. I don't know yet, but when I do, I'll let you know. You just be ready when I do."

Witters stood, mashed his burning cigar into the desktop next to Ferguson's outstretched hand and walked to the door. "Just stay cool my friend, just stay cool." Witters left Davis's office and strolled across the lobby. As he reached the entry, he turned and stared at Davis Ferguson.

Witters cold gray eyes conveyed a message to Ferguson even across the lobby. Ferguson was scared both of Witters and the runaway chain of events which tied him to Jeremy Witters. As Witters left, Ferguson began to wonder just what he had gotten himself into. He knew deep down inside that Witters was right. His only way out was to get enough money to go someplace where no one knew him to start again. Not that it mattered much to Davis. There was nothing left in Caribou and he knew it. Even his father could not bail him out this time. He was the cashier of Ferguson Federal only because his father suffered it not because he had any talent for banking. He thought he could live like a king in some other country if he only had enough money. Just like his great-grandfather, he could be a success in another land. If only he had enough money.

The small sums he was able to lift from the vault were not enough and would soon be discovered by the examiners if the accountant didn't find it first. He opened his desk drawer, removing the travel folders from within. He was so intent upon his thoughts of faraway places he did not notice the careful scrutiny Witters gave him through the window by his side.

Satisfied with what he observed, Witters, strolled across the lawn and down the adjoining alley. Near the opposite end of the block sat a new Lincoln Continental, steel gray, and driven by a tall man in western clothes. As Witters approached, the tall man ran the electric window down.

"Pat, this guy is flaky, but I think we have him hooked. Keep an eye on him for a while. I'll come back and pick you up after I run a few errands."

Exchanging places, Pat leaned in the window, "ok boss. Check on the horses, will you? They need to to be fed. That piebald keeps getting loose too. That could cause some trouble if he wanders too far."

Witters drove off while Pat sat down on a convenient park bench to read his newspaper and keep an eye on the unhappy banker.

Chapter 15

Witters strained under a load of hay he was distributing to the horses tied in the barn's spacious stalls. Dressed in blue jeans and a plaid cotton shirt he did not resemble his earlier appearance in the bank. Here he looked like a cowboy. The resemblance ended there. He was obviously afraid of the horses he was feeding. Timidly he would ease between the stall wall and the horse to a point where he could throw the hay into the manger. The effect was to startle the horses which in turn got them to moving around the stall and frightened Witters even more.

"You wouldn't have so much trouble with them horses if you would carry the hay clear up to the manger. You're just spooking em up when you throw hay at their heads. Might get stepped on this way."

"Look, Pat, I know we need these things to make this bank deal work, but I just don't trust them. Too bad we have to have them around all the time. I guess it's better nobody knows we have them, but I could live without having to be around them."

"Well, I guess we could try and use motorcycles through the mountains or just use the car. That bank guy might stick out like a sore thumb though. Besides, I like horses. You just need to get acquainted better with them."

Witters stormed out of the last stall. "No way! You like the damn things; you take care of feeding them. I'll ride one cause it's necessary to my plan, but that's why I have you here to put on the saddles and pack the equipment. That's your area of expertise, not mine."

Pat finished putting out the hay and began distributing grain to each of the horses. One quart of grain went on top of the hay before each horse. The only sound for several minutes was the sound of horses chewing grain and the rustle of hay as a horse nuzzled deeper into the hay for the remaining grain. Occasionally a horse would stomp a foot as he moved about or a tail would swish toward a bothersome fly. Pat learned many years ago that you had to have patience with animals to get the most out of them. He leaned against a stall divider with one foot raised against the wood as he pondered the outcome of Witters's latest venture. Pat had been an active partner with Witters for 12 years and was remarkably satisfied with the results of that partnership. He had a large bank account, lived well and only worked a small part of each year. Witters was a genius when it came to hitting banks. Part of that success came from constantly changing his method of operation. Each job was conducted differently from any of the previous hits.

This gig had a different feeling though. Witters didn't know horses. It was a crazy getaway. They planned to make their hold-up at the bank, drive to where the horses were and ride across a vast wilderness area in the mountains to a location on the north face of the Rockies near the Canadian border where they had another vehicle located. If it was done right, no one should suspect where the bandits had gone. Taking that banker along was downright foolish. The fat slob probably can't ride a horse any better than Witters. That would leave the whole getaway operation in Pat's lap. No sir, Pat didn't like the feel of this one at all.

"Jeremy don't be smoking in here," exclaimed Pat as he rushed up to Witters and took the cigar from his mouth. "You drop some hot ash into this dry barn, and we won't have any horses. Probably have all the neighbors and maybe even the cops here too. In this part of the country, everybody will turn out to fight a fire."

"Sorry, wasn't thinking. Let's get this done pretty soon.

I've been around all these sorry horses too long. Starting to get on my nerves." Witters looked tight as he paced back and forth in the narrow walkway.

"I'm ready when you are. Not too late to change our minds. Maybe we should start over with something new."

Witters grinned, the tension seeming to flow from his body. "No. This should be the easiest profit we have ever turned. For a small bank, they keep plenty of money laying around loose every Friday. We couldn't find a better target. Just load the money up and take a ride through the mountains," he drawled slowly.

"Ok, Jeremy. When you're ready, I'll be right with you."

The two men left the barn through a small door cut into the large double sliding doors and walked across the yard to the little house. Witters is again lighting a cigar. Pat pushed his cowboy hat further back on his head and lowered himself into the lawn chair on the porch.

"One of us needs to go back into town and check up on the fat boy."

Witters took a deep draw on the cigar. "I'll go in. I need some more cigars anyway. See you in a few hours." With that, he walked to the Continental, settled himself behind the wheel and drove down the dusty lane to the paved highway two miles away.

In the Ferguson Federal building, Davis Ferguson was seated at his desk going through bank records. Actually, he was altering some of the accounts in the hopes his earlier thefts would go unnoticed for a while longer. He ardently wished for Witters to hurry up with the plans for robbing the bank. It was melodramatic but it was also his only way out. Maybe he could hurry Witters up. If Davis's manipulations were found out, it might mess up Witters's plans as well although perhaps that was what Witters wanted. Then he wouldn't have to share with Ferguson. Davis decided he would warn Witters against that. If he got caught before Witters acted maybe he could trade the information to the prosecutor in return for probation. He leaned back in his chair and contemplated his options. There didn't appear to be many.

Davis Ferguson was a dreamer and inherently a con man. He grew up as the only child in a well to do family with a sweeping family tradition. Old Man Ferguson set a standard for his children, grandchildren, and great-grandchildren to attempt to live up to. Silas had been hugely successful. Looked up to by all in the community made it difficult for those who followed to live up to the community's expectations. With each generation, there was less to accomplish and more to live up to. By the time Davis was a child, Ferguson Federal Savings and Loan was an established institution in Caribou. The financial fortune of the Ferguson family was made. Davis's mother spoiled him with everything money and position could purchase. That may have affected his personality. In school, Davis was the typical spoiled rich kid. If he didn't like the game, he would literally take his football and go home. As an older child, he was the neighborhood bully, taking his frustrations out on those who were smaller or lesser than he. Perhaps the rod would have helped, but it was spared.

Don't fault his mother or even his ancestors exclusively. They meant well. Davis suffered from diabetes. The disease contributed to his frustration and pain. Insulin shots were necessary every day of his life just to keep him alive and well. One of the natural consequences was his tendency towards fat. Teasing from his contemporaries about his baby fat was always present in his life. Whether it excused his final development as a person is questionable. Others have had more significant challenges and have risen above handicaps. Davis Ferguson did not.

Most diabetics avoid alcohol. Ferguson did not. As a teenager, he was arrested on a frequent basis for being a minor in possession of alcoholic beverages. His driver's license had been suspended more than once for driving while under the

influence. Usually, daddy's money and position could miti-
gate the consequences. Even when he was responsible for
the death of one of his friends and severe injuries to another,
the power of the Ferguson family kept him out of jail. Money
was paid. Families failed to prosecute. In the process, Davis
learned that money could do almost anything. Totally irre-
sponsible in every way he became what he was today. Given
a responsible job with the family bank he was still protected
and allowed to get away with more than he should. His father
was well aware of the juggling of the bank's books. Davis did
not know that. His own past had led him to his present state
of mind. Witters counted on that state of mind to help him rob
this bank. Keeping Davis off balanced and thinking he had no
choice was essential. As a result, either he or Pat kept a fairly
close watch on Davis Ferguson.

Ferguson was startled by the tapping on his window.
Jumping up from the desk he quickly shut the account book
and stared out the window into the gathering dusk. Witters
motioned for Davis to open the side door. As Witters stepped
into the bank, he increased the pressure on Davis. "You idiot.
Why are you in the bank after hours with all the drapes open?
Close them."

What thoughts Ferguson had weren't expressed, but
he hurried to comply with Witters's order. As he pulled the
drapes shut in the office, Witters slid into the chair behind the
desk. "Looky, looky. The busy bank executive is busy altering
the books. Maybe I should just take these with me."

"What are you doing here? We shouldn't be seen together,"
Davis stuttered out.

"You dummy. Are you trying to call attention to yourself
before we can put our operation together? You're worried
about this little penny ante stuff you've been pulling off, and
in the process, you're going to ruin the big chance. I ought to
call this whole thing off and just let you sweat."

Pacing the floor, Ferguson looked like he was about to cry.

"I just didn't want this other thing with the books to foul us up. I often work here at night so that wouldn't be unusual even if someone looked in." Then in a rash moment, he blurted, "let's get the show on the road."

Witters got up from his chair and crossed the office to Ferguson. Grabbing him by the lapels of his coat he forced Ferguson into one of the two desk chairs. "I told you before. I make the decisions on timing, not you. Park your ass and wise up. You be ready. Quit doing stupid things like doing more book alterations and get your equipment ready. I'll tell you when we get the show on the road."

Witters left the office in several quick strides, slamming the office door behind him. Leaving the bank, he got into the Continental, made a u-turn in the alley and pulled onto the main street.

The sheriff's patrol car coming the opposite direction noticed the Continental pull out of the alley next to the bank. Noting the license number he reached for the microphone on the dash. Before he could speak into the mike, his radio conveyed the message that there was a prowler in the backyard of a house about three blocks away. He acknowledged the radio transmission and forgot about the steel gray Continental with out-of-state plates.

CHAPTER 16

I awoke to the hiss of the TV. Probably a good thing it was on. The only light in the room was the blue-white flicker of a television tuned to a channel that had long since signed off the air.

Just as I got comfortably settled into bed, the phone began to ring. Could have been worse. Usually, callers wait until I'm sleeping well before they call. It was the dispatcher with a request to make a blood run. Why call me you may ask. After all, I had done my shift last night. The main reason, in fact, the only reason they called me, is that I am the department's best pilot. I'm also the only one. Most of the time it's a real benefit. Getting paid to fly is even better than driving a patrol car. At 5:00 a.m. the rewards are less enticing.

Being out in the sticks has its advantages and disadvantages too. One of the benefits was that it justified the department's operation of an airplane. The downside was that the hospital rarely had blood on had hand, which requires a flight to Billings each time an emergency comes up. The life of a small town cop!

After calling flight service, one of the better services provided by the federal government, and getting the current weather reports, I filed a tentative flight plane and drove over to the hospital to pick up the ice chest for keeping the blood preserved during the flight back from Billings. It's an easy job. The hospital makes arrangements for the blood, and the blood bank delivers it right to the airport. Because it's a medical mission, the flight gets expedited through the system, and all I have to do is fly up and back.

Some people must work weird hours like mine. When I walked into the hospital, Cheryl was talking on the phone at the main desk. She covered the mouthpiece and yelled across the lobby at me. "The ice chest is on the table in the lab. I'll be right there."

I was getting to where I almost liked coming to the hospital. The pretty lady made being here downright enjoyable. I grabbed the ice chest and started across the lobby area as she left the phone and came to meet me. "Are you going after the blood yourself?"

"Thought I would. I'm the only pilot they could get out of bed this early. What's the emergency?"

"Single car turnover about an hour ago. Maybe a ruptured spleen, so they need some standby blood when they start surgery." She smiled at me, making my knees do their wobble act again.

"You fly airplanes too? I thought you would have to go in your car with all the red lights flashing and then park in front of the door again."

I grinned back. "I did park in front of the door. Some of the lights are blue." Surprising even myself I said, "flying's quicker though. Want to go along?"

"You're in luck. I'm only here to take care of the blood when you get it to the hospital. Can I go along?"

"Sure, come on let's get to the airport. Got a coat?"

She did. Soon we were in the Pontiac and headed up the hill to the hanger. Nice to have such cute company along. Besides, it helps to have someone to push on the other wing to get it out of the hanger. Didn't tell her that until we got to the airport. As I pushed the big doors open I let her in on that part.

"That's not very nice. I thought you wanted my company."

"Oh, but I do. A little extra muscle always helps though."

We pushed the department's Cessna 206 onto the pad in front of the hanger, and I did a quick pre-flight. Although I'm about the only one to ever fly the 206 and I keep a close eye on the maintenance, I always like to know if something has gone wrong since the last time I used it. Hangar rash, those scratches, and dents that appear once in a while because someone was careless and pushed one plane into the other can ruin your day if the flight characteristics of the airplane are affected. Everything looked good. Cheryl had stowed the ice chest in the cargo area, and I crawled through the right side front door and slid into the left seat. Cheryl climbed into the right seat as I started through the checklist. I learned a long time ago your life expectancy is better if you use the checklist. Even if you are familiar with the operation of a plane you use all the time, you can forget little details that can get you hurt. Once on a military flight in a little Cessna spotter plane, I landed at a small strip to let off a passenger and then took off with the carburetor heat still on. Carb heat keeps the carburetor from freezing on landing but takes a lot of the power away on takeoff. Fortunately, I was the only one in the plane. As they say, there are old pilots and bold pilots, but no old, bold pilots.

Cheryl noticed my use of the checklist as I set switches, adjusted instruments and started the engine. "Do you know how to fly this thing? I'm not encouraged to see you using the instruction book just to get it going!"

I smiled. "Too early in the morning to remember everything. I think we have the book on how to land in the briefcase behind you." She didn't look too happy. "Shucks, even you could fly this little old 206."

I relented a little and told her why I use a checklist, got her seatbelt fastened for her and started the engine. After doing a run-up engine check and searching the area for other traffic, I taxied onto the active runway and eased the throttle forward. At eighty knots I eased the wheel back, and we were flying. With a few quick adjustments to engine RPM and getting the prop pitch into the green, I settled into a climb to altitude while I contacted center for my clearance.

Center must not have been very busy this morning. Almost

immediately they came back with "Lifeguard November Three Three Sierra Delta, Salt Lake Center; cleared as filed, climb to and maintain one five thousand, squawk one seven six seven, report Lido intersection. Altimeter two niner niner four."

"Roger Salt Lake. Lifeguard Three Sierra Delta, amend flight plan to two souls on board." That took care of the formalities. The day was dawning with a beautiful sunrise, the air was clear and smooth, and except for the drone of the engine, everything was serene.

Cheryl had never flown before, so I enjoyed myself showing her how the different gauges and instruments functioned and explaining the little details of our flight and the conversations with Center as we went along. Flying is unique. There is nothing like it. Maybe that's why I like to teach others how to fly.

On a clear morning like this, you can see for miles across the mountain peaks and into the valleys. The air is smooth, and you feel like you are hanging above the top of the world.

We could have flown without filing any flight plans and certainly without submitting the instrument flight plan we were not following, but I've found it helps expedite the route into large airports like Logan International in Billings and Stapleton International in Denver. Today's flight could be lifesaving even if we were only transporting blood. Hence the formal instrument flight plan and the prefix of "Lifeguard" in front of the plane's identification number.

"Lifeguard Three Sierra Delta, Salt Lake Center. Contact Billings approach on one twenty point five."

I thumbed the transmit button on the wheel. "Roger Salt Lake. Lifeguard Three Sierra Delta leaving your frequency. See you on the return."

I switched the radio to Billings approach, advised them I had the field in sight and got clearance to land on two seven right. For a change, I greased the landing. Impressed Cheryl to no end. As we taxied up to the terminal, the blood bank fellows brought out the blood, and we made a hot load that is with the engine still running. Nice to work with the same folk all the time. They know the drill better than I do. In a short time, we were back in the air and headed for home.

Cheryl smiled over at me. "I'm impressed. You really do know how to fly this airplane. I'm glad I could come along."

"I'm glad too. I like having company especially when it's a pretty lady. Someday we'll go out flying when we can sightsee. Maybe I can introduce you to the mile high club."

She looked puzzled, "what's that?"

I figured I'd better soft sell that idea before I got into trouble. The mile high club is only for those who are very, very close friends. It involves some activities that are better left for the bedroom. I was just kidding her, but somehow I figured I had better leave well enough alone. "I'll show you someday," I hoped.

We landed at Caribou. Another great landing. Two in a row is sometimes pretty hard if you have someone in the plane you want to impress. Guess I was just relaxed and comfortable with her. I haven't felt that way in a long time. Maybe time does heal. Perhaps it was just her. Time also will tell. We parked in front of the hanger and moved our cargo into the Pontiac. With no wind, I could let the plane sit until I could come back to refuel and hanger it. Figured we had better get the blood over to the hospital and let Cheryl get back to work.

I parked in front of the emergency room doors again. "There you go, pretty lady. Hope it helps."

"I'll let you know. Thanks for taking me along."

"My pleasure. I'll pick you up later unless you've changed your mind.

She gave me a look, like that you'd give a momentarily misbehaving child. "No way. I'm looking forward to it. Take care."

I got the plane fueled, hangered and ready to go if it was again needed in a hurry. Blood runs and looking for lost hunters were the most common uses. Occasionally we transported prisoners and even carried some patients once in a while. That's how we justified the six-place airplane to the county commissioners. You need that extra room for a stretcher. Other than the extra room, it was about as cheap to fly as a four place.

Today was my day off, but since I had shot most of it already, I went by the office to see what was going on. Not much! The Sheriff and I had coffee and talked over some shift changes. He didn't say anything about the Undersheriff job, and I didn't remind him. Puttered the rest of the day around the trailer cleaning up. Even washed the Blazer. Finally laid down and took a nap. Good thing I set the alarm or I would have been late picking Cheryl up

CHAPTER 17

Tom Flanigan leaned back in his chair, put his feet up on his desk and thought about himself and his job. His eighth term as Sheriff of Banner County would end in two more years. Thirty-two years as Sheriff. That was a record almost anywhere. It was legendary in the west where the voting public had a tendency to change elected officials every term or two. Generally, an Undersheriff stood a pretty good chance of succeeding the Sheriff if he had a few years in the job. That wouldn't work in Banner County. His Undersheriff of many years was going to retire and move to Arizona in two months.

Flanigan hated to just walk away from the job without having some input as to the next Sheriff. Jerry Burkley would be perfect for the job, but somehow he lacked the desire. Tom had been unable to even convince him to do the Undersheriff's job. Of course, Flanigan hadn't told him the reason he wanted him to, but it would undoubtedly influence the voters. Maybe I should run one more time he thought to himself. No, can't keep the job forever. Time he retired as well.

Tom thought back to his first meeting with Jerry. The Sheriff had been cleaning up some paperwork in his office when the dispatcher came in with a request for advice. All the deputies were pretty far out in the county, and the Fireside Bar had a fellow trying to create a disturbance. Rather than call someone in, Flanigan decided to run on over himself. When he got there, he discovered a six foot, dark-haired fellow in cowboy clothes running his mouth and trying to start a fight. No damage had been done, but all the necessary elements were present. The Fireside catered to a rougher crowd who were always eager for some excitement. Later in the evening when everyone had a little more to drink, one or more of them would be happy to oblige the mouthy cowboy. Years of handling people gave Sheriff Flanigan the edge. He was able to talk Burkley into leaving the bar with him. Once they were on the sidewalk, he was able to speak with Jerry meaningfully. They sat in the Sheriff's patrol car and spoke for over an hour. Something in Jerry stirred an urge in Big Tom Flanigan to try and help him.

After the initial belligerence wore off, Jerry poured out many of his frustrations, some of his problems and a lot of his prior background. Big Tom was a good listener. His demeanor and appearance often led people to confide in him. Jerry was no exception. Jerry's ramblings gave the Sheriff the insight to help Jerry salvage himself. It had turned out to be the best investment of time the Sheriff had made in a long time. Jerry was probably the best deputy he had ever hired with the possibility of being one of the best law enforcement officers in the country.

Jerry's story was typical in many respects. After Vietnam, he went to college, graduated with a degree in business. After leaving college, he discovered the job market was severely restricted both as to availability and desirability. He took the entrance exams for the Denver Police Department just to get a job. Graduating first in his class at the Police Academy, he was soon working as a patrolman. For more than a year he worked the swing shift, the hours from four in the afternoon until midnight. Sometimes he had a partner but more often was left in a solo environment. He was finding the job challenging and exciting. So much so that he began studying for the sergeant's exam to be given the following September.

Before college, he received a brown envelope from the government which like for so many other young men changed his life dramatically. The draft notice was the generic type which could have placed him in any of the services. The typical choice of his generation was to either accept the draft call or head for Canada. He did neither. After talking with the recruiters for each branch of service, he enlisted in the United States Army.

Qualifying for Warrant Officer training as an aviator, Jerry was immediately inducted and sent to basic training. He did well in all aspects of basic although not the very best. His request for flight training was granted, and Jerry soon found himself at the Army's WOC aviation training center. He excelled in all aspects of flying; a natural flier if there is such an animal. He completed rotary wing and instrument training.

He was sent to train in fixed-wing airplanes, big and small. That's not a lot since the Air Force has all the really big aircraft but the twin-engine Caribou, a troop and equipment transport plane isn't all that bad. No further use was to be made of his advanced qualifications even though there was a shortage of Army multi-engine pilots in Vietnam.

Jerry didn't talk much to Sheriff Flanigan about his Vietnam experience, but the Sheriff had a chance to see Jerry's DD Form 214, the summary of a person's military experience given to the veteran when he is discharged. Tom noted that the 214 showed the award of the Silver Star, two Bronze Stars (one with a V for valor), ten Air Medals and the Army Commendation Medal. These were in addition to the general array of decorations given to all who were in Vietnam for any length of time. Burkley was discharged as a WO3 after serving another year at Fort Carson, Colorado. He then returned to Wyoming and Denver police departments to pick up life where he had left off.

Well, not exactly where he had left off. While still at Fort Carson, he wooed and married an Army Nurse who was discharged the day after he was. They honeymooned by moving to Denver. She went to work at Fitzsimmons Army Hospital in Denver as a civilian nurse. Jerry went to work as a cop. He passed the sergeant's exam, was assigned to supervise a day shift and started studying for the lieutenant's examination. On his days off he taught flying at one of the regional airports.

Everyone figured he was moonlighting. He wasn't. Jerry did it because he liked to fly not for the money. At least, not at first. His wife liked to spend, and she didn't like working all that well. They didn't fight when she quit her job; conversations just didn't take place. It was a subject they avoided. She because it was easier and Jerry because he cared deeply for her. Money then became a real problem. Cops don't make good money even at lieutenant rank. Neither do flight instructors.

Salesmen, however, do make good money. So do successful businessmen. Everyone knows that. Why not just become a business tycoon. It sounded simple when they first talked about it. It being a business venture. One of Jerry's fellow cops, Fred Hanks, suggested that he and Jerry go into the police supply business. After all, both of them used and understood the equipment they used on the job. They knew the people that bought equipment, both in their department and many others in the front range region, and they had the knowledge to run a business. At least they thought they did.

Using their limited savings, a generous Small Business Administration loan and their contacts, they both threw themselves into the business. Surprisingly they were moderately successful.

Unfortunately to achieve that success they both were away from home most of the time. Fred was single, so it didn't cause him any problems, but Jerry's wife was openly hostile about his absences. She returned to work as a nurse, a job she had never been real thrilled about, and six months later advised Jerry she was divorcing him. Pleading, crying and promising didn't change anything. She pursed the divorce.

Jerry kept with the business for a while, but his heart wasn't really in it. He had started it primarily for her benefit and without her to share the rewards, just didn't care. Jerry finally sold his share of the business to Fred on easy monthly payments and hit the road in a used Chevy Blazer. He had enough income from Fred to pay his expenses, giving him the ability to just wander with his thoughts. He went where the moods took him. After traveling around a large part of the country, Jerry ended up in Caribou.

Sheriff Flanigan didn't get all of that from their conversation in the patrol car, but he got enough of the story that he decided to invite Jerry home to stay with him for a while. They talked more as the days passed. After checking Burkley out with the Denver Police Department and talking to Fred on the phone, Sheriff Flanigan offered Jerry a job as one of his deputies. By then Jerry was about traveled out, and the idea of being a cop again was appealing. He took the job.

That was five years ago. Jerry was now one of three lieutenants on the department. The Undersheriff supervised the three lieutenants. Jerry went to all the advanced qualification schools he could get into and helped innovate several new concepts in the department. He was studiously single and rarely dated. The fact that he worked swing shift contributed, but basically, he just didn't want to get hurt again. Everyone should get married once, but no one should do it more than once. At least that was a philosophy that kept him safe from further hurt.

Now if the Sheriff could push him along just a little more, he would have a successor. In five years Jerry had become the son the Sheriff never had. Like all parents he wanted his son to succeed. Look at how many companies are named 'and Son.'

Turning from his thoughts, the Sheriff began to work through his monthly report to the County Commissioners.

CHAPTER 18

The dispatcher sounded bored when she answered the phone. All dispatchers sound bored. It's part of the job description. They also sound calm and unruffled when they use the radio, even if the world is coming to an end as they speak. Our dispatchers are pretty good. They keep track of the various field units, know the geography of the county well enough to be able to send the closest unit on a call, and best of all they worry about the safety of the guys in the field. Just be late responding to a radio call for a status check or take longer than usual on a car stop and you will find they have already started a backup unit in your direction. We give them a bad time every once in a while and complain about how slow they are, but every veteran cop knows what angels they are. They get even once in a while too. Jenny Abbote did. "What are you calling in for? I thought you were out of our hair for the night."

"I am. Just thought you'd worry if you couldn't talk to me. I'm going to leave the portable in the car while I'm at dinner, so you'll have to call the Rusty Nail if you want me for anything."

She laughed. "Why would we need you, fearless leader? You know we do better on your nights off. Keeps things smooth. Have fun." Then said, "hey, how come you aren't taking your portable? Got a date or something?"

"Or something." Dispatchers always think they need to know everything.

Guess it was kind of different. Most times I live with the portable. I kind of like to know what all's going on too. It's not that I don't trust the guys on my shift to be able to take care of business. I just like to know. Sergeant Falls can handle whatever comes up. Any of the experienced deputies could supervise if we were both gone. Years of not having anything better to do makes you a busybody.

I like the Rusty Nail. It would be a first class restaurant anywhere in the world. The service is attentive, the food is excellent, and the people that go there are friendly. You can sit in the bar and talk if you want or you can curl up in a soft chair next to the fireplace and read a book if you feel like it. No one cares. Ed Plant, the guy who owns the Nail figures you should be able to treat the place like your home away from home. Cheryl should like it. Fancy but not snobbish.

When you enter the Nail, you come into a large room with a high vaulted ceiling supported by massive, rough beams. The smoke from the fireplace over the years has given them a black appearance that gets lighter as you get farther away from the fireplace. A massive bar runs along the length of one side of the room. On the other side is a rock wall with a massive fireplace. Leather comfortable chairs and a couch surround the front of the fireplace in the open area between the bar and the wall. High wood stools line the bar itself. It gives the appearance of being someone's recreation room rather than being a bar. The closest tables are in the next room, and they are for eating rather than drinking. Trophy heads of elk, deer, and moose decorate the stone wall above and around the fireplace. Comfortable and quiet. No jukebox, no TV. You can talk to someone, and they can hear you.

The restaurant is similarly done. Comfort, not high style. The tables have red tablecloths with real candles. An extensive wine rack with some outstanding wine lines one wall. The other walls show the log structure of the building. The most amazing aspect is the cooperation of the help. If your water glass is empty, whoever has the pitcher will fill it and all the rest in the room who has a similar need. You don't ever know who your waitress is because they all help each other out.

I discovered the Nail shortly after I came to Caribou. It's a little out of the beaten path just outside of town. Actually, it's part of a dude ranch operation. You might say I'm a regular customer. Ed treats me like part of his family after all these years. Think I surprised him a little tonight though. I've never brought a date there. That's not surprising. I haven't dated much since I got to Caribou. Just me and my portable most times.

Ed noticed right away. "Who is this charming young lady and where have you been hiding her? Now I know why you haven't been in all week."

"This is Cheryl. She's been holding me prisoner at the hospital this week." That comment got me an elbow in the ribs from Cheryl.

"He just can't do his job right. Keeps falling down. Sheriff Flanigan thought he needed to be institutionalized." She grinned impishly, "now I can't get rid of him. He keeps hanging around the hospital all the time. Said he likes the food!"

Ed kept the exchange going. "Good thing. I may not feed him at all tonight if that's the kind of food he likes. I'd hate to have my cooks all quit so they wouldn't have to dish up that stuff."

Ed slapped me on the back and took our drink orders. As he made the request to the bartender, Cheryl and I settled down on the couch. Ed returned and added wood to the fire. "Take your time Jerry. Billy's out finding a cow that wants to be your dinner. We've got a band at nine. Maybe if you don't step on the lady's feet, she'll dance with you later."

Just what I needed, two on one. Cheryl thought he was charming.

We did take our time. It was one of those comfortable times when you could just sit in front of the fire and talk. I don't remember what we talked about, but I sure did enjoy it. Ed finally chased us to our table. He had ordered for us and dinner was already there when we got to the table. I think he enjoyed spoiling us.

We ate and talked and enjoyed each other's company. Ed came by every once in a while and poured more wine into our glasses. As I said, the service at the Nail is superb. Friends are special. Ed is one of those kind of friends. Cheryl and I were able to get well acquainted without any distractions while Ed mothered us.

The band was as good as Ed had indicated. They played the kind of music you could dance to all night. Dancing with Cheryl was very pleasant. She kind of flowed into your arms and followed you every step of the way, even with a dancer as miserable as me. I don't remember having such a compatible time in a long while. We sat and talked during the band's intermissions and danced most of the dances.

I told her about my job, a little about my past and she listened, even laughed at my stories of the routine that was not always routine in a small town cop's life. Maybe it was a night of illusions; I don't know. I do know it ended all too soon.

We bid Ed a good night and went out to the Blazer hand in hand. The portable was making noise when I unlocked the Blazer door, but I ignored it. Opening the passenger door for Cheryl, I pulled her close to me and kissed her. She returned my kiss and pressed close to me. We stood next to the Blazer with the door open and explored each other's lips while the portable blubbered on. Then Ed came out to lock up for the night.

"Why don't you two go somewhere a little more private than right here under all the lights?" Ed laughed and soon the Nail's lights went out.

"Guess maybe we should," I whispered, "but I sure am comfortable where I am."

"Me too," murmured Cheryl.

I helped her into the car, gave her another kiss, and started to close the door. She looked at me and smiled. "It's been a lovely evening."

She reached across the Blazer and opened the lock on my

door. As I got in, the portable slid off the center console and dropped to the floor. I reached down to get it and could no longer ignore the sounds coming from it.

"Officer down, needs assistance," came the dispatcher's excited voice. I pulled the portable off the floor and demanded information.

"Charlie 27 and Charlie 15 responded to the Highway Mini-Mart on a reported robbery in progress. Shots have been fired, and 15 called for backup and an ambulance. No further transmissions."

"Roger SO, I'm rolling in my own vehicle. Advise Charlie 1." That's the Sheriff. "What other units are in the vicinity?"

"Charlie 5, none close. Charlie 17 and 18 are in a double car about fifteen miles out. The rest are thirty or more. City is also responding."

I slammed the Blazer into gear and headed for the Mini-Mart on the opposite edge of town. There aren't any lights or sirens on my Blazer, but I can generally get through traffic about as well without them anyway. "Cheryl, you stay in the car no matter what happens. Do you know how to work the radio?"

"I can. Please be careful."

"Not to worry. I got over being a hero in Vietnam."

The Mini-Mart came into view as I crested over the hill. The lights were all on, and there was activity inside. Two patrol cars were parked at angles to the front with the overhead lights still turning. I pulled in behind them and told Cheryl again to stay in the car. As I stepped out of the Blazer, I reached under my coat and pulled out the off-duty Beretta automatic from the small of my back.

I was vaguely aware of another patrol car pulling into the lot as I ran crouched over to the side of the closest parked car, putting it between me and the store and away from the Blazer. I assumed the other car was the Sheriff or one of the off-duty supervisors but didn't take the time or attention to check. My whole focus was riveted on the storefront. I checked the chamber indicator on the Beretta to be sure a bullet was in place and moved from the car to a position behind the gas pump. Not a great place to be standing if someone did start shooting but better than being in the open.

A figure in uniform stepped from between the shelves and came to the door. Sergeant Falls yelled to me, "we're code 4. Come on in."

I holstered the Beretta and waved to the other patrol car. It was the Sheriff. We went into the store together. A youngster in jeans and a sweatshirt was lying on the floor in front of the counter with his hands handcuffed behind his back. The glass doors on the display refrigerator were shattered; glass was everywhere. Mick was talking to an older man wearing an apron who was sitting on the floor behind the counter.

Jack Falls grinned at the Sheriff and me. "The kid decided to hold up Pop Martin but got the surprise of his life. You know that old shotgun he keeps under the counter. Well, when the kid pointed his gun at Pop, Martin dived under the counter and came up with the shotgun blasting. Lucky. The kid hit the floor right away, and the only damage was to the refrigerator and some of the canned goods. The red all over is only tomato sauce. When we got here, Pop was standing over him with his shotgun."

"Why didn't you call it in," asked the Sheriff, "we got a report of shots fired and then nothing."

"Guess cause Jerry got here too soon. You did too. We heard the shots as we drove in and Mick called it in. By the time we got it sorted out you were here."

"You both have portables; next time use them."

"Yes, sir. Only trouble is, mine is on the charger at the station, and I think Mick left his in the car."

"No, I didn't," exclaimed in Mick from across the room, "I dropped it coming across the lot."

I told him to find it before it walked off. "Do you need any help, Jack?"

"No, we've got it in hand."

I borrowed the Sheriff's portable and called in Code 4 to dispatch, then went back to the Blazer.

"Nothing like a little excitement to settle your dinner. Ready to go home?"

Cheryl looked worried. "Are all your nights like this?"

"No. Usually, we're bored to death," I explained what had happened as we drove back to her apartment. "Since we're usually spread out all over the county, it can get pretty hairy. Everyone knows that help can be a long way off if you wait for a regular backup or a city unit. They don't come real fast to help us out. You might have noticed they were just arriving as we drove off. I guess that's why most of us keep our portables with us when we aren't on duty."

"Does the Sheriff work this shift too?"

"No. He monitors calls too. Always shows up when there is trouble. He was probably on his way before we were."

"I'm glad to know that. It makes me feel more comfortable to know you have help when you need it." Cheryl's smile was back but still showed some of the strain of the last half hour. Kind of gave me a warm feeling that she worried about me. Julie never did.

I took Cheryl back to her apartment and kissed her again at the door. Her kiss was soft and full of promise. "Dinner tomorrow," I asked as I held her. "I have the night off again."

"Tomorrow or today?"

"I guess it is tomorrow already isn't it. Dinner tonight."

"Ok, but you come here, and I'll cook for you. I have tomorrow, or rather today, off too. I think I'd like to spoil you with a home-cooked meal."

I kissed her again and wandered back to the Blazer. The drive home was disconnected. Guess my circuits were overloaded. I went to bed with a feeling of warm happiness.

CHAPTER 19

"They look like a happy couple don't they Sheriff?"
"Yup, sure hope it lasts. Jerry needs something good in his life for a change."

"He sure works fast. Cheryl's only been in town for a week or two, hasn't she?"

"That's true Jack. I guess you could say his hard head helped him out for a change. I introduced them at the hospital the night Conners hit him with the chair over at the Moose. He managed to pass out right in front of her. Things like that help bring out the maternal instinct. Well, you've got the situation in hand here. Think I'll go on home."

"Have a good night Sheriff. Hopefully, I won't see you again until morning."

Rolling a cigarette as he walked back to his patrol car, the Sheriff reflected on the night's events. Mainly the attentiveness paid Cheryl by his favorite lieutenant. The Sheriff had some inside information that wasn't common knowledge. Cheryl was really a local gal. She lived in Banner County until she was sixteen or seventeen. Cheryl moved with her parents to Boise, Idaho. She had attended high school in Caribou.

Sheriff Flanigan knew her parents well. Cheryl's father had been Big Tom's closest friend for many years. Larry Hefner had been a rancher during those years. Tom and his wife, Edna, had spent many a pleasant day at the Hefner ranch helping Larry brand, moving cows, and just enjoying each other's company. Ester, Larry's wife, and Cheryl's mother were as friendly and outgoing as Edna, and the two were as close as Tom and Larry.

Ester's parents had homesteaded Piney Creek back in the late eighteen hundreds, and the entire family had worked the ranch over the span of time before the Hefners moved to Boise. Larry had the misfortune of developing a late allergy to hay, horses, and cows. Not the best situation for a rancher. Drawing on his business education Larry was able to land a job in Boise with one of his old college classmates building and selling prefab log homes. Larry headed up the sales division and reports were that he was very good at what he did.

When Cheryl wanted to return to Caribou and work at the hospital, Larry contacted his good friend, Tom Flanigan, to look after her. It was a chore that Tom looked forward to doing. Tom had watched Cheryl grow from a freckle-faced little girl to a young woman. She was a typical tomboy. On a ranch, a girl, especially an only child, learns to ride and rope just like the young boys do. You had to admit she was pretty good as a ranch hand. She was also a lady to the core. The transformation from tomboy to lady was magical. Cheryl had charm to Tom's way of thinking.

Tom backed the patrol car into the drive and stretched. It had been a good night, and he was relaxed as he went into the house. Edna, as was her habit, was waiting up for him. "Any problems honey?"

Tom shed his gun belt. "Nope, in fact, it looks like maybe some of our concerns over two young people we care about may about be solved. Jerry seems to be pretty taken over Cheryl."

"That's nice. You should be pretty happy. Your almost son hitched to your best friend's daughter. Think it will change Jerry's mind about accepting the responsibility of being Sheriff?"

"I hope so. Don't tell Jerry about being Sheriff though. I've only been working him on Undersheriff. At any rate, they seem happy together. Jerry took her out to dinner at the Rusty Nail tonight and left his portable in the car. First time he's been without a radio since he went to work for me."

Ester ripped out some stitches that were not just right. "I saw Sarah at the grocery store today. She said Jerry took Cheryl along with him when he went after the blood yesterday. He even held the door for her at the airport."

"Hope it works out for both of them. Ready to hit the hay?"

Edna put down her sewing and taking Tom by the arm kissed him on the check. "Of course. When are you going to quit trying to organize everyone's life for them?"

"Ah, I just want 'em to be happy and satisfied like I am."

As was his habit, Big Tom liked to be in the office as the midnight shift came off duty and the morning shift started. Although his presence wasn't needed, he could get the feel of the county as he listened to the reports, the briefing and the general conversations around him. Tom did it because he liked the involvement. Most of the other shift supervisors did it because Sheriff Flanigan did. Most mornings would find all three lieutenants hanging around too. Of course, it was no big deal for the morning and midnight supervisors since one was coming, and one was going, but for the swing shift supervisor, it meant getting up early after having worked past midnight. Jerry was generally there. Jack would occasionally show up if he had been the supervisor sergeant on Jerry's night off. When it was said that Jerry was usually there, it should be noted that the only times he wasn't was when he was out of town or tied up on a case.

"Jack, where's Jerry?" queried Lynn Tibbets, the day shift supervisor.

"Don't know lieutenant. As far as I know, he's in town."

Tom just smiled as he listened to the exchange. "Some

cops you guys are. He went fishing up the canyon this morning about daybreak. It seems like one of you would have noticed the Blazer as I did."

"Shucks Sheriff," pointed out Jack Falls, "we don't keep track of him as you do. It's probably the other way around. He's getting that bad habit of yours of turning up just when you least expect him. One set of cat's feet around here is enough."

Lynn Tibbets poured himself a cup of coffee and snagged the last donut. "Jerry don't fish. How come he's got the bug now?"

"Well Lynn," opined the Sheriff, "I think he wants to show the little lady with him some of the scenic spots in the canyon. At least I think that's what they had in mind since they got Bertha to make them up a sack lunch over at the diner."

"Same one he had last night Sheriff?"

"Looked like her to me Jack but who knows, maybe our fair-haired lieutenant is coming out of his social shell."

"OK with me Sheriff, I could use a little less official supervision on his nights off. I never know whether I'm supervising or he is. Gets kind of confusing."

Sheriff Flanigan left the room chuckling to himself. He, as one of his favorite TV characters, was fond of saying, loved it when a plan comes together. Now if nature would just cooperate a little, he could retire with a happy mind.

While the Sheriff was chuckling to himself, Jerry and Cheryl were laughing over Cheryl's antics with a rainbow trout. She had hooked it, but the fish had gone under a log, taking the trailing fly line with it. The fish was on one side of the log and Cheryl was on the other. Try as she might, she couldn't coax the fish back under without breaking the line. Jerry was no help to her as he lay on the bank laughing and holding his sides.

"Who caught who?" he laughed.

"The proper sentence is who caught whom, not who. You could at least help. I'm going to lose that big trout if you don't."

"That's alright. There's more in the stream. Besides, if you keep it, you'll have to clean it."

"You mean you won't clean it for me."

"Nope, that's woman's work. Even if it wasn't, you would have to clean your own. I only clean what I catch."

"You haven't caught anything yet."

"See, I won't have to clean anything."

At that point, the trout slipped the hook free, and Cheryl's line went slack. "I lost it." She reeled in the line, laid the pole across a rock and tackled Jerry as he lay on the bank. She tickled him until he was able to grab her hands and hold her still.

"Give up?" he asked as he gave her a gentle kiss.

"No, but it was the only way to get your attention away from that silly fish and back to me. I like the way you hold me. It's almost worth being wakened before morning by some idiot who wants to go fishing."

"I'm glad you were willing to come. I haven't been fishing in a long time but when I woke up this morning it seemed like a really good idea. Besides, it was the only thing I could think of to invite you to that early in the morning."

"If you'll let me up I want to try and catch another trout. I haven't been fishing since I was in high school. Not too many opportunities when you live in the big city and even less when you're going to school."

She kissed him and hopped up to retrieve her pole. She cast out into the stream and thought about how comfortable she was with this quiet, shy man. He's what I've been looking for all my life and just when I quit looking, he literally falls into my arms.

Others were up and about on this clear, warm morning. Our friends, the bank robbers, or should I say prospective bank robbers, were up and about too. They weren't as happy as Jerry and Cheryl, but they were indeed up.

"Where the hell is that damned horse? They're all in the barn but that one."

Pat eased himself out of his sleeping bag, lite the fire in the stove, and drawled, "That piebald? Probably slipped through that gap in the fence again and grazed out into the big pasture."

"Well, go get him. We can't have people commenting on the number of horses around this supposedly deserted building."

"Right away Jeremy. Do you suppose you could handle breakfast while I'm away?"

Pat slipped on his boots and a coat. Going out the door, he picked up a lariat. In a manner of minutes, he was back with the missing horse. It had been an easy job to locate the horse and throw a rope around its neck. He let it back into the barn and securely tied him in the stall with a nylon halter and lead rope.

The odor of eggs, bacon, and coffee greeted Pat as he entered the ramshackle building. "He's back in the barn."

"Good. Let's put this show on the road tomorrow afternoon. The payroll will be in the bank by then. I'm tired of waiting around."

"Sounds good to me. Want me to tell Ferguson?"

"Not until tomorrow. Ferguson couldn't keep it a secret for longer than thirty minutes. He'd either tell someone or do something to give it away. We'll go by and get him just beforehand. You can tell him to stay home from work tomorrow though. Tell him to call in sick."

CHAPTER 20

I awoke to the sounds of birds chirping, the trees were gently rustling and the early morning sun was streaming in my bedroom window. It was one of those rare, beautiful mountain mornings. The alarm said 5:00 a.m. I was awake and well-rested even with the late hours of the night before. That's what contented thoughts and feelings will do for a night's sleep. I rolled out of bed and went through the motions to make a pot of coffee. I was standing in front of the open refrigerator trying to decide what to have for breakfast when I thought of Cheryl. Cheryl and a beautiful morning. Two beautiful things should go together. I slammed the refrigerator shut and made my way across the room to the telephone.

"Hi there pretty lady. Are you up for the day?"

"It's all right. I had to get up to answer the telephone anyway."

"That's great! How would you like to go fishing?"

"Now?"

"No, the second Tuesday of next week. Of course now. This morning. It's beautiful out. Might even get lucky and not catch any fish."

"Let me get dressed, and some breakfast and I might be able to make it. At least if I can get some coffee pretty soon."

"Just get dressed. I'm on the way to get you. We can get breakfast and some lunch to go at Bertha's Diner."

I gathered up a pair of fishing poles from the equipment shed and got the Blazer pointed towards Cheryl's. She was standing on the porch waiting for me. What a lovely sight.

After getting her situated in the Blazer, we drove over to Bertha's. Bertha's place isn't fancy. It's far from fancy. Just a lunch counter with stools but the food is wonderful.

As usual, the Sheriff was seated on his customary breakfast stool. He eats here most mornings, so it wasn't much of a surprise. If you want breakfast in Caribou, you have to go to Bertha's or the truck stop outside of town. Since the food there would kill a mule, the only choice is to go to Bertha's. I eat here quite a bit too. Makes me a regular. Besides my cooking is not much better than the truck stops.

"Howdy Sheriff. You're up kind of early. Must have gone right home last night."

"That's for sure. Probably got home before you did. Good morning Cheryl. You sure are looking pretty this morning."

"Thank you, Sheriff. I'm glad somebody noticed."

I had noticed. Just couldn't get it out as ably as the Sheriff seemed to be able to do. It always sounds dumb when I say it even when I mean it very much. I think it; I just have a hard time saying it.

"You don't look any different than you did yesterday," I said, feeling dumb again.

"Thank you very much I think," Cheryl said teasingly. "What kind of a compliment is that?"

Once again the Sheriff saved my bacon. "I think what he means is that you are as lovely today as you were last night. He's just getting jaded by being around such a vision of loveliness all the time. In fact, I hear you two stole the department plane for a joy-ride yesterday," he chuckled.

"Now Sheriff," I protested, "it was official business. Cheryl just went along to make sure the blood was handled properly."

Cheryl looked at me and smiled. "Why Sheriff, he told me he just didn't know what to do with that blood and could I explain it to him. After the third explanation, I told him I would go with him since he couldn't understand a simple explanation."

Tom laughed, "Cheryl, I'm sure after flying blood runs routinely for several years that he knows the procedure. He probably just wasn't concentrating."

They went on in this vein for quite a while. I seemed to be the butt of all their remarks. Gives a guy such a warm feeling to know they care. We hustled through breakfast and got Bertha to make us up a couple of sack lunches. I paid the check, left a tip and started out the door with my arm around Cheryl.

The Sheriff's voice boomed across the diner. "Going somewhere? You'll miss morning shift change."

"My day off Sheriff. See you tomorrow, if not before. We're going fishing."

"Have fun kids. Keep him out of trouble Cheryl. He's not much of a fisherman so you may have to show him how." Both of them laughed out loud. I just had a big grin on my face.

We saw a herd of deer just outside of town as we started up the canyon. The deer were working their way back up the hillside after watering at the creek. Next month when hunting season starts they won't be so casual about the trip. You would probably be hard pressed to see even one on the hillside in the daylight after opening morning.

I have a favorite spot to fish. After wandering around the timber for a while on old logging roads, you come out on a high hill with a stream running along the bottom. Near the foot of the hill is a large beaver pond. It was sparkling in the morning sun as we started down the hill. Cheryl did teach me how to fish. I've never been enthusiastic about fishing. If the fish are biting, then I like to fish. If not, then I can think of plenty of other things to do. She makes an art of it. Just like a fish mind-reader, she could cast a fly right to an open mouth. After a while, I just leaned back against the tall grass on the bank and watched.

The only one she had trouble with was a fish that took her line under an old log. You could see the fish on one side trying to shake loose and Cheryl trying to get him back under the log without breaking her line. The fish won, and I got the best laugh I've had in a long time. She decided to help me with the laughter and started tickling me. It took me a few minutes to get her corralled and then with a quick kiss on her part; she went back to her fishing. Nice way to spend the morning.

After lunch, we hiked for a while in the hills and enjoyed the changing colors of the aspen trees. I ended up cleaning Cheryl's fish. Must be the gentleman in me. We took a leisurely drive back to town, and I dropped Cheryl off at her place.

"Come over around six," she informed me. She gave me a kiss that said don't bother to leave. Six was a long ways off.

"I'll be there with bells on." Actually, I was probably hearing bells at that point. I drove away in what was rapidly becoming my own personal fog. It's a nice feeling. I was beginning to feel like I was falling in love with her. Not good. A guy can get hurt pretty bad that way. I remembered my few years with Julie. They started out all right but got pretty colorless and then pretty unpleasant. I guess I had a few scars left over from the one and only marriage. Made a mental note to myself to watch out. Self, I said, don't get too involved. She's a nice gal, so let's keep it that way. Sure do like her company though. Have to think about it some more. Went by the office. Got ragged by the guys. You'd think they never went fishing themselves. The Sheriff was out so I went home and cut the grass.

Dinner was exquisite. At least I think it was. I don't remember what we had. When I got to Cheryl's, she met me on the porch with a martini in a metal glass. What strength it was I don't know, but it was one of the smoothest, most powerful martinis I had ever had. And I've drunk my share. I relaxed in a comfortable chair which faced the kitchen, drank my martini and conversed with Cheryl. She created some magic with the food. Chicken, vegetables, and rice. Kind of diet Chinese food. After dinner, I helped wash the dishes. Well, at least I dried them. Almost more than I do at home. When the dishes were done, Cheryl came into my arms and gave me a long, deep kiss.

"Thanks for the help with the dishes."

"It was my pleasure. I can't remember when I've had such an enjoyable evening."

We resumed where we had left off. Eventually, we move to the couch, although we never let go of one another long enough to count. Clothes began to disappear as we explored one another. Last night I commented that it had been a night of illusions. Tonight was not an illusion. We became one. One in body, one in emotion and one in spirit.

I held her close as she murmured into my ear, "my darling, I love you so."

I felt the love as well, but I had a hard time expressing it to her. I held her for a long time, feeling her warmth against me. Finally, we moved to her bedroom. She cuddled into my arms and rested her head against my shoulder. We held each other through the long night, and when morning came, she was still there in my arms.

"You look lovely my pretty lady." I was enjoying the sight of her as she slept close to me.

"You look pretty good to me too. I love you," she whispered.

Once again I sidestepped that issue, but I was kind of feeling it too. Something special only happens once in a while. Cheryl was special, very special.

We were part way through breakfast when the telephone rang. I let Cheryl answer it. After all, it was her house. Could have saved the trouble. It was the Sheriff. I asked him how he knew where to find me. He never gave me an answer and his first statements took away my desire to know. "Ferguson Federal's been robbed. One of the robbers is dead, and Mick has been shot. He was in the bank when it went down. He tried to stop it and caught a load of buckshot in the chest. It doesn't look good for him."

"What can I do?"

"Get in the plane and check for them by air," he ordered. "They went west in a late model Continental, gray in color. Shouldn't be too many of them around. Three robbers originally. Now there's two," he added.

I gave Cheryl a quick kiss and a hasty explanation as I went out the door. The Blazer would pick this morning to be temperamental, but I got it going and headed for the airport. Tom must have made some other calls as well; the plane was out of the hangar and ready to go when I got there. Cecil Atwell was pushing another single-engine Cessna out of the hanger when I drove up.

He yelled across the ramp, "I'll go east, Jerry. Sheriff thinks they went west, but one more set of eyes should help."

"Thanks, Cecil. I'll stay on the Unicom frequency and pass any information I get from the SO net to you.

A quick preflight and I was soon in the air climbing toward the canyon.

CHAPTER 21

There are times that try any man's patience. It wasn't the times that were trying Jeremy Witter's patience though. It was Davis Ferguson. First, Davis wanted to wear his usual suit, then when it was explained to him that he would be easily recognized in his regular clothes, he wanted to wear the dark pants and black turtleneck that Jeremy had forced him to purchase earlier in the week. Finally they, Jeremy and Pat that is, got him dressed in western attire and a plaid wool coat. The three then looked like hunters jumping the season a little or cattlemen in from the ranch for a day in town. In other words, they looked like they belonged in town. At least they looked like they belonged in this town.

The three drove to town in the steel gray Lincoln Continental in the alley behind the bank. Both Pat and Jeremy were armed. Pat with an illegally shortened 12 gauge shotgun and Jeremy with his .45 automatic. Neither trusted Ferguson with any type of weapon. He would be just as likely to shoot one of them as to accomplish any good by having one. As is stylish with bank robbers, each pulled a nylon stocking over their respective heads and faces. The stretch nylon distorted the facial features significantly. Of course, fat, foolish Davis Ferguson looked like fat, foolish Davis Ferguson with a stocking over his head, but you can't have everything. Using Ferguson's keys, the trio entered the rear door of the bank and quickly took their positions around the bank lobby. Pat moved to the front door and after locking it with the key supplied by Ferguson turned to the few customers in the bank and pointed the shotgun in their general direction. "Everybody on the floor." Everybody got on the floor. Such a simple request when someone is holding a loaded gun.

Witters covered the teller area while Davis Ferguson entered the vault and began to gather the currency contained therein. The job took several large deposit bags of the sort used by the armored car services. Deep bags with zippered tops and handles. Ideal for transporting money. Davis loaded only paper currency and did not weigh himself down with change. Pursuant to Witter's plan Ferguson attempted to distribute the weight in the bags evenly. Pat had explained that when they put the money on the pack horses that the weight on each side had to balance. If it didn't, they would spend a lot of time trying to adjust pack saddles; time they would not have to spend. As Ferguson got the bags loaded, Witters transferred them to the back door and stacked them in the hall. Six bags in all were filled.

Witters and Ferguson then carried the bags to the waiting Continental while Pat covered the customers and employees of the bank. He had slowly herded them together in one corner of the lobby while Ferguson had filled the bags. Now standing near the front doors, Pat could watch them and at the same time watch the street. The plan called for Witters to pick Pat up at the front after he had stashed the money in the car. In that way, the car would not be exposed for long in front of the bank and Pat could keep everyone in line until they were ready to depart.

Unfortunately, Witter's plan was not foolproof. No one had thought to check the customers for weapons. Who expected a bank customer or even a bank employee to have a gun? Mick Larson was in the bank when the three robbers entered. Mick had been thinking about buying a new car for several weeks and finally got the time to go to the bank to see about a loan. He hit the floor with everyone else when Pat made his request, but he continued to watch for an opportunity to take some action. Most cops dream about the chance to catch an armed bank robber in the act. Most just get to fantasize about it particularly in a small town. The opportunity to be a hero sometimes affects your good judgment.

Mick took his chance when Witters and Ferguson went out the back door. As Pat turned to unlock the front door in anticipation of his imminent departure, Mick drew his off-duty revolver from its belt holster and rose to his feet.

"Police," he yelled, "drop your gun." He took the appropriate stance to fire but was exposed in his standing position. Pat did not hesitate but turned and shot the 12 gauge in Mick's direction. Mick took the force of rounds squarely in the chest. With a reflex action, he squeezed the trigger of his gun. The bullet took Pat through the side of the head spraying blood and gray brain matter over the doors and wood paneling. People began screaming and crawling for better protection. One teller had the presence in mind to push the alarm button and later to call the police station and request an ambulance. The action probably was instrumental in saving Mick's life.

Pat's lifeless remains were visible from the door as Witters drove off. Having heard the shots reverberating through the bank as he drove off, he knew there were complications, but he was loyal to Pat and would have made any reasonable attempt to help him. One look was all it took to convince Jeremy that his long partnership with Pat was over. Ferguson did what would be expected of him. He gagged and began to throw up. The action almost did him in as well until he could finally pull the stocking from his face. The odor of fresh vomit permeated the car. Rolling down the electric windows of the Lincoln, Witters demanded that Ferguson lean out the window if he was going to continue heaving.

Heading west out of town, Witters began to worry about his getaway. The plan had been to use horses and trail across the wilderness area to another county. Pat was the expert with horses, however, and Witters could barely ride, much less get pack saddles and equipment on the other horses. He doubted that Ferguson was much better. Witters decided to stay away from horses for the time being and see how much distance he could put on between there and the town. He hadn't seen any police cars, and he wasn't being followed, so he continued to press on. With a little luck, no one could identify the Lincoln or the two passengers.

CHAPTER 22

Quickly flipping switches and checking instruments as I taxied away from the hangar, I did a quick preflight inspection, turned onto the active runway and shoved the throttle forward. The little 206 lunged forward, and I was soon airborne. Making a turnout of the pattern I headed up the canyon. My preflight had been a little skimpy. I looked to see if the wings were still on and got underway. I figured that there wasn't much time if the suspects had headed up the canyon and took one of the many side roads into the trees. If they stayed on the highway, I thought I had an excellent chance to catch up to them. Even climbing I could make about 120 mph and with winding roads, they would be lucky to average 65-70 mph. I could see Cecil lifting off the end of the runway as I adjusted the engine settings for climb configuration. "Cecil, take a close look around the junction area. They could turn either way there, but you may be able to get to the forks before they can."

"Roger Jerry. Keep me posted. I'll stay on the Unicom frequency as well."

"10-4", I replied and set up my second radio to Center frequency as I tried to simultaneously hook up the external antenna for my portable. Can't do that and still fly but it keeps you occupied. Naturally, my field glasses were far in the back in my extra flight bag. I hoped that Lincoln wouldn't be that hard to spot on the road.

"Charlie 5, SO."

"Go"

"Reports from the Chevron station west of town that your Continental headed up canyon about ten minutes ago. We'll get a unit headed that way as soon as possible but most of them were east and south so it may be a while. Sheriff says to use your own discretion." I clicked the transmit button twice, changed frequency, and relayed the word to Cecil on the Unicom.

"Cecil, stay east for now. This may not be the right car." Just then I caught sight of a silver-colored car going through the right turns where the road corkscrews through the canyon. "Disregard, I've got the one we're looking for about 20 miles up the canyon. Move on back this way if you can." I could see Cecil in the distance making a turn back toward me as he acknowledged. I switched back to the portable. "SO, five. I've got the suspect vehicle in sight, twenty miles up canyon. What have you got on the other side?"

"Nothing nearby. I'll try patrol and see if they can block for you," replied the dispatcher, "try to keep them in sight."

Sheriff Flanigan broke in on the radio, "Jerry, see if you can identify any of the occupants at least. Can you land ahead of them?"

"Negative Sheriff. No clear areas that will take the plane and still allow me to fly it back out. Not sure I could get it into most of these clearings anyway. Sure would help to have some cars on the road. Some of our cars that is!"

"Big country, Jerry. We're trying." The Sheriff sounded tired and concerned both. Big responsibility, small department.

Passing over the car I kept my altitude and moved further up the canyon. Lots of pilots buy the farm when they find out the plane won't climb as fast as the canyon walls do. By going up ahead of them, I would be pointed down the canyon as I came back low over the car. It would also make it easier to see through the windshield of the Lincoln. Circling back I reduced the power and eased the stick forward. Actually, it's a wheel, but all of us airplane drivers call it a stick. Dropping down quickly, I leveled off about a hundred feet off the highway and began to follow it down the canyon. Abruptly the silver-colored car came into view. I could see two people in the front seat, but no way could I get a proper identification on either. One appeared to be pretty heavy set and the other average, but I couldn't tell at that altitude and speed even if they were male or female. With a maneuver I never figured to use for anything serious except to pass my flight instructor's test, I put the Cessna into a chandelle. It's a graceful, quick way to turn the airplane around without breaking the fool thing. This was not the place to bend the frame.

On the right were the steep walls of the canyon. Moving left I again caught sight of the car twisting up the road. Climbing for altitude and pulling ahead of the Continental I turned back once more and put it down on the deck. The people in the car had to know something was up by now, and I soon found out they did. They had speeded up as fast as the road would allow and our combined speeds had me past them in a rather hurry. Sort of like the passenger I had one day when we met an eagle flying in the opposite direction. From inside the plane, it looked like the bird was moving along. My passenger commented, "I didn't know they could fly that fast." I was about as low as I could get without impacting the car. They must have thought I was low enough to hit them because they fishtailed all over the road trying to get it stopped. I was pretty low. Too low in fact. Something grazed the wheels. I could feel the shock in the plane. Struggling to get everything under control. Hang in there, don't lose it. There we go, flying speed and some altitude.

Don't think I want to do that again. Looking back as I turned up canyon again I could see the Continental. The top of the roof had a pretty good crease down the center. No wonder I had trouble. Wondering if I had broken anything I circled over the location. Suddenly the car turned around and started back down the canyon. Trying the portable, I couldn't get any response. It took a little while to register. The antenna for the portable is mounted underneath the plane. Must have damaged it or lost it with my close in flying. Got to remember this isn't an attack plane.

"Cecil, can you hear me."

"Roger Jerry, loud and clear."

"I've lost my ability to communicate on the SO frequency, and I may have some damage to the plane. The Continental is headed back down the canyon."

"OK. I'm about five east of the airport. I'll land and call it into the SO."

That would help. "Thanks, Cecil. When I'm ready to come back in, I'd appreciate a visual on the plane before I land. Will you stick around?"

"Sure. Good luck. I'm on final now. Call on Unicom when you're ready."

The Continental was rapidly moving down the canyon. I was just setting up a position on their backside when I saw the tail lights come back on. The car slid to a stop, and the driver stepped out of the car. I knew I wasn't going to like the reason for his top when he pointed at the plane. I could hear a bullet strike metal somewhere on the plane. Discretion being the better part of valor I shoved the throttle to the firewall and made a hard left turn. Sheriff Flanigan was not going to be pleased when he got the bills on this one. I wasn't real thrilled myself. Fuel was pouring out of the underside of the right wing.

Oh great! A quick glance at the fuel gauge confirmed my immediate fears. It was going from full to empty at a rapid rate. Probably a hole clear through the tank and the surrounding wing which would let it siphon out the top faster than it would leak out the bottom. I shifted the fuel selector valve to the left tank and began to climb for altitude. Either that guy is very, very lucky or one heck of a good shot! Out of his way is where I wanted to be at the moment. Plenty of fuel in the left tank but if anything else is damaged or if the right decides to flame, I'm going to be in a real world of hurt. "Cecil, can you copy."

"Roger Jer. Where are you?"

"Still up the canyon. I've got problems. Son of a bitch tried to kill me. Took a hit from a handgun of some sort. Losing fuel at a rapid rate out of the right tank. The car is headed down the canyon still. I'm afraid if I go on down as well he'll turn back up. I won't be able to follow him for long if that happens. Advise the Sheriff that I'm going to set down at the forest service field above Challenge Creek. Tell him to send a car for me as quick as he can."

"10-4 Jerry. Good luck."

The next few minutes were pretty busy. I was still worried about the damage to the wheels. Actually, it didn't feel like I hit any harder than you sometimes do with a marginal landing. As the forest service field came into view, I started flipping switches and making the adjustments for landing. Flaps down. Fuel on the fullest tank. In fact, the only tank with much fuel. Throttle and RPM set. Eased her on down and coaxed the little Cessna gently onto the grass runway. Mighty thankful that the gear held and seemed to function alright. I shut everything down in a hurry and got out as soon as I came to a stop. No fire but it would be poor form to still be inside if it decided to blow up.

The rest of the morning was like being back in the Army. Hurry up and wait. About thirty minutes after I landed a highway patrol car drove up. Leaving my examination of the large hole in the wing of the Cessna, I trotted over to the car. "Which way did you come in?"

"From the west. You sure do look funny standing there. Come on I'll give you a ride on down. SO indicated you might like a ride." I climbed into the passenger side and reached for his mike. He commented, "you might want to change to SO frequency. It's channel two on this rig."

"Thanks."

I called the SO, "SO, Charlie 5. What's the situation?"

The Sheriff broke in and told me. It wasn't good. Unless we caught sight of the Continental on our way down he had probably gotten back through town. Cecil was back in the air but no luck so far. I thought that was probably correct from where I saw the car last. "Sheriff, make sure everyone knows that they are armed and very, very dangerous. There was no hesitation about shooting. He just stepped out, aimed and fired."

I urged Grant, the patrolman, to hurry us down the canyon. By now we should have plenty of manpower, both from the field and all the off-duty people. I was mentally figuring out some search patterns and roadblocks when I got the news that totally ruined my day. "Charlie 5, SO."

Snatching the mike out of the holder and flipping back to channel two I answered. The news was all bad. The Continental had indeed made it back to town. They had careened down main, grabbed a girl on the street and roared off. The girl was Cheryl. It was like being hit in the stomach.

CHAPTER 23

Jeremy Witters swore as the plane thumped against the roof of the Continental. "What's that sonofobitch trying to do?" He slammed on the brakes and reached for the automatic under his arm. The car was barely stopped when he stepped out and aimed the Colt at the fast approaching airplane. Ferguson jumped as the gun roared. Witters snapped two shots at the plane and still swearing leaped back into the car and put it in gear. With tires spinning he backed onto the shoulder, shifted into drive and squealed in a tight circle fighting the car as it fishtailed down the asphalt.

"What are you doing?" exclaimed Ferguson. "Are you try to get us killed?"

"Shut up. That bastard has got to be a cop. The first time over might have been some dumb pilot flying too low, but when you come back and almost run into a car on the road, you aren't out for the scenic flight. Either we ditch him, or we go to jail. Think you can handle that?"

Davis flushed white. "It's probably that deputy the Sheriff brought in a few years ago. I think he flies." Ferguson shook visibly. "What are you going to do?"

"With a little luck, I hit his plane or at least made him keep his distance. We'll run back down the canyon and see if we can get to the horses."

Ferguson ran his hand through his thinning hair. "Can you get them loaded with supplies without Pat? I can saddle a horse, but I can't pack one."

"We'll do what we have to. Shut up and let me concentrate

on the road." Witters needed to concentrate. He was barreling down the winding road at speeds never contemplated for by the builders. Davis shut his eyes and slumped down in the seat whimpering to himself. Witters shouted to him, "Keep your eyes open and see if you can see that airplane. We need to know where it is." Davis struggled to bring himself upright and began to scan the sky behind them.

"I don't see anything."

"That's good I guess. Keep looking."

Witters flew through the curves, tires squealing. Ferguson cringed in his seat but continued his watch for the airplane. Fishtailing out of the last curve, Witters aimed the car down the straightaway into town. Fortunately, the traffic was light. The Continental roared into the center of town. Suddenly Witters braked to a stop throwing Ferguson onto the floor.

Cheryl was coming out of the drug store as Witters was making his charge through town. She watched in amazement as he swerved to a stop across from her. Witters leaped from the car, crossed the street to where Cheryl was standing and grabbed her by the wrist.

As he started pulling her to the car, he snarled, "you're coming with me."

Cheryl lost her hold on the packages she was carrying and pulled away from Witters. As she turned to run from the crazy man accosting her, Jeremy tripped her and grabbed her by the hair. Pulling her to her feet, he grabbed an arm and twisted it behind her. With one hand holding her hair and the other twisting her arm he half carried her to the car and pushed her into the front seat. Ferguson sat and stared at this development.

"What are you doing," Ferguson exclaimed, "we've got to get out of here. She'll only slow us down."

"Maybe." Ferguson slammed the car into gear and with wheels spinning he sped down the roadway. Cheryl hit him and started moving toward the back seat. Jeremy reached out with his right hand. Cheryl was crammed back against the windshield as Witters strained to regain control of the car. "Hold on to her," he directed the shaking Ferguson, "she's our guarantee that we get out of town. I can't drive and hold her too so you've got to get with it."

Still stunned by the blow to her head, Cheryl was unable to effectively fight Davis, but she continued to struggle with her hands and feet, kicking Jeremy and scratching Davis until Ferguson was finally able to pin her arms behind her back and force her down onto the floorboard. His weight was sufficient to hold her firmly in place.

"You could have at least picked a tamer one." Ferguson rasped, his breath coming in gulps. He was bleeding steadily down the face where Cheryl had deeply scratched him during the struggle.

"Just hold on to her. Do you see anyone following?" Witters pushed the car to its maximum, heading into the hills to the north. "We'll go to the horses and go out over the range as Pat advised."

"Nothing coming. Can we get rid of her now?"

"No, let's keep her until we know we've gotten away without any company. Someone might still show up, and if we let her out, then they will know for sure which way we went."

Thirty minutes later Witters drove the Continental into the barn and went to close the doors. "Hold on to her for a few more minutes until I can get something to tie her with."

Cheryl had ceased her squirming some time ago but knowing that one of her captors was occupied, and out of the car she was determined to try once again to free herself from these two men. She felt Davis begin to move his bulk onto the car seat and as he did, she scooted backward across the floor toward the driver's side. Ferguson reached for her, but the steering wheel impeded his attempt. Cheryl slid out the door and slammed it shut. Turning she ran toward the open barn door. Witters, on the outside, saw her coming and as she reached the door, he shoved it into her knocking her back into the barn. Cheryl was halfway to her feet when Witters clubbed her across the side of the neck with his fist driving her to the dirt. He pulled her to her feet by the front of her blouse and hit her solidly across the face with a swinging backhand. Blood spurted from her nose and splattered down the white blouse.

Witters brought his hand back to strike her again. "Settle down, or I'm going to beat it out of you. No more fighting, no more running, or you are going to get hurt." Cheryl's arms were crossed in front of her face; the fight had gone out of her. She hung limply by her blouse. Ferguson ran up with fear in his face.

"What are you doing? Don't hit her anymore."

"Would you rather I hit you. I should! You were supposed to be watching her. You dumb shit. Can't you do anything right." Witters let Cheryl fall to the floor. Half sitting, half reclining, she brought her hands to her battered face. "Tie her up, and do it right."

Davis could tie knots. You had to give him that. Cheryl thought she might be able to wiggle out of the ropes but found after some experimentation that her struggles just drew them tighter. She watched from the corner as Jeremy and Davis began their attempts to saddle the horses they would use to carry themselves, their supplies and most importantly the cash recently liberated from the bank. To her experienced eye, it was apparent that neither Ferguson nor Witters were very familiar with the equipment and how it went on the patient animals. Davis Ferguson had little trouble putting saddles on the waiting animals and had two saddled when Witters ordered him to saddle a third. Cheryl surmised that she was not to be left behind as she had hoped but was going to occupy the third saddle.

Ferguson had greater difficulty with the pack saddles. A pack saddle is quite simple, a crossbuck that goes on the horse's rump to keep it from sliding forward and a breast collar to keep it from slipping back. Ferguson was having trouble figuring out what went where. Witters was of no help. He could hardly ride a horse much less get them saddled properly. That had been Pat's job. Since Pat was probably dead, Witters knew they would have to get along the best they could. He would have preferred to forget the horses and only the thought of the airplane and the likely roadblocks kept him on his present course. After the pack saddle is correctly placed on the horse, there are two panniers, large bags that hang on each side of the horse suspended by the wooden crossbucks. There is an art to tying the ropes that hold the bags in place. With a light load, there is not too much problem but as the load increases so does the need for an adequately tied hitch. Cheryl had packed into the mountains with her parents and her friends for years. She quickly figured out as she observed the two inept men that they would not be able to carry much in the way of supplies and make any time. That might work to her advantage. She determined to keep the information she had to herself. She leaned against the barn wall and rubbed some of the now drying blood on the shoulder of her blouse. Closing her eyes, she thought of Jerry. Would he know she had been taken by these two men? Very few people had been on the street, and it had all happened so quickly.

Ferguson and Witters continued to work. Even though they lacked the wisdom of Pat when it came to packing the horses, both were intelligent men and soon had most of the mechanics worked out. They began loading food and equipment onto the two pack horses. The supplies had been worked out earlier by Pat and had been placed in piles which were of equal weight. This foresight on Pat's part made it easy for the two remaining bank robbers. Neither was aware of the need to balance the load on each side of the horse to keep it from slipping as the horse carried it along the trail. It was luck that Witters put half the money on each side. There just wasn't room for all of it on one side, so he split the sacks, two on each side of one horse and one on each side of the other. Soon they were ready to travel. Witters brought Cheryl to one of the saddled horses and untied her hands and feet. Retying her hands in front of her he helped her onto the horse. He then tied her hands to the saddle horn and ran the end of the tape behind her back and then down to the stirrup where he securely tied it. "You better hang on, or you'll just end up hanging from your hands. I trust you won't be able to untie the rope without me noticing it and if I see you try, I'm going to bloody your nose again. Ever ride a horse before?"

Cheryl considered her options before answering. "Once or twice back east but not lately." She figured her movements on a horse might be too easy if she got distracted and it would be better if these two didn't know she had been raised on a horse. She had been watching them as they worked and had about decided that the fat one was one of the bank officers. She seemed to remember a chubby kid in school whose father was the bank president. Seemed like a funny situation for him to be in if he was indeed the same person.

Ferguson had tied the two pack horses together, head to tail, and mounted his horse. After closing and locking the barn door, Witters took the lead rope for Cheryl's horse and mounted his own, wrapping the lead rope around the horn and starting his horse out the gate. "With the barn locked it should slow them down even if they check the place out. The longer it takes them to discover we aren't in the car, the better. I'd like to get clear across without them knowing we are going through the wilderness area."

Ferguson fell into line behind Cheryl. "Hope so. This has been a lot more complicated than I ever expected." Both men ignored Cheryl as they started up the trail into the trees. Ferguson was busy watching the two pack horses as they followed him and Witters was feverously trying to remember all that Pat had told him about the trails across the top. He had only half listened when Pat was explaining them weeks ago. Witters had depended upon Pat for too many years to get worked up about learning all he could. Pat would be there to show him the way. Except now Pat wasn't there to help, and he was suddenly cold with the realization that there could be problems he couldn't anticipate. The trail sloped steeply upward. The parade moved steadily forward, each of the three lost in their own thoughts.

Although the robbery had occurred early in the bank's business day just after opening at 9:00, the subsequent events had used up a lot of the remaining daylight hours. It was already getting late in the afternoon as Witters lead his little band up the mountain trail. He knew they would have to find a place to camp before long. Jeremy knew that he could not lead them with any certainty after dark. He was hungry, he was tired, and he was definitely concerned if not outright worried about this operation. Nothing had seemed to go right from the time they settled on Ferguson Federal Savings and Loan as the target. Ferguson himself had been a problem right from the start. Afraid of his shadow and a deterrent to every action Jeremy had initiated. The horses were a mistake. Always before they had used conventional transportation. It was only because this bank was in such a remote area that they had even been considered. It was a shame Pat was a frustrated cowboy at heart. If he had Jeremy's distrust of horses, they would never have even thought of this unique escape. Probably nobody since the days of Butch Cassidy and the Sundance Kid, had anyone robbed a bank at gunpoint and then ridden away on their trusty steed. Now to top it off he had lost Pat, who was the expert on horses, and who knew the way across the mountain to where the pickup truck was parked, and he was stuck with Ferguson and some dame he'd never seen before. He had to admire her spirit though. She had tried every trick to resist until he punched her. I'd like to dump her, he thought but if I do she may get back to where she can give our plans away. The slick thing about Pat's design of this departure was the multitude of routes out. The cops could not cover every possible way out of the area without bringing in a sizeable army. Maybe he could dump her way up high. The only other alternative would be to kill her. That might be the answer. If Pat was dead, he probably already faced a murder charge of some sort. What a screwed up mess.

Sometime later Witters found the area he was looking for. There was shelter of sorts under the rocks, a place to tie the horses where they could graze, and water for them all. He stopped and gestured to Davis to begin setting up a temporary camp. Jeremy stepped down from his horse flexing his knees to get the feeling back into them after several hours of cramped riding. He untied the tape from Cheryl's saddle and told her to get down. She gripped the horn with her tied hands and swung her leg over the saddle. As she started to step down, Jeremy placed his hands on her sides just under her breasts and let his hands slid upward to steady her as she slid down from the horse. Her fears were calmed as Jeremy turned her toward him, untied her hands and told her to turn around. He then firmly tied her hands behind her and after having her sit on the ground tied her feet securely to her hands. Leaving her, he went to help Davis unsaddle the remaining horses. Soon they had a fire, had some food cooking for dinner and had settled into a reasonably comfortable camp.

CHAPTER 24

Going up the stairs to the Sheriff's office I alternated between being mad, scared, and worried. Mad at myself for losing the Continental. Thinking about how I missed it scared me and I was concerned about Cheryl. I was anxious about her. And that just made me mad again. If I hadn't misjudged the altitude when I hit their car or hadn't stayed so low that I picked up bullet holes, maybe they would have kept on the other way. Then Cheryl would be safe. Thinking about the bullet holes in the fuel tank got me scared again, and then the cycle would start all over again. I was so caught up in my feelings that I ran right into the Sheriff.

"Easy boy. You might knock someone down that way." The sheriff's face showed his concern too.

"Sheriff, what's the situation now?"

He eased his hat back on his head. "Not much different. Everyone's out looking but no sign yet. From the reports we got downtown, they just drove into town fast, hopped out of the car and grabbed onto Cheryl. Then drove off again."

"Are you sure it was Cheryl?"

"Yup. Sorry, Jerry. She was positively identified by Mrs. Jenkins. She works at the hospital and knows Cheryl pretty well. She had on one of those white coats she always wears when she's working. There's no doubt it's her." He took me by the arm and guided me back to his office. I didn't resist. "We have every available car out on the street, and Cecil is back up in the air. He was down for a while to get fuel but is making an orbit around the area. We should know something soon. They can't get out of the area now anyway. By coming back to town, we got the time we needed to block every road with either our units or ones from the Highway Patrol. The area is secure. We just need to get them located."

I sat down in one of the big arm chairs. "What do you want me to do now? The Cessna is out of commission for this chase. May have to do some work on it up there before it can even be flown out."

"What happened?"

"I got too low and slow, and one of those guys is a pretty good shot. He got at least two into the wing before I could get turned away. I say at least two because there are two big rivers of gas running out. At least there were when I left." I was too anxious to sit still. Pacing back and forth in front of the Sheriff's desk I used his phone and called the airport. After getting one of the mechanics to go up and secure the Cessna, I turned to Big Tom. "I'm worried. Someone should have seen something by now. Maybe they pulled in at one of the ranches and are laying low."

"Possible. Go get something to eat. Sandwiches and maybe still some fried chicken in the coffee room. I'll get someone checking by phone to those that are closer in. We can pull some of the city units to check those that don't answer. You can coordinate it after you get some food."

The radios in the dispatch office were crackling. I could hear units checking in with dispatch and talking to each other. The sandwich was dry in my mouth. The coffee was cold. Not up to the department's usual standard. Then it happened. "SO, City 6 on mutual aid channel. We have the Continental."

"Where," I yelled, running into the radio room. Before Sally could answer my question or ask it of City 6, I was pressing the button on the mike. "City 6, this is Charlie 5. Where is it?"

"Inside the barn at the old Ortiz ranch. Doesn't look like anyone's around."

"Any sign of Cheryl Hefner, the girl they took in town?"

The wait was interminable. "No sign Charlie 5 Looks like there may have been some horses stabled here. Lots of fresh manure. Tracks going out of the corral and no horses in sight."

No one was in my way as I ran for the front, grabbing a set of keys to the patrol car in the lot. Good thing too. They would still be wondering what hit them. My exit from the lot would not have done much for the department's public relations with the city either. With lights flashing and siren screaming, I pushed the car toward the Ortiz ranch as hard as it would go.

"Charlie 5, SO. Sheriff says for you to coordinate the crime scene investigation. He'll have backup when you determine actions taken by the perpetrators." I acknowledged. Darn nice of him to be so understanding. I hadn't even thought about cop work as I went out the door. I just knew I couldn't wait for someone else to give me the information I so desperately wanted. As I drove, I alternated between hoping that nothing had happened to her and raging that if something had, I would break some heads. Actually, I think I said I would kill them. Slowly.

Len Cody, the city cop, had things pretty well in hand when I got there. He's a good policeman, and it was evident that he had been exercising those skills. "Jerry come over here. It looks like someone was tied up here in the corner for a while. See the rub marks in the dirt like someone had their hands and feet close together. There are some white threads in the wood along the wall and some fiber that looks like hemp."

"I think you're right." Looking around I could see that several horses had been tied in the barn recently. There were piles of fresh manure in five of the stalls. Normally that wouldn't tell you much, but the Ortiz place had been vacant for two or three years now. It was good luck or good police work that had led Len to this location. We went out into the yard and looked at the tracks. They were pretty messed up. Len had unwittingly driven over a lot of them when he drove up to the barn, but it looked like several different size feet for the people tracks. There were a lot of horse tracks but nothing unique I could spot. "Len, I think they rode out of here on horseback."

"Why would they do that? Horses are a lot slower and should be easy to catch." Len walked part way up the trail toward the trees. "I think you're right though. These tracks look pretty fresh."

Ok, Sheriff. Get the posse. This was crazy. I agreed with Len. Why go anywhere on horseback if you're trying to get away from the law enforcement agencies. They have fast cars, airplanes, and radios. At least we did have airplanes, plural. All we had right now was Cecil in his plane. I got back on the radio. Several minutes later I had part of the answer. Cecil was overhead but reported that the trees were too thick to see through clearly. The rest of the solution was given by the forest service map. Once in the area, there were unlimited directions to go. It would be almost impossible to get enough manpower to cover the possible exits. The realization of what we faced was just beginning to dawn on me when the Sheriff drove up. His analysis of the situation was the same as Len's and mine. Now what?

"Jerry, I think we better locate some horses," said Sheriff Flanigan. "The only way to locate them for sure is going to be to follow them."

I was flabbergasted. "You mean we're going to follow the outlaws on horseback like in the old days." Here we had all the modern law enforcement equipment, and we were going back to the horse and buggy days, or maybe I should say the Sheriff and his posse days. He was right. It just took me a while to realize that we could travel at as good a pace as they did and would stand a better chance of determining their direction of travel. We also had the advantage of being able to utilize our modern tools as well. The most logical areas could be blocked or watched, the plane could still spot, and we could communicate information quickly. It made sense.

Going back into the barn I noticed a bridle hanging in one of the stalls. It still had the sales tag on the bit. Giving it to Len I suggested he check with the store that sold it and see if there was any other equipment sold with it and to find out what the clerk might remember about who bought it. The tag was still bright and shiny, so it wasn't something left from the Ortiz era. He went to call it into his office while I continued to poke around. Not finding anything else of interest I wandered back out in front. The Sheriff was talking on the radio with someone, and from the look on his face, I thought the news might be encouraging. He called me over just as I was starting to go his way.

"Carl Tafoya has some horses in his corral we can use and has all his packing gear ready. In fact, he was working on it to get it ready for hunting season. Says we can use any we want and will go along with us if we need him." The Sheriff grinned at me, "I assume you want to go along." It was a statement, not a question. He was entirely correct. Nothing could have kept me from this assignment even if I had to walk, and I hate to walk any farther than I have to. Why do you think I park in front of the door where I'm going!

"That's great. Hope Carl has that big sorrel horse he calls Red for me. I rode him one year when I guided hunters for him. One heck of a horse. How about supplies?"

"Already being sent out along with the winter equipment packs from the Army Guard. Everything will be taken to Tafoya's barn, and we can meet them there. Ideally, we should start from here, but I think we can cut across from Carl's and intercept the trail from here without any trouble." The Sheriff was already fastening his seat belt as I went around his car and got in.

"Len, see that somebody takes the other patrol car back in will you? I left the keys in it." Len nodded and turned back to the plaster cast he was making of some of the tracks. I admired his dedication to doing a good job of investigation but doubted that any of the painstaking evidence would be necessary. If we caught up to our bad guys, they would have the money with them. That, together with the pictures at the bank from the automatic machines, would probably be enough for even the most conservative court. Besides, I swear if they hurt Cheryl, they probably wouldn't even get to trial.

The Sheriff did his usual Indy 500 job of getting us over to Carl's. You could tell he was intent on getting underway too, cause he forgot entirely to use the siren and lights. Strange behavior from the man who generally uses them to go to lunch.

"Jerry, I'm worried about Cheryl. I've known that girl since she was just a little tyke and I'd hate like everything to have anything happen to her."

"Me too Sheriff, more than you can believe. I haven't known her as long, but I really care about her. Looks like they're holding her as a hostage though, rather than anything else. Might not be any problem until we catch up with them."

Tom shook his head slowly back and forth. "I hope so, but this has been a unpredictable bunch. Look at the cool way he stopped and shot at you then lost his cool in town."

"Maybe he didn't lose his cool. I think he saw a hostage and computed it into his plans. Apparently, the horses were his primary escape route, and for some reason, he made the run up the canyon. Has anyone turned up anything on the one that was killed at the bank?"

"Not yet. You may have something there. What if the one at the bank was the horse expert? Maybe these other two don't know much if anything about using horses. If so, that would explain the initial attempt to go up the Canyon. When you cut them off, they went back to plan one."

The Sheriff turned into Tafoya's ranch yard and cut the engine. "Could be Sheriff. Or it could be that the horses were a backup. I'd hate to underestimate these two."

Carl already had two horses saddled and was leading two

more out of the corral. I went over to help him saddle while the Sheriff checked on our other supplies. "How's it going, Carl?"

"Pretty good, Jerry. You want that red horse again." He grinned and spit a stream of tobacco into the dust. Carl is your typical cowboy. The first thing he puts on in the morning is his hat, and it's the last thing he takes off at night. Chews tobacco and would saddle a horse to ride from the house to the barn if it kept him from having to walk. Knows his horses and his job. He's one of those guys you like to have around, especially if you've got trouble. As they use to say in the western movies, he's a man to ride the river with.

"You bet I do. That's one fine horse. You going with us?" I took the leads for the two horses he had and tied them to the hitch rail.

We walked into his tack room and gathered up the gear to put on the two tied in front. "Thought I might. Haven't been for a ride in the hills since last season. Didn't even get up there for any fishing this summer."

Gathering up a saddle I thought the Sheriff would feel comfortable in; I went back to the horses in front. "That's what you get having rodeo fever."

"True, how true. Made a little at it though."

"Yeh, I heard you did well on the circuit. How many pack horses are we taking?"

Carl chuckled. "No one does well. By the time you pay travel expenses and entry fee, you kind of use up the long green. I came home with some extra and ate pretty well, so it probably was a good year." He brushed off the bay horse and swung the blanket over the horse's back. As he lifted the pack saddle into place and adjusted the rump straps, he said, "depends on how much equipment you're taking. I've got more than we can handle so take all you need." He swiftly adjusted the straps and was hooking the breast collar as the Sheriff came up.

I finished adjusting the saddle on the Sheriff's horse,

slipped on the bridle and handed the reins to him. "How much gear Sheriff?"

"Probably two horses worth. Let's take three in case we need more out there." He pointed with his chin toward the mountain trail we would soon be traveling. "Here comes the gear. Need a hand with the horses?"

Carl tied the pack horse to the rail and pointed at the tack room. "Why don't you and the deputy get the gear in the pack saddles while Jerry and I get the rest of the horses ready. There's a set of scales in the cupboard."

I caught up the red horse and got him saddled while Bill saddled his own gray saddle horse. That gave us three saddle horses and three pack horses. By then the first set of panniers were ready to be put on the horse. Carl grabbed the strap on one end while I got the other and we carried it over to the right side of the first pack horse. With Carl at the head and me at the tail, we just lifted it up and slipped the straps over the cross buck. We slid the second on the other side, and I moved across to the other side to hand Carl the cinch and tie straps from my side. With smooth moves, Carl soon had the horse packed, and we moved on to the other two. Within a short time, we were ready to ride. I slipped a rifle with a scope into the saddle scabbard on Red. Bill has a unique way of naming his horses. He just goes with what is convenient. The better the horse, the shorter the name. Hence Red for the sorrel or red horse that I was riding and Grey for the one he was riding.

Each of us led one of the pack horses and started up the trail. Bill took the lead since he knew the area better than either the Sheriff or me. That says a lot because both of us have covered this area a lot, both officially and when we've been hunting. Our mood was optimistic as we moved out.

CHAPTER 25

Cheryl slumbered fitfully as the night drug on. She was covered with a sleeping bag and near the fire, but the ropes dug into her wrists and ankles and made sleeping difficult. She was stiff and sore from laying in the confined position. It was hard to turn to ease her stiffness. Witters and Ferguson had alternated between sleeping and keeping watch during the night. She could hear Witters prowling around the perimeter of the camp. The ropes remained as tight as they had been before. She was curious about the two men who had abducted her. They were both as opposite as could be. She wondered what had drawn them together and for what purpose. They had not disclosed to her the reason for having taken her from town nor had they revealed a reason for this strange journey into the mountains. Perhaps she would learn more in the morning. She knew it was vital to watch for any chance she had to escape her captivity. If she could get loose, it would be easy to elude the two men in the mountainous terrain. She was confident she could make her way back to help if she could get even a little head start on them.

Ferguson was not sleeping well either. He had been unable to get to sleep after he had stood his watch. His mind was in a turmoil. At first, it had seemed so easy to agree to help Witters rob the bank. He knew the robbery would cover his own embezzlement, would give him the freedom from the discovery he desired. Unfortunately, he did not consider the consequences of his active participation with Witters. He knew deep in his own heart that he could never go back to Caribou even if his prior embezzlement was never discovered. He had crossed the divide between honest and dishonest a long time ago but now he had definitely passed to the other side of society. At least one person was now dead. It was doubtful that he wasn't recognized. Now that he thought about it he knew that his absence would identify him just as readily as his picture on the bank's photo monitor system.

Witters was confident, however. The loss of Pat hurt him more than he thought was possible, but he was supremely sure that the plan he and Pat had devised would be sufficient. Jeremy Witters had the money. He had the horses, and he was well into the mountains. The only problems would be Ferguson and the girl. He was undecided about her. Should he keep traveling with her or should he do something to ensure she could not identify him? The question raged on in his head. An accomplished crook, at least of the robbery variety, Witters was reluctant to kill. Perhaps because he had never had to in the past. Or maybe he wasn't quite as bad as he would sometimes like to believe. She could identify him. That was the problem.

Morning came, and the rising sun found each of the three with the same thoughts they had worried over during the night. Ferguson discovered another problem shortly after that was of much more consequence to him. Ferguson was a diabetic who used insulin on a daily basis. The self-contained vials of insulin and needle had been crushed by the pack load on the horse as they had traveled. Only six had survived the trip. Witters was less concerned or maybe unconcerned would be a more appropriate description of his feelings about Ferguson's predicament.

"What do you want me to do about it? Maybe ride back to town and pick up a new supply for you? What are you worried about anyway?. We should be out of here in a week without any problems. Then you can get some more."

Davis blanched, "I don't know if they'll last a week.

Sometimes when I'm under stress or my diet is off I need more than one shot a day."

"Can't you salvage anything from the package?"

Ferguson threw the pan he was holding across the clearing. As it bounced off a tree, he turned and almost whispered, "no." Clearly, he was stunned by the prospect of being without his insulin. Cheryl saw a possible advantage for her. With a little luck maybe she could get the two men slowed down until someone could catch up with them. She was certain the Sheriff would send someone after them. Maybe Jerry would be able to spot them from the airplane. She had noticed the good view that could be had from the cockpit of the airplane when she flew to Billings with Jerry just the day before. Only a day, it seemed much longer. She spoke to Witters but in such a way that Ferguson would be swayed to help her with her silent plan to attract attention from any rescuers. "With the right meals and proper rest he could go for more than a week."

Witters snarled at her. "What do you know about it? You a doctor or something."

"No. But I am a trained laboratory technician. I know quite a little about diseases like his."

"Great," Witters exclaimed, "just what I need. One sick and one to nurse him along. How do you think we're going to get out of here if we just lay around camp and eat our gourmet meals?"

"It won't help me much if I'm not around to get out." Davis turned to Cheryl, "how much do you know? Can you help me stretch my supply?"

"Sure. It's not hard. Just a few simple tricks with the food intake to keep your blood sugar in balance." She looked at Witters, "if you untie me, I can cook something for him that will help."

"At least that's a good idea. You can cook for all of us. Davis, untie her."

Cheryl felt a thrill of excitement run through her. They

were going to free her. Perhaps she would have a chance to run. If not, she could do little things to help those following. If anyone was. Her hands stung with the resurgence of blood into them. The ropes had cut off part of the circulation during the night. She rubbed them and watched the color come back into the fingertips. "Show me what you have for supplies so I can figure out the best long-range diet for him."

Ferguson almost sprang at her in his haste to have her view the supplies carried in the panniers. Cheryl took her time going through each of the panniers. Sensing Witters impatience to get underway she gathered what she needed for breakfast. "I'll need a fire and that pan you threw over there."

"Get them for her. I'll start saddling the horses." Davis hastened to comply. Cheryl eased over towards the trees and started picking up sticks for the fire. Before she could get very far though, Witters ordered her back.

"I'll get your wood. You just stay right there by the fire where I can see you. I don't want you running around in the woods. You might get lost or something." Cheryl was disappointed, but not entirely. At least he wasn't getting the horses ready if he was gathering wood for her. A small delay but they could add up.

She took her time cooking over the fire. Periodically she would add some of the greener wood so the fire would become smoky. She knew she would only be able to delay so much before Witters would become suspicious. Ferguson was too concerned with his own problems to give her activities a second thought. When the coffee was ready, she poured a cup for each of the men and started to take it to them.

"I told you to stay put." Witters grabbed her by the arm spilling the coffee down his arm. He jumped away holding his burned arm. "What in the hell are you trying to do."

"I was just bringing your coffee. If you weren't such a gentleman, you would be drinking it instead of wearing it." She didn't know how far she could push him, but now was as good a time to find out as any.

"You just stay put. We can get our own coffee. And our own food."

Cheryl moved back to the fire. As she broke the eggs and dropped them into the pan, she decided to keep on pushing. So far he had only yelled. If he started hurting her as punishment, she would change tactics, but for now, she would keep up her course of passive resistance.

The day was well advanced by the time breakfast was eaten, the horses loaded and the three were mounted and underway. Witters continued to lead the way with Cheryl in the middle. Witters had relaxed his guard to a certain degree. He still led Cheryl's horse but had failed to again tie her hands to the saddle. A thoughtful observer might have noticed the differences in the way each of the three rode. Ferguson, who was fat and heavy, had a great deal of difficulty finding a comfortable way to sit in the saddle. Witters was starting to find aches and pains in places he never imagined. He was basically in good physical shape, but his inexperience as a horseman was going to make horseback riding more difficult as the day wore on. Only Cheryl had no problems. For her, it was more like a pleasure ride. The day was pleasant. The sun shining on her back warmed her almost to the point of contentment. She rode as one with her horse, and so was the only relaxed one of the three. As a child, she had spent many long hours on a horse on rides such as this. Well, not exactly like this. Never before had anyone forced her to travel against her will. Never had her life been placed in jeopardy. Continuing to conceal her knowledge of horses and the mountains, she joined in Davis's request to stop and rest. She could have ridden on, but neither of the other two was of such a mind, so she groaned and limped with the other two as they dismounted. Walking around to ease the kinks out the two men did not notice the methodical way in which Cheryl was stacking rocks on top of each other near the trail where it would be seen by anyone riding along behind them. Again, not much but a little.

"Do you want me to fix something for lunch while we're stopped?" Cheryl was standing on the trail leaning against the pack saddle looking for all the world like the last thing she wanted to do was more cooking.

"Just some cold sandwiches," said Witters, "we need to keep moving."

"Ok with me." Cheryl started unbuckling the panniers. "Kind of hard on your buddy though."

Ferguson looked up from his seat on the ground. "What do you mean, hard on me?"

"Well, you're the one that's short on insulin. Sandwiches will probably throw your balance off more than a regular meal will. Course maybe you'll get out of the mountains in time."

"Knock that off. Make wimpy a meal. Hurry it up though. I'm not going to sit around here all afternoon." Jeremy tied his horse to a nearby stump and eased himself down onto the ground. "Your lunch Ferguson. You get the firewood."

Davis got a fire going with a quickness that surprised even him. Some of the old boy scout training must have stuck with him.

Cheryl delayed as much as she could, but Witters drew the line at waiting while she washed the dishes and pans. She was able to create a large smoke cloud when she threw water on the fire to kill it. It was a clear day, so maybe it would be seen. She hoped so.

Remounting the horses, the trio moved on up the trail. For the time being, they were on a well-traveled portion of the path. Even so, it was a little more than a well-worn track in the dirt where the previous horses and mules had dug up the grass where they walked. Parts of the trail that Witters hoped to use had not been used enough to make a very distinctive path. In fact, he would find that in places he would have to guess where the trail had gone. Today though he felt good about his progress in the mountains. The day was bright, crystal clear, and warm. They had not traveled as far as he would have wished but he was having no trouble finding his way, and the animals were going smoothly.

Travelers in the mountains should never get complacent though. The weather can get pretty tricky during the fall. It can be a beautiful day one minute and a blinding blizzard the next. Witters didn't know that. Hard to teach a city boy those things when they have never experienced it. Cheryl and Ferguson had both grown up in the mountains or at least near them and subscribed to the old adage if you don't like the weather wait a few minutes and it will change. Witters was going to get a lesson in mountain weather before he got out of the area. Today he and Davis were lucky. The weather held and he even found a comfortable spot to camp before it started getting dark.

The area was a small meadow with good grass. The edge of the field was lined with aspen trees just starting to turn from green leaves to a golden and red riot of color. The silver trunks of the trees contrasted gently with the colored leaves. Many had fallen in prior months, and firewood was not only plentiful but easy to get. Falling into a sort of routine, the horses were unloaded and tied to trees and bushes near the camp area, Cheryl began to sort through the supplies for the evening meal, Davis got the fire going, and Witters saw to unsaddling the horses and picketing some on the tall grass. It almost appeared as if this was a friendly group out for some late year camping. It was only through the tenseness and the almost eerie silence of the group that identified it as something entirely different.

Following a quiet dinner, Cheryl was again tied hand and foot and placed in a sleeping bag between the two men. The ropes were not as tight as the first night but still were sufficient to hold her securely. She was encouraged by the day's events. She now had some measure of freedom and was confident that she could obtain more as time went along. In one way though she had made herself more firmly a prisoner than before. Davis Ferguson was not about to let the person who could help prolong his life out of his sight. He would not hurt her, but he would be very cautious that he did not lose her until he could get more medicine. She was to him anyway his medicine. That was not lost on Witters. He knew he could relax his vigilance a little bit insofar as the girl was concerned because Ferguson would keep an eye on her whereabouts.

What a group. No one trusted the other, and yet each was somewhat dependent on the others for their own well-being. Witters was the least dependent since he could go on by himself, but he kept Cheryl as a hostage to bargain with if he was not successful in slipping away over the mountains. He knew full well that pursuit would be inevitable. The only factors on his side were the time it took to find the Continental and for the police to figure out his new means of travel. He had tried to stay inside the trees as much as possible as he climbed into the high country and was secretly pleased that no airplanes had gone overhead; that told him that was evidence that his plan had not been discovered.

CHAPTER 26

I don't mind telling you I was plumb worried about my pretty lady. No indication of what those two had in mind for her. And if that wasn't enough, the mountains around here in late September can be downright dangerous. They're alright if you have the right equipment and you know what you're doing. Otherwise, you can get hurt pretty bad. Each year we have hunters hurt or killed from just plain being stupid. They get lost, or they go out on a pretty day, and the weather turns nasty. Then someone has to look for them. Sometimes it's an ugly picture when you do find them. I was glad to have Sheriff Flanigan and Carl Tafoya with me. I've hunted with both of them, and they know what they're doing.

We didn't know what gear the robbers had with them. Just that they had both saddle and pack horses and had planned to go into the hills. I hoped they had warm clothes for Cheryl. From the description in town, it didn't sound like she had on winter weather clothes or for that matter very appropriate clothes for riding in the fall.

Carl led us over a trail that would tie in with the one from the Ortiz place. It climbed up steeply across the side of the hill. Soon the horses were blowing hard, and Carl reined in for a breather. The only sounds were the heavy breathing of the horses and the creak of saddle leather. You could hear the wind work its way through the trees. There's something unique about that sound. If you've ever heard it, you never forget it. You can almost hear the route the wind takes through the treetops like a wave over the ocean. The aspen trees mixed in among the various evergreen varieties cast a festive color over the hills. Sort of like they dress up for you in the fall. I've never tired of seeing them or of riding through the mountain hills each fall. Sheriff says that's the only reason I go elk hunting each year. Could be he's right. If it weren't for that empty feeling in my stomach, it would be a good day for packing into a hunting camp. Carl started up and ol' Red pulled off a last clump of grass and lunged up the grade. We dropped into a little valley and up the other side onto a mesa. Across the center of the mesa ran the trail from the Ortiz ranch into the National Forest. We rode up to the trail and parallel to it. We could see fresh tracks in the dirt.

Tracking is kind of a lost art. In all the cowboy westerns you read the hero can tell you how many in the party, how much they weigh and sometimes what color shirt the rider is wearing just from studying the tracks for a few minutes. None of us were quite that good. I stepped down from my horse and handed the reins to Tom. Carl and I spent several minutes studying the trail.

"Looks to me like there are five horses. Three with shoes all around, one with a shoe missing and one with no shoes." Carl pointed out each of them as he listed them for me.

"I think you're right. At least that one set of shoes leaves a pretty distinctive track. Hope they're the ones we're looking for and not some bunch from the dude ranches down there." I tightened my cinch and climbed aboard. "Let's go find out."

Carl led out again, riding along the side of the tracks so we could recheck the trail without our tracks being mixed with their tracks.. Just in case we lost track of where they were going. So far they were going steadily up the mountain. The trail leveled out going along the top of the ridge, and we could make pretty good time. Suddenly Carl stopped.

"What's yuh got?" I asked as I rode up beside him. He pointed off to the left towards the trees. "Looks like they're headed into the timber."

"Yup, that's what I think. I almost missed where they turned. He led them across where the area is pretty hard. Either he's lucky, or he has given some thought about tracks and people following him." Carl took a drink from his canteen and passed it over to me. I almost choked on it.

"What have you got in there? It's sure not water."

"Just a little tequila. The other one has water if that's what you want." Carl was laughing pretty hard, so I had a little trouble understanding him.

"That's OK. I'll try this again. Sort of surprises a guy when he expects water."

Sheriff Flanigan laughed too. "Come on Jerry, share the wealth." I passed it on to him. "Got about three hours till dark. Let's push on and see how far into the trees they went."

Carl and I nodded, and after getting his canteen back from the Sheriff, he led off into the trees. The drink must have helped. I wasn't quite as keyed up. Maybe it helped to know that they were still moving, or at least they had been up till now. As long as they were riding Cheryl would probably be alright. The tracks went about ten feet into the tree line and then basically followed the tree line and the trail off to the right. It dawned on me that whoever was leading them was trying to stay out of sight. Being in the trees would have made it hard to spot them from an airplane. All they had to do was stop, and they would blend right into the trees. It would make it harder to see them from the trail too. I was right happy I was out here on a horse following on the ground rather than up in the air where I wouldn't have been able to see a thing.

We pushed on until we could hardly see any tracks. Finally, the Sheriff decided we had better stop for the night. Just our luck to have a dry, dry camp, on the top of a windy ridge with no water except what we had carried with us. Fortunately, we had been able to water the horses as we crossed a stream at the base of the ridge not too long before. There was plenty of grass to hold the horses for the night. We stripped off the packs and saddles in the dark. Tom started some dinner over a Coleman stove while Carl and I picketed the horses. He tied his grey to a tree and gave it some grain.

"Just in case some of them critters decide to wander off during the night we can ride after them. Hate to walk after a horse that doesn't want to go back to work."

I thought that was a pretty good idea as well. I've had to go clear back to my last camp for horses that have wandered in the night. Usually, they will stick around with one that's tied if they typically run together. I didn't want to lose time chasing loose horses at this point in the game.

I've got to admit the Sheriff did a pretty good job with the dehydrated army surplus meals. He has a real knack for cooking. Tom didn't take too kindly to my suggestion that he take it up as a retirement job. Don't rightly know if he was upset at the idea of cooking or retirement. May have been some of each. We were all asleep almost as soon as we were in our sleeping bags. It had been a long day.

I woke up before daylight. My watch said 4 a.m. It was probably right. I lay in the sleeping bag and looked at the stars overhead. Just stars. The moon had disappeared in the early morning hours, and the sun had not peaked out at us yet. After wasting some time thinking about Cheryl and some more worrying about her, I rolled out of the sack and pulled on my boots. I grabbed my coat and hat, buckled on my gun belt and started saddling horses. I had them all saddled and the pannier ready to load by the time false dawn began to lighten the darkness. The sky gets kind of light colored, but no sunlight can be seen. It's a quiet time of night, but you can hear the rustle of small animals in the trees and occasionally the sound of something bigger, deer or elk, moving through the trees. And, of course, you could hear the Sheriff snoring. I don't know how Edna puts up with it every night. The smell of coffee woke both of them up. Even if you don't like coffee, the smell first thing in the morning helps you get started on the day. Even Carl complained about granola bars for breakfast, but I was ready to go. We tightened the cinches on the pack horses and lifted the panniers on, lashing them tightly in place. I pulled my own cinch tight and stepped up to the stirrup. Red was awake for sure. Good thing I had a good grip on the horn or he would have left me standing there. I swung into the saddle and reined him around in a tight circle. Could have sworn I heard both Carl and the Sheriff chuckle, but they both had nutural expressions on their face as I turned back to them.

"Come on you guys, Let's go. We're burning daylight." Both of them came, but at their own speed. Hard to rush a guy that doesn't want to be rushed.

Carl led out studying the trail. I had two of the pack horses tied together right behind me, and Sheriff brought up the rear with the remaining pack horse. Without the packhorse to slow him down, Carl could make better time up the trail as he could study it and ride ahead without thinking about what the pack horse may have been up too or worrying about a pack slipping. Tom and I could follow quickly behind him because we didn't have to watch the tracks as we moved forward. Only had to observe where Carl went and follow him. It was just getting light out as we rode away from our camp. What we would call shooting light during hunting season. I hoped there wouldn't be any shooting on this ride.

Carl stopped near the crest of a hill and motioned for us to come forward. As I rode alongside him, Carl pointed down the valley to our right side. Moving down the far side of the valley was a line of elk going back into the tree line and probably from there up into the higher mountain country. With my field glasses, I could see the herd bull. At least six points on each side and a heavy rack of horns. What a beauty. It's rare anymore to see a large herd so I couldn't begrudge Carl the time we took to watch the regal procession. Although I was in a hurry, it was worth the wait. A grand, majestic animal even in groups of two or three.

There were probably 75-100 in this herd. The large 6-point bull, several smaller bulls, and many cows and calves. Truly a wondrous sight. We watched until they disappeared into the trees and we lost sight of them. Silently Carl moved out again. No one had said a word the whole time. We just watched in awe. I've been told that large herds use to be the rule. Now they don't herd up thanks to civilization. Not only do all the people in the backwoods break up the herd, but the game and fish departments intentionally split up the herd with airplanes each fall so the hunters won't decimate the herds all at one time. It's too bad. What a sight.

So far they were keeping to the main trail, although they were staying under trees whenever possible if the trail didn't actually run through the trees. Carl was doing an excellent job of keeping their tracks in sight, and we made good time all morning. Towards midmorning, we came across an area where someone had camped recently. The embers were still warm in the fire pit. Like a lot of people, they had left garbage behind. We took the trouble to pack ours out, but lots of folk just dump it wherever they feel like it. You can tell you're near civilization even in the mountains. Just look for the empty beer cans. Garbage in the mountains is generally something that will make me mad, but this time I was glad to see it. We learned a little about what our two robbers were like. Unlike us, they were packing perishable food. At least the remains of what looked like two meals were. If that were true, they would have a tough time keeping it from spoiling for many days. The most interesting find was a bunch of broken hypodermic syringes though. The label identified them as insulin. It made a connection for the Sheriff.

"Jerry, isn't Davis Ferguson a diabetic?"

I thought about it for a few minutes. "I'm not sure. I know Davis has some sort of a health problem that he takes shots for, but it could be allergies for all I know." Then I started making the same connection the Sheriff was working on. The description of one of the bank robbers could fit Ferguson. I was about to speculate on it to the Sheriff when he got out his portable radio and tried to make contact with the office. The range wasn't right or something because he got no answer. We could try again later when we got higher up. In the meantime, we got Carl and had a little pow-wow. If the other male was Ferguson, we would have some valuable insight into the tactics of the two men we were following. In fact, we would know a great deal about at least two of the three persons in the group. That could be an advantage later.

The western novels always emphasize the importance of knowing the person you are tracking. Placing yourself in their boots if you will. We didn't need the information to track them. We wouldn't know how to apply it even if we had a lot of it. As policemen, however, the information could be helpful. Knowing something about how a person thinks can help you predict what they will do in a given situation. Then you can alter the conditions to the extent possible to give you the advantage. It doesn't always work though. Remember, I used that type of process when I dealt with Conners in the bar. I got a sore head for my trouble that time. Generally, it works though and can be applied to assist in a tight spot. That's the idea the western novels try to expand on when the tracker knows his target and can figure out what he will do to his trail as he attempts to elude his followers. I don't think it would help in following these two since they weren't hiding their trail and may not know how to hide it anyway. I'm not sure I could hide my own.

We put our heads together and started trading what information we had. In a small town, some generally know all about everyone else. Your past might be a secret before you got there, but everyone seems to know all about what you've done since you arrived. Sometimes that is an aggravation, right now it could be helpful. Ferguson had been in Caribou since he was a baby and his family was one that everyone talked about. Couldn't help it. They were prominent and well known by everybody. As a result, we could put together a lot between the three of us. Basically what we had was a spoiled mama's boy who wasn't very active physically. He worked in the bank but wasn't very adept at that. He'd gone to a junior college and taken some banking and accounting courses. Rumor had it that he had majored in parties. It would help to know if he was still in town. If he were, it would rule him out as the second man. If not, he was a prime candidate. It was time to split up.

Carl and I would take all the packhorses and follow the trail. The Sheriff would ride high on the ridge and try to make radio contact with the office. Then he would catch up with us. I had a roll of florescent engineer tape with me that I could tie strips on trees for him to follow. Old habit from hunting. If you have ever left an elk or deer in a heavy timber so you could get a packhorse and then tried to find it again, you always remember the orange tape. It shows up for a long way and gives you a trail to follow. Sort of like street signs in the city.

We got lucky. Twice. Sheriff Flanigan was able to get through to the office. I could hear his half of the conversation on my own portable. When he cleared with the office, I called him on the radio. He filled us in. Ferguson was not in town and had not been seen since the night before the robbery. The insulin was for him. He had just filled a prescription for the same brand as that we found in the campsite. Odds were pretty good that Ferguson was one of our suspects. The Sheriff had directed the office to alert all law enforcement authorities to pick him up for questioning. No big deal if he was one of the ones in front of us, but we would know for sure if he got picked up somewhere else while we were running around the hills.

I was just riding up to Carl to talk about Ferguson when I saw the rocks piled up next to the trail. It was a fresh pile. Some of the stones still had wet dirt on them. You could see where they had been pried out of the soil near the trail. To folks in the mountains rocks piled on top of each other like columns are in the direction of travel, but rocks piled up like a hill mark a trail. It looked like Cheryl was trying to help us locate her. I was sure of it when I took a close look at the pile. Sticking out near the top was a plastic name badge with her name and the hospital's on it. We were on the right trail and hopefully getting closer. I called the Sheriff on the portable but got my answer in person as he rode down the side of the hill to us.

"Jerry, they cooked here too. Look at the fire and the garbage over by the big tree. Horses were tied here for a while too. The grass is grazed down around several trees." Carl started throwing their garbage onto the empty pack horse panniers. "Good thing we brought an extra horse. I'm getting kind of tired of hauling their trash too. What does the cooking here mean? Made sense at an evening camp, but not too wise here if they're trying to make any time."

"Maybe it does make sense," said Tom, "diet is an important part of any diabetic's health. If it gets out of whack, they can go into a coma or pass out. Maybe Ferguson engineered the stop." I shoved my hat back on my head and squatted down. "What if Cheryl convinced them to eat. She should know about diabetics, and most of Ferguson's insulin is down the tubes. It sure would slow them down."

Carl cut through the rhetoric. "What difference does it make? Whoever called the stop is slowing them down. We ought to get going rather than sit here and talk about it."

CHAPTER 27

Witters awoke with a start. He had been dreaming of days and places long ago. Or maybe long in the future. As with many dreams, it was hard to remember exactly what he had been dreaming about. At any rate, it was an enjoyable, pleasant dream. Movement from the girl had jarred him from his sleep. Cheryl was squirming against her ropes trying to loosen them. Quickly emerging from his sleeping bag, Witters grabbed her by the hair and twisted her head towards him.

"Just what do you think you're doing?" He knotted the hair in his hand and bent her head backward stretching her neck and arching her back against the ropes.

Cheryl struggled to speak. "My arms are going to sleep. The ropes are too tight," she rasped. "Please loosen them."

Witters relaxed his hold on her head and unzipped the bag. Rolling her over he could see the swelling that had begun in her wrists. Whether from the rightness of the ropes or her struggling, he could not determine. Untying the ropes brought almost instant relief to Cheryl. She brought her hands in front of her and began to massage them. "Thank you. That helps. Would you loosen my feet too?"

Witters complied. "I'll leave them loose for a while, but no moving around or I'll tie you back up. Understand?"

Cheryl pulled the sleeping bag around her to ward off the chill of the night. "Yes, I'll be quiet."

Slowly Cheryl was obtaining little freedoms that would add up as time went along. With freedoms went a similar relaxing of Witter's guard. She was sure he would be watching her closely tonight, but there was a good chance she would be able to stay untied most of the time. That would give her an opportunity to slip away sometime soon. Worming down into the warm sleeping bag, she drifted happily off to sleep. Her dreams were happy ones as well. She dreamed of Jerry and their short time together. Sometimes in the rest of the night, the dreams moved on into a future together with him. Unlike Witters, she remembered the dream vividly the following morning.

Cheryl was not a city girl. It was true she had lived in large cities for a while, but her background and her childhood were country. Her grandparents had homesteaded near the mountains where she was now held captive. Fred and Kathleen Henderson were part of a wagon train traveling across the area in the late 1800's. The newlyweds liked the looks of the area and stayed behind to begin a modest ranching operation. They too were familiar with Old Man Ferguson. Silas Ferguson had loaned Fred $3,000.00 to purchase his first livestock. For those days, $3,000.00 was a small fortune. Fred made it work though. He drove cattle into the fertile valley where he began his home and after shipping some of the older cattle to market a year later was able to pay off Ferguson and still have a good nucleus of animals to build upon. Fred and Kathleen did not have to fight Indians, the Battle of Little Big Horn has been long over and all the problems associated with it in the surrounding area pretty well settled. That didn't mean Fred and Kathleen didn't have their own issues. They had to deal with nesters, other ranchers who would like to own the Henderson water and all the typical day to day problems of trying to operate a successful ranching operation. After two miscarriages, Kathleen finally gave birth to their first child. A pretty little girl they named Ester. Ester signaled the beginning of the end of the Henderson problems. She was a healthy, quiet girl who was as home in the kitchen as she was working cattle with her father. The tomboy soon gave way to the lovely young lady she was to become. The belle of the ball in Caribou, she had thus far rejected the advances of several potential suitors. Just as her parents were resigning themselves to the prospect of having an old maid on their hands for the years to come, she became head over heels in love.

Not that the situation made her parents all that happy. She was in love with Larry Hefner, a perennial bachelor ranch hand on one of the neighboring ranches. They met at a barn dance one Halloween night, and by Christmas, the two were almost inseparable. Fred finally bowed to the inevitable and hired Larry to work on the Henderson Ranch. Wedding bells soon followed. Although both Larry and Ester were well into their thirties, they were happy together. For Fred and Kathleen, it was the answer to all their dreams and hopes for their daughter. Larry was a top hand on any ranch and soon was supervising all aspects of the Henderson ranching operation, giving Fred and Kathleen the opportunity to travel and vacation away from the ranch. Something they had never been able to do while they were actively engaged in the ranching operation.

Larry and Ester were just starting to build a home for themselves a short distance from the Henderson headquarters when Ester discovered she was pregnant. Like her parents, this was her one and only child. And like her mother, Cheryl was a tomboy who loved the ranch and all the activities involved in its operation. What she loved most though was the fall hunting trips with her father. Ranching was a sometimes dubious occupation as cattle prices fell and costs rose. Guiding hunters was a means of supplementing a rancher's income each year. Larry was no different than other ranchers of the time. Extra cash came in real handy. Guiding hunters was an enjoyable way to earn extra cash. Hunters were fun-loving and had the money to spend. Sometimes the tips were as large as the charges for being guided to some of the best big game hunting in the Rocky Mountains.

Cheryl was a big help to her father. She could wrangle horses with the best of them, could help with cooking and had a sixth sense about game and where they would be on a given morning. More than one eastern hunter could credit his trophy elk to Cheryl's guiding talents.

Then tragedy struck the Hefner household. At least it was a tragedy to them. Larry developed a late, but intense allergy to hay, horses, and cows. For many people, this would be an inconvenience, but for a rancher like Larry, it was the end of a lifestyle. Neither Fred nor Kathleen could continue to operate the ranch. Age has a way of catching up as well. The ranch was leased to others with Fred and Kathleen remaining in the old headquarters building which had been their home for so many years. Larry, Ester, and Cheryl moved out of their home, seeing it go to the family leasing the ranch. It was a traumatic time for Cheryl, but to her credit, she weathered the time with grace and poise. Perhaps she inherited the trait from her parents. Larry and Ester had a lot of adjustment to live through as well. Neither had been away from the ranch in many years. Larry had not always been a cowhand. For a short time anyway, he had gone to college. Those college years were the basis for their new life. Larry's college roommate and good friend was living in Boise, Idaho, and operating a successful business building and selling prefabricated log homes. Larry went to work for him as a salesman. Soon he was heading up the sales division.

Cheryl attended college in Boise and worked there in the hospital for several years after graduating. Finally, the pull of the area where she grew up became overpowering. One day she was reading the Caribou newspaper and noticed the county hospital was looking for a lab tech. She immediately called the hospital and landed the position. From her perspective, it had been a fantastic move. She spent long hours visiting with her grandparents at her old home and was planning on spending much more time at the ranch. Even though it was leased out, it was still part of her family and part of her heritage. Then she met Jerry. That had to have been the most important reason for coming home to Caribou even if she didn't know it at the time. She knew immediately that he was the one for her, even as he was busy falling down at her feet. The look in his eyes told her the feeling was mutual.

This background she now was desperately hiding from Witters and Ferguson. She wanted to give the impression of being a helpless city girl, new to the mountains. She had a good idea of who Davis Ferguson was. She remembered him from her high school days in Caribou. He had been two or three grades ahead of her. It took some time to make the connection since it was hard to believe one of the Fergusons would be involved in robbing Ferguson Federal Savings. When Witters called him Davis, she intuitively guessed he meant Davis Ferguson. As she waited for the two men to wake to the morning sun, she tried to determine if there was any way she could use the information to her advantage. She certainly did not want to have the knowledge used against her. Davis was unpredictable in school. The typical spoiled, rich kid. Use to getting his own way in everything and indulged by parents who were not much better. She wondered if Davis would recognize her. So far neither one had even asked her name. Time would tell.

Gradually the two men began to stir. Ferguson crawled out of his sleeping bag and walked into the woods. Soon he came back with some more wood for the fire. He shook Cheryl by the shoulder.

"Are you ready to start breakfast?"

She nodded her head. "He told me not to move. Is it alright if I get up?"

Witters spoke from within his bag. "Go ahead and get breakfast. We need to get going so make it a fast breakfast." He pointed at Davis. "Feed each of the horses a can of grain and take them down to the stream for water." With that, he slid out of bed and added wood to the fire. He then sat next to the warmth of the fire and took his automatic from beneath his arm. Removing the clip and working the slide to remove a bullet from the chamber he began to clean the gun with materials in a small kit as he watched Cheryl fix breakfast.

"What's your name?"

Cheryl paused in her preparations. Was he a mind reader or was it only coincidence he asked her name so soon after she had wondered about the lack of interest on his part. She compromised by saying just, "Cheryl."

"Well Cheryl, you can make it easy or hard on yourself. Your choice. You're going to be with us for a while. If you cooperate and make yourself helpful to me going across the mountains, things will be more comfortable for you. If not, you aren't going to enjoy the trip very much at all." Witters had come to the conclusion that Cheryl would be taken along to the end. To turn her loose was too risky and he didn't want to kill her.

Cheryl discerned the compromise in Witters' speech. "I haven't caused you any trouble."

"Just see that you don't. I don't have time to worry over you all the time, and I'm not going to turn you loose up here where someone might find you."

"You wouldn't leave me alone here in the woods would you?" Cheryl turned her head toward her cooking so Witters would not see anything in her face that would give him any indication of how much she would like to be left in the forest "I'll cook meals for you and try to help the man with his medications, but please don't leave me alone here."

The Brier Rabbit in the briar patch gamut did not work, but perhaps it would help her later. She felt more confident that she was conveying a sense of helplessness to him. Again, Cheryl delayed as long as she thought was safe in preparing breakfast for the two men. Once again Witters pushed her to get underway and would not let her clean up the pans and dishes before moving on. Soon the three were mounted, and Witters led Cheryl's horse up the trail as Davis brought up the rear with the two pack horses. Moving single file, they entered the pine trees.

"Watch the limb," Witters warned Cheryl as the horses moved under a low branch of a pine. Cheryl did not pass the warning to Davis Ferguson. Intent upon watching one of the pack horses he was leading Ferguson did not see the tree branch until it was too late. He was just turning his head to the front as his horse carried him into it. Ferguson's face hit the thick limb knocking him to the ground. His anguished yell of pain caught Witters' attention.

"Are you all right?"

Ferguson laid on the ground holding his face with both hands. Witters turned on the narrow trail. There was not enough room for Cheryl's horse to turn with Witter's horse wedging in alongside. Ferguson continued to roll and moan on the ground.

Cheryl was next to Witters. "Aren't you going to help him," she asked, "he looks like he's hurt."

"You get down and check him. You're the nurse."

"I'm not a nurse, just a lab tech. I'll try and help him, but you'll have to move out of my way so I can get off the horse."

Witters backed his horse away from hers giving room to dismount. Cheryl slid off her horse and went to Ferguson. He was making a lot of noise, but she could see that his injuries were mostly superficial. He had split his scalp open on the branch, and the wound was bleeding massively. Cheryl knew that head wounds bleed impressively, but were generally not serious. Blood was flowing freely down Ferguson's face and around his hands. He looked like he was bleeding to death.

"I'll need some bandages. Is there a first aid kit?" Witters tied his horse to a tree and attempted to catch the pack horses.

"There's a kit in one of the pack saddles. I'll have to catch them first."

Cheryl watched with interest as Jeremy tried to catch the loose horses. The pie-bald pack horse bolted in fear as he ran up to it. With luck all the horses would run after the skittish pie-bald and Cheryl would have an opportunity to run. Unfortunately, the others stood fast, and Witters was able to hold onto the other pack horse and the horse Ferguson had been riding. He quickly tied them to trees and located the first aid kit.

"Here. Get him fixed up." Cheryl took the kit from Jeremy and began to work on Ferguson. Witters sat and watched her work. She cleaned around the gash as she held a compress against the wound to stem the flow of blood. Only after she had wrapped a bandage around the compress and Ferguson had ceased his whining did Witters move. "Watch her Davis. I'm going to get that other horse. Make sure she doesn't try anything foolish."

Mounting his own horse, Witters rode back down the trail after the pack animal. He hoped that it would stop soon. He didn't relish wasting much time looking for it. Mentally he began reviewing the contents of the pack horse's panniers. If he didn't catch it soon, he might have to abandon it. At least it didn't have any of the money on it. He had put it all in the lead pack horse when they saddled them that morning. What he was trying to remember was what other supplies it did carry. He was sure they could survive even if they went hungry for a while.

CHAPTER 28

It appeared we were slowly gaining on them. The distance between camps was becoming shorter and shorter. One of them was apparently hurt some from the looks of the blood and bandage wrappings we found in one place. Still, we didn't have them in sight, and it had been four long days following them. Their direction of travel took them higher and higher into the Rockies. The days were still warm and comfortable for travel, but the evenings and nights were developing a distinct chill.

I was shaking off some of the morning chill as we crested out into a long, vast meadow and rode into the welcome sunshine. It was a cool, clear morning and you could hear the Meadowlarks singing. I stretched in the saddle and urged Red along. Just as I turned to check on the progress of Carl and Tom, shots reverberated through the peaks. It was a long way to the ground off the red horse, but reflexes from Vietnam took precedence. I rolled off the left side and scurried behind a nearby log. The horses scattered back down the trail, two of the pack horses bucking as they went.

The shots quit as suddenly as they began. They had been the sharp crack of a handgun, not the bellowing thunder of a large caliber rifle. As the echoes faded and died, I took stock of our situation. The horses were scattered, probably in different directions too. My rifle was on my horse, and I assumed that Carl's and the Sheriff's were on theirs as well. My Barretta was in my hand, and my left side hurt from the fall. Everything was still working. Carl's yell broke into my assessment of the situation.

"Jerry, the Sheriff's hurt." I started towards Carl and got another shot for my trouble. I could swear I heard the bullet as it went by. Rolling into a tuck, I threw myself to the ground again and began shooting in the general direction of the shots. Then I thought of Cheryl and immediately ceased. Edging back to Carl I could see why he was excited. Sheriff Flanigan was laying on his back in the edge of the trees with blood spurting from his left leg. I made a quick dodging run to his side without attracting any more shots. Using my handkerchief, I covered the wound and applied pressure just like they taught us in all the first aid classes I was forced to sit through in the Army and throughout my career as a policeman. Using the Sheriff's belt, I tied it in place and began checking him out for other injuries. He was breathing loudly through his mouth and nose, so I knew there was no problem there. He was unconscious but otherwise appeared alright.

Carl startled me when he came up to me. "I think they're gone. At least no one's shooting anymore."

"I think you're right Carl. Why don't you see if you can find some of the horses? Be careful though. The guy's either good with that handgun or lucky." I eased the Sheriff into a more comfortable position and slid my coat under his head as a pillow. Then I conducted a more thorough examination to ensure he didn't have any more injuries that could be life-threatening. Although as deep in the mountains as we were, what he had could be pretty dangerous.

We had been both stupid and lucky so far. Dumb not to have been aware that an ambush could be set for us at any time. We had been blindly following the trail of a felon who had shown himself to be intelligent and ruthless enough to have taken a hostage for protection. We were lucky that only one of us had been hurt. That was bad enough as the Sheriff would be lucky not to lose his leg or at least the use of it. We were a long way from medical help, and I wasn't much of a doctor. I doubted that Carl was much better for something like gunshot wounds. My worries about the Sheriff were lessened as he regained consciousness.

"What are you doing down there Sheriff?" I asked him remembering a similar greeting from him a couple of weeks ago. "How do you feel?"

"How the hell do you think I feel? Kind of like a Mack truck drove over me a couple of times. How's Carl?"

I checked his leg. "Carl's Ok. He's trying to round up a horse or two, so we can function. What happened to you?"

He growled, "I got shot, you dummy."

"I know that. I meant did you get shot first or fall off the horse first. You were unconscious when I got to you, and you shouldn't have been just from getting shot in the leg."

Tom gingerly rubbed the side of his head. "I must have hit it when I went off the horse. I was trying to hang onto him when the shooting started. He jumped about the time I felt the slug hit my leg. Don't remember going down."

"Ok. At least we have someplace to work from. It doesn't look like the crack in the head hurt you much anyway. Can you move your foot?"

He grinned a little, "can't hurt me much by hitting me in the head."

"I'm glad you said that and not me."

Carl chimed in, "How's the hardhead?"

I was glad to see that he had our entire string of horses with him. "Tom's alright, I think." Turning back to the Sheriff, I repeated my question about his foot.

"I'm pretty sure nothing's broken. It sure hurts like hell though."

There was no exit wound that I could see. The only blood was on the front of the thigh. "Let's get your pants down and see what we can do about patching you up." Carl brought over a first aid kit. That man impresses me. Seems to be able to read your mind most of the time. He was carrying his hunting rifle and a pair of binoculars.

"I'll go on up ahead a little and make sure we don't get any repeat company." He walked up the trail keeping low as he moved into the meadow and then angled off to one side to keep to the tree line.

"Jerry, I don't think anyone will be close by. That was a long shot just to give him time. We've been closing for the last day or two. Now he will have us being super conscious of another attack. That will give him some edge," the Sheriff said.

We got his pants down so I could check the wound. The bleeding had slowed and was starting to clot around the entry site. It didn't appear to have penetrated very far into Tom's leg. "I think you were just in the wrong spot at the right time Tom. That bullet was just about spent when it hit. The Thing is, I don't want to fish around in there for it."

"I think you're right. From the size of the hole, it must be large caliber. It would have penetrated all the way if he had been within a reasonable range. Going to slow me down though."

I was busy thinking the same thing. As I washed and bandaged Tom's leg, I considered our options. While Tom could probably continue on, it would not be comfortable for him and might even be dangerous. Sounds funny talking about hazardous when you are hunting for an animal that can shoot at you, but the odds were different. Not only was there the problem of infection, but there was the possibility that the bullet had done some damage that we couldn't see which would manifest itself at some later time. Perhaps under the exercise necessary to ride through rough terrain and maybe even the need to walk or run in some instances.

"Sheriff. I think you and Carl should go back to town and get your leg cared for while I follow Ferguson and his friend."

"Like hell. This is my job, and the wound isn't much." The Sheriff got pretty worked up and made quite a speech about duty and responsibilities and such. Under other circumstances, it would have made a pretty good campaign speech for him. We argued for quite a while. We were still "discussing" the options when Carl walked back into our temporary camp.

"They've moved on up the hill. I found where they stopped. Looks like he hit you with a .45, Sheriff. Eight empties about two hundred yards up the trail."

"Hard to hit anything with a .45 up close. No one can be that accurate at two hundred yards with most pistols. Especially not with a .45 automatic." The Sheriff was back on his soapbox.

"How do you know it was an automatic," asked Carl. "Might have been one of those long barreled pistols."

Even I could guess the reason. "Because the empties were on the ground and because of the number. The automatic spits them out as you fire and eight is probably about right for one clip load."

Tom nodded his head. "That's about what I figured."

Carl joined in on our conversation about the Sheriff and Carl going back to Caribou or at least to some place where a chopper could pick Tom up. I had tried several times to get someone on the portable radio but only got static. Tom convinced himself that he would probably Ok, but changed his mind when he tried to stand up. The pain in that leg must have been pretty intense even for someone like Sheriff Flanigan, the original iron man. He sat back down slowly. Through clenched teeth and a pale white face, he conceded my plan.

"You be careful though. I'll get someone else started back to join you as soon as possible."

I thought about what I still had to do. Nothing serious, just ride out alone, find Cheryl, get her away from the bad guys, arrest both of them and bring them back to Caribou. Like I've said before, don't ever get out of the patrol car. Carl and I consolidated what supplies I felt I should take onto a single pack horse. He and the Sheriff started their slow descent off the mountain with the rest of the horses. The Sheriff gave me a wave that was almost a salute as he rode into the trees and down the trail.

Riding carefully and trying to watch every bush, tree, and rock in front of me I spurred Red along across the meadow. The pack horse was a special horse, a stocky black who was the best of the pack horses we had with us. Not only was he trail wise, but he was close enough to the ground to make it easy to load and unload him by myself. I was carrying only the meagerness of rations, a bedroll and little else besides my guns and a change of clothes. The problem was in knowing how much longer I would be out in the open. It was quite a change from fall hunting trips. Then you know how long you will be there, where you will be at any given time, and your quarry doesn't hunt back. Guess John Wayne said it best. "Courage is being scared and saddling up anyway." I never thought of myself as being brave. I'd seen combat, and I've been in a few tense situations as a cop, but I was always just doing the job. This was different.

Not just in the fact that I was riding around after the bank robbers on a horse like a character in a western novel, but because a pretty lady I thought an awful lot of was mixed up in it. Pretty bizarre. A bank robber who drives a Lincoln Continental makes his getaway on horses across a mountain wilderness area where there aren't any cars or any roads either for that matter. One of the robbers appeared to be an officer of the bank and one owned by his father to boot. They aren't satisfied with simple robbery; they have to take a hostage. A hostage who couldn't be better if they only knew. This was no simple hostage situation to keep the police at bay. They had taken the only girl I had really cared about in more years than I can remember. I was glad the Sheriff and Carl had agreed to turn back. Not only would I feel better about the Sheriff, but I could move faster and more effectively by myself. With only two horses I would move more silently.

Carl and the Sheriff were going to make lots of noise going down. Hopefully, the two I followed would think I was with them as well. Now was the time to gamble. I was going to leave their trail and try to get ahead or alongside them with my own ambush. I didn't think about what I would do if they had hurt Cheryl.

Riding easy in the saddle I led the black horse up through a stand of aspen on the north side of the meadow and drifted upslope winding my way through the deadfall and darker timber gradually working my way up the grade of the ridge. I intended to cross over the ridge and work my way up a valley that paralleled the one the others were following. In this way, I hoped to be able to get into a position where I could at least observe them. It was also a protective move as I would not be continuously riding along a trail that might be under their gun sights. I didn't think they would use another ambush right away, but I wasn't going to take a chance on what they might do since the gamble would be to my detriment.

I had begun thinking of them collectively as the Ferguson Gang. If I was going to be in an old west story, the name tags might as well fit right in. I was sure that only one person had been shooting. That might have been on purpose, but I began to wonder if only one had a gun. That would be most fortuitous for me.

I rode until it got too dark to continue. Rubbing down the horses after stripping off the saddles kept me occupied for a while longer. Finally, I ate a cold meal and rolled into my sleeping bag. Sleep was a long time in coming. Pleasant dreams kept turning into nightmares as my short past with Cheryl merged into fears about the future.

It was just getting light enough to find my way through the trees as I rode out the next morning, urging Red through the thick stand of pine. Even with the time I had lost tending to Tom, I was closing the interval again. Toward noon I glimpsed the movement of a horse on the ridge across from the one I was traveling. They were holding to the main trail where it crossed the east ridge. I knew it would dip down into the valley between us several miles away and would then follow the valley bottom to the pass where the trail could cross into the drainage on the other side. Red could feel the excitement, and he stepped up his gait to a trot along the narrow game trail we were following. I intended to be in front of them before they reached the pass. Some of the chill lifted from my chest as we hurried through the swales among the trees.

CHAPTER 29

Cheryl watched in horror as Witters began shooting at the three horsemen following them. Although it was over in seconds, the entire episode was carried out in slow motion for her. She saw the horses leap at the sounds of the explosions and saw several horses bolt as the bullets tore furrows in the ground near them. She saw Jerry jump from his horse and strike the ground awkwardly on his side. She saw Sheriff Ferguson clutch his leg and fall sideways from his horse. His body seemed to bounce as it struck the ground. It reminded her of the slow-motion movies of the dummies striking the windshields of the test crash automobiles. Only Carl got off gracefully. One moment he was sitting on his horse holding the lead ropes of two pack horses and the next he had stepped down from his horse in the fluid motion used by calf ropers in the arena at a rodeo.

"You bastard. You'll kill them." Cheryl screamed!

Jerry was moving toward the Sheriff. Cheryl could see Witters raising his automatic to aim at Jerry. She dove at him hitting Witters across the back of his shoulders as the gun started to fire. She was conscious of other shots being fired from down the mountain as she beat her hands against Witters head and shoulders. Witters ceased shooting and backhanded Cheryl with the .45 Colt. The front sights raked across her cheek drawing blood. As she fell to the ground, Witters dropped behind a rock. He continued to hit at her with the Colt and his hands until she curled into a ball and lay silent next to him.

"You stupid broad. Don't you ever do that again."

Cheryl remained on the ground, keeping her silence against the rage that burned within her. A senseless ambush that accomplished very little in her estimation.

Ferguson watched with favored interest. He was fascinated by the panorama before him. Simultaneously revolted by the thought of more killing and thrilled by the violence of the shooting and the combined fury of the girl and Witters, he watched and waited for the next chapter to unfold. Rather like watching television, but much more exciting. He could feel the adrenaline flow as he watched. Being a confirmed coward he did not participate, but the voyeur in him was sated by what he observed.

Witters, his temper abated by the knowledge that they must be moving on quickly, turned his attention back to the three lawmen sprawled out below him. He observed Jerry attending to Sheriff Flanigan and marveled at the smoothness with which Tafoya melted into the trees and suddenly disappeared. Grasping Cheryl by the arm he half pulled and half drug her to the horses tied nearby. "If you don't want to be hurt anymore, get on that horse and get ready to ride out of here."

Cheryl, stunned by the shooting and the subsequent violence directed at her person, docilely climbed onto the waiting horse. She was shaking so much her teeth chattered, but whether from fear or rage she wasn't exactly sure. Witters and Ferguson quickly mounted their horses. Leading Cheryl's horse, Witters lead the way into the trees and down into the open meadow leading away from the Sheriff's group. He kicked his horse into a run. They raced along the length of the meadow and into the trees at the far end. The branches hit against Cheryl's face as her horse was pulled along behind Witters. Finally, he slowed his flight allowing the horse to slow to a walk. With heaving sides, the horses moved along the dim trail, the sounds of their labored breathing loud in the quiet of the forest.

"Can we stop?" Cheryl pleaded. "I think I'm going to get sick."

Witters continued his solid pace along the wooded ground. "You just keep on with me, or I'll tie you back on that horse. If you're going to be sick, get sick over the side. We aren't going to stop for anything for a long while. They're too close for me to feel much like stopping."

The queasy feeling soon passed for Cheryl. She rode stolidly along, her face a mask of dulled emotion. At least two of the lawmen following them were close to her. Sheriff Flanigan had been like an uncle for many years, helping her grow up and assisting her when she moved back to Caribou. Her feelings about Jerry Burkley were not as fixed but were just as strong. She loved the shy, strong man, who was such a mixture of conflicting emotions and diverse accomplishments. She had not admitted it even to herself that she loved him until this time. She had made love to him but did not realize that she had committed her entire life to him until right this moment. It was not a bad feeling she had to admit. If only they were together and not both facing danger from the madman, who alternately beat her and charmed her. Her captor was a strange and driven individual.

They rode solidly for four hours. Witters pushed them along the faint trail that looped through the valleys and across ridges. Once Cheryl thought she saw a large group of horses and riders moving down the mountain. Away from her and not toward her. She had a barrage of emotions at the sight of the departing horsemen. Was she being abandoned? Even worse, were one or more of the men badly hurt? So badly hurt they would have to leave her here alone with Ferguson and Witters. She desperately hoped not.

Witters saw the riders too. "Ferguson, is that them going down that open area over there?"

Davis turned in his saddle and scanned the mountainside. "Sure does look like it. Does that mean they're going to turn back and let us alone?"

"I doubt it. Maybe they're scared we will shoot again. Whatever it is, the cops aren't following us right now, and that means we can get some distance between us." He spurred his horse forward and led off at a fast walk.

Ferguson strained to keep up with Witters and his captive. Davis felt exhausted and was developing a terrible headache. From experience, he knew his blood sugar balance was off. He needed insulin soon. His repeated pleas to Witters seemed to fall on deaf ears though. Witters continued his headlong plunge through the trees ignoring all distractions in his haste to place distance between himself and the following lawmen. Finally, he brought the tiring horses to a stop in a heavily wooded and secluded area far from the main trail. Davis moved quickly to get his insulin from the pack horse. With horror, he realized that he was down to one injection. The stress of the past few days had increased his need and therefore his consumption of the vital insulin.

"Witters, we've got to get out of here. I'm out of insulin. I can't go on any longer out here. Please get us off the mountain and near a drugstore. Please!" Ferguson was almost on his knees as he pleaded with Witters. The plea fell on the same deaf ears.

Witters slowly prepared himself a sandwich from the supplies Cheryl had unloaded from the panniers. "You can go back if you want. I'm going on over the mountain, with or without you. The money goes with me though."

Cheryl decided she might have an advantage if they split up or if the dispute between the two men escalated. She remarked, "He'll surely die if he doesn't have medication. He is too far advanced to go without his insulin. Even a day without it could put him in a coma."

Ferguson paled. "See, I need insulin. Let's get off the mountain and back to some sort of civilization."

"No way. Hit the road on your own if you want off so bad." Witters finished his sandwich and tightened the cinch on his saddle. He motioned for Cheryl to repack the pannier as he started adjusting packs to continue on his way.

Perhaps it was the strain of the last week. Maybe it was fear of his own death or illness. Whatever it was, Davis Ferguson developed some bravado. He made his clumsy way back into the saddle and grabbing the lead rope for the pack horse carrying the bank money, he kicked his horse and ran down the trail leading the money away from Witters.

"Come back here you son of a bitch." Witters leaped into the saddle and started after Ferguson. Cheryl was momentarily left with her own horse and a pack horse with food and bedding on its back. This was the opportunity she had watched for all week. Cheryl quickly fashioned a set of reins with the lead rope and halter on her horse and stepped into the saddle. Leading the remaining pack horse she angled into the trees and began working her way down the steep slope into the adjoining valley. The trees were close together and the hill so steep in some places that the horses were almost sliding on their tails as they worked their way down, the horse she was riding picking his way carefully down the rocky hillside. The horse often brushed her legs against the trees and brush as he half walked, half jumped down the hill. Cheryl held on carefully and trusted the horse to get her safely down the embankments.

Witters was caught on the horns of a real dilemma. His captive was going one direction and his money the other. Greed won out. He continued to follow Ferguson noting as he did so, the direction Cheryl had taken. He had become convinced that she could not function in the woods by herself and so felt that he could catch up with her later. Jeremy divided his anger between Davis and Cheryl. He would make them pay for this. He whipped at his horse and continued his pursuit of the fat man taking his money.

Ferguson could hear the crashing of tree branches as Witters chased him through the trees. Davis could only plunge ahead. There was no visible trail. Just the headlong racing of the horses through the trees. Branches slashed at his face and body. He gripped the saddle horn in a stranglehold as he tried to keep his balance on the horse. His horse was running out of control by this time. Davis had one hand occupied in holding onto the pack horse and the other trying to stay on the horse. The excitement of the running horses charged both horses into higher speed. One excited the other, and then they could hear another horse running behind them. The race was on. Ferguson was powerless to influence the race. To use the reins which were loosely held in the same hand holding the horn, he would have to turn loose of either his establishing grip or the pack horse. The decision was taken out of his hands suddenly. His galloping horse ran under a tree limb of gigantic proportions. There was plenty of clearance for the horses to get under, but not much left for the hapless passenger. The limb caught Ferguson squarely in the chest and stripped him off the horse. The horses continued their mad passage through the trees. Ferguson's luck was just not with him at all today. He fell under the feet of the following pack horse. Although not trying to hurt Ferguson the horse managed to trample him with almost direct strikes of his hoofs hitting him in the chest and along the side of his head. Davis was knocked almost immediately unconscious by the combined effects of the branch, the fall, and the running horse.

Witters saw only the final trampling of Ferguson but could see the tree limb in time to avoid the same fate. He pulled his horse up briefly seeing the battered, bleeding banker lying face down under the trees. He then continued his pursuit of the all-important pack horse. The money meant more to him than the supplies on the other horse or the fate of the other two persons. In time he caught both the pack horse and the riding horse that Ferguson had used. It was deceptively simple. He broke out of the thick trees into a grassy clearing surrounded by thick timber. The two horses had tired of their romp through the trees and were contentedly eating grass when Jeremy rode into the clearing. He was able to ride up to the two horses and take up the lead ropes without any difficulty. It was getting darker as Witters sat there, the sun dropping down below the tops of the trees and the shadows growing long. He realized he did not have the faintest idea where he was. He thought he could follow his trail back the way he came in the daylight, but daylight was rapidly diminishing and the day was growing cold.

It was growing cold and dark where Ferguson lay as well, but he did not notice. He was unconscious. Later in the night, Davis would regain consciousness only to go into hysteria over his predicament. He spent the night huddled under the trees, shivering with the cold and tortured with specters of his fate in the woods all alone. Slowly the insulin wore off. At a time when he needed more insulin to compensate for both injury and the severe emotional stress he was under, he had no medication, no proper diet, and no idea of where he was. Walking in circles, he tried to get to some location where he would know how to get back to some form of civilization. When morning came he was still traveling in larger and larger circles; still lost and becoming more so.

Cheryl had spent the night in relative comfort. She had reached the foot of the steep hill and intercepted a fairly old trail running along the bottom of the valley. Cheryl could see the faint outline where hunters or fishermen of years ago had traveled. It gave her something to follow which was going in the approximate direction she wished to move. She did not want to follow the trail they had followed coming in, but she wanted to go back toward Caribou. She was in no particular hurry as she had adequate supplies and warm clothing. Of one thing she was positive. She had no intention of letting Witters retake her captive. Towards nightfall, she had located a secluded grove of aspen partially surrounded by walls of granite rock. The area provided shelter, some grass for the horses, and best of all a good view of anyone approaching her camp. She did not risk a fire, knowing it would show for a long distance at night and could be smelled by anyone passing nearby. She ate a cold dinner and settled into a warm sleeping bag for the night.

Morning dawned crisp and clear. Cheryl decided to risk a small fire to make coffee and something warm for breakfast. She had just placed the coffee pot over the flames when a man stepped out of the trees at her back. He stood and watched her work at the fire and then spoke.

"Cheryl, are you all right?"

Cheryl knocked over the coffee pot as she spun around to the voice behind her. "Oh, Jerry. I'm so glad to see you.!" She ran to him and threw herself into his arms. "How did you find me?"

"Saw the movement of the horses and worked my way into the grove. Where are the others?"

"Chasing each other around the top of the mountain trying to see who gets the money. When Ferguson took off with the pack horse and all the money, Witters followed him. I just took off down the side of the embankment." She turned her face up to Jerry and gently kissed him. "I love you!"

"I've missed you, too. I didn't know how much I needed you until I thought I might have lost you. I was lonely and didn't even know it until I met you." Jerry returned the kisses passionately, holding Cheryl close to him. Soon they broke apart to move on with the horses. Jerry thought to send Cheryl back off the mountain, but she wouldn't listen.

"I know the mountains, can handle the horses and I want to be with you. Please don't send me away. I'd feel more comfortable with you than by myself. I'd keep worrying that Witters would be right behind me." Cheryl's eyes studied him intently as she spoke to him.

"Ok. I'll feel better if you're with me too, but I've got to keep after them. Some of the duty that Sheriff Flanigan impressed on me. Besides, I think the one you call Witters may be dangerous to anyone who comes across him. After he gets over the pass and starts down the other side, there will be other people around. That could be rough." Jerry saddled Cheryl's horse as he talked. Soon they were ready to move on. Jerry led Cheryl's pack horse and he led the way to where his horses were picketed. Soon they were working their way toward where Cheryl had last seen Ferguson and Witters.

CHAPTER 30

The relief I felt when I discovered Cheryl in the secluded little nook of the valley was like nothing I had ever experienced before. I couldn't believe my eyes. There she was making coffee like nothing had ever been any different. I knew she was alone. Riding along the upper edge of the ridge I had seen movement in the trees below. I pulled Red up and sat still, unmoving except for the swishing of the horses' tails at an occasional fly. One of the horses tied below moved around the tree. The aspen were turning from green to a variety of reds and yellows, but in the one spot where the horse was standing the leaves had already begun to drop off or else that section of the tree had no foliage. I couldn't tell from where I sat several hundred feet above, but I could see that it was a horse. Gently I eased Red and my pack horse away from the edge and tied them away from eyes which might be looking up.

I then indianed my way along the ridge, down into the valley and up to the nook. Scouting around, I discovered that only two horses had been ridden in. There weren't any sign of tracks other than by the horses. It looked like a single person. Only one size boot print. The right boot had a cut in the heel, and each set of tracks had the same cut impressed in the dirt. I watched Cheryl for a long time before I stepped out of the trees. She was alone. I would bet on it. In fact, if I was wrong, I could end up betting my life on it. The desire to see her and hold her was strong. Finally, I was satisfied that she was in this lonely spot by herself. Circling around the campsite, I could find no other sign.

It was a most satisfactory welcome. Cheryl ran to my arms and professed her love for me. I wasn't quite ready to make the total commitment but told her how I missed her. Someday I hope I'll be able to tell her how much I love her as well. While I would have liked to delay our departure from her hidden location, I knew that it would not be wise to delay locating Witters and Ferguson. Witters was a dangerous animal. Slow to anger, he had demonstrated how ruthless he could become. The beatings of Cheryl, the ambush that resulted in the Sheriff's wound. He was a cunning adversary.

Cheryl filled in some of the missing information for me. We had surmised that Ferguson was one of the two. It was helpful to have the information confirmed. Interesting also was the knowledge that not only was Ferguson suffering from diabetes but was short of the necessary insulin to adjust to any situation. Kind of like a chameleon. It would be helpful to know if he caught up with Ferguson and what had happened. I wanted more than anything to just turn around and take Cheryl off the mountain. We might be able to find Witters and Ferguson anytime. Only trouble was, I didn't believe that myself.

We had been alone in the wilderness area for the last week, but after crossing over the pass, we would soon wind our way out of the wilderness on that side and move back into areas of population. Not a lot of population by eastern standards, nor even by the standards of the west, but more people than we had seen lately. There would be remote cabins at the very least. Some or all would be occupied for another month or so. The end of the summer and the beginning of the fall hunting season would make them very desirable locations. Witters could take other hostages if he desired. The people in those locations would be sitting ducks for Witters in his bid for escape. I had to stay behind at the very least. I could still try to cut him off, but first I had to relocate him. It appeared that he was off the main trails and would be harder to locate.

Of Witters, I knew very little. From Cheryl, I now had a

physical description. I also knew of his reactions to various situations as Cheryl was able to describe them. I didn't know anything about his background though. He was just a man who had robbed a bank and taken a strange means of escaping the consequences of his acts. I wanted to catch up with him. Not just for what he had done to Cheryl, although that was a large part of it, but also to satisfy my curiosity about the man himself.

Soon we arrived near where Cheryl had ridden over the edge of the embankment and down the steep slope into the valley floor below. We could see the marks of the horses, especially the deep indentations made by running hoofs going down the same path. There was no trail except the tracks made by the running horses. I was leery of going blindly down that trail. Either of the two men could be anywhere along the length of it or even coming back along it. From Cheryl's description, neither was really at home in the mountains or on a horse. After studying the nearby area for a while, I decided the best course of action would be to move Cheryl and the horses out of the general area and then scout it out on foot before riding along their tracks.

We moved carefully back into the rocky ridge to our north. Leaving Cheryl with the horses and my rifle, I eased along parallel to the churned trail of Ferguson and Witters. I had changed into a pair of thick-soled moccasins, the better to creep through the pines. By moving slowly and being careful where I placed my feet, I could travel almost soundlessly among the trees. Boots did not give me the sensitivity to determine when I was going to break a twig and tended to scrape as I crossed rocky ground. The moccasins gave me that much more advantage. I could glimpse the route they had traveled without actually being on the same pathway. Often I stopped to listen. All I heard was the sound of the wind through the trees and the scurrying of smaller animals such as squirrels and chipmunks.

I had crept alongside their trail for better than a mile when I heard the sounds of horses moving. Easing behind a group of rocks I peered out at the trail I had been following. The sounds grew louder, and soon Witters rode into view. He was leading a pack horse, with the pack slipping badly, and a saddle horse that I presumed was Ferguson's. He was still about a quarter of a mile away from me, but moving closer. With a little luck, he would ride up right beside me. I settled back to watch as he climbed steadily up the trail towards me. Well, maybe not calmly settled. My breathing was kind of fast as the tension, and the excitement of the end of the chase started to build in me. Cheryl was safe, soon I would be able to arrest Witters, and then it would be a mop-up operation to find Ferguson. Since Witters had all the horses, I assume he also had the money from the bank.

My well-laid plans, as with a lot of my well-laid plans, simply disintegrated in front of me. Witters turned west and started up the mountainside into the trees. Carefully, but with all the haste I could muster, I moved through the trees to try and intercept him. Good plan. Bad terrain. The deadfall of trees in the area I was trying to cross almost stopped me entirely. Big trees, little trees, and middle-sized trees were lying on the ground like the pieces of a pickup sticks game. You couldn't walk through or around them, only over and under them one at a time. I soon decided that the best route might be to go back the way I came and travel down the trail to where Witters turned off.

I was pretty well out of breath and sweating heavily by the time I got back to the trail. Off in the distance, I could see the three horses working their way toward the ridge outlined on the distant horizon. It was easy to see why Witters turned when he did. It was an almost straight shot to the top from where he turned, the natural slope of the terrain making a virtual roadway to the top. From there he would only have to cross the rocky area above timberline, cross the ridge and start down the other side.

Wasted more time getting back to Cheryl and the horses, cussing myself all the way. Just got too smug and let him get clean away. As I tightened the cinches, I explained to Cheryl just what had happened.

She was kind. "Don't blame yourself. There's no way you could have foreseen where he would go."

"I know, but it galls me to be that close and then lose him entirely."

We mounted up and started up the mountain. I didn't want to follow Witters on the trail he was following, but we would have to cross at about the same place near the top. I worried about another ambush.

The higher we went, the tenser I became. Part of it was not knowing where Witters was or what he was doing. The rest was the change in the area we were crossing. As we got higher, the trees began to thin out. Soon there were only a few straggly looking specimens. The windswept trees above timberline had foliage only on the downwind side. What few of them there were anyway. They looked like something out of a nightmare or a science fiction movie backdrop. Even in the sunlight, the entire area is cold looking. The grey-white granite cliffs loomed up on one side with an unlimited view to the other. Kind of like being on top of the world. In a way, I guess we were. You could look across the vast expanse to view different mountain slopes and valleys. There were numerous rocky outcrops making the footing for the horses more difficult. I was glad I was riding Red. It makes for a calmer ride when the horse is surefooted and confident.

What little grass there was between the rocks was small and fragile looking with lichen growing on the rocks. It develops that way because the area has snow banks on it for most of the year. There were glaciers and snowbanks on the rocky walls above us. Numerous snow-fed lakes with cascading streams bubbled around us.

"What a fascinating area," Cheryl noted.

"I like it, but it always seems too alien, especially after being in the trees for so long. Kind of cold and sterile." I was scanning the slope above us for any sign of Witters, or even Ferguson for that matter. Most of what bothered me about this majestic chunk of mountain was the exposed feeling I had being in the middle of it. I suppose I might have been more appreciative of the scenery if I wasn't worried about us both being targets in the middle.

As we crested over the top, feeling very exposed, I saw movement in the tree line far below us. At least I think I did. It could have been Witters and his horses, or it could have been my imagination or an elk. If it was Witters, I hoped he kept right on riding. We would be just as exposed coming down on this side as we were going up the other wide. I led us down through the boulders, trying to keep solid rock between us and the tree line below. Probably more psychological than real, but it did ease my mind some.

From our elevation, you could see the slow-motion sway of the pine trees below. I headed toward the area where I thought I had seen the movement before. It would probably be necessary to find Witter's tracks or some evidence of his travel before we could determine where he had headed. From this point he had a multitude of options, being able to travel in many different directions as he moved down off the mountain pass.

Part way down I remembered my portable radio. From the top, I might have been able to reach the Sheriff's office. Good time to remember! Supercop in action, right? I tried it with the expected lack of results anyway. Decided to keep on going. Might not have worked up on top either. The batteries seemed to be pretty weak.

Cheryl spotted the trail first. Witters had finally lost his pack and spilled gear and food all over. It was easy to figure out what happened. Even though the packs weren't heavily loaded, the trip up and down the mountain with a pack that was already slipping finally caught up with him. He must have repacked in a hurry because he hadn't bothered to get a lot of it back. The horse must have spooked or else he didn't even realize the pack had slipped over to the side of the horse. Probably a little of each. He had stuff spread in a line for about a hundred feet. We found where he had tied the horses and redone the pack cinches.

I didn't know if he was in a hurry, if he even knew we were still right behind him or if he was just about to some destination he was aiming to reach. It would have been nice to know. At any rate, we didn't have any trouble finding where he had entered the trees again. Guess I needed a little luck at this point.

Chapter 31

After finding the horses, Witters spent the night in a cold, dry camp. He wasn't sure where he was. He was reluctant to light a fire. He didn't have any water. It was a long miserable night. As he sat wrapped in a sleeping bag, he thought more about Ferguson. If Davis had been there, Witters would have beaten him to death. What kind of a foolish stunt that had been. He wondered if Ferguson was still by the tree where he fell. Witters hoped so. At least he was relatively warm, and he had the money. Ferguson had nothing. That suited Jeremy. On that happy thought, he dozed off. He awoke to the sounds of the horses moving. Quickly he checked to ensure he still had the reins and lead ropes firmly grasped in his hands. He had not bothered to unsaddle any of the horses the evening before. They were becoming restless.

Between the horses moving about, Witter's own fears in the long dark night, and the thought that Ferguson might be close enough to hear kept Witters awake throughout the remainder of the night. As the morning light began to peak into the valley, Witters spirits began to rise. Soon he would be out of these damn mountains and back to civilization. He had more than enough of horses.

Throwing his sleeping bag into one of the panniers he mounted his horse to begin the rest of his journey. To Jeremy, it was starting to feel like a never-ending journey. As he rode, he concentrated on what Pat had told him about the trail over the pass. He knew he should be getting close to the top. From there it would be a short ride to the pickup truck the two had parked in the mountain campground some three weeks ago. What Witters didn't know was that the Forest Service had towed that pickup truck away some two weeks ago thinking it was an abandoned vehicle. So much for that great escape plan. Witters wasn't there yet, so the vehicle factor wasn't one he considered.

One question was answered for him though. Ferguson was no longer under the tree as Witters rode by. He spent only an instant in looking around for him, then continued. Witters chuckled to himself. Too bad, Davis was a good old boy. No money, no horse, no supplies. Tough!

Witters continued to look about as he rode along the trail. There were too many people he didn't want to see. Ferguson was only one. He wasn't sure if the cops were still on the mountain. If so, he definitely wanted to avoid them. That gal though. He figured he wouldn't mind seeing her again. After the way she had run off, Jeremy would have been happy to have a little revenge. Besides the nights were getting colder and it might be nice to have a little warmth in the sleeping bag. As he was fantasizing about future deeds, Witters glanced up the hill to his right. There it was. A pathway clear to the top. It boded of good things for Jeremy. Up to the top and down the other side. Yes, sir. Maybe Davis had done all right for Jeremy. Witters had the money, the horses and just a little more riding to finish this up. No one to split with made retirement a real possibility. Relax in comfort for many years. Sounded real good to Jeremy Witters.

The euphoria lasted until the pack saddle slipped. Even the ride through the funny little trees made him happy. He was on top of the world, literally and figuratively. When the horse bolted just as he was entering the trees, he was caught unaware. He was pulled partly from the saddle as the panicking pack horse hit the end of the lead rope Witters was holding. He managed to hang onto the pack horse and remain on his own, but it was touch and go for a few minutes. His arm hurt from the impact.

His whole body was starting to develop new pains as he vainly tried to get the pack saddle and panniers pushed back into position. Only after a great deal of struggle did Jeremy get the cinches loose enough for him to slide the pack saddles back into position on the horse's back. He was fortunate to have a very gentle horse to work with. Some would not have put up with his struggles for long. Witters discovered the hard way that you should always fasten the pannier shut. He had not done so when he put his sleeping bag in that morning. Now Witters had gear spread all over the faint trail through the trees. He walked up the trail to the ever important money bags, hefting three of them and walking back to the tied horses. He was just too tired to make more trips for the other items. Soon the trip would be over. He would just keep on going.

Within an hour Witters was rethinking his decision to abandon his equipment and supplies. The air was turning chilly. As the wind increased, Witters comfort and happiness sped away. He thought about turning around, but decided not to waste two hours up and back. He was firmly fixed on his direction. In his haste to keep moving, he put himself at a real disadvantage.

Storms in the mountains come swiftly and viciously. This one was no exception. One minute it was clear and serene. The next was a raging snow storm. The large white flakes fall slowly at first then more intensely. Witters was lost in a world of white. Somewhat like the little crystal balls you shake to create a snowstorm over the figures within. He lost all sense of direction when the wind began to blow the snow in swirling waves. The bitter wind-driven snow attacked his exposed skin turning it into intense pain. He wanted shelter desperately but knew not how to find it. He gathered the horses around him and used them for a haven from the storm. The horses, however, were not so cooperative. The natural instinct of the horse is to turn into the storm to get the maximum effect from the hair on their bodies. By facing into the weather, the wind pushes the hair flat against them to lock in the warmth. When turned away, the wind and snow get under the hair. Witters' three horses were no exception. They wanted to get faced in the right direction, even if Witters was not sheltered. Witters consistently found himself standing in the biting wind in front of the horses, rather than between them as he wished. Eventually, Witters crawled into the protection of a bush and there he suffered as the storm raged on. His hands were frozen into a cramp as he tried to hold the horses and his precious money.

Some fall storms end in a hurry. This one didn't. It raged on through the rest of the afternoon and most of the night. Witters raged on through the night as well. He screamed his frustrations back at the wind until he was hoarse. Finally, the storm blew itself out. It was morning light before Witters became aware that it was no longer blowing snow about him. He was pretty well covered with snow. That was probably why he suffered no more damage than he did. The pile of snow helped insulate him from the chill of the night.

The furious storm was hard on the horses as well. They were strong mountain-bred horses used for arduous pack trips in and out of the mountainous areas of their home range. They were also used to proper care, adequate food and sufficient rest. Witters had burned them out. He had been keeping them saddled all the time, gave them little opportunity for grazing the foliage that keeps them fueled and had quit feeding them any grain. He could not, for all the grain was on the pack horse Cheryl had taken with her. The pack horse stopped first. He simply would not move on the morning after the storm. He stood with his feet apart, his head down and would not move, even when Witters hit at him. With tears of rage forming in his eyes, Witters removed the bank bags from the worn horse and tied them to the saddles of the other two. He left the tired packhorse to fend for himself. Mounting his horse and adjusting the bags comfortably around his legs Witters led the other horse away from the site, moving slowly down the mountainside. He followed the faint trail as it weaved between the trees. The snow was quickly melting even as he rode. It was astonishing to Jeremy to see the sign of his misery the night before evaporating before his very eyes. The storm had come and gone. In a few hours, the snow would be melted into the sparse grass leaving no evidence of its earlier violence.

The day had dawned bright and clear and now was developing into a warm, pleasant day. Witters soaked up the warmth of the sun on his back as the horses plodded along. He was hungry, his clothes were still wet, and he was furious over the events of the last two days. In this unsettled mood, he saw the cabin in the middle of the meadow he had just entered. It was time for Witters to make other decisions. Should he approach the cabin or fade back into the trees and detour around it. He stopped the horses and considered his options.

CHAPTER 32

The storm moved in on us in a hurry. Riding down through the trees, we could see the clouds rolling across the tops of the mountain the falling snow visible from a distance. I knew from experience that we would have only a short time to find shelter from the storm. Luck was with us. As we moved down the trail, we came to a fresh deadfall of trees. The fallen trees formed a cave large enough for the horses and us. Cheryl and I quickly unsaddled the horses and crowded them into the natural corral created by the trees.

Covering our sleeping bags with a large canvas, we huddled together as the storm reached us. A regular 'blue norther', the windblown snow howled at us. We were warm, dry, and most important, together. Nor did we need to worry any about the Ferguson gang, either of them, since there wouldn't be anything moving in this storm. Kind of like being in the patrol car. If I hadn't been worrying about catching up with Witters and Ferguson, I wouldn't ever want to move from this location. Cheryl was cuddled up against me. We were both comfortable in each other's arms, trading kisses, touching and talking. Happy to be together after the strain of the last few days. In a way, it was almost as if we hadn't been apart. We had been through a lot, and now we could make up for it. We did.

The next day dawned bright and clear. We were buried under several inches of snow and were warm and toasty is in our little cave. We unwound from each other and crawled out to greet the bright new day. The sun glistened on the fresh snow creating a winter wonderland for us. The horses were covered with snow. It took a while to get them brushed off sufficiently to saddle. While I took care of that chore, Cheryl made breakfast for us. Nice way to start the day. The smell of bacon and coffee, mixed with the pleasant odor of the horses. All in all, it was a perfect morning.

Duty calls, however. It was time to get on with the job at hand. We moved out, carefully looking for any sign of the bank robbers. Cheryl noticed the movement first. "Look, isn't that a horse standing in the trees?"

"You've got good eyes, pretty lady," I responded, seeing what she had noticed first. "Get off your horse, quick," I urged her, wondering if one of the robbers was nearby. I swung off Red, drawing my Barretta as I did.

Leaving Cheryl with the horses and my rifle, I crept up on the lone horse, watching all around for another ambush. By the time I got to the bay pack horse, I was dripping wet, more from worrying about an ambush than from exertion. I could see the horse clearly from where I was watching. After scanning the area for a long time, I moved up to that poor animal. Standing with his feet spread and head low, it was clear that the horse was just used up. There were lots of tracks, some animal and some man-made around the bay. I could see where someone had mounted a horse and the tracks of at least two different horses trailing out of the area. I followed them far enough to make sure they hadn't gone out a short distance and turned back. When I was sure they had continued, I returned to Cheryl and our horses.

"Looks like someone pulled out of here. You can see where someone bedded down during the storm. The pack horse is pretty tired out. Probably wouldn't move out this morning, although it's got a pack-saddle on," I explained to Cheryl as I came back. "Let's move ours over there and see what we can do for the horse."

"That's one of the pack horses that were with us. Where are Witters and Ferguson?"

"Don't know for sure. Looks like only one of them was here," I observed.

"Well, last time I saw this horse, Ferguson was running with it. Do you think he was here?"

I wasn't sure. Either Ferguson was here, or Witters had gotten it back. Since there were probably three horses here together, it was hard to tell for sure in the loose snow; they must have gotten back together somewhere along the line. It would have had to been before the snow storm since the tracks leave from here, but none come in except ours. Time would probably tell.

We stripped the pack gear off the bay horse and gave him some grain. He was already looking like he felt better. I tied his halter rope to our two pack horses, and we started out along the trail left by one of the bandits. It would have been a pretty day for a ride if it were not for the worry of what lay ahead. The day was warming up, the snow was starting to melt and except for water dripping off the trees, it was a good day to move down the mountain.

It was easy tracking in the snow and mud left by the storm. The horses we were following left clear, unmistakable tracks for us to follow as we wound down the forest trail. It was a good, wide trail, which allowed for Cheryl and me to ride side by side with the three pack horses following along in a line. All we could hear was the creak of the saddle leather, the noises of the horses and the quiet roar of the wind through the trees. The wind seemed to move across the tops of the trees to us, and you could almost see the wind shift in the slow-motion sway of the tall pine trees.

As we came around a bend in the trail, we could see a mountain valley spread out below. The trees gave way to a broad meadow. A small herd of elk grazed its way along the grassy edge of the field. "Oh, look Jerry." Elk, lots of elk ,started getting up from where they had been laying and began moving over the next ridge.

"We're too far away to have started them moving. Keep a close watch for our friends, either or both," I warned Cheryl. "Something moved that herd, and it wasn't us."

"They sure are pretty to watch though," Cheryl commented. "They probably sat the storm out there."

I reined Red in and reached for my field glasses. Slowly scanning the area, I finally found movement other than the elk. Coming into the meadow was a single rider with two horses. From the general size, I figured it was probably Witters. He didn't look pudgy enough to be Ferguson. I could make out the bags tied to the two saddle horses. "Looks like Witters got his money back. I wonder where Ferguson is," Cheryl observed. I wondered too. I felt better it was Witters I could see, rather than Ferguson though. Cheryl's description of Witter's shooting was still a little too vivid in my mind. It also made me wonder how the Sheriff and Carl were doing. With any luck at all, they would be off the mountain by now. I hoped they were sending someone in from this side. A little help would sure be appreciated along about now.

Keeping to the tree line so that our movement would be less noticeable, we continued down the tree-covered slope. I was concerned that we would be seen and have a repeat of being a target. Particularly now that Cheryl was with me. It wouldn't do for her to get shot, or me either for that matter.

As we moved lower, I could see a cabin sitting in the far end of the meadow. That gave me mixed feelings. If it was empty, Witters might stop there. But if it were not, the hostage problem would start all over again. I was too far away to see if it was even a good cabin. There are a lot of old, abandoned cabins up in the area, more since the wilderness area was established some years ago.

I lost sight of the other group of horses for a short while and then as I came around a curve in the trail, could see the horses standing by the house, but no one around them. I stopped and glassed the house with the binoculars but saw nothing. The horses were grazing in the tall grass, but nothing else was moving. The bags, I figured they were probably the money bags, were still tied to the saddles of the two horses. It didn't make sense that Witters if that were actually he, would leave the horses standing loose by themselves. I needed to be closer to the house, but was afraid to move much closer without knowing where Witters had gone.

When the shots rang out, I slid off Red, grabbing Cheryl on the way past, dragging her off the horse and pulling us both to the ground. Everything got a little wild at that point. All the horses bolted and ran, ours and Witters's. His horses ran to the right so I looked to the left of where they had been. There was movement in the small nest of rocks near the house. Now I knew where Witters had gone. I still didn't know where Ferguson was, but Cheryl had noticed that only Witters had a gun. That helped a little, but not much.

"Are you OK?" I asked Cheryl, lying half on top of her. It would have been a nice position under different circumstances. "Yes," she breathed in a low voice. "Can you move off me, I can hardly breathe." Oh, well, I thought it was a good position. I rolled to one side; Cheryl rolled over onto her stomach so she could see down the hill as well. As usual, my rifle had gone with the horses. So much for being a well-prepared law enforcement officer. The range was much too far for a pistol, mine or his. Should have thought of that before the horses all left. Getting off the horse probably fits in the same category as getting out of the patrol car, but too late now.

CHAPTER 33

Witters cursed his own stupidity. He hadn't tied the horses and his shots not only sent the horses running off, but his money was still with them. He had just thought to check out the deserted cabin when he had observed the horses moving on the mountain above. Even more stupidly, he had fired the remaining cartridges for the automatic. On foot, no ammunition and no money. Things were not going well.

If Jeremy Witters thought things were going badly, things were even worse for Davis Ferguson. Or at least, things had gone worse. It was over now. Lost and getting more confused and tired by the moment, Davis had slipped in the rocks and fallen into a deep ravine. He tried to crawl out, but the blinding snow and his weakened condition simply did not allow it. Davis Ferguson died from exposure to the wind and snow during the night. He slipped into a coma and never awoke.

Witters was a survivor. He accepted as a fact the money was gone. He didn't waste time looking for the money or trying to get a horse. He had all he could take of horses anyway. On foot he moved away from the cabin, using it to shield his movement from those on the hill. In short order, he made it to the tree line and moved through the woods to a game trail. He followed it for several miles until he came to a stream that Jeremy followed downhill. Without the money and short two partners, one he missed and one he was sorry he ever met, Witters steadily worked his way out of the mountains and back to civilization. Or at least as much civilization as you can find in that part of the west. Eventually, he made his way to a town and after making some collect telephone calls, got some help in getting out of the state.

Sheriff Flanigan and Carl reached town much more quickly than it took them to get up the mountains earlier. Even while being treated at the hospital, Big Tom set up the necessary coordination with Sheriff Les Bowdon. Les was the Sheriff of Canyon County and could come from the other side to go up and meet Jerry with whatever help he would need. It was frustrating to know Jerry was alone on the hill without help and not knowing what Cheryl's fate was to be. He did everything possible to get help on the way as quickly as it could be arranged.

The Sheriff from Canyon County, Les Bowdon, was every bit as competent as Big Tom. He likewise determined that the best course of action would be to send a mounted posse, just as Big Tom had done from the other side. His posse missed Jeremy Witters but was most pleased to find Jerry and Cheryl moving carefully down the mountain after having recovered the horses, and the money, but not Witters. Cheryl had actually caught their horses while Jerry moved down to the cabin. After ascertaining that Witters was gone, she and Jerry rode up to the other horses and grabbed the money carrying stead about a mile away. As is usual, after getting over their fright at the gunshots, the horses were grazing and easy to catch.

It took several days to wrap up everything on the mountain, no mean feat in itself. Ferguson was found by a group of hunters even before all the equipment was brought out of the wilderness area. The bank was happy, or at least the depositors, the banking commission and the Federal Deposit Insurance Corporation. Davis Ferguson's parents were deeply hurt and upset. They fussed and fumed at Big Tom for months after, insisting that Davis had been kidnapped by the robbers and was a victim, rather than a perpetrator. Money and power play a big part in the scheme of things and this time was no different. Most folks didn't know, nor care, what Davis Ferguson's role in the drama involved.

CHAPTER 34

I enjoyed the trip off the mountain. Cheryl was with me, and we could just ride along and be with each other. We went back the way we came. The weather was warm; we had the horses and just the two of us. We saw some of the same elk, or maybe they were different elk. We didn't care. It took only two days, and one too short night to come back to Caribou. It was great!

Les Bowdon, the Sheriff from Canyon County, had things well in hand when Cheryl and I left. He is one of those quiet, competent county Sheriffs like Big Tom. His team of deputies had already taken charge by the time we left, but we were both pleased to see him arrive. Witters had only been gone for a while when Les and his "posse" rode up to us. It was a good thing they were in the open cause I was really on edge and expecting another shot or something from Witters.

"Hello the camp," yelled one of Sheriff Bowdon's deputies. "Are you all right?" He rode up cautiously, but without pointing any guns at us.

"Yup," I replied. "Witters went that direction." I pointed out where he had gone.

Sheriff Bowdon pointed at two of his officers and commanded, "check it out." They rode off ready to do battle with Witters if they located him.

I didn't know about anyone else there, but I was weak with relief. It had been a long time, under a lot of pressure and worry, particularly about Cheryl. Now the pressure was off. I could unwind, and I did. I stood and shook for several minutes. Cheryl noticed and took me in her arms and held me. I was probably over my shakes long before I let go of her. That was when I started to relax, and get back into the proper mindset to finish up this case. Little did I know that it would be a long time to the end.

I checked the saddles, and after tightening up some cinches, Cheryl and I were ready to head back. Sheriff Bowdon had the bank money with his team, and I had horses to return to Carl Tafoya. Besides, I was looking forward to having Cheryl with me for the long ride back. I was really looking forward to it.

After helping Cheryl onto her horse, I stepped into the stirrups and swung into the saddle. It was starting to feel comfortable again. I was still worried about Witters being out there somewhere but didn't think he was anywhere close. I kept my eyes open anyway. You never can tell. I gathered up the lead rope from Les and led the way out of the open meadow where we had been operating.

"Thanks, Les, see you again sometime. Really appreciate your help", I told the Sheriff as Cheryl, and I started out.

"Any time," he replied. And with a wave from all of us, Cheryl and I were off for a long, lonely ride back to Caribou. Just the two of us, our horses and wild animals along the way. With a lot of luck, there wouldn't be the other wild animal, Witters.

The horses were panting hard by the time we gained the ridge, but not straining awfully hard. The creak of the saddle leather and the sound of the wind in the trees kept us company. Cheryl and I didn't talk much, just rode along side by side holding hands. It was a beautiful day! We ran into the elk herd about an hour after we started out. They were resting on the face of the mountain, lying down in the sage. When we rode up, they started getting up and slowly moving away from us. It was a pretty sight to see, more than a hundred elk moving up the mountain away from us, not in any real hurry, but covering a lot of ground in a hurry. We stopped and just watched them go, the warm sun on our backs making us lazy and contented to just be there.

"How far are we going today?" Cheryl asked.

"Just till late afternoon. We can stop early today and set up camp. There isn't any real rush. Tom won't expect us to move along very fast. The horses have been used hard. In fact, so have we. So I think we will set up early and maybe even get a late start in the morning.:

"Ok," Cheryl replied, squeezing my hand.

We stopped about four, after riding into a small clearing with a stream running through it. There was feed for the horses, water and a nice place to camp. I stepped out of the saddle, and my knees told me we had been riding long enough. I helped Cheryl down, and together we unloaded the pack horses. I stripped off the saddles and put them over a downed tree limb. Cheryl was already starting a fire by the time I finished staking out the horses. It wasn't much of a camp since we only had sleeping bags and what was left of the cooking supplies. I liked it. Cheryl was there.

Just my luck, the sleeping bags wouldn't zip together. Different brands. I was cussing out the situation when Cheryl pointed out that one of them was big enough for both of us, especially if the weather was cold. I hoped it was frigid.

After dinner, cold canned stuff, we crawled into the larger sleeping bag and cuddled. It was really nice. Even more comfortable than during the blizzard. And then I amazed myself. I didn't know I was going to say it until I did.

"Cheryl, would you marry me?" I whispered into her lovely ear.

"Sure, why not?" she laughed. Then a few minutes later she pulled me into her arms and kissed me hard. "Oh, yes, I will, I will."

"Good, it will save me a lot of commuting time," I laughed. That got me an elbow in the ribs. The question was only a formality though. I think both of us had known for quite some time that we belonged together. We kind of celebrated the honeymoon early.

The next morning dawned bright and cold. We missed most of it. By the time we got up, it was starting to warm. The horses were grazing on the meadow grass and were probably as content as we both were. I caught up the horses and brushed them down. The Bay horse the Sheriff had been riding seemed to be mine now, and he really liked the feel of the brush over his back. You could just see him bend with the brush as I rubbed him down. I put on blankets and saddles and cinched them loosely.

By the time I was done, Cheryl had fixed up something for breakfast. I don't remember what it was, as I was so involved with just being with her. We stepped onto our horses, and leading the pack horses; we set off down the other side of the mountain. It was a delightful day to ride. Nothing really to worry about, except a vague concern about where Witters might be, and the morning sun to warm our backs. It was a nice ride down the mountain to Caribou.

I gave a lot of thought to the past few days. Although I expected some help eventually, the sounds of the riders coming towards us yesterday spooked me a little. Didn't know if it was Witters, Ferguson, or what when I first heard the creak of saddles and the clop of horses coming up the trail. We holed up behind some boulders until we could tell who was coming. Then we carefully let them know we were there. For all I knew, they may have been shot at as well. They hadn't been. We hadn't seen any sign of Ferguson, and nothing of Witters since he last shot at us. I was getting tired of him taking shots at me. I thought about Witters and worried about his location all the way back down the mountain. I would have liked to locate Ferguson but wasn't worried about him like I did Witters.

The final mile into Caribou was anticlimactic. No one shot at us. We didn't chase anyone, and there wasn't anyone there to greet us. We were unsaddling the horses when Sheriff Flanigan drove up to the barn.

CHAPTER 35

"**G**lad to see you back," said the Sheriff. "I see, like usual, you took your own sweet time doing it.

"Less than two days, Sheriff. I think your own trip took longer than that as I recall from the radio messages," I replied.

Cheryl just gave Tom a big hug. "He doesn't have a good sense of time down does he, Sheriff?"

"Nope probably slacked off all the way back," the Sheriff commented.

"Well!" said Cheryl. "He had a lot of things on his mind. Oh, maybe he was just out of his mind, which would explain a lot. He proposed to me on the way back"

The Sheriff laughed, "what did he propose?"

"Well, he asked me to marry him. He hasn't backed out yet."

The Sheriff hugged Cheryl, then grabbed Jerry in a big bear hug. "Congratulations Jerry. This is just great! Just wait until Edna hears. She will be pleased. What a great outcome."

Larry and Ester, Cheryl's parents, didn't have a chance. Edna supervised all the details of the wedding, except that she called the Hefners once a day, the bride's parents and the adopted son's parents conspiring to make it a wedding worth remembering by the bride and groom. The wedding was set for June because that is when new brides get married and the heck with the groom's impatience.

Jerry spent the time in his patrol car.

The wedding was nice. I think. About all I remember was shaking hands with about everyone in Caribou at the reception. Didn't know so many people lived there. Finally, all the hands got shook, and we got away for the honeymoon. A short flight in the Cessna to Billings and then a longer trip through Salt Lake to San Francisco.

What a neat town. The city by the bay! You can see San Francisco, the bay and the ocean as the airliner lands several miles south of the city. You can see the Golden Gate Bridge, the Bay Bridge, and the skyline made familiar on many TV programs as the plane turns to base and final over the ocean to land at San Francisco International. It was hard not to try and fly the airplane down; I don't like being a passenger on a plane. Probably left footprints on the bulkhead trying to help the pilot land it.

There are people everywhere. Lots of slidewalks, the kind of flat escalators that move people in the airport. A flat moving surface that lets you walk twice as fast as you can walk. Makes it easy to cover a lot of distance. Cheryl was getting pretty good at it. Suddenly Jerry exclaimed, "that's Schrader and Weisberg!"

"Who are they?"

"Two of the guys from Vietnam. The one on the left is a guy from the ships, Bob Weisberg; he is a doctor. The other one is the Medical Service Corps Officer who handled some of the missions and worked for General Burks. I think he is going to Rucker. Hey! You two, assemble on me."

(Warrant Officers don't give orders to officers, but this was a whole new situation.)

"I'm not sure how to put this Doc," Bob said, poking Dr. W. on the arm. "That sure looks like a mission coordinator from a certain officer named Burks, who we didn't always want to show up."

"Mr. Burkley, is that you?" yelled Doctor W.

"Yes, sir!"

The three men ran together, hugged, and were introduced to Cheryl; then caught up on what the others had been doing. Information was eagerly exchanged:

"Rios got shot down twice while riding along on Dustoff missions."

"General Burks got his 3rd star."

"Rios is doing for General Burks what you were doing, Bob."

"Bill Jones bought the farm!"

"Flagg is flying for Southwest Airlines."

"The Benewah left for Subic Bay and the Colleton is back on the Mekong."

"Quincy made O-6 (Full Colonel) and has been given a new Aviation Battalion at Riley."

Cheryl was astonished and somewhat bewildered by the close association the three men displayed, and the rapid flow of information traded in acronyms and shorthand language she couldn't always decipher.

When the conversation slowed, all adjourned to the Mark Hopkins Hotel on California Street. They took the elevator to the iconic bar on the top floor, quaintly called the Top of the Mark. After some negotiation with the Maitre d, the men acquired "loaner" sports coats and ties so they would comply with the dress code. They were escorted to a table next to the window and ordered drinks.

"Do you have Famous Grouse?" Jerry asked.

"Of course Sir. We are a very high-class establishment."

The men all ordered Grouse on the rocks. Cheryl ordered Chablis, and the far-ranging discussion continued far into the evening. After dinner at The Montclair, an Italian Restaurant north of Broadway, where the waiters were all men in tuxedos and the atmosphere made you think 'Godfather' and expecting other Mafia figures to be in attendance in one of the curtain enclosed dining table areas. Stuffed with French bread, soup with cheese, antipasto, dinner and after dinner drinks, they separated and went back to their respective quarter with promises to stay in touch.

Jerry was somewhat surprised anyway when he got a call from Major Schrader a few months later. Lieutenant General Burks was still directing Jerry's future in ways Jerry didn't always appreciate.

"Jerry, Colonel Schrader. How's married life?"

"Pretty nice," Deputy Burkley responded, "I thought you were a Major, not a Colonel. Are you still in flight school?"

"Nope, graduated, got instrument and weather qualified; got promoted to telephone Colonel (a reference to the fact that over the telephone Lieutenant Colonels generally referred to themselves as Colonel). General Burks has me doing some errands for him."

"That can't be good news. Working for the General I mean. Congratulations on instrument weather and the promotion. That's good news! Why are you calling me?" Jerry demanded, concerned about why Schrader was calling and what the General might have in mind for him.

CHAPTER 36

Fighting broke out near a small town in a small country with no armed forces or even an efficient police department. The invaders were a well-armed insurgent army unit sent to overthrow the tiny country's government. Near the town was a medical school specializing in training doctors and nurses. The school was a target for the insurgents. Students were captured and held hostage.

Jerry reported to General Burks at his office in the Pentagon. He knocked and when was told to enter, walked in, closed the door, marched to the center front of General Burks' desk, saluted sharply, and announced, "Warrant Officer 4 Burkley reporting Sir!"

"At ease Jerry, have a chair."

"Thank you, sir. I think you have an assignment for me," Jerry blurted.

"Why do you think that?"

"Colonel Schrader called and told me to report to you."

"You are correct. I, indeed, do have a job for you. An essential job at that. I assume you are aware of the student hostage situation," the General stated.

"Yes Sir, that's all that is on the news."

"I need to know more about the situation on the ground, the conditions of the students, and also to have some electronics placed near the school."

"Sir, I only know what's in the news, and I know next to nothing about electronics."

"Not to worry son," General Burks smiled and said,

"I only want you to fly some people in and take a look around."

Sure thought Jerry, and personally carry all the students under my arms to my Medivac and fly them to safety. But he said, instead, "Ok Sir, what are my orders?"

"There are several:

1. Fly into safe proximity of the school.

2. Insert an Air Force Forward Air Control Team, who will install a laser landing system for C-130s near the school. Then you will extract them.

3. If possible, you and your crew are to recon the area around and in the school area for pertinent future mission information and requirements.

4. Return all personnel safely to CONUS (Continental United States). You may use your own discretion about the mission, but the Air Force mission is primary."

"Wow. I assume you want me to use the 1022nd Blackhawk, Rios and I flew here, but I will need more crew."

"Since you don't have a 1022nd crew here, except Rios, I have laid on a crew from 247th Med. You won't like the AC (aircraft commander), but it is the best I can do. Rios can go as a medic."

"Who is the AC?" Jerry requested?

"Major Moore," replied the General.

Oh, shit, Jerry thought, just what I need is old heavy hands, who can't find the airport with a map, or his six (reference to his posterior) with both hands and a flashlight. This could be a hairy mission. FUBAR (messed up beyond all recognition) before we even get off the ground. Jerry did what all good soldiers do. He said, "yes sir," and set off to do the best he could do to carry out his orders. Cowboys would have called it 'riding for the brand'. In Jerry's case, the brand was the United States Army, duty honor and country. Jerry and Rios went to the airfield, met the crew and began preparations for departure.

Jerry sat in the left seat of the Sikorsky LAH-60 Blackhawk, fastened his seat belts, put on his helmet, and began the pre-start checklist, flipping switches, setting instruments and radio frequencies with the assistance of Major Moore. Rios connected his helmet to the ship intercom system via a long cord which allowed him to move about inside and for a short distance outside the Blackhawk. He keyed the mic and reported, "crew strapped in, cargo secure, and ready." Others in the crew did the same. The Air Force FAC leader said they were also secured and good to go.

Jerry turned his communications switch to radio, and called ground control, "Andrews ground control, Cowboy two six, light on the skids and ready to move from transit rotary wing parking to active runway for departure."

"Cowboy two six, Andrews, Roger, low hoover to heli-pad approved. Contact tower with information Bravo." (Low hoover meant Jerry could lift the helicopter off the ground and move it to the helipad area. Information Bravo was the current information about weather, altimeter settings, and such).

Jerry called the tower when he reached the helipad and was cleared for departure. He increased power with one hand, changed pitch with the other, and used both feet to keep the helicopter correctly aligned (kind of like patting your head and rubbing your stomach circularly in one direction than reversing the direction for each hand in random intervals while tapping a foot.) He flew nose low until he gained speed then lifted up and turned to his departure direction. The flight lasted several hours and included two landings for fuel before they reached the school destination.

During the flight planning session for the mission, Jerry and Major Moore consulted with the Air Force FAC Team and studied the available charts for the best place to safely insert the FAC Team. Now Jerry was carefully maneuvering up a winding, unpopulated valley to the insertion point. He skill-fully landed. Rios and the rest of the crew assisted the FAC

Team to unload their equipment and phase one of Jerry's unorthodox mission was successfully completed.

Jerry once more put Cowboy two six in the air, without any radio transmissions to give away their position, and moved to a nearby mountain-side where they could both observe what was occurring, and would allow them to walk around the area, concealed from enemy (and friendly, for that matter) observation.

Jerry had a crew chief, two medics, CPT Rios, and Major Moore. Although Moore was the aircraft commander, and therefore the senior officer on the aircraft, Jerry, only a WO4 (probably equal pay to a Major, but not a Commissioned Officer as were Major Rios and Major Moore) was in charge. The General had put him in overall command of the operation. Jerry, as unorthodox as it was, commanded the mission. (Generally, Warrant Officers were in kind of a never-never land; they had all the rights and prerogatives of a Commissioned Officer and were treated as such by all enlisted soldiers, but had no command responsibilities.)

Jerry selected Rios, Moore, and one of the medics, Randy Billings, to go with him to recon, leaving the crew chief, Luther King, and a Combat Medic, Dale Steiner, to guard the Blackhawk and work the radio if necessary. Jerry didn't intend to get too far from them, since the successful completion of the mission, getting everyone safely home, largely depended on having the Blackhawk for transportation. Even with this restriction on his movement, he managed to place his three extra eyes in strategic locations. Each of them was equipped with a handheld radio which was encrypted to secure the privacy of their communications, as was Jerry. All could communicate with each other and the Huey. Jerry also had an encrypted channel allowing contact with the FAC Team. Leaving his crew members, Jerry walked though the medical school campus. It was empty. Not another person was present, no students, no soldiers, and no one! This worried

Jerry. He was aware the General would want to know where the students were being held.

"Cowboy 6 (the call assigned to Major Moore, the AC), Cowboy 5, (the call assigned to Jerry as the Pilot), I'm going to move into the town a few clicks and see if I can locate the students."

"5, 6, Roger. Any other orders Mister," the Major, obviously upset with the command chain as it was now set-up.

"No Sir. Please have all hold positions," Jerry carefully responded.

As Jerry encountered the town buildings, he observed a group, presumably the students, under the guard of several heavily armed troops. That's what I need to know, time to get out of here, Jerry told himself. He followed his own advice and made his way back to his Blackhawk, advising the rest of the crew by radio to do the same.

"Charlie-Charlie (the FAC Team), Cowboy 5, about ready to go?"

"Cowboy, ready to go."

"ETA. five mikes, (estimated time of arrival five minutes)," Jerry advised.

When Jerry got to the Blackhawk, Major Moore was not present. "Where's Moore?" Jerry asked the crew.

"We saw about a dozen insurgents on the way back, and he went into a concrete barn about 2 klicks back," Rios advised Jerry.

"Why are you here and he isn't?"

"We took cover, then crawled away. The Major wouldn't follow us," SPC4 Billings stated with contempt in his voice. The insurgents weren't ever a problem as long as we stayed concealed."

"Ok, you all wait here. Get the blades turning. I'll be back as soon as I can get Moore rounded up."

Jerry saw Major Moore and called to him. Moore ducked behind a short wall and curled up in a fetal position. "Moore, come on, we need to go. Come with me to the chopper".

Moore eased himself from behind the wall, looked warily about, and then fell to the ground. Jerry heard the gunshot at the same time. A lone soldier, with a rifle held to his shoulder, was trying to chamber another round. Jerry pulled a .45 Pistol from his holster and fired several semi-automatic rounds at the solder. One of them hit a vital point; the soldier dropped.

Jerry hurried to Major Moore but discovered there was no pulse. He dragged the Major to the wall, got him in a standing position, the dead (literally) weight hard to maneuver, and got the Major in a fireman's carry. He was struggling to get to the chopper when Rios and the crew chief arrived to assist. They got Moore's body into an olive drab body bag, zipped it closed and onto the chopper. Jerry strapped into the AC's seat and got them airborne in short order. He was able to successfully extract Charlie-Charlie Team. WO4 Burkley ordered one of the FAC (Forward Air Controllers) into the Pilot's chair, swiftly lifted off, and turned the helicopter towards safety.

When the FAC put on a headset and indicated he was on the intercom, Jerry told him, "Put the radio on the command frequency, and advise our situation."

"What is our situation, Sir?'

"Sorry, forgot you just got on board. One U.S. KIA, all on board, mission successful. RTB (return to base)."

SSG Kline, the FAC, complied, and gave Jerry a thumbs-up. Jerry could monitor the transmissions, but needed both hands to fly the Blackhawk.

Safety was a long time in coming. Several kilometers from take-off Cowboy Two Six flew over a company of insurgents. The combined rifle shots hit and disabled the Cowboy Two Six Blackhawk. Jerry managed to fly the crippled helicopter over the hill, and away from the insurgent troops before he had to auto-rotate. When the chopper hit the ground, slowed somewhat by the autorotation maneuver, it rolled to the right and pinned Jerry between the door and his armored chair, then continued over to leave all the doors exposed.

Rios was the first to recognize Jerry was hurt. "Medics, attend the AC, now!"

They complied, and the entire crew and the FAC's struggled to free Jerry, remove him from the crippled medivac, and get him laid out in a secure place on the ground. Rios, who had been on the Benewah and learned a lot from observing the surgeons and the medics began working on Jerry. The FACs set up a security perimeter. The Crew Chief scrounged equipment from the crashed helicopter and prepared the Blackhawk to be destroyed by thermite grenades. (The aircraft would be valuable to the insurgents, and it wasn't going to be left intact.)

Jerry had a massive and deep cut on his right upper arm. Rios cleaned the wound as well as possible with the supplies in the field medic pack and using a suture kit carefully closed the incision with precise sutures. The two medics then dressed and bandaged the wound, arranged a sling, and then helped Rios get Jerry back to his feet.

"Now what, Mr. Burkley?" asked SSG King respectfully.

"Now we walk. The map indicates the LZ is in that direction," Jerry said looking at both his topographical map and a military compass he had been carrying on a pouch on his belt.

"Torch the bird and let's go," ordered Jerry.

Once again the military chain of command was ignored. Major Rios outranked Jerry, but Jerry had been the officer in command and the others respected his ability to lead. The explosion of the thermite grenades, the heat, and glare from the burning helicopter gave them the incentive to move quickly out of the area. They knew the insurgents would hear and probably see the explosion and would be coming that way. Jerry led the small group into a gulley that wound upward. SSG Kline was busy on the radio. "Mr. B. There is a Jolly Green (an Air Force Rescue Helicopter), supported by some Fast Movers (Jet Fighter Planes) coming our way."

The entire group started grinning and began to prepare for pickup. MAJ Moore's body bag was ready for pickup by a winch to the Jolly Green if it couldn't land at the LZ. The designated LZ was 2 klicks west. The team quickly moved to the location and started to prepare the LZ for the pick-up. A few trees were tall enough and close enough to cause helicopter problems. SSG King and SSG Kline wrapped det-cord, a rope-like explosive around each tree, the number of wraps determined by the size of the tree trunk. A detonator was attached to each and hooked to a switch that would make the det-cord explode and cut the tree trunk in two, clearing the LZ for landing.

When the sounds of the rotor blades were heard, Jerry ordered, "cut the trees." The cords exploded, and the trees fell as planned. The large Helicopter was able to land, get everyone loaded, and out of the area as the fast movers begin dropping ordinance (bombs) on the approaching insurgents.

CHAPTER 37

NOBODY CARES!

**NOBODY CARES,
NOBODY,
THEY JUST USE ME
AND THEY DON'T CARE HOW I FEEL.
THEY BREAK MY HEART IN TWO,
BUT THEY DON'T CARE.
WHY CAN'T THEY CARE FOR ME,
I'M ONLY HUMAN
AND I NEED SOMEONE TO CARE FOR ME,
BUT NOBODY CARES.
NOBODY!**

* Anonymous

"Great job Jerry," said General Burks, "you, your crew, the FACs and the rescue crews did extremely well. Because of your efforts, all the student and staff hostages were freed. Some of them didn't believe anyone cared about them. Turns out your team, rescue crews, and the President did care!"

"So did you, Sir," Jerry pointed out. "You put this operation together and made it work. Does someone care enough to get me out of this hospital and back to Wyoming?"

"What does Dr. Weisberg say?"

"He says I am ready for discharge, but since he is only the Flight Surgeon for 1022nd Medical Helicopter Company, and a Doctor with Caribou Hospital, he doesn't have admitting or discharge authority at this facility."

"Ok, I'll see what I can do," promised General Burks. "Take care, and I will be seeing you."

"As long as it isn't another job like this one, I would look forward to seeing you and Mrs. Burks," said Jerry, part joking and part solemn.

The geese were circling high above Caribou. They were beautiful, almost all making goose noise, and almost flying in a Y, rather than a V, as they lined up to land on the lake. Dr. Robert Weisberg and WO4 Berkley had flown from the military hospital to Cheyenne in a new UH-60 replacement for the 1022nd Blackhawk destroyed in Jerry's last mission. From Cheyenne, the Wyoming Air National Guard, both as a courtesy to the 1022nd, and as an add-on to a 187th Aeromedical Evacuation Squadron training mission, flew the two returning combat officers to Caribou. "Look at the geese, Doc," said Jerry, pointing to the circling birds.

"Awesome, good to be back home!'

Sheriff Flannigan was parked next to the active runway with two deputies in another car to handle their luggage. "Hi, boys, nice to see you back. Doc, do you need Jerry, or can I finally have him back?"

"Oh, you can have him, Sheriff. He is fit to work again, and I am tired of his oft-repeated jokes, especially those he makes up on the spot."

"Yup, I've traveled with him before," the Sheriff responded.

Doctor W's wife, Bonnie, was there to pick him up, and after everyone greeted and chatted for a while, she drove him off.

"Hop in Jerry," the Sheriff said, pointing at his cruiser which had its lights flashing to indicate he was on official business on the airport runways. "We can run over to the office, and I'll bring you up to date."

ORDERS EXTRACT
(Multiple Commands)

Burks, John R., Retired as General (o-10); Transferred in grade to Ready Reserve [General Officer]; proceed to Home of Record: Pauls Valley, OK, For Discharge United States Army.

Schrader, Robert W., Colonel (06); Transferred in grade to Ready Reserve,[Field Grade Officer]; proceed to Home of Record, Cheyenne, WY, for Discharge United States Army.

Rivera, Rios NMI: Major (04): Transferred in grade to Ready Reserve [Field Grade Officer]; proceed to Home of Record, Casa Grande, AZ, for Discharge (Honorable), United States Army.

Sheriff Tom continued, "We have made a few changes since you left Jerry," pointing at a chart on the wall across from his desk.

SHERIFF TOM FLANNIGAN
UNDERSHERIFF – JERRY R. BURKLEY
CAPTAIN – RIOS RIVERA

LIEUTENANT #1	*LIEUTENANT #2*	*LIEUTENANT #3*
Mick Nicholson	*Joe Pawlik*	*Sid Koslowski*
(0800 – 1600)	*(1600-2400)*	*(2400-0800)*

SERGEANT #1	*SERGEANT #2*	*SERGEANT#3*
Fred Carson	*Casey Brown*	*Don Fredericks*

CHIEF OF RESERVE DEPARTMENT
Lieutenant Robert W. Schrader
DEPARTMENT MEDICAL OFFICER
CPT Robert Weisberg, D.O.

"We also have a new deputy. Her name is officially Carlita Christina Camino, but she goes by Chris Roads. Camino is Spanish for Road. I looked up the meaning of Carlita. In Spanish it means 'manly,' a leader, rather than a follower, resents authority, unique, creative and stubborn, bored and inpatient. I think she may fit the definitions. Anyway, she is going to be called Chris."

"What's her background?" Jerry asked, more interested in facts than what her name meant, the one she wasn't going to be using anyway.

"She is a qualified EMT, volunteers for the Ski Patrol at Banner Ski Area, and was an Ag Teacher before she got a divorce and came to us. She is a friend of the Sheriff's wife and was recommended by Schrader. Oh, yeah, her uncle was a cop killed on duty with the Casa Grande PD."

"Sounds solid. Where is Roads assigned?"

"I put her on swings with SGT Brown. You can reassign if necessary."

"Joe and Casey will give her good training. Anything else, I want to get home to Cheryl."

"Nope," Sheriff Flannigan smiled, "you might as well get on home. Your car is on the lot."

Jerry drove home, just a little over the speed limit. He gathered Cheryl into his arms and kissed her for a long time. Dinner was slightly delayed that evening.

"Roads, get in here," Lieutenant Joe Pawlik said, waving at her from his office door. "Sergeant Brown, I need you too."

Both Deputies entered the Lieutenant's office, sat down on the two visitors chairs facing the Lieutenant's deck, and awaited his orders. "What's up Boss?" Sergeant Brown asked.

"Deputy Roads has just returned from the Academy (The Wyoming Law Enforcement Academy at Douglas, Wyoming).

She graduated, not sure how! She managed to pass everything and graduated second in her class. Congratulations Chris! You did well! Do you think you are ready to work in a patrol car?"

"You bet, Yes Sir!" Chris exclaimed.

"Good," Lieutenant Pawlik responded. "Sergeant Brown will be your field training officer. He's been there, done that, and is a street-wise deputy. Listen to what he tells you. She's all yours, Casey."

Thanks, Boss." Just what I need, thought Casey, a rookie to train. "Let's go Rookie."

Sergeant Brown took Roads to the Patrol Briefing Room. "Looks like either the Academy or the Lobotomy (what the trainees called the bar in the Labonte Hotel in downtown Douglas) trained you well. What are you carrying?"

Chris assumed he meant what weapon and replied, "Model 19 Smith and Wesson, 4-inch barrel."

"That's a start, what else are you carrying?"

"Handcuffs, .357 shells in a speed loader, mace, a Keli-Lite 5 cell law enforcement flashlight instead of a nightstick, a Motorola brick (two-way handheld radio), cuffs, car keys, and a citation book."

"And."

"And a Sig Sauer P-238."

Sergeant Brown continued his questioning. "Why carry a Keli-Lite flashlight, it's pretty heavy?"

Chris explained, "I can hold it in my hands, and no one gets upset like they would if I held a nightstick that way. The stick is offensive, the flashlight is just a flashlight, except it is heavy and can be used as a stick or a light."

"Great! Explain the Sig."

"It has a six round magazine with rounds that are almost .38's. It is light and easy to carry concealed."

"I might have made some different choices, but yours are fine. Go check my Pontiac out of the motor pool, run a pre-patrol checklist, and pick me up at the front door in 15 minutes."

"Jerry," called Sheriff Tom. "Would you like to have a Jet Ranger?"

"What?" Jerry replied, not sure he was hearing the Sheriff correctly.

Sheriff Tom leaned back against the counter, made flying movements with his hands and arms, and repeated his earlier question, "do you want a Jet Ranger (a civilian helicopter similar to the military Huey)?"

"Sure, I would like a new Cessna Citation too!"

"Can't do the Citation, but I have a grant for a helicopter, and there is a Jet Ranger available in Buffalo. The owner of the flying service is upgrading and is willing to make a good deal for law enforcement on the sale of the Ranger."

"Great!" Jerry grinned. "When do I leave?"

"You can take Schrader if you want to let him fly it back. If you want to fly the Jet Ranger, take Camino, I mean Roads. She has a commercial pilot's license."

Jerry pointed a finger at Sergeant Brown and said, "Let me borrow your Rookie for a while."

Sergeant Brown, who had been clued in by the Sheriff, grinned and said, "Sure Jerry!"

Undersheriff Burkley directed Roads to his patrol car and drove to Caribou Air Field. The Cessna 206 was on the pad west of the hangar. After Chris and Jerry performed a comprehensive preflight check (Jerry hadn't seen the plane, much less flown it in several months and he wanted to ensure everything had been repaired and was up to his standards), Jerry took Chris by the arm and pointed to the left seat. Chris climbed into the command pilot position and fastened her seat belt. Jerry joined her in the right side co-pilot seat. The checklist went smoothly and quickly. Soon the six place plane was pointed towards Buffalo.

The Bell 505 Jet Ranger was in impeccable condition with low hours on the engine. There were dual instrument and radio systems. In other words, it was perfect for the Banner County Sheriff's Office. Search and rescue, medical evacuation, transportation, and transfer of people and equipment, as well as many other uses, could be utilized by the Department. Jerry thought it would be a perfect partner for the fixed-wing Cessna 206. He called the Sheriff on his cell, got approval for the major purchase. Jerry sent Chris back to Caribou in the 206. The fixed base operator completed the paperwork to sell the helicopter to Banner County and Jerry signed the grant papers to authorize payment.

It was a great solo flight back to Caribou. Jerry thought about an excuse to take Cheryl up in the new addition to the Banner County Sheriff's Office. He was pleased to discover Chris, Rios and the Chief of the Reserve Department, Bob Schrader, a former military fling wing (rotary wing or helicopter) pilot, who was the third pilot in the department, were waiting to help hangar and admire the Jet Ranger. Bob was drooling over the new Ranger. Jerry promised him a check ride in the morning. The chopper and the 206 were carefully hangered by the three pilots

Rios notice the new Deputy right away. She was cute, especially in her uniform, gun belt and wearing a badge. Not many cute women wearing a badge! Rios was to later learn Carlita was as tough as she was cute. Rios was single, and so was Chris, but he was not only her supervisor, number 3 in the chain-of-command, but she was the newest and first female Deputy in Banner County's history. He thought about this dilemma as he drove to Caribou Air Field to pick up Chris and help her hangar the 206.

"Hi, I'm Captain Rivera," he announced as if Chris couldn't tell from his uniform. "I'm your Patrol Supervisor, your ride to the SO (Sheriff's Office), and your helper to hangar '33SD' (the registration number painted on the tail of the Cessna 206)."

"Pleased to meet you, Sir," smiled Chris as she tossed her hair back. "I appreciate the ride and the help. Sheriff Tom briefed me on the staff assignments, made me feel like I already know you."

"Well, I hope to get to know you better!" said Rios as he simultaneously realized he meant to meet this goal.

CHAPTER 38

D r. Weisberg and Jerry were enjoying lunch when Rios and Schrader came rushing in and loudly announced, "The General is running for the United States Senate in Oklahoma!"

"He would be a good one," Dr. W. opined.

"Yup, but we're in Wyoming, so not much we can do about it," Jerry said as he bit into his hamburger."

"True," said an excited Rios, "but it's going to cost the Department a Reserve Deputy!"

"Who?" inquired Jerry.

"That one," Rios said, pointing at Bob.

"Why?"

"The Old Man asked me to serve as his Chief-of-Staff," advised Bob. "He is unopposed, will win in November, and Betty and I are moving to D.C."

HEADLINES FROM CARIBOU BULLETIN

- ROBERT SCHRADER JOINS SENATOR'S STAFF
- SHERIFF TOM TO RETIRE – BURKLEY TO RUN
- NEW SHERIFF IN BANNER COUNTY
- TRUCK DRIVERS STRIKE
- DEPUTY CRASHES PATROL CAR DURING CHASE

Roll Call was almost over when Lieutenant Pawlik announced, "Deputy Roads, you are with Sergeant Brown tonight. He will administer your final field training test, and if you pass you will be in a solo car next shift."

Applause from the other Deputies made Chris blush. She was finally going to be a fully qualified Banner County Deputy.

Sergeant Brown brought Chris back to earth. "Well Deputy, get my patrol car ready and then meet me in the Lieutenant's office."

Chris completed her check of Sergeant Brown's car and almost ran to Lieutenant Pawlik's office. She was anxious to get her final Field Training Test behind her. "Your car awaits Sergeant Brown. All checked, all equipment in place and ready to go!"

"Thanks, Chris, but there may be a slight delay before we can go on patrol. Lieutenant Pawlik has some reservations about some of your training," SGT Brown said, his eyes avoiding Chris.

"Sadly, Chris, that is where I stand. You have had some problems during training that bring into question your qualifications for being a Deputy Sheriff in this County," advised Joe.

Chris was dejected and completely depressed by this turn of events. "What did I do wrong? I've done my very best in every assignment." She felt she was about to cry.

Joe eased Chris's worries somewhat, "Casey and I both feel you have worked hard and deserve full qualified status, but I do have some concerns. We can go talk to the Sheriff and see what he wants done, after all, it is his decision. We all need to go over to the Sheriff's Office."

Lieutenant Pawlik led the way to Sheriff Burkley's new office. The new office was necessary because Big Tom was officially "Consultant" to the Sheriff. Tom keep his old office, and new space was constructed for Jerry. Actually, Sheriff Burkley's new office was his old Lieutenant's office with some expansion to make it more serviceable as a public access administrative office.

Jerry Burkley, the newly elected Banner County Sheriff, was seated behind his desk. Three chairs had been placed before his desk. Chris was sitting in the middle chair with LT Pawlik and SGT Brown on either side (kind of like guards, body-guards or bookends).

"Chris," Sheriff Burkley solemnly intoned, "there are some concerns about all the negative publicity the Sheriff's Department received in the newspaper involving you. First, there was the incident with a car chase which ended with you driving Sergeant Brown's patrol car into the rear of the car you were chasing. It was a spectacular ending to a routine traffic stop. Do you have any comment?"

"Yes Sir, the perpetrator had run four traffic lights and six stop signs at a fairly high rate of speed. He was a danger to everyone on the road. At the end, he slammed on his brakes and stopped dead in the middle of the road. I just couldn't get the car stopped in time to avoid hitting him."

Jerry looked at Casey. "Sergeant you were in the car too. What do you have to offer?"

"Sheriff, there wasn't anything she could have done differently. If I had been driving, I probably would have hit him too. She did everything she could afterward, checking on everyone's physical condition, arresting the perp, giving him his rights from a Miranda Card, and getting him booked into the jail."

"Was there anything she could have done, but didn't?"

"She should have written one more traffic citation."

LT Pawlik interjected, "For what violation?"

SGT Brown laughed, "Stopping too fast for conditions."

This got a chuckle from everyone, even Chris.

"OK," Jerry said, "that might be acceptable. On the other hand, there is the trucker situation! Chris, you got to respond to the 911 truck call. What happened there?"

"Well, we were briefed at roll call that there was a national trucking company on strike and only supervisors were to respond to any calls regarding them unless additional back-up was requested by the supervisor. Sergeant Brown and I received a radio call from dispatch advising a fight at the State

Motor Vehicle Check Station was in progress. When Sergeant Brown and I arrived, we discovered a union trucker and an independent trucker were arguing and fighting. The union trucker believed the independent trucker was a 'scab' (a non-union member doing a striking union member's job). It turned out the independent had purchased a used truck from the national trucking company, and it still had that paint pattern. The union guy thought he was a strikebreaker. That's when the fight broke out."

"That's right Sheriff," said SGT Brown. "You and Tom were there. The problem came up when the union guy tried to slug Tom. It took five of us to get him arrested and into the patrol car. The problem wasn't him, or Chris though. It was the guy's wife."

"True story," said Joe, "the wife raised a fuss at the SO (Sheriff's Office) and demanded access. Tom told her no way. She said she paid taxes and had the right to be there. Tom threw her a quarter and told her that was a refund of any taxes she may have paid in Wyoming. The newspaper headline the next morning was 'Sheriff Calls Woman Two-Bit Whore!'. Chris helped defuse the publicity in an interview where she defended Tom and explained the facts."

"Very good. That was kind of the way I remembered it too. Chris, you handled both situations calmly and professionally. Both Joe and Casey have recommended waiving your final training test and giving you fully qualified Deputy status."

Chris thought I'm not toast! "Why did you make me feel like I failed?"

"Part of it is tradition. It makes the presentation that follows more meaningful for the recipient. It also makes you mindful of the awesome responsibility you are undertaking as a law-enforcement officer in this Department. We want you to always be cognizant of your duty to the job and the people we protect," Jerry pontificated. "Joe, will you and Casey do the honors." It was an order, not a request.

Sergeant Brown announced, "Deputy Camino, sorry Roads, congratulations, you are now assigned Banner County Badge C-40, which is also your radio call-sign."

Lieutenant Pawlik presented Chris a badge with both her name and her badge number inscribed upon it. "Wear it proudly, and carefully."

"Ok Chris, get on patrol. Your car is on-the-lot. It has your number painted on the left rear. Be careful and have a good evening," said Jerry.

Chris was floating on air. It had been an interesting and memorable experience.

"Sheriff, important call on 5," shouted his secretary.

Jerry picked up his phone and punched 5. "Burkley."

"Jerry, this is Les Bowdon."

"Hi Les, what's up?"

"I think two of my deputies may have located our mutual friend, Jeremy Witters."

Jerry's heartbeat got faster, "When, where?"

"There is a cabin on the Canyon County/Banner County border up north. My Deputies think he is holed up there, and on foot."

"What kind of access is there?"

"Air, horse, or on foot. Can't even get four-wheelers through some of that timber. Kind of reminds me of where we left off," Les commented.

"I'll get my guys ready and fly over in the Ranger. Should be at your airport in about 25-30 minutes."

"See you soon. Thought you might be interested."

"Thanks, Les, I am. Maybe together we can get this guy!"

Jerry called in all his supervisors, both on and off duty. "Gentlemen, Bowdon's Deputies may have located Witters. I am going to fly over and meet Les to start coordination. We may be able to capture Witters. Rios has the basic information and will brief you. I want a command post here at the Sheriff's Office and a mobile unit that can be loaded on a plane or horses. We may have to do some walking too, depending on how events shape up. Please get everything organized. I am authorizing you to call in both off-shift and off-duty officers as necessary. We need to be able to continue day-to-day operations and have people in the field. It may stretch us some, but I know we can do it. Rios, see what kind of support we can get from PD (Caribou Police Department), WHP (Wyoming Highway Patrol), and Guts and Feathers (Wyoming Game and Fish Department). Keep me updated."

Jerry jammed his hat on his head, turned and ran to his Patrol Car. Within the ETA (estimated time of arrival) he had given to Les Bowdon, Jerry landed the Banner County Jet Ranger and met with Les. The two Sheriffs agreed on a coordinated approach to the area where Witters had last been seen, and planned methods to cut off any escape in any direction.

Jerry flew 3320SD, the Department's new Jet Ranger, back to Caribou Air Field. At the SO he discovered former Sheriff Big Tom Flannigan busy organizing the dispatch/command center and helping Undersheriff Rivera orient everyone. "Hey Tom, how are we doing?" said Jerry."

"Bout done; coming together well. Schrader has all the Reserve Deputies on deck, except for two. One is sick, and one is out of the area. Schrader and Camino are taking care of Aviation. Tafoya has horses ready. Shifts have been adjusted so we can fully cover normal operations and jail requirements."

"Overtime might be outrageous," the Undersheriff commented, "but it is manageable."

"Great," praised the Sheriff. He went on to bring everyone up to date. "We will use the mutual aid radio frequency for the

Witters operation. That will allow everyone in both departments, including Patrol and Jail, to monitor progress and changing requirements. Patrol and Jail frequencies for both Departments will be open for regular communications.. Both our aircrafts are equipped to use Mutual Aid. Former Sheriff Flannigan will be 'Sierra 1'. All others will use badge number call with a county prefix. For instance, I am 33C1. Sheriff Bowdon is 26C1.

Sheriff Bowdon has already started a horseback patrol south towards us. We will prepare a horseback patrol but hold in place until after we have done air surveillance of the area. Lieutenant Schrader and I will fly the Jet Ranger. Deputy Camino will fly the Cessna. Undersheriff Rivera will fly with her as an observer. She will be the Aircraft Commander in charge of decisions regarding aircraft operations. When Witters is located, and he shall, an assessment of options will be made. One options is to bring many officers in on horseback and surround him. Another option, and one Sheriff Bowdon and I favor, is to deploy Deputies from the Jet Ranger and perhaps from an Army Guard Blackhawk to surround and capture Witters. We have made a formal request to the Wyoming Army National Guard for support, and have been informed two helicopters are being sent from Cheyenne to assist. The only downside is the travel time from there to here.

Supervisors have copies of the mission orders and will complete individual briefings."

The meeting broke up. The pilots and those assigned to the air insertion mission were quickly transported to the Air Field. Equipment and personnel were loaded.

"Charlie 40, Charlie 1. What do you observe?"

"Just coming over the ridge. The cabin is in sight. Rios, sorry, C-2 observed tracks around the cabin, and one set from the north,and one set to the west."

"Ok, Bob and I will come around and move towards you from the west going east. We are over Granite Peak right now. There is a valley that leads up to your location." Jerry thought that is probably ideal for Witters. He can move down the valley from the cabin with an almost easy walk out. Or it would be easy if there wasn't so much snow.

"Got him," Schrader shouted, "up under that scrawny lodge pole just under the ridge!"

"Yup," Jerry observed, looking intently through his field glasses, "that's him." " Joe," the Sheriff said pointing at LT Pawlik, and then his headset, "you, Fred, Casey, and Don will come with me. Bob, put us down about a klick above Witters. When we unload, go get another field team. Charlie 40, assist 26C1 to move as many of his people as you can to the Forest Service Corrals at Tie Camp."

Deputies were deployed, the aircraft hustled on their assignments and the capture was almost anti-climactic. Witters was still under the scrawny tree. He was wrapped in a tarp and sound asleep. He had no weapon and was suffering from exhaustion. After a careful check, Jerry pulled Witters to his feet and cuffed his hands behind him.

Les Bowdon arrived on Schrader's second flight into the area. Jerry and Les took great pride in having captured the bank robber/kidnapper and were quite pleased to see their Deputies thoroughly check Witters for weapons and contraband, load him into the Jet Ranger and transport him to the Banner County Jail.

CHAPTER 39

PRESIDENT ENDORSES SHERIFF FOR RE-ELECTION

PRESIDENT BURKS NOMINATED FOR SECOND TERM

BANK ROBBER/KIDNAPPER CAPTURED BY SHERIFF
- NOT GUILTY PLEA
- JURY TRIAL DEMANDED

HOSPITAL CHIEF OF STAFF WEISBURG RETIRES

SHERIFF'S OFFICE ROMANCE = MARRIAGE
- UNDERSHERIFF AND CHIEF DEPUTY WED
- PRESIDENT PERFORMS WEDDING

POSTHUMOUS MEDAL OF HONOR FOR VIETNAM PILOT

"Sheriff, phone for you on one," his secretary announced. "Thanks," Jerry picked up the phone and said, "Sheriff Burkley."

"Good morning, Sheriff. My name is Pruter. I'm with the Secretary of the Army's office in Washington, D.C., I'm trying to located Warrant Officer 4 Jerry Burkley, Colonel Robert A. Weisburg, and some others who were with Chief Warrant Officer Burkley in Vietnam."

"Interesting. What did you say was your name?"

"I'm Colonel Don Pruter. I am Chief-of-Staff for the Secretary of the Army."

"I'm Jerry Burkley. I am a Warrant Officer 5. I served in Vietnam with the 191st Assault Helicopter Company and some missions for your Boss's Boss, then Major Burks. He has my number, so I'm not too hard to find. I am also the Sheriff here. What can I do for you?"

"Thank you, Sheriff. I'm just using the information I was given from the files. Sorry I didn't make the connection. You, your wife, and Colonel Weisburg, and others are being invited to the White House to attend a presentation of the Medal of Honor to Warrant Officer 3 William H. Jones."

"That is fantastic, and long past due. Dr. Weisburg is in my Reserve Department. I can get that message to him. Who else are you looking for?"

"A Major Moore, a Warrant Officer Rivera, Bob Schrader, and Dan McKane. I understand all of them served with him."

"Moore bought the farm (got killed) in a Desert Storm mission. Rivera works for me. I don't know McKane's location. Colonel Robert Schrader was the President's Chief of Staff when he was a Senator and for part of his first term as President. Bob is Chief of my Reserve Department so I can also let him know," replied Jerry.

"Thank you, Sheriff. If you could provide me with address or contact information, I will see that invitations are promptly sent by the Secretary of the Army," Colonel Pruter smoothly closed.

"I will, and thanks for the information. Bill was a great friend, a good soldier and a solid pilot. I would be pleased to be present when he receives the Medal." He hung up, feeling a warm feeling for his old friend.

"Sara," he called to his secretary. "I need you to send some information to the Pentagon."

**THE PRESIDENT
OF THE UNITED STATES
OF AMERICA**

JOHN R. BURKS

~

**REQUESTS YOUR
ATTENDENCE IN THE
WHITE HOUSE ROSE GARDEN
FOR THE PRESENTATION OF THE
MEDAL OF HONOR
TO**

~

**WILLIAM H. (BILL) JONES
Warrant Officer 3
United States Army**

[Formal attire; military or civilian]

Enclosed with the invitation were the time, date, and directions to the Rose Garden. Access passes were also enclosed. Jerry heard from everyone who received the elegantly engraved cards, not in the U.S. Mail, but hand delivered by Deputy United States Marshals from the Cheyenne Office of the U.S. Marshals Service. This was a special event, and President Burks wanted everyone to recognize the distinction. The President had known Bill personally, and they had worked together several times. The invitees were aware of the Sheriff's Vietnam service and that Bill and Jerry had been roommates who flew missions as a team. They weren't all aware of Bill's total devotion to duty!

Bill's wife Kathleen, her three children and four grandchildren were the first notified. The President appeared at Kathleen's front door of her home near Oracle, Arizona. "Mrs. Jones, my name is Burks, John R. I would like to consult with you on a matter of importance."

Kathleen immediately recognized the President. "Please come in Mr. President. What can I do for you? Would you like a cup of coffee?"

Kathleen opened the door wider and gestured for the President to enter. His Secret Service agents slipped between Kathleen and the President, casually checking out the situation inside the house. Finding all was secure, led the President into the Jones home. "Please excuse my detail. They have their jobs to do and weren't able to do it in advance as they normally would. I would love some coffee if you will allow my staff to serve us while we talk (the President having already been briefed, Mrs. Jones was alone in the home)."

"Of course, let's sit on the couch."

After they were settled on the couch and served coffee from an Air Force One (the Presidential Airplane) thermos in Kathleen's cups, the President told Kathleen the reason for his visit. "Kathleen. May I call you Kathleen?"

"Of course, Mr. President."

"Good! I first met Bill when he and Jerry Burkley reported to Rucker for WOC Flight Training class. I helped them move their contraband refrigerator into WOC quarters. Bill was a brave, no-nonsense pilot. In Vietnam, he volunteered for many life-saving missions, not his job to perform. The last cost him his life. He gave all for his fellow soldiers."

"I know that Sir," Kathleen said with tears running down her face."

President Burks handed her his handkerchief. "I'm sorry, I didn't mean to make you cry. My mission today is to honor Bill. May I have your permission to upgrade his award of the Distinguished Service Cross (the second highest valor award given to soldiers) he was awarded earlier with the Medal of Honor?"

"Yes, yes! He was recommended for the Medal at the time you know!"

"I do. The award of the Distinguished Service Cross has

been upgraded to the Medal of Honor. I would like to present it to you, your children and grandchildren, in Bill's honor in a White House Rose Garden Ceremony. You and the children would be flown from Davis Monthan Air Force Base at Tucson to Andrews Air Force Base and would stay at the White House with my wife, Rose, and me overnight before returning. This is a list of people I want to invite." The President handed her a short list typed on a slip of paper with the Presidential logo engraved at the top. "Do you have any additions or deletions?"

After perusing the short list, Kathleen pointed out, "Dan McKane was killed during an airshow accident two or three years ago."

"Sorry to hear that. Good man, great pilot."

"I hope all the rest can be there," Kathleen said, handing the paper back to President Burks. "They were all Bill's friends."

Jerry got telephone calls from SGT Billings and SSG Satterfield expressing happiness that Bill was finally going to get the Medal. Jerry spoke for a long time with each. Billings had remained on active duty as an Army medic and retired as a Master Sergeant (MSG). He was now living in Billings, Montana. "Great," said Jerry. "just what Montana needs is a Billings living in Billings." They made arrangements to get together in Caribou. "I'm flying several of us to D.C., so plan on going along."

"Thanks sir, will do."

SSG Albert Satterfield was discharged from the Army at the end of his Vietnam tour of duty. He and two other door gunners channeled their interest in weapons in aviation into a very successful business, United Firearms, which developed and sold helicopter mounted automatic weapons to the U.S. Military. Al Satterfield was now the President and Chief

Executive Officer of the Company. He was living in Maryland, not far from Washington, D.C., where he lobbied Congress on behalf of his company. They agree to meet before the White House ceremony. Jerry finally assembled the remaining invitees, all of whom either worked for Banner County Sheriff's Department or had a close connection. They were Bob Schrader and his wife Betty, Rios Rivera and his wife Chris Roads, Dr. Bob Weisberg and his wife, Bonnie, and Jerry's wife, Cheryl. All were friends and were chatting excitedly about the D.C. trip. Jerry leaned back against a table at the front of the room and looked at the seven smiling faces. "For a change, I have some good news about death." As you know, Bill Jones is getting the Medal. President Burks is going to present it. Bill was nominated in-country for the award, but it was downgraded to the Distinguished Service Cross. Burks got it upgraded back to the Medal of Honor. Most everyone who was involved with Operation Freedom Win in the Cam Son Secret Zone with us will be there. Major Quincy made full Colonel, but sadly had a fatal heart attack shortly after retirement. Dan McKane got killed in an airshow flying an experimental airplane. Billings, the medic is a retired Master Sergeant and will be traveling with us. Satterfield, the crew chief/door gunner, now makes guns and will meet us in D.C. The rest of us will be there. I am also pleased to announce we are all invited to a private reception for us in the President's quarters. I mean the White House." That comment got laughter from everyone. Jerry went on to brief everyone on travel and hotel arrangements.

For Washington, D.C., the weather was good. A slight breeze made the hot day bearable, especially for those wearing military dress uniforms. The crowd was a small, select group. President Burks wanted to keep this presentation intimate. Everyone present were wives or soldiers who had served together and belonged to the brotherhood of warriors bonded by combat.

The Marine Band provided Sousa marches before the ceremony, prompting a snide comment by someone who had been an Army troop who had served with the Navy in the Mobile Riverine Force, "pretty good music for a bunch of seagoing bellhops."

"Shut up," Larry whispered. He was wearing his Army Warrant Officer 5 Dress Blues, with all his decorations. "Show some respect. The band is here for Bill." The room was quiet for a minute;then the band began to play 'Hail to the Chief'. Everyone rose to attention as the President and his wife, Rose, Kathleen and her family, entered the Rose Garden from the White House. The music ended, President Burks asked all to be seated and started the Medal of Honor Ceremony.

John R. Burks, President of the United States, was the only Army veteran in the Rose Garden area who was not in military uniform. He was dressed in a tuxedo, the dress uniform of the President. "Warrant Officer William H. "Bill" Jones was not a regular medical evacuation Huey helicopter pilot in Vietnam. He was assigned to the 191st Assault Helicopter Company. That unit flew Cobra Gunships, helicopters with machine guns and rockets that can be fired at enemy forces. Bill's quarters when in Dong Tam, were next door to the 247th Helicopter Ambulance Company, Detached. The pilots in both units knew each other and were friends. Bill had flown Dust off medical missions before. One fateful day, because Bill was the person he was, volunteered to fly a Medical Evacuation mission because bother soldiers needed him. Bill put on his flight gear, reported to flight operations, and started flying missions. The helicopter he and his new co-pilot were given didn't have machine guns or rockets like his normal assault helicopter. The assigned helicopter was an older model HU-1D slick with red crosses painted on the nose and both side sliding doors called aiming points by non-medical helicopter crews. He used four that day!

"Bill and his crew successfully evacuated maximum patient four times, refueling, sometimes moving to a replacement helicopter (one without major holes from enemy weapons) and returning to hot LZs where the Division was heavily engaged. Each time they flew into landing zones which were under enemy fire, receiving small arms hits to the helicopter coming and going. Five was an unlucky number!"

"Departing with a full load of wounded, Bill's Huey was hit by an RPG (Rocket Propelled Grenade) killing all. Bill's voluntary participation as a Dustoff pilot not only saved many lives but enabled United States Forces to prevail in a major military action. Bill was an unselfish hero who went where he didn't have to go. He knew it was a dangerous mission before he flew the first mission flight. Six medical Hueys and thirteen troop Hueys had already been downed. Three more Medivacs were shot down during the time he was flying missions. Bill elected to press on. That, my friends, is a true hero," concluded President Burks!

The Adjutant then read the formal citation. President Burks presented the Medal of Honor with the Five-Star Crest in a presentation box to Kathleen. Hugged her and the children. Rose and the President then escorted the Jones family back to the White House. Aids to the President led Jerry and the other invited guests to the President's residence in the White House. The President poured his special Martini into glasses with the Presidential Seal engraved upon them and proposed a toast to Bill, "to a true hero, a friend, and a fellow warrior!"

"Here, Here!" replies echoed around those assembled.

The gathering went on for quite some time, with many stories told and sometimes retold with different endings!

CHAPTER 40

"Sheriff," his secretary called, "Ms. Ray on one."

Jerry picked up the handset, punched #1, and greeted Carol Ray, the County and Prosecuting Attorney, "howdy Counselor, how's the legal eagle?"

"Pretty good right now. Judge Brodrick set a trial date for Witters."

"That's pretty quick!" Jerry exclaimed. "Any problem with that?"

"I don't think so. It's a pretty straightforward trial. We only have five witnesses. Defense has only had one listed so far; Witters and he may not take the stand. I want to brief all our witnesses on Wednesday if you can get them all served right away."

"When you have papers to serve, I'll send a deputy to pick them up and serve them," offered Jerry.

"Thanks, I thought you would. Papers are ready. Send your deputy, and I will see you Wednesday at 9 a.m.," replied Carol. She said "good-by" and hung up.

Well, that was fast, thought Jerry. The first Deputy walking past Jerry's office was Chris Roads. "Forty (a reference to her badge number) run over to Ray's office and serve the papers she has for you ASAP (as soon as possible)."

"On the way, Sheriff."

(Service of Process, such as a Witness Subpoena to compel attendance at a trial, casually called 'papers', was the providence of the Sheriff's Department and have to be given in person to the witness by a Deputy Sheriff. The Deputy then fills out a 'return of service' which states the time, date and location it was given to the person subpoenaed and filed with the Clerk of Court as part of the trial record. Failure to appear can be punishable by the Judge. This action was probably not necessary for the prosecution witnesses in the Witters trial since all, except maybe the Ferguson Federal Savings and Loan employee, Terrance Fordham, were ready and willing to testify.]

Roads knocked on Jerry's open door and reported: "Everyone served, Boss!"

"Good job, Chris. Appreciate the quick work."

"Well, all served but one!"

"Who?"

"No one now," Chris laughed, handing him his subpoena, "now everyone is served!"

Jerry too chuckled, "outstanding job, Deputy!"

The Prosecution witnesses were all seated around a conference table in the elected County Attorney's private law office. Due to Banner County's small population, the County Attorney, even though an elected County Official, was a part-time job. Carol didn't have a County Office; she used her private practice law office and the courtroom for her elected and private practice duties, as was the custom in many Wyoming Counties.

"Morning Cheryl, and the rest of you guys," Carol cheerfully greeted the assembly of witnesses!

"Morning!"

"Hi."

"Morning Carol."

"Too early for this!"

"Ok," Carol grinned. "I just wanted to brief you and set up some interview times. Happy you could all be here. Trial is in three weeks. The Judge will be The Honorable James F.

Brodrick, who has been on the bench for seven years. He is a good Judge, fair but strict. Do as the Judge says and follow his instructions. Stand when he enters or leaves the courtroom, or if you are speaking to him unless you are on the stand (the witness chair), then remain seated. His Court Reporter is Tashana Gonzalo. Some call her 'TG', you won't. Speak slowly and loudly, or she will hand you your head on a platter. Don't interrupt anyone or speak at the same time. If you do, you will discover the real meaning of `madder than a wet hen`. Same thing if you crowd her space or get between her place in front of the bench and her line of sight to the Judge. She is really a nice lady!"

The Defense Attorney is Harley Chatman, of Chatman, Ford, and Jones. Many have used the old joke about the similarity of his name and the legendary firm of Dewey, Cheatham, and Howe."

Chuckles and laughter broke out, many having heard the joke before, and all actually knowing the respected Defense Attorney. "Please use all due respect during the trial," Carol smiled!

Carol and the witness group arranged times to go over testimony, and everyone went back to their jobs.

Cheryl and Jerry walked out of Carol's office hand-in-hand. Cheryl commented, "She's nice!"

"Yup, She sure is until she goes into the courtroom, then she becomes a legal bulldog, not like the nice Labrador puppy you just saw," Jerry cautioned. "She knows the law, is fantastic in court; she can read a witness, and can present her case effectively. She really hates criminals, but can also be fair and reasonable. She would be a great Judge!"

"Wow," was Cheryl's response. "What's the deal on Chatham?"

"Harley is also a good attorney, probably not as good as Carol, but then I'm prejudiced, the guy is a defense attorney!"

Cheryl and Jerry laughed.

Witters and his attorney, Harley Chatham, also met. The atmosphe was not as light as Carol's meeting with her witnesses, it was downright tense. Both men knew Witters was guilty. Witters spun his version, "Look, I was the fall guy. Pat and Davis already had it set up. I was just supposed to go along to drive the car and be a lookout."

"OK, we'll approach it that way, but since capital crimes are charged because Pat was killed at the bank, the Sheriff was shot which will be argued was attempted murder, and a bank robbery and kidnapping occurred, you can be convicted even if you didn't do the acts."

Witters was horrified, scared and willing to do anything to get off. "So what do you suggest?"

"Plead guilty and hope for mercy. "

"No way! Pat and Davis did it all. I'll take my chances on a Jury."

Good luck thought Harley. Harley then began planning the best defense he could fight.

Outdoor light is different in the fall. It is more subdued than the bright light of summer. The shadows in the evening are longer. The air is colder too. The day of the trial was like an October day in Wyoming; probably because it was an October day in Wyoming!

The courtroom was crowded. But then, it looked crowded when Hollywood made a movie there and had a hard time getting all the city council cast around the council tables.

The Judge and his Court Reporter had office space behind

the front of the courtroom and could enter through doors directly into the courtroom. The Jury had to traverse the hallway from a small Jury Room to the Court. The attorneys had either the courtroom or the law library to share. The attorneys used counsel tables in the courtroom, rather than walk the short hallway, go outside, or back to their law offices if there was time.

"All rise, District Court for Banner County, Wyoming, is now in session, announced the Court Bailiff, The Honorable James F. Brodrick, presiding."

Everyone rose to a standing position as the Judge and TG, his Court Reporter entered. The Judge sat in his high backed chair and waited until Tashana Gonzalo, his Court Reporter sat and adjusted her stenographer equipment. "Please be seated. The case before the Court is State of Wyoming v. Jeremy Witters. The Defendant is present with his Defense Attorney, Harley Chatham of Chatham, Ford and Jones, Caribou, Wyoming. The State is represented by the Banner County and Prosecuting Attorney, Carol S. Ray. The Defendant and the attorneys are present in the courtroom. Are all parties prepared to proceed?"

The Judge and both attorneys had just come from a hearing in the Judge's Chambers (Office), so the Judge knew they were prepared to start, but he asked the question for the official trial record, which TG duly recorded with nimble fingers pushing keys on her stenograph.

"Prosecution is ready, Your Honor," answered Ms. Ray.

"Ready for the Defense," said Harley Chatham.

Looking at Chatham, the Judge inquired, "And?"

"Excuse me, Your Honor," Chatham apologized for his error in addressing the Judge correctly.

"Very well, you are excused. We will now proceed with jury selection."

Judge Brodrick addressed the Clerk of the District Court, Tina Black Eagle, "Please call the names of the first thirteen names on your jury roll. She complied, and with the assistance of Deputy Roads, the acting Court Bailiff assembled and seated the prospective Jurors in the jury box. The other members of the jury panel were sitting in the first rows of the spectator section of the courtroom.

"Ladies and Gentlemen of the jury panel, each and every one of you are to pay close attention to questions put forth by me, and also those of the County Attorney and the Defense Attorney. Some of you may be called to replace those already in the Jury Box. This is a process we call Voir Dire, which is the method we use to obtain a fair and impartial Jury for this trial," explained Judge Brodrick.

"The Defendant, Jeremy Witters, has been charged in an Indictment which alleges Jeremy Witters . . . (and the Judge read the formal criminal indictment). In simple language Witters was accused of:

1. Two charges of Felony Murder – the deaths of Patrick Torkelson, who was killed during the bank robbery, and Davis Ferguson, who died in the mountains while engaged in escape from the armed robbery. Felony murder is a legal concept which holds all the parties to a criminal activity equally guilty of any death which occurs during the commission of that crime as if they actually killed the person. The penalty is the same.
2. Kidnapping Cheryl Hefner.
3. Three charges of attempted murder – a. shooting Nick Nicolson at Ferguson Savings & Loan; b. shooting Sheriff Tom Flannigan; c. shooting at Jerry Burkley d. shooting at Cheryl Hefner. The law imputing the concept the shootings were intended to kill
4. Bank Robbery of Ferguson Federal Savings and Loan.

Judge Brodrick went on to explain to the Jury the legal concept of felony murder and gave them some preliminary

Jury Instructions, as well as information they may need such as how to get to the restrooms, and so forth.

The Judge began the questioning of the prospective jurors, with preliminary questions about their qualifications:

"Do any of you know Jeremy Witters?"

"Do any of you know Carol S. Ray, the County Attorney, or members of her staff?"

"Do any of you know Harley Chatham, or any members of his Law Firm, Chatham, Ford, and Jones?"

These types of questions went on for a substantial time, with follow up questions if someone answered yes. Some of those resulted in a Juror being excused, either peremptorily or for cause. When the Judge concluded his line of questioning, both attorneys were given the opportunity also ask qualification questions. A panel of twelve primary and two alternate jurors were selected, sworn in as Jurors, and excused for the day following an admonition by Judge Brodrick not to discuss the case with anyone.

"Trial will convene at 9 a.m. tomorrow in this courtroom. Please be on time." The Judge and his Reporter rose and left the courtroom.

CHAPTER 41

"All Rise" announced Deputy Roads, the acting Bailiff. Chris was getting pretty good at being Bailiff for the District Court. She was fearful Sheriff Burkley would make it permanent. Had she asked, Jerry would have told her, "I need you on the street more than Judge Brodrick needs more acting senior citizens." And he would have been truthful and correct. The bailiff was a short, part-time assignment. Deputies on the street in a patrol car keep Banner County safe!

"Have you selected a foreperson?" Judge Brodrick inquired. He was politically correct, as there were men and women on the panel.

An elderly gentleman seated in the left front seat next to the Judge's bench arose and advised, "I have been elected by my fellow Jurors to serve as such, Your Honor."

"Your name for the record Sir?" asked the Judge.

"My name is Franklin Roosevelt, Sir. Most folks call me Frank."

"Thank you, Mr. Roosevelt. The, Court is appreciative of your service and will usually refer to you as Mr. Roosevelt. The Judge continued, "we will have opening statements. What the Attorneys say is not evidence, and you should not consider it as such. Only the sworn testimony of witness's testimony and any physical evidence admitted into evidence by the Court should be considered by you when you begin deliberations at the conclusion of the trial."

"The Prosecution, Ms. Ray is allowed to go first because the State has the burden of proving to you, beyond a reasonable doubt, the Defendant is guilty of each charge. That will be defined for you later in the proceedings. Ms. Ray, you may begin your opening statement.

"Thank you, Your Honor! May it please the Court?" Carol moved behind the podium in front of the witness chair. "As you all know, I am Carol Ray. I have been elected as your County and Prosecuting Attorney. The County part is the non-criminal aspects of the law, such as zoning and advice to county officials and civil lawsuits about traffic accidents involving county vehicles."

The Second part is why several of Sheriff Burkley's Deputies and I are here today. Our job is to keep the peace. It is my job, as your elected Banner County Prosecuting Attorney, when a Defendant is apprehended, to prosecute criminal activities in Banner County in the name of the State of Wyoming. The Defendant in the pending case has been captured and incarcerated in the Banner County Jail. The Judge has informed the Defendant of pending charges."

"This part of the trial is termed 'opening statements' and as Judge Brodrick has instructed you, are not statements constituting evidence, but simply what the Lawyer thinks. Opening statements are simply a statement of what the Attorney for each party, the Prosecution and the Defense expect to prove The Prosecutor must prove guilt beyond a reasonable doubt for each charge. The Defense may demonstrate reasonable doubt as to the Defendant's guilt on each count."

Carol addressed the jury, and said, "the Prosecution intends to show . . . ." (Carol went on to outline the State's evidence about each charge). "When all evidence has been properly put before you, I would expect you to return a Verdict of 'Guilty' on all charges."

Carol returned to her chair, and before seating herself,

she addressed Judge Brodrick, "My opening statement is complete!

"Thank you," replied Judge Brodrick. Mr. Chatham, if the Defense is ready, you may proceed."

"May it please the Court. Ladies and Gentlemen of the Jury. My name is Harley Chatham. I am Counsel for Mr. Jeremy Witters, the Defendant in this case. Mr. Witters has pleaded not guilty to all charges. There were other individuals involved, who may be the guilty parties, but we may never know. Patrick Torkelson was killed during the bank robbery of Ferguson Federal Savings and Loan. Jeremy Witters will testify Torkelson was the mastermind of this bank heist and was helped by a bank employee insider, Davis Ferguson. Ferguson could have been the leader, it was his families' bank after all. He knew when money was going to be in the vault, and how the bank was protected. Who Knows! Jerry Witters remembers he was just a lookout who also drove a car. The car was soon abandoned and horses obtained by Patrick Torkelson were used in an attempt to escape."

Harley paused to drink part of a glass of water. "All of this seems to raise reasonable doubt that Jeremy Witters committed any crime other than being present when crimes were committed."

The Defense Attorney continued in this vein, raising possible areas of 'reasonable doubt' to all of Witters actions and ended his lengthy opening by asking the Jury members to find Jeremy Witters 'not guilty on all charges.

Judge Brodrick adjourned the court for a brief, but late lunch for the Jury and to give Counsel some time to prepare for witness direct and cross-examination.

The trial progressed, as did most major criminal trails, slowly and usually dull. Carol put her witnesses on the stand, elicited what had occurred at the bank, in the streets of Caribou, and on the mountain pursuit. The last Prosecution witness, Sheriff Burkley, was cross-examined by Harley Chatman and dismissed. Carol addressed the Court, "Your Honor, the Prosecution rests, but reserves the right to recall any of the Prosecution witnesses for rebuttal if necessary."

"Thank you, counsel. Witnesses shall be subject to recall and shall continue to be recused from the courtroom, except Sheriff Burkley who has been Designated as Prosecution lead and may continue to assist with the Prosecutor's case. Mr. Chatman, please call your first witness."

Harley called Jeremy Witters, the Defendant, to the stand. After Witters had testified to his version of the facts, blaming Davis Ferguson and Pat Torkelson for everything, Carol began her cross-examination. She started asking Witters about his involvement in the bank robbery, but Witters interrupted and blurted, "Davis and Pat did all that. They made me go along because I had a car!"

"So you participated, but on a limited basis," Carol smoothly got Witters to talking.

"Yeah, that's right!"

"Were they both smarter than you, or just one of them?"

Before Harley could even form an objection to the question, Witters snarled, "hell, if their brains were dynamite, neither one of them would have the brains to blow his nose."

Carol quickly asked, "but you couldn't plan this robbery, could you?"

Again, Harley didn't get the opportunity to object before Witters boasted, "not only could I, but in spite of those two I did!" Witters' voice got quiet as he realized the trap the wily prosecutor had led him into. "Shit," he mouthed, and put his head in his hands!

"No further questions Your Honor!" Carol returned to her place at the Prosecution table, sat down and grinned at Jerry, who was seated next to her. Jerry and most everyone in the courtroom was amazed at the Defendant's outbursts.

Harley Chatham did the only thing he could do at that point. "Defense rests, Your Honor."

"Nothing further from the State, Your Honor," echoed Carol.

A brief recess was called by Judge Brodrick. When the Court was back in session, both Carol and Harley made short closing arguments. There wasn't much to add to Witters outbursts. Judge Brodrick gave the lengthy general instructions to the Jury, and they recessed to the Jury room for deliberations.

"What's keeping them," Jerry asked Carol. "They have been out a long time."

"Don't know, maybe they heard something we missed. I didn't think there was any doubt as to Witters guilt, much less any reasonable doubt." (Jurys who are having trouble deciding on a verdict usually take a long time, as they discuss, argue, and try to arrive at a unanimous decision as to the verdict.)

This jury didn't have any problem reaching a verdict. They all probably already had their collective minds made up before the jury instructions were given. Even without Witters performance in court, the evidence of guilt was overwhelming. The delay was most likely caused by the smell of fresh coffee brewing in the Jury room and the large box of fresh donuts resting in the middle of the long jury table. A quick vote found Witters guilty on all charges. The foreman, Franklin Roosevelt, then reasonably suggested that they probably would not be provided lunch that day, since the trial was going to end midmorning anyway, and perhaps they should delay return to the tedium of the court proceedings until after they had a break. After all, the coffee and donuts would just go to waste if they didn't.

While the Judge, attorneys, witnesses, and spectators speculated on what the Jury was doing, Jury members were having friendly conversations and enjoying their break. Eventually, the Jury returned to the Court-room, announced the verdict, and returned to the normalcy of Caribou.

The Judge was ready to pronounce sentence immediately and did so. "Jeremy Witters. You have been found guilty on all counts in the criminal indictment with which you were charged. I find there is no need to delay sentencing. I hereby sentence you as follows:

Count Number 1 – Armed Robbery of Ferguson Federal Savings and Loan. I sentence you to serve not less than 15 years, nor more than 20 years, in the Wyoming State Penitentuary.

Counts Number 2 and 3 – Felony Murder of Patrick Mahoney Torkelson and Felony Murder of Davis Ferguson. I sentence you to Life in the Wyoming State Penitentuary without the possibility of Parole, on each count.

Counts Number 4, 5, 6, and 7 – Attempted Murder of Mick Nicholson, Tomas Flannigan, Jerry Burkley, and Cheryl Hefner. I sentence you to Life in the Wyoming State Penitentuary.

Count 8 – Kidnapping of Cheryl Hefner. I sentence you to Life in the Wyoming State Penitentuary.

"Mr. Witters, your total sentence is seven times the rest of your life plus at least 15 years. Since two of those sentences are without the possibility of parole, you will die in prison. I order that these sentences be served concurrently, rather than consecutively. This means that you will only have to serve one lifetime in prison, not that it probably makes any difference."

Sheriff Burkley, the prisoner is remanded to the Banner County Sheriff's office for transportation to the Wyoming State Penitentiary at Rawlins, Wyoming, in the manner, and at a time you deem appropriate."

"Yes, Your Honor. It shall be done!"

"This Court is now in recess," announce Judge Brodrick as he rose and exited to his chambers.

Witters was transported to Caribou Field under heavy guard. The Sheriff's Department Cessna 206 was on the pad in front of the hangar door. The two cargo doors in the side of the cabin were open and ready to receive the prisoner. Former Sheriff (and advisor to Sheriff Burkley) volunteered to be part of the escort to Rawlins. Jerry assigned Bob Schrader, C-20, and Chris Roads, C-40, to pilot the mission in N33SD (which Chris finally figured out stood for Banner County Sheriff's Department, 33 is the number at the beginning of Banner County automobile license plates, each county having a different number 1 to 33.

Jerry assigned Lieutenant Joe Pawlik and the Undersheriff, Rios Rivera, as guards. Witters was placed in a middle seat away from the cargo doors, with Tom Flannigan between Witters and the door, and two Deputies in front of and behind. No chances were being taken.

The plane was met at the Rawlins Airport by Wyoming State Penitentiary staff. The Lieutenant in charge greeted Big Tom as he exited the Cessna. "What have you got for me Sheriff," inquired his old friend, Lieutenant Casey Foster?"

"A very long-term resident. The prisoner has almost a cat's life minus two lives plus fifteen to twenty years sentence, although the Judge made them Concurrent, so only one life with no possibility of parole. He should be with you for quite a while and he's not that old!"

"Past my retirement probably. Ok, we will take him off your hands." The papers were signed and exchanged; the prisoner exchange was made.

Jerry's instructions to his two fixed-wing pilots included a second mission. "Put Rios in the left seat and make him fly home." He told Chris, "You are an IP. Start getting Rios dual qualified (Rivera was a highly qualified helicopter pilot, and there was no reason he should not be flying the Department's fixed-wing plane as well.)"

"That should be fun," Bob laughed.

"You'll think fun, while you are in the back of the plane and can't reach the controls while the Undersheriff tries to prove he can actually fly a plane where the wings don't spin around in circles. It really should be lots of fun," joked Chris.

EPILOGUE

CODE OF THE WEST

1. Live each day with courage;
2. Take pride in your work;
3. Always finish what you start;
4. Do what has to be done;
5. Be tough, but fair;
6. When you make a promise, keep it;
7. Ride for the brand;
8. Talk less, say more;
9. Remember that some things are not for sale;
10. Know where to draw the line.

*-Derived from the book, Cowboy Ethics by James P. Owen,
and summarized as the official state code of Wyoming.*

Cheryl was reading the Caribou Bulletin when she noticed the Wyoming Legislature had adopted a Code of Conduct, The Code of the West, as the Wyoming State Code. "Jerry, the Legislature has finally figured out what makes you tick," she laughed. "Read this!"

"Hah. No way is that me!" But it was, and although President Burks had never seen Wyoming's Code of the West, he did know Jerry Burkley well. He had a present of sorts for Jerry too. He called the Pentagon and asked for Colonel Pruter.

"Colonel Pruter Sir," Don answered the phone not knowing who was calling.

"Don, John Burks. How are you doing?"

"Very well Mr. President. What can I do for you today?"

"Something nice for someone else. Do you remember the

group you got together for the Medal of Honor ceremony for Bill Jones?"

"Certainly do. That was an interesting group, especially the Sheriff from Wyoming. He was certainly an original."

"Well, that Sheriff is why I'm calling. I am going to present him with the Presidential Medal of Freedom. Can't give him the other one, but he certainly qualifies for the civilian equivalent! I would appreciate having you get hold of that group you put together before, find an appropriate date that fits my calendar, sometime on or around the 4th of July; you can check with Sara on that, and get invitations out. Talk to the Sheriff's wife, Cheryl, rather than the Sheriff until you get it put together, then you can call Jerry and let him know he is ordered by his Commander-in-Chief to attend. He might not otherwise."

Don chuckled and said, "I think he is the kind to duck out if he could. I'll get right on it Mr. President!"

John R. Burks laughed out loud. "Yes he would!"

Colonel Pruter anxiously waited in the ante-room to the Oval Office in the White House. President Burks had sent for him. Don didn't know why. The President's Secretary rose from her desk, smiled at Colonel Pruter and gestured for him to enter the Oval Office. Don moved directly to the front on the President's desk, saluted sharply and reported, "Colonel Pruter reporting as ordered Mr. President."

The President smiled, returned Don's salute, although he didn't have to, and walked around to the front of his desk to shake Don's hand and say, "you were asked, not ordered you know!"

"A request from my President is always an order, Boss," countered Colonel Pruter.

"Thank you for that honor, Don! I appreciate your long-time support. What do you have for me on Burkley?"

"Probably the longest guest list you have ever seen. He has

friends, co-workers, and relatives out the ear. He is a retired Chief Warrant Officer who has served all over the world. He made a lot of friends in the Army. He is also a long-term politician, and he made a lot of friends along that path."

"Did you ask him to cut the list?"

"Right away! And he simply said, if the old man wants to tell someone to stay home, he can tell them."

John Burks grinned. "I knew he would. He's never left anyone behind! Ever."

"What would you like me to do, Sir?"

"Well, we have here what some may call a situation. We have a grand award to present. We have a bunch of civilians and military, many of whom are well connected politically, and would be highly disappointed, if not just plain hacked off, to be left out of the party. Let's try this; use a C-17 Globemaster for elected and appointed government officials, all active, retired military, guard and reserve and one guest each for transportation. Use the VOQ (visiting officers quarters) at Andrews for all of them. Arrange for guest privileges at the O-Club (Officer's Club) for any that need it. Bus everyone from Andrews to here for the ceremony. We can probably get a meeting room comped by one of the hotels for the ceremony and reception."

"Probably manageable, Sir. I would suggest however you use the White House for both the Ceremony and the Reception, even if you have to use two or more rooms to handle the overflow. Less opportunity for criticism."

"Thanks, Don, do it," the President ordered.

"Phone for you on two, Sheriff," his secretary shouted. "Some guy named Pruter!"

"Thanks," Jerry acknowledged. Wonder what he wants? "Morning Colonel, what can I do for you, Sir?"

"Actually, not much Mr. Burkley," Don replied, using WO5

Burkley's military title, rather than Sheriff. "I think I have all my targets located. I just wanted to pass on a VOCO (verbal order of Commanding Officer) to you."

"I'm retired," rejoined Jerry. "Who is the Commander?"

"You poor boy! This VOCO is from the big commander, our Commander-in-Chief, President John R. Burks. His instructions to me were to order you to appear at an award ceremony in your honor and that you should be in Dress Blue with all your decorations attached, no ribbons. (Decorations were awards that had a medal hanging from a ribbon which was pinned to the uniform in order of importance; ribbons were used in place of the medals on a service uniform and for other awards for which there was no medal. Most ribbons were of the 'I was there' or qualification indicators.)

"Well then Colonel, all I can say is Yes Sir, and do my best to carry out the order!" Both officers chuckled, and the Colonel hung up his phone.

THE PRESIDENT
UNITED STATES OF AMERICA
JOHN R. BURKS

INVITES YOU TO ATTEND
A PRESENTATION OF THE
PRESIDENTIAL MEDAL OF FREEDOM
TO
JERRY R. BURKLEY

Enclosed: Pass to White House
Date/time/location details

DRESS: Tux
Mess Dress Uniform
Formal Attire for the ladies

The chatter of voices outside Jerry's office was loud and getting closer. "Sheriff, what's this Freedom thing."

"Do we get time off?"

"How are we getting to D.C.?"

And many more questions, comments, and congratulations. Incoming phone calls almost forced the system to shut down. This continued far into the night and into the next couple of days. Jerry intended to speak to each shift during the briefing, but that didn't work out. His explanation to the assembled Deputies and staff at the first briefing was to say, "The Presidential Medal of Freedom is just another decoration, only the President gives it instead of the military."

That explanation didn't fly. The first time Jerry used it, Rios almost shouted, "bullshit, that thing with the funny name is about the same as the Medal of Honor. The only real difference is this one is for civilians and military, and the Medal of Honor is only for the military. Own up, Sheriff."

"Ok, the Undersheriff is correct. I didn't want to have people make a big deal out of it." After that, Rios gave the briefings and answered the phone inquiries.

THE WHITE HOUSE
FOURTH OF JULY
FORMAL DINING ROOM

Colonel Donald Pruter shook hands with Jerry, sincerely congratulated him and walked center stage to the microphone. "Welcome to the White House. Today we honor a Sheriff, a Chief Warrant Officer, and one of our nation's heroes.

[Actually, you read this in the Preface at the beginning of the story. If you wish to refresh your memory, please feel free to re-read it, but stop before you reread the whole story. You will just end up back here!!!]

As the President was leaving, he took Jerry by the arm and said, "stick around after the reception. I have a project to discuss with you."

Jerry sighed, "I think this is where I came in!!"

PREVIEW

READ THE BEGINNING OF ANOTHER
ONE OF JERRY'S STORIES

TUNNEL SECRETS

Two dead bodies. One in Banner County. One in Cheyenne. No identification on either. Strange causes of death. Many suspects. City, County, and State Law Enforcement Agencies competing with FBI, CIA, and other 'Initial Designated' governmental agencies perhaps involved. A "Who Done It" Wyoming style.

READ ON!

PROLOGUE

"911, what is your emergency?" asked the dispatcher at the Banner County Sheriff's Office.

The phone line went dead. "Sergeant Carson," said Jenny Abbote, the night dispatcher. "I feel like we may have a problem!"

"What?"

"Hang up!"

"So, we get a lot of those."

"True, but I heard a gunshot!"

"Trace it back if you can." Sergeant Fred Carson used his department cell phone to call the Sheriff. "Hey Boss, we may have a shots fired 911 call."

Sheriff Flannigan said, "more!"

"Nothing yet, but Jenny is trying to trace it."

"OK, let me know, and thanks," said Big Tom.

Sheriff 'Big' Tom Flannigan was the Sheriff of Banner County, Wyoming. The county seat is Caribou, Wyoming, with a population of about 5,000 people. The whole county may have 40,000 people. The low population probably accounts for the number '33' as the prefix for automobile license plates. The County north of Banner County, Canyon County has a license prefix of '26'. Cheyenne, the capital city of Wyoming, has a '2' prefix.

Banner County is small, but a tremendous place to live. There is virtually no crime, probably due to Sheriff Flannigan and the Caribou Police Chief, Stands Tall Ferguson. Stand Tall's mother was Cheyenne Indian. His father was "Old" Silas

Ferguson. Ferguson owned and managed Ferguson Savings and Loan. Silas built a fortune making small loans to local farmers and ranchers. He was wealthy!

"911, what is your emergency?" Jenny was both ready and surprised at the caller's answer.

"I am hiking along Antler trailhead to Anthem Peak. My cell phone keeps going out."

"Did you call earlier?" asked Jenny.

"Yes, but the phone dropped out!"

"What can I do for you?"

"There is a dead body about a mile back. I'm a nurse, so I know it's a dead body."

Stands Tall is not rich. He is an honorable man and an extremely proficient Police Chief. Stands Tall and Tom work as a team to shield Banner County residents from danger. A dead body in Banner County motivates Stands Tall and Tom to high alert.

Jenny advised, "please stay where you are. I will send a helicopter for you." And she did! The Banner County Sheriff's Office had just acquired a Bell Jet Ranger using federal grant money. The Department had three deputies who were qualified and licensed as Commercial Pilot who flew aircraft for the Banner County Sheriff's Department. Jerry Burkley, Carlita Camero (aka Chris Roads) were licensed fixed wing pilots and could fly the Cessna. Bob Schrader, who like Jerry was a former Army Helicopter pilot was licensed and qualified to operate the Jet Ranger. Jerry Burkley was authorized to fly both the Jet Ranger and the Cessna 206. Schrader was the Chief of the Banner County Sheriff's Reserve Department and worked as a volunteer. Chris was a full-time Deputy, but couldn't fly the Jet Ranger. That left Jerry, who was a full-time Deputy and a shift Supervisor. Guess who got called? Jenny liked waking up the new Lieutenant.

Jerry didn't like his sleep disturbed. "What do you want?" he growled into the phone.

"Want to fly?" asked Jenny?

Jerry liked flying, fixed or rotary-wing, and his tone softened. "When, where and why?" he answered.

"There is a lady hiker near Anthem. She has a dead body," Jenny explained.

"On the way."

Jerry loved to fly. Jerry enjoyed being in law enforcement. He especially favored mixing both activities. As a Lieutenant Jerry had his own patrol car, a new Pontiac with lights, siren, and radios installed. He quickly drove to Caribou Air Field. After opening the hangar doors, he pushed N3320SD, the Banner County Jet Ranger, onto the pad in front.

Lights swept across the pad area. Sheriff Tom Flannigan, who monitored all the radio traffic, drove in. "Hi Sheriff," Jerry greeted him, "I didn't know this assignment was on the radio."

"It wasn't. Jenny thought you might need some help."

"I did before you got here! Two Zero Sierra Delta is hard to push. You had great timing."

"Well, my intentions were good. Where are we going?"

Jerry knew he was going to have company. Sheriff Tom liked to fly too but as a passenger. On the other hand, having an experienced investigator along was beneficial. Four eyes were better than two and Tom could help load the body. Thank you, Jenny thought Jerry to himself.

Jerry completed his pre-flight walk-around of the Jet Ranger, seated himself in the right seat (the Aircraft Commander's station), fastened his lap and shoulder belts while Sheriff Tom buckled into the left side seat. After using a checklist to ensure all systems were adequately checked, Jerry yelled, "clear!" Jerry started the turbine engine and carefully watched his engine instruments for any problems.

Sheriff Tom, although not a licensed pilot, had been on many flights with Jerry and the other Department pilots. Tom turned the radio to 122.8 MHz, the Unicom (plane to plane) frequency used at airports without working control towers. Tom keyed the radio mike with a push switch on the control stick and transmitted, "November 3320Sierra Delta light on the skids for takeoff on Runway Two Six."

"Hey, you're getting the radio work Sheriff?"

"Thanks."

Jerry adjusted pitch and collective, made a 360-degree pivot to watch for other aircraft and hoovered. He then angled forward to gain airship and lifted into the night sky.

The rotatable spotlight mounted underneath the Jet Ranger illuminated a woman waving. She was wearing outdoor gear and a backpack. Jerry landed the helicopter softly on the ground in a clearing nearby.

"Howdy mam, my name is Flannigan. I'm the Banner County Sheriff. The pilot of that contraption is Lieutenant Burkley. Did you call about a dead body?

"Yes, I did. It's about a hundred yards that way," she said, pointing west.

Jerry shut down the helicopter. He and the Sheriff walked to the body.

"Not good Sheriff. That's a bullet shot to the head."

"Better call for a forensic team and the coroner."

"Yup," said Jerry as he turned and walked back to the Jet Ranger, knowing his portable radio wouldn't be effective.

CHAPTER 1

The American was pleased with himself. After only three weeks in a foreign country, he felt confident enough to travel alone, order meals, and pass unnoticed. He sought housing in a hotel in the Schwarzwald Region of southern Germany. Months of language training had given him the faculty to speak the German language. The last three months gave him the gestures, mannerisms, and customs of the people where he was living. Only last week while skiing at Davos, Switzerland, about a three-hour drive from his hotel, he was able to pass himself off as a German to another.

It was snowing as he returned to the Hotel Zer Sonne and let himself into the small hotel room. Flakes of snow fell in gentle puffs as he looked from the window to survey the scene before him. Soon it would be too late to turn back.

The Bar and Restaurant in the Hotel Zer Sonne in Donaueschingen, Germany, was cozy and relaxing. The American, Cecil Winegar, locked the door to his room, walked down the narrow stairway, and entered the bar area. He seated himself at a table for four, where he could sit with his back to the wall. Winegar could observe both doors and everyone in the room from this location. He ordered 'Furstenberg' draft beer. Getting the beer prepared for him was a lengthy process. The foam was allowed to settle several times before the liquid was even with a mark engraved on the beer glass with almost no foam. Then, and only then, would the proprietor bring Cecil his beer.

"Dr. Livingston I presume," said the slight man before

him. The man was wearing a Bavarian-style cap and an over-coat. He was carrying a large briefcase held shut with two large straps.

"And you must be Henry Morgan Stanley!" This and several other equally corny exchanges were the passwords and responses used to authenticate each other's identity.

Herr Rudolph Gulde was an Anwalt (lawyer) in a large legal firm in Stuttgart. His function in this transactions was to convey information to Cecil so sensitive it could not be mailed or even put in written form. Thus, the need for two strangers to meet face-to-face.

Rudy Gulde told Cecil everything he knew about a tunnel leading to an underground vault. Inside the vault was possibly the most important, most vital and most valuable object imaginable.

"Be very careful my friend," warned Rudy. "If you move it, hide it well! Tell no one what I have told you!:

"Thank you. Watch your back. You too are in danger!"

The two men parted and went their separate ways. Cecil did not return to his room. He hiked cross-country, avoiding congested areas and shunning both public and private transportation. Several weeks later Cecil boarded a commercial air flight from Amsterdam, Holland, to Toronto, Canada, using a different name and identification.

"Banner County Sheriff's Office, Lieutenant Burkley. What can I do for you?"

"Jerry, this is Hank Toshman."

"Good morning Doc, or should I call our new Banner County Coroner Doctor? You can call me Jerry. Welcome to Caribou."

"Either is fine. I answer to Hank, Dr. T, Doc, Doctor Toshman, or most any other friendly greeting. Its nice to be here, thanks."

"What can I do for you Hank?" Jerry earnestly replied. Jerry already liked the guy.

"Your John Doe from Anthem Peak may or may not have died from a gunshot to the head."

Jerry was puzzled. He had seen the wound in the forehead. "Sure looks like he was shot!"

"Oh, he was shot. The bullet was a .45 calibre, probably from a model 1911. I recovered the round and it looks like a military issue slug. The problem is the autopsy suggests the cause of death was from being frozen. This is August, and it has been hot!"

Jerry leaned forward in his desk chair and started making notes on his desk pad. "Strange. Any theories?"

"A couple; shot first and put in a freezer; put in a fridge and then shot. Maybe died on his own, iced and then shot. My problem is the autopsy results don't support any of my speculations. I'll keep looking, but I thought you should know."

"Thanks, Hank. I'll let Tom know. Maybe our investigators will find something to help fill in the blanks. Nice talking with you. Hope we can meet face-to-face sometime soon."

Jerry hung up the phone and went to find Sheriff Tom. Jerry was sure Big Tom would be interested in this development. And the Sheriff was very interested. "Let me get this straight. We have an unknown person found dead in Banner County. No one knows how he died. We don't know who done it, or why. It that about it?"

Jerry shook his head. "We don't know how he got to the Peak either."

The Sheriff shook his head too. "Ok, send Carlita Roads to interview the lady who found the body, Ms. Carmichael. Have Casey (Sergeant Casey Brown) use some of his shift deputies to recheck the area to see if they can find any witnesses. Put a request for information on NCIS (National Crime Information System, a computer system for law enforcement)."

"On it," responded Jerry. "And Carlita is called Chris Roads."

"Oh, see if you can get the feebies (FBI) out of first gear. They should have been able to provide an identity by now," the Sheriff growled. "And I know her name is Chris."

"My pleasure Boss," chuckled Jerry, who was well aware of the high regard and praise Tom had for Federal Agencies, particularly the mighty Federal Bureau of Investigation (FBI).

In this instance, the FBI was of some help. The feebies actually called Banner County. "Sheriff Flannigan, the is SAC (Special Agent in Charge) Cheyenne, Zeke Flores."

"Good afternoon," responded Sheriff Tom Flannigan. What can I do for you today?"

"I think I can do for you today. Your John Doe, Case #331507UP, is Elmer Palmer based on prints you sent."

"Well, thanks. The SAC doesn't usually call us with lab results. Does the FBI have some interest in this case?"

"Not at this time, but the CIA (Central Intelligence Agency) had a flag on the name. As you are aware, CIA doesn't do in-county investigations, the FBI does. Thought I might get ahead of anything going."

"Right now all I know is Banner County has a dead body. Might have been shot, may have been frozen or some other cause of death. Coroner hasn't decided. We are looking into it."

"Please keep us informed," demanded the SAC.

Sure will though Tom, when something freezes over next summer. Tom walked across the hall to Jerry's office. "Be cautious. Looks like the FBI and the CIA and probably other Feds want to run our office!" Tom was indignant and probably with good reason. Federal agencies had intruded on his turf many times in the past and rarely with good results. This case was Banner County's to solve. Not black suit outsiders.

Jerry noted the Sheriff's agitation and was well aware of how Tom felt about Federal intervention. "Sure Sheriff. Let me take the next call. I do have some information though."

"What," Sheriff Tom said, calming down?

"Well, not to get you riled up again, but WHP (Wyoming Highway Patrol) and CID (Wyoming Criminal Investigation Division, a state agency) want to be involved too."

"Why? Neither has any jurisdiction."

Jerry shrugged his shoulders. "The motorized meter maids and speed trap boys and girls, sorry the Highway Patrol, just want something else to do. The CID has a better reason. The FBI gave CID our DB's (dead body) ID. The CID has been investigating an Elmer Palmer for some time. CID isn't interested in cause of death, but want information."

Sheriff Tom pushed his gray Stetson back on his head and commented, "Sounds fair. Help CID, tell Highway to go back on patrol."

"Jerry laughed, "sure Boss!"

Lightning Source UK Ltd.
Milton Keynes UK
UKHW041017110219
337097UK00001B/135/P